Praise for #1 *New York Times* bestselling author

NORA ROBERTS

"When Roberts puts her expert fingers on the pulse of romance, legions of fans feel the heartbeat."
—*Publishers Weekly*

"A superb author... Ms. Roberts is an enormously gifted writer whose incredible range and intensity guarantee the very best of reading."
—*Rave Reviews*

"Her stories have fueled the dreams of twenty-five million readers."
—*Chicago Tribune*

"Nora Roberts is among the best."
—*The Washington Post Book World*

"Roberts' style has a fresh, contemporary snap."
—*Kirkus Reviews*

"With clear-eyed, concise vision and a sure pen, Roberts nails her characters and settings with awesome precision, drawing readers into a vividly rendered world of family-centered warmth and unquestionable magic."
—*Library Journal*

Dear Reader,

You know that feeling...that it was meant to be, it's written in the stars, you just *know* he's the one! The idea of fated love is what bestselling author Nora Roberts explores in this collection of classics about couples who couldn't be more different from each other, but are eventually drawn together by an irresistible attraction.

Some men make your pulse hammer, your heart flutter. In *Best Laid Plans,* structural engineer Abra Wilson finds architect Cody Johnson to be just such a man. Though Cody is utterly distracting, Abra has no time for romance...especially with a charmer like him. But the irrepressible architect has intentions that may even put Abra's steel will to the test....

In *From This Day,* hotel manager B.J. Clark meets her match in Taylor Reynolds—the establishment's new owner. B.J. likes her sleepy little inn the way it is and wants nothing to do with Taylor's plans to modernize it. Yet, despite their differences, sparks fly, and B.J. finds her loyalties divided between her beloved hotel and the torrid kisses she's sharing with her boss!

Even when two people seem worlds apart, these truly romantic tales prove that one unforgettable kiss can bring them together forever!

The Editors
Silhouette Books

NORA ROBERTS

Change of Heart

Silhouette Books

Published by Silhouette Books

America's Publisher of Contemporary Romance

SILHOUETTE BOOKS

CHANGE OF HEART

ISBN-13: 978-0-373-28168-8

Recycling programs
for this product may
not exist in your area.

Copyright © 2013 by Harlequin Books S.A.

The publisher acknowledges the copyright holder of the individual works as follows:

BEST LAID PLANS
Copyright © 1989 by Nora Roberts

FROM THIS DAY
Copyright © 1983 by Nora Roberts

Visit Silhouette Books at www.Harlequin.com

Printed in U.S.A.

CONTENTS

BEST LAID PLANS

For Bruce,
who knows how to build and make it last.

Chapter 1

She was definitely worth a second look.

There were more reasons—more basic reasons—than the fact that she was one of the few women on the building site. It was human nature for a man's eyes to be lured by the female form, especially when it was found in what was still predominantly a man's domain. True, a good many women donned hard hats to work construction, and as long as they could hammer a nail or lay a brick it didn't matter to Cody how they buttoned their shirts. But there was something about this particular woman that pulled his gaze back.

Style. Though she wore work clothes and stood on a mound of debris, she had it. Confidence, he mused as he rocked back on the worn heels of his boots. He supposed confidence was its own brand of style. It appealed to him as much—well, nearly as much—as black lace or white silk.

He didn't have the time to sit and speculate, though. He'd been almost a week late making the trip from Florida to Arizona to take over this project, and there was a lot of catching up to do. The morning was a busy one, with plenty of distractions: the noise of men and machines; orders being shouted and followed; cranes lifting heavy metal beams to form the skeleton of a building where there had been only rock and dirt; the vivid color of that rock and dirt under the white sun; even his own growing thirst. But he didn't mind distractions.

Cody had spent enough time on building sites to be able to look beyond the rubble, through what to the uninitiated might seem like confusion or even destruction. He saw instead the sweat, the strain, the thought and the possibilities.

But just now he found himself watching the woman. There were possibilities there, as well.

She was tall, he noted, five-nine or five-ten in her work boots, and lean rather than slender. Her shoulders looked strong under a dandelion-yellow T-shirt that was dark with sweat down the back. As an architect, he appreciated clean, economical lines. As a man, he appreciated the way her worn jeans fit snugly over her hips. Beneath a hard hat as bright as her shirt was a thick short braid the color of polished mahogany—one of his favorite woods to work with because of its beauty and richness.

He pushed his sunglasses farther up on his nose as

the eyes behind them scanned her from hard hat to boot tip. Definitely worth a second look, he thought again, admiring the way she moved, with no wasted gestures as she leaned over to look through a surveyor's transit. There was a faint white outline worn into her back pocket, where he imagined she tucked her wallet. A practical woman, he decided. A purse would get in the way on the site.

She didn't have a redhead's pale, fragile complexion, but a warm, golden tan that probably came from the blistering Arizona sun. Wherever it came from, he approved, just as he approved of the long, somewhat sharp angles of her face. Her tough-looking chin was offset by elegant cheekbones, and both were balanced by a soft, unpainted mouth that was even now turning down.

He couldn't see her eyes because of the distance and the shade from the brim of her hat, but her voice as she called out an order was clear enough. It sounded more appropriate for quiet, misty nights than for sweaty afternoons.

Tucking his thumbs in the pockets of his jeans, he grinned. Yes, indeed, there were endless possibilities.

Unaware of his study, Abra continued to frown as she swiped an arm over her damp brow. The sun was merciless today. At 8:00 a.m., it was already blistering. Sweat rolled down her back, evaporated, then rolled again in a cycle she had learned to live with.

You could only move so fast in this heat, she thought. You could only haul so much metal and chip so much rock when the temperature hovered in the nineties. Even with water barrels filled and salt tablets dispensed, every day was a struggle to stay ahead of the clock. So far they were pulling it off, but… There couldn't be any buts, she reminded herself. The construction of this resort was the biggest thing she'd been involved with in her career, and she wasn't going to mess it up. It was her springboard.

Though she could have murdered Tim Thornway for tying Thornway Construction, and her, to such a tightly scheduled project. The penalty clauses were outrageous, and in the way Tim had of delegating he'd put the responsibility for avoiding them squarely on her shoulders.

Abra straightened as if she could actually feel the weight. It would take a miracle to bring the project in on time and under budget. Since she didn't believe in miracles, she accepted the long hours and hard days ahead. The resort would be built, and built on time, if she had to pick up hammer and saw herself. But this was the last time, she promised herself as she watched a steel girder rise majestically into place. After this project she was cutting her ties with Thornway and striking out on her own.

She owed them for giving her a shot, for having enough faith in her to let her fight her way up from assistant to structural engineer. It wasn't something she'd forget—not now, not ever. But her loyalty had been to Thomas Thornway. Now that he was gone, she was doing her best to see that Tim didn't run the business into the ground. But she'd be damned if she was going to baby-sit him for the rest of her career.

She took a moment to wish for one of the cold drinks

stashed in the cooler, then picked her way around and over the rubble of construction to supervise the placing of the beams.

Charlie Gray, the ever-eager assistant Cody had found himself stuck with, all but tugged at his shirt. "Want me to tell Ms. Wilson you're here?" Cody tried to remember that he, too, had once been twenty-two and annoying.

"Got her hands full at the moment." Cody pulled out his cigarettes, then searched through two pockets before he found some matches. They were from some little hotel in Natchez and were damp with his own sweat.

"Mr. Thornway wanted you to get together."

Cody's lips curved a little. He'd just been thinking that it wouldn't be such a hardship to get together with Abra Wilson. "We'll get around to it." He struck a match, automatically curling his fingers around the flame, though there wasn't a breath of wind.

"You missed yesterday's meeting, so—"

"Yeah." The fact that he'd missed the meeting wouldn't cause him to lose any sleep. The design for the resort was Cody's, but when family problems had cropped up his partner had handled most of the preliminary work. Looking back at Abra, Cody began to think that was a shame.

There was a trailer parked a few yards away. Cody headed for it, with Charlie scrambling to keep up with him. He pulled a beer from a cooler, then pried the top off as he walked inside, where portable fans battled the heat. The temperature dropped a few precious degrees.

"I want to take a look at the plans for the main building again."

"Yes, sir, I have them right here." Like a good soldier, Charlie produced the tube of blueprints, then practically stood at attention. "At the meeting—" he cleared his throat "—Ms. Wilson pointed out a few changes she wanted made. From an engineering standpoint."

"Did she now?" Unconcerned, Cody propped himself on the thin, narrow cushions of the convertible couch. The sun had mercifully faded the vivid orange-and-green upholstery to a nearly inoffensive blur. He glanced around for an ashtray and settled on an empty cup, then unrolled the blueprints.

He liked the look of it, the feel of it. The building would be dome-shaped, topped by stained glass at the apex. Floors of offices would circle a center atrium, giving a sense of open, unstructured space. Breathing room, he thought. What was the use of coming west if you didn't have room to take a breath? Each office would have thick tinted glass to hold out the brilliance of the sun while affording an unhampered view of the resort and the mountains.

On the ground level the lobby would curve in a half circle, making it easily accessible from the entrance, from the double-level bar and the glassed-in coffee shop.

Patrons could take the glass elevators or the winding staircase up a floor to dine in one of three restaurants, or they could venture a bit higher and explore one of the lounges.

Cody took a long swallow of his beer as he looked

it over. He saw in it a sense of fantasy, even of humor, and more basically a marriage of the modern with the ancient. No, he couldn't see anything in his basic design that needed changing, or that he'd allow to be changed.

Abra Wilson, he thought, was going to have to grin and bear it.

When he heard the door of the trailer open, he glanced over. She was even better close up, Cody decided as Abra stepped inside. A little sweaty, a little dusty and, from the looks of her, a lot mad.

He was right about the mad. Abra had enough to do without having to chase down errant laborers taking unscheduled breaks. "What the hell are you doing in here?" she demanded as Cody lifted the can to his lips again. "We need everyone out there." She snatched the beer away before Cody could swallow. "Thornway isn't paying you to sit on your butt, and nobody on this project drinks on the job." She set the beer on the counter before she could be tempted to soothe her own dry throat with it.

"Ms. Wilson—"

"What?" Her patience in tatters, she turned on Charlie. "Oh, it's Mr. Gray, right? Hold on a minute." First things first, she thought as she rubbed her damp cheek against the sticky sleeve of her shirt. "Listen, pal," she said to Cody, "unless you want your walking papers, get yourself up and report to your foreman."

He grinned insolently at her. Abra felt reckless, unprofessional words bubble to her lips and battled them back with what control she had left. Just as she battled back the urge to jam her fist into his cocky chin.

A good-looking sonofa— She caught herself there, as well. Men with those kind of rough-and-ready looks always thought they could smile their way out of trouble—and they usually could. Not with her, though, Abra reminded herself. Still, it wouldn't do any good to threaten a union employee.

"You're not allowed in here." Frustrated, she bit the words off and snatched up the blueprints. Maybe if the morning had gone more smoothly she wouldn't have been ready to bite someone's—anyone's—head off. But he was in the wrong place at the wrong time. "And you certainly have no business poking around in these." She wondered what color his eyes were behind his dark glasses. If for no other reason than his continued grin, she would have been delighted to blacken them.

"Ms. Wilson…" Charlie said again, desperately.

"What, damn it?" She shook off his hand even as she reminded herself to be polite. The devil with polite, she thought. She was hot, tired, frustrated and delighted to have a target. "Have you got that illustrious architect of yours out of his hot tub yet, Gray? Thornway's interested in seeing this project move on schedule."

"Yes, you see—"

"Just a minute." Cutting him off again, she turned to Cody again. "Look, I told you to move. You speak English, don't you?"

"Yes, ma'am."

"Then move."

He did, but not as she'd expected. Lazily, like a cat stretching before it jumps off a windowsill, he unfolded his body. It appeared that most of him was leg. He didn't look like a man afraid of losing his job as he sidled between the table and the sofa, plucking his beer from the counter. He took a long, easy sip, leaned against the compact refrigerator and grinned at her again.

"You're a tall one, aren't you, Red?"

Barely, just barely, she caught herself before her mouth fell open. Building might still be primarily a man's trade, but no one Abra worked with had the nerve to be condescending. At least not to her face. He was out, she told herself. Schedule or no schedule, union or no union, she was going to issue him his walking papers personally.

"Find your lunch bucket, get in your pickup and make tracks, jerk." She snatched his beer again, and this time she poured the contents on his head. Fortunately for Cody, there was only a swallow left. "File that with your union representative."

"Ms. Wilson…" Charlie's face had gone bone white, and his voice was shaking. "You don't understand."

"Take a walk, Charlie." Cody's voice was mild as he lifted a hand to tunnel his fingers through his damp hair.

"But…but…"

"Out."

"Yes, sir." More than willing to desert a sinking ship, Charlie fled. Because he did, and because he'd called the lanky, pretty-faced cowboy "sir," Abra began to suspect that she'd taken a wrong turn down a blind alley. Automatically her eyes narrowed and her shoulders tensed.

"I don't guess we've been introduced." Cody drew

his shaded glasses off. She saw that his eyes were brown, a soft, golden brown. They weren't lit with anger or embarrassment. Rather, they assessed her with a flat neutrality. "I'm Cody Johnson. Your architect."

She could have babbled. She could have apologized. She could have laughed off the incident and offered him another beer. All three options occurred to her but, because of his calm, unblinking stare, were rejected. "Nice of you to stop by," she said instead.

A tough one, he decided, despite the hazel eyes and the sultry mouth. Well, he'd cracked tough ones before. "If I'd known what a warm reception I'd get, I'd have been here sooner."

"Sorry, we had to let the brass band go." Because she wanted to salvage her pride, she started to move past him, and discovered quickly that if she wanted to get to the door, the sofa or anywhere else she'd have to move through him. She didn't question why the prospect appealed to her. He was an obstacle, and obstacles were meant to be knocked down. An angling of her chin, very slight, was all she needed to keep her eyes level with his.

"Questions?" she asked him.

"Oh, a few." Like who do I have to kill to have you? Does your chin really take a punch as well as you think? And since when is a hard hat sexy? "Do you always pour beer on your men?"

"Depends on the man." Leaving it at that, she started by him again—and found herself lodged between him and the refrigerator. He'd only had to turn to accomplish it. He took a moment, keeping his eyes on hers.

He didn't see fear or discomfort in them, only a spitting fury that made him want to grin again. So he did.

"Close quarters in here...*Ms.* Wilson."

She might be an engineer, she might be a professional who had come up the hard way and knew the ropes, but she was still a woman, and very much aware of the press of his body against hers, the hard line of hip, the solid length of thigh. Whatever her reaction might have been, the glint of amusement in his eyes erased it.

"Are those teeth yours?" she asked calmly.

He lifted a brow. "Last time I checked."

"If you want to keep it that way, back off."

He would have liked to kiss her then, as much in appreciation for her guts as in desire for her taste. Though he was often impulsive, he also knew when to change tactics and take the long route. "Yes, ma'am."

When he moved aside, she slipped past him. She would have preferred to walk through the door and keep going, but she sat on the sofa and spread the prints out again. "I assume that Gray filled you in on the meeting you missed?"

"Yeah." He slid behind the table and sat down. As he'd said, the quarters were close. For the second time, their thighs brushed, denim against denim, muscle against muscle. "You wanted some changes."

She shouldn't be defensive. It did no good to be defensive. She couldn't help it. "I've had a problem with the basic design from the beginning, Mr. Johnson. I made no secret of it."

"I've seen the correspondence." Stretching out his

legs was a bit of a trick in such cramped quarters, but he managed it. "You wanted standard desert architecture."

Her eyes narrowed fractionally, and he caught the glint. "I don't recall the word *standard* coming up, but there are good reasons for the style of architecture in this region."

"There are also good reasons for trying something new, don't you think?" He said it easily as he lit another cigarette. "Barlow and Barlow want the ultimate resort," he continued before she could comment. "Totally self-contained, and exclusive enough to draw in big bucks from the clientele. They wanted a different look, a different mood, from what can be found in the resorts sprinkled around Phoenix. That's what I'm giving them."

"With a few modifications—"

"No changes, *Ms.* Wilson."

She nearly ground her teeth. Not only was he being pigheaded—a typical architect—but it infuriated her the way he drew out "Ms." in that sarcastic drawl. "For some reason," she began calmly, "we've been unfortunate enough to have been chosen to work together on this."

"Must have been fate," he murmured.

She let that pass. "I'm going to tell you up front, Mr. Johnson, that from an engineering standpoint your design stinks."

He dragged on his cigarette, letting the smoke escape in a slow stream. She had amber flecks in her eyes, he noted. Eyes that couldn't make up their mind whether they wanted to be gray or green. Moody eyes.

He smiled into them. "That's your problem. If you're not good enough, Thornway can assign someone else."

Her fingers curled into her palms. The idea of stuffing the plans down his throat had a certain appeal, but she reminded herself that she was committed to this project. "I'm good enough, Mr. Johnson."

"Then we shouldn't have any problems." He crossed his booted ankles. The noise from the site was steady. A productive sound, Cody had always thought. He didn't find it intrusive as he studied the woman across from him. It helped remind him that there was a time for business and a time for... pleasure.

"Why don't you fill me in on the progress?"

It wasn't her job. She almost snapped that at him. But she was tied to a contract, one that didn't leave much margin for error. By God, she'd pay her debt to Thornway, even if it meant working hand in glove with some overconfident, high-flying East Coast architect. She pushed the hard hat back on her head but didn't relax.

"As you've probably seen, the blasting went on schedule. Fortunately, we were able to keep it to a minimum and preserve the integrity of the landscape."

"That was the idea."

"Was it?" She glanced at the prints, then back at him. "In any case, we'll have the frame of the main building completed by the end of the week. If no changes are made—"

"None will be."

"If no changes are made," she repeated between clenched teeth, "we'll meet the first contract deadline. Work on the individual cabanas won't begin until the main building and the health center are under roof. The golf course and tennis courts aren't my province, so you'll have to discuss them with Kendall. That also goes for the landscaping."

"Fine. Do you know if the tiles for the lobby have been ordered?"

"I'm an engineer, not a purchaser. Marie Lopez handles supplies."

"I'll keep that in mind. Question."

Rather than give him a go-ahead nod, she rose and opened the refrigerator. It was stockpiled with sodas, juices and bottled water. Taking her time with her selection, she opted for the water. She was thirsty, she told herself. The move didn't have anything to do with wanting to put some distance between them. That was just a side benefit. Though she knew it was nasty, she screwed the top off the bottle and drank without offering him any.

"What?"

"Is it because I'm a man, an architect or an Easterner?"

Abra took another long sip. It only took a day in the sun to make you realize that paradise could be found in a bottle of water. "You'll have to clarify that."

"Is it because I'm a man, an architect or an Easterner that makes you want to spit in my eye?"

She wouldn't have been annoyed by the question itself, not in the least. But he grinned while he asked. After less than an hour's acquaintance, she'd already damned him a half-dozen times for that smile. Still, she leaned back against the counter, crossed her own ankles and considered him.

"I don't give a damn about your sex."

He continued to grin, but something quick and dangerous came into his eyes. "You like waving red flags at bulls, Wilson?"

"Yes." It was her turn to smile. Though the curving of her lips softened her mouth, it did nothing to dim the flash of challenge in her eyes. "But to finish my answer—architects are often pompous, temperamental artists who put their egos on paper and expect engineers and builders to preserve it for posterity. I can live with that. I can even respect it—when the architect takes a good, hard look at the environment and creates with it rather than for himself. As for you being an Easterner, that might be the biggest problem. You don't understand the desert, the mountains, the heritage of this land. I don't like the idea of you sitting under an orange tree two thousand miles away and deciding what people here are going to live with."

Because he was more interested in her than in defending himself, he didn't mention that he had made three trips to the site months before. Most of the design work had been done almost where he was sitting now, rather than back at his home base. He had a vision, but he was a man who drew and built his visions more than a man who spoke of them.

"If you don't want to build, why do you?"

"I didn't say I didn't want to build," she said. "I've never thought it necessary to destroy in order to do so."

"Every time you put a shovel in the ground you take away some land. That's life."

"Every time you take away some land you should think hard about what you're going to give back. That's morality."

"An engineer *and* a philosopher." He was baiting her, and he knew it. Even as he watched, angry color rose to her cheeks. "Before you pour that over my head, let's say I agree with you—to a point. But we're not putting up neon and plastic here. Whether you agree with my design or not, it is my design. It's your job to put it together."

"I know what my job is."

"Well, then." As if dismissing the disagreement, Cody began to roll up the plans. "How about dinner?"

"I beg your pardon?"

"Dinner," he repeated. When the prints were rolled up, he slid them into their cylinder and rose. "I'd like to have dinner with you."

Abra wasn't sure it was the most ridiculous statement she'd ever heard, but it certainly ranked in the top ten. "No thanks."

"You're not married?" That would have mattered.

"No."

"Involved?" That wouldn't have.

Patience wasn't her strong suit. Abra didn't bother to dig for it. "None of your business."

"You've got a quick trigger, Red." He picked up his hard hat but didn't put it on. "I like that."

"You've got nerve, Johnson. I don't like that." She moved to the door, pausing just a moment with her hand on the knob. "If you have any questions that deal with the construction, I'll be around."

He didn't have to move much to put a hand on her shoulder. Under his palm he felt her coil up like a cat ready to spring. "So will I," he reminded her. "We'll have dinner some other time. I figure you owe me a beer."

After one self-satisfied glance at the top of his head, Abra stepped out into the sun.

He certainly wasn't what she'd been expecting. He was attractive, but she could handle that. When a woman took root in male territory, she was bound to come into contact with an attractive man from time to time. Still, he looked more like one of her crew than a partner in one of the country's top architectural firms. His dark blond hair, with its sun-bleached tips, was worn too long for the nine-to-five set, and his rangy build held ripples of muscle under the taut, tanned skin. His broad, callused hands were those of a working-man. She moved her shoulders as if shrugging off the memory of his touch. She'd felt the strength, the roughness and the appeal of those hands. Then there was that voice, that slow take-your-time drawl.

She settled the hard hat more securely as she approached the steel skeleton of the building. Some women would have found that voice appealing. She didn't have time to be charmed by a southern drawl or a cocky grin. She didn't, when it came right down to it, have much time to think of herself as a woman.

He'd made her feel like one.

Scowling against the sun, she watched beams being

riveted into place. She didn't care for Cody Johnson's ability to make her feel feminine. "Feminine" too often meant "defenseless" and "dependent." Abra had no intention of being either of those. She'd worked too hard and too long at self-sufficiency. A couple of...flutters, she decided, just flutters...weren't going to affect her.

She wished the can of beer had been full.

With a grim smile she watched the next beam swing into place. There was something beautiful about watching a building grow. Piece by piece, level by level. It had always fascinated her to watch something strong and useful take shape—just as it had always disturbed her to see the land marred by progress. She'd never been able to resolve that mixture of feelings, and it was because of that that she'd chosen a field that allowed her to have a part in seeing that progress was made with integrity.

But this one... She shook her head as the sound of riveting guns split the air. This one struck her as an outsider's fantasy, the domed shape, the curves and spirals. She'd spent countless nights at her drawing board with slide rule and calculator, struggling to come up with a satisfactory support system. Architects didn't worry about mundane matters like that, she thought. It was all aesthetics with them. All ego. She'd build the damn thing, she thought, kicking some debris out of her way. She'd build it and build it well. But she didn't have to like it.

With the sun baking her back, she bent over the transit. They'd had the mountain to deal with, and an uneven bed of rock and sand, but the measurements and placement were right on. She felt a tug of pride as she checked angles and degrees. Inappropriate or not, the structure was going to be perfectly engineered.

That was important—being perfect. Most of her life she'd had to deal with second best. Her education, her training and her skill had lifted her beyond that. She had no intention of ever settling for second best again, not for herself, and not in her work.

She caught his scent and felt the light tickle of awareness at the back of her neck. Soap and sweat, she thought, and had to fight not to shift uncomfortably. Everybody on the site smelled of soap and sweat, so why was she certain Cody was behind her? She only knew she was certain, and she determinedly remained bent over the eyepiece.

"Problem?" she said, pleased with the disdain she was able to put into the single word.

"I don't know until I look. Do you mind?"

She took her time before stepping back. "Be my guest."

When he moved forward, she hooked her thumbs in her back pockets and waited. He'd find no discrepancies—even if he knew enough to recognize one. Hearing a shout, she glanced over to see two members of the crew arguing. The heat, she knew, had a nasty way of bringing tempers to a boil. Leaving Cody to his survey, she strode across the broken ground.

"It's a little early for a break," she said calmly as one crewman grabbed the other by the shirtfront.

"This sonofabitch nearly took my fingers off with that beam."

"If this idiot doesn't know when to get out of the way, he deserves to lose a few fingers."

Neither man had much on her in height, but they were burly, sweaty and on the edge. Without thinking twice, she stepped between them as fists were raised. "Cool off," she ordered.

"I don't have to take that sh—"

"You may not have to take his," Abra said levelly, "but you have to take mine. Now cool off or take a walk." She looked from one angry face to the other. "If you two want to beat each other senseless when you're off the clock, be my guest, but either of you takes a swing on my time, you're unemployed. You." She pointed to the man she judged the more volatile of the two. "What's your name?"

The dark-haired man hesitated briefly, then spit out, "Rodriguez."

"Well, Rodriguez, go take a break and pour some water over your head." She turned away as if she had no doubts about his immediate obedience. "And you?"

The second man was ruddy and full-faced and was smirking. "Swaggart."

"Okay, Swaggart, get back to work. And I'd have a little more respect for my partner's hands if I were you, unless you want to count your own fingers and come up short."

Rodriguez snorted at that but did as he was told and moved away toward the water barrels. Satisfied, Abra signaled to the foreman and advised him to keep the men apart for a few days.

She'd nearly forgotten about Cody by the time she

turned and saw him. He was still standing by the transit, but he wasn't looking through it. Legs spread, hands resting lightly on his hips, he was watching her. When she didn't make a move toward him, he made one toward her.

"You always step into the middle of a brawl?"

"When it's necessary."

He tipped his shaded glasses down to study her, then scooted them up again. "Ever get that chip knocked off your shoulder?"

She couldn't have said why she had to fight back a grin, but she managed to. "Not yet."

"Good. Maybe I'll be the first."

"You can try, but you'd be better off concentrating on this project. More productive."

He smiled slowly, and the angles of his face shifted with the movement. "I can concentrate on more than one thing at a time. How about you?"

Instead of answering, she took out a bandanna and wiped the back of her neck. "You know, Johnson, your partner seemed like a sensible man."

"Nathan *is* sensible." Before she could stop him, he took the bandanna from her and dabbed at her temples. "He saw you as a perfectionist."

"And what are you?" She had to resist the urge to grab the cloth back. There was something soothing, a little too soothing, in his touch.

"You'll have to judge that for yourself." He glanced back at the building. The foundation was strong, the angles were clear, but it was just the beginning. "We're going to be working together for some time yet."

She, too, glanced toward the building. "I can take it if you can." Now she did take the bandanna back, stuffing it casually in her back pocket.

"Abra." He said her name as if he were experimenting with a taste. "I'm looking forward to it." She jolted involuntarily when he brushed a thumb down her cheek. Pleased with the reaction, he grinned. "See you around."

Jerk, she thought again as she stomped across the rubble and tried to ignore the tingling along her skin.

Chapter 2

If there was one thing she didn't need, Abra thought a few days later, it was to be pulled off the job and into a meeting. She had mechanics working on the main building, riveters working on the health club, and a running feud between Rodriguez and Swaggart to deal with. It wasn't as though those things couldn't be handled without her—it was simply that they could be handled better with her. And here she was cooling her heels in Tim's office waiting for him to show up.

She didn't have to be told how tight the schedule was. Damn it, she knew what she had to do to see that the contract was brought in on time. She knew all about time.

Her every waking moment was devoted to this job. Each day was spent sweating out on the site with the crews and the supervisors, dealing with details as small as the delivery of rivets. At night she either tumbled into bed at sundown or worked until three, fueled by coffee and ambition, over her drawing board. The project was hers, hers more than it could ever be Tim Thornway's. It had become personal, in a way she could never have explained. For her, it was a tribute to the man who had had enough faith in her to push her to try for more than second best. In a way, it was her last job for Thomas Thornway, and she wanted it to be perfect.

It didn't help to have an architect who demanded materials that made cost overruns and shipping delays inevitable. Despite him and his marble sinks and his oversize ceramic tiles, she was going to pull it off. If she wasn't constantly being dragged into the office for endless meetings.

Impatient, she paced to the window and back again. Time was wasting, and there were few things that annoyed her more than waste of any kind. If she hadn't had a specific point to bring up to Tim, she would have found a way to avoid the meeting altogether. The one good thing about Tim, she thought with a humorless smile, was that he wasn't really bright enough to recognize double-talk. In this case, she wanted to make the pitch herself, so she'd come. But—she glanced at her watch—she wasn't going to twiddle her thumbs much longer.

This had been Thornway's office. She'd always liked the cool, authoritative colors and the lack of frills. Since Tim had taken over, he'd made some changes. Plants, she thought, scowling at a ficus. It wasn't that she disliked plants and thick, splashy pillows, but it annoyed her to find them here.

Then there were the paintings. Thornway had preferred Indian paintings and landscapes. Tim had replaced them with abstracts that tended to jar Abra's nerves. The new carpet seemed three inches thick and was salmon-colored. The elder Thornway had used a short-napped buff so that the dust and dirt wouldn't show. But then, Tim didn't often visit the sites or ask his foremen to join him for an after-hours drink.

Stop it, Abra ordered herself. Tim ran things differently, and that was his privilege. It was his business in every way. The fact that she had loved and admired the father so much didn't mean she had to find fault with the son.

But she did find fault with him, she thought as she studied the tidy, polished surface of his desk. He lacked both the drive and the compassion that had been so much a part of his father. Thornway had wanted to build first for the love of building. With Tim, the profit margin was the bottom line.

If Thomas Thornway had still been alive, she wouldn't have been preparing to make a break. There was a certain freedom in that, in knowing that this current project would be her last for the company. There would be no regrets in leaving, as there might once have been. Instead, there was excitement, anticipation. Whatever happened next, she would be doing it for herself.

Terrifying, she thought, closing her eyes. The idea was as terrifying as it was compelling. All unknowns were. Like Cody Johnson.

Catching herself, she walked back to the window. That was ridiculous. He was neither terrifying nor compelling. Nor was he an unknown. He was just a man—a bit of a pest, with the way he kept popping up on the site. He was the kind of man who knew he was a pleasure to look at and exploited it. The kind who always had a line, an angle and an escape route.

She'd seen men like Cody operate before. Looking back, Abra considered herself lucky that she'd only fallen for a pretty face and a smooth line once. Some women never learned and kept walking blindly into the trap again and again. Her mother was one, Abra thought with a shake of her head. Jessie Wilson would have taken one look at a man like Cody and taken the plunge. Thank God, in this way it was not "like mother like daughter."

As for herself, Abra wasn't interested in Cody Johnson personally and could barely tolerate him professionally.

When he walked in seconds later, she wondered why her thoughts and her feelings didn't seem to jibe.

"Abra, sorry to keep you waiting." Tim, trim in a three-piece suit, offered her a hearty smile. "Lunch ran a bit over."

She only lifted a brow. This meeting in the middle of the day had caused her to miss her lunch altogether. "I'm more interested in why you called me in from the field."

"Thought we needed a little one-on-one." He settled comfortably behind his desk and gestured for both her and Cody to sit.

"You've seen the reports."

"Absolutely." He tapped a finger on a file. He had a nice, engaging grin that suited his round face. More than once Abra had thought he'd have done well in politics. If anyone knew how to answer a question without committing himself, it was Tim Thornway. "Efficient, as always. I'm having a dinner meeting with Barlow senior this evening. I'd like to give him something more than facts and figures."

"You can give him my objections to the interior layout of the main building." She crossed her ankles and spared Cody the briefest glance. Tim began to fiddle with one of his monogrammed pens.

"I thought we'd settled all that."

Abra merely shrugged. "You asked. You can tell him that the wiring should be completed on the main structure by the end of the week. It's a tricky process, given the size and shape of the building. And it's going to cost his company a fortune to cool."

"He has a fortune," Cody commented. "I believe they're more interested in style than saving on the electric bill."

"Indeed." Tim cleared his throat. The way things stood, the Barlow project was going to bring him a tidy profit. He wanted to keep it that way. "Of course, I've looked over the specs and can assure our client that he's receiving only the best in materials and in brainpower."

"I'd suggest you tell him to come see for himself," Abra said.

"Well, I don't think—"

Cody cut in. "I agree with Ms. Wilson. Better he

should buck now about something that doesn't suit him than buck later, after it's in concrete."

Tim frowned and backpedaled. "The plans have been approved."

"Things look different on paper," Cody said, looking at Abra. "Sometimes people are surprised by the finished product."

"Naturally, I'll suggest it." Tim tapped his pen on his spotless blotter. "Abra, you have a suggestion in your report about extending the lunch break to an hour."

"Yes, I wanted to talk with you about that. After a few weeks on the site I've seen that until and unless we get some relief in the weather the men are going to need a longer break at midday."

Tim set down the pen and folded his hands. "You have to understand what a thirty-minute extension means in terms of overall time and money."

"You have to understand that men can't work in that sun without a reasonable reprieve. Chugging salt tablets isn't enough. It may be March, and it may be cool inside when you're having your second martini, but out there it's a killer."

"These men get paid to sweat," Tim reminded her. "And I think you can only agree that they'll be better off to have the buildings under roof by summer."

"They can't build if they drop from heat exhaustion or sunstroke."

"I don't believe I've had any reports of that happening."

"Not yet." It would be a miracle if she held on to her temper. He'd always been pompous, she thought.

When he'd been a junior executive she'd been able to skirt him and go straight to the top. Now he *was* the top. Abra gritted her teeth and tried again. "Tim, they need the extra time off. Working out in that sun drains you. You get weak, you get sloppy, then you make mistakes—dangerous mistakes."

"I pay a foreman to see that no one makes mistakes."

Abra was on her feet and ready to explode when Cody's calm voice cut in. "You know, Tim, men tend to stretch out breaks in the heat in any case. You give them an extra thirty minutes, makes them feel good—obliged, even. Most of them won't be as liable to take more. You end up getting the same amount of work and good PR."

Tim ran his pen through his fingers. "Makes sense. I'll keep it in mind."

"You do that." With an easy smile, he rose. "I'm going to hitch a ride back to the site with Ms. Wilson. Then we can discuss that idea about our working more closely together. Thanks for lunch, Tim."

"Any time, any time."

Before Abra could speak, Cody had her by the elbow and was leading her out. They were in front of the elevators before she managed to jerk away. "I don't need to be shown the way," she said through clenched teeth.

"Well, *Ms.* Wilson, looks like we disagree again." He strolled into the elevator with her, then punched the button for the parking garage. "In my opinion, you could definitely use some guidance—in how to handle birdbrains."

"I don't need you to…" She let her words trail off,

glancing over at his face. The hint of amusement in his eyes matched the reluctant smile in hers. "I assume you're referring to Tim."

"Did I say that?"

"I have to assume you were—unless you were talking about yourself."

"Take your choice."

"That leaves me with a tough decision." The elevator shuddered slightly when it reached the parking level. Abra put her hand out to keep the door from sliding shut again as she studied him. There was a sharp intelligence in his eyes, and an easy confidence around his mouth. Abra nearly sighed as she moved through the doors and into the garage.

"Made up your mind?" he asked as he fell into step beside her.

"Let's just say I've already made up my mind how to handle you."

The slap of their boots echoed as they walked between the lines of cars. "How's that?"

"You've heard of ten-foot poles?"

His mouth quirked at the corners. She was wearing a braid again. It gave him the urge to loosen it, strand by strand. "That's downright unfriendly."

"Yeah." She stopped in front of a compact station wagon. Its white paint was scarred and dusty, and its windows were tinted violet to combat the merciless sun. Thoughtfully she dug out her keys. "Are you sure you want to go to the site? I could drop you by your hotel."

"I do have a mild interest in this project."

She moved her shoulders in a quick, restless gesture.
"Suit yourself."

"Usually do."

Once in he cocked his seat back and nearly managed to stretch out his legs. When she turned the key, the engine coughed, objected, then caught. The radio and air conditioner sprang to life. Music jangled out, but she didn't bother to turn it down. Scattered across the dashboard were a family of decorative magnets—a banana, an ostrich, a map of Arizona, a grinning cat and a lady's hand with pink fingernails. Scribbled notes were held in place by them. As far as Cody could make out, she had to pick up milk and bread and check on fifty tons of concrete. And call Mongo? He narrowed his eyes and tried again. Her mother. She was supposed to call her mother.

"Nice car," he commented when it shuddered and bucked to a stop at a light.

"Needs a tune-up." She shifted into neutral to let the engine idle. "I haven't gotten around to it."

He studied her hand as she jammed the car into first and accelerated. It was long and lean and suited her build. She wore her nails short and, unlike the plastic depiction of a lady's hand, unpainted. No jewelry. He could imagine those hands serving delicate cups of tea—just as he could imagine them changing spark plugs.

"So how would you handle Tim?"

"What?" He'd been lost in a quiet little fantasy about how those narrow, competent hands would feel stroking along his skin.

"Tim," she repeated. She gave the car more gas as they headed south out of Phoenix. "How would you handle him?"

At the moment he was more interested in how he was going to handle her. "I take it you two don't always see things the same way."

"You're the observant type, Johnson."

"Sarcasm, Red." He didn't ask permission to smoke, just rolled the window down an inch and began to search through his pockets for matches. "Personally, I don't mind it a bit, but when you're dealing with Thornway you'll find oil does better than vinegar."

It was true, absolutely true. It annoyed her that she'd put herself in a position where she'd had to be reminded of that. "He doesn't recognize sarcasm if you pour it over his head." She punched in the car lighter for him.

"Not nine times out of ten, maybe." He touched the tip of the lighter against his cigarette. "It's that tenth time that could get you in trouble. Before you say it, I already know you don't mind a little trouble."

Despite herself, she smiled, and she didn't object when he turned the radio down. "You know those horses, the parade horses that wear blinders so they'll follow the route and not look around and get spooked by crowds?"

"Yeah, and I've already seen that Thornway wears blinders so that he can follow the route to profit without being distracted. You want better working conditions for the men, a higher grade of material, whatever, you've got to learn how to be subtle."

She made that quick, restless movement with her shoulders again. "I can't."

"Sure you can. You're smarter than Thornway, Red, so you sure as hell ought to be able to outwit him."

"He makes me mad. When I think about—" She shrugged again, but this time there was sorrow in the movement. "He just makes me mad. When I get mad, whatever I think comes out."

That was something he'd already figured out for himself. "All you have to do is use the common denominator. With Thornway, that's profit. You want the men to have an hour lunch break in the heat of the day, you don't tell him it's for their benefit, you tell him he'll get higher efficiency and therefore higher profits."

She scowled for a minute, then let out a long breath. "I suppose I'll have to thank you for talking him into it."

"Okay. How about dinner?"

She cast him a short, level look. "No."

"Why not?"

"Because you've got a pretty face." When he grinned, she granted him the briefest of smiles. "I don't trust men with pretty faces."

"You've got a pretty face. I don't hold it against you."

Her smile widened for a moment, but she kept staring at the long road ahead. "There's the difference between you and me, Johnson."

"If we had dinner, we could find others."

It was tempting. And it shouldn't have been. "Why should we want to find others?"

"Passes the time. Why don't we—" He broke off

when the car swerved. Abra swore and wrestled the car to the shoulder of the road.

"A flat," she said in disgust. "A lousy flat, and I'm already late getting back." With that, she slammed out of the car and stomped around to the back, swearing with admirable expertise. By the time Cody joined her, she'd already rolled out her spare.

"That one doesn't seem to be in much better shape," he commented, eyeing the tread.

"I need new ones all around, but this one should hold awhile." She hauled out the jack and, still muttering curses, hooked it under the bumper. It was on the tip of Cody's tongue to offer to change it himself. Then he remembered how much he enjoyed watching her work. He hooked his thumbs in his belt loops and stayed out of her way.

"Where I come from, engineers do pretty well for themselves. Ever think about a new car?"

"This one does the job." She spun the lug nuts off. With easy efficiency she pulled off the flat and rolled the spare into place. The breeze from a passing car fluttered through her hair.

"This is bald," Cody said when he took a look at the flat.

"Probably."

"Probably, hell. I've got more tread on my sneakers. Haven't you got more sense than to drive around on bald tires?" Even as he asked he started around the car to examine the tread on the remaining three. "These aren't much better."

"I said I needed new ones." She brushed the hair

out of her eyes. "I haven't had the time to take it in and deal with it."

"Make time."

He was standing behind her now. From her crouched position, she aimed a look over her shoulder. "Back off."

"When I work with someone who's this careless personally, I have to wonder how careless they might be professionally."

"I don't make mistakes on the job." She went back to tightening the lug nuts. He was right. Because it embarrassed her, she refused to admit it out loud. "Check the records."

She stood, and was more annoyed than surprised when he turned her around to face him. It didn't bother her to be close. It bothered her to *feel* close. "How many do you make off the job?"

"Not many." She should move away. The warning flashed in and out of her mind as her throat went dry. They were standing toe-to-toe. She could see the light sheen of dampness on his face and throat, just as she could see, whether she wanted to or not, the flicker of desire in his eyes.

"I don't like to argue with a woman who's holding a tire iron." He took it from her and leaned it against the bumper. Her hands curled into fists at her sides, but it was nerves, pure nerves, and had nothing to do with anger.

"I've got an inspector coming this afternoon."

"At two-thirty." He took her hand, turning the wrist up to glance at her watch. "You've got some time."

"Not my own," she said evenly. "I'm on Thornway's clock."

"Conscientious." He looked down at the bald tire. "Mostly."

It was uncomfortable and unnerving to feel her heart thud against her ribs. As if she'd been running, Abra thought. She didn't want to admit that she'd been running since she'd first laid eyes on him.

"If you've got something you want to say, say it. I've got work to do."

"Can't think of a thing at the moment." But he still held her hand. His thumb lightly grazed the underside of her wrist, where her pulse beat hard and steady. "Can you?"

"No." She started to move past him and found herself brought up firmly against his chest. She'd always been lousy at chess, she thought, flustered. Never looking past the immediate move to the future consequences. It took more effort than it should have to keep her voice steady. "What's your problem, Cody?"

"I don't know." He was every bit as intrigued as she. "There's one way to find out." His free hand was on her face now, not resting there but holding her still. "Do you mind?" Even as he spoke, his lips lowered toward hers.

She wasn't sure what made her pull back at the last moment—or what made her able to pull back. She lifted a hand to his chest and pressed firmly, even as she tasted the warmth of his breath on her lips. "Yes," she said, and was amazed to realize that it was a lie. She wouldn't have minded. In fact, she'd wanted the feel and taste of his mouth on hers.

There was only an inch separating them, perhaps less. He felt, unexpectedly, a churning, a tug, a heat that drew together and centered in his gut. It was more than curiosity, he realized, and he found himself not entirely comfortable with the knowledge. When he stepped back, it was as much for his own sake as anything.

"I shouldn't have asked," he said easily. "Next time I won't."

She'd start trembling in a moment. It stunned her to realize that any second her system was going to betray her and shudder and quake. Again, not from anger. She held it off through sheer will and bent to the ruined tire. "Go find someone else to play with, Cody."

"I don't think so." He took the tire from her and stored it in the rear of the car. Before she could see to it herself, he had lowered the jack and stored that, as well.

Taking slow, steadying breaths, she walked around to her door. A tractor-trailer rattled by, and the force of the air it displaced hit her like a wall. She braced herself against it, as she had braced herself against him. Her palms were sweaty. Carefully she rubbed them against the thighs of her jeans before settling inside and turning the key.

"You don't strike me as the kind of man who keeps knocking at a door when no one answers."

"You're right." He leaned back again as she pulled onto the road. "After a while I just open it myself." With a friendly grin, he turned the radio up again.

The inspector had come early. Abra swore about it but couldn't do much else, since the wiring passed. She walked through the building, which was already taking shape, and climbed to the second and third floors to supervise the insulating and the first delivery of drywall. It was moving like clockwork, and she should have been more than satisfied.

All she could think of was how she had felt standing on the shoulder of the road with Cody's lips an inch from hers.

She was an engineer, not a romantic, she reminded herself as she stood on a platform twenty feet up and unrolled a drawing. The cooling system, she thought as she went over the specs again. That was going to take enough of her time and energy over the next few days. She didn't have the time or the inclination to stand around and wonder what it would have been like to kiss Cody Johnson.

Hot. Hot and exciting. No woman could look at that mouth and not see the kind of damage it could do to the nervous system. It had already jangled hers, and without even making contact. He probably knew it. Men like him always knew what kind of effect they had on a woman. They could hardly be blamed for it, but they could—and should—be avoided.

With another oath, she rolled up the drawings. She wouldn't think about him or what would have happened if she'd said yes instead of no. Or if she'd said nothing at all and had moved on instinct rather than brainpower.

There were the elevators to consider. It wouldn't be long before they'd be going in. She'd worked hard and long with another engineer on the design. What was now on paper would be reality soon enough, running up and down the walls, glass glittering as they rose and fell without a sound.

Some men could do that—make your heart rise and fall, make your pulse hammer though it couldn't be heard by anyone but you. No matter how you tried, how you pretended it wasn't happening, inside you'd be shooting up and shooting down so fast that a crash was inevitable. No matter how clever you were with a calculator, you could never quite fix the kinks in the system.

Damn him. Damn him for that—for taking that one step beyond and making her vulnerable. She couldn't forget the way her hand had felt in his, the way his eyes had looked when his face had been that close. So now she would wonder. The blame for that was his. She'd do well to remember that.

Glancing down, she saw him on the first floor, talking with Charlie Gray. Cody was gesturing toward the rear wall, where the side of the mountain sloped in to become part of the building—or the building to become part of the mountain. There would be long panes of glass there to form the ceiling, curved glass that would blend the line from the rock to the dome. She'd already decided it would be ostentatious and impractical, but as she'd been told, it was her job to make it work, not to approve.

Cody shook his head at something Gray told him, and his voice rose a little, enough to carry but not enough to make the words clear. Annoyance was there. It pleased her.

Let him be annoyed, she thought. Let him go back east and be annoyed where he would be out of her way.

She started down, using the temporary stairs. She had the progress on the health club to check out, and the excavation work on the first set of cabanas. As long as they could keep one job overlapping the next, they'd be all right. Tim should have been there, overseeing the scheduling. Abra moved a shoulder to work out a kink. It was better that he wasn't, that he had left the responsibility to her. He had a way of irritating the men when he showed up on the site in his expensive suits.

Just as she checked her watch, she heard a shout from above. She had enough time to see the metal stud falling toward her before she was grabbed by the waist and dragged aside.

The stud landed inches from her feet, spewing up dust and clattering. Hard hat or no, she'd have been taking a trip to the hospital now if she'd been under it.

"You all right? Hey." Arms were still around her waist, but now she was turned and pressed against a hard male body. She didn't have to see to know who was holding her.

"Yes." But her voice wasn't steady. Neither were her hands. "I'm okay. Let me—"

"Who the hell's responsible for this?" Cody shouted up, still holding Abra against him. He knew now what it meant to be sick with fear. He'd moved instinctively, but the moment the stud had hit harmlessly his stomach had heaved. Looking at it, he could envision her lying there, bleeding. Two men were already scurrying down the ladder, their faces as white as his.

"It got away from us. God, Ms. Wilson, are you

okay? There was an electric box on the floor. It tripped me up, and the stud just went."

"It didn't hit me." She tried to move away from Cody but didn't have the strength.

"Get up there and make sure those floors and platforms are clear. If there's any more carelessness, people are going to be out of a job."

"Yes, sir."

The hammering, which had stopped dead, resumed hesitantly, then with more vigor.

"Look, I'm all right." She had to be. Even if her hands were clammy, she had to be all right. "I can handle the men."

"Just shut up." He fought back the urge to pick her up, and pulled her along instead. "You're white as a sheet." He shoved her down on a crate. "Sit."

Because her legs felt like rubber, she didn't argue. A few deep breaths, she told herself, and she'd be fine.

"Here." Cody pushed a cup of water into her hand.

"Thanks." She drank, forcing herself to take it slow. "You don't have to bother."

"No, I could just leave you in a puddle on the ground." It hadn't come out the way he'd intended, but he was angry, as sick with anger as he'd been with fear. It had been too close, way too close. If he hadn't glanced over at her... "I could've stood there and watched you get smashed, but it seemed a shame to get blood all over the fresh concrete."

"That's not what I meant." She swallowed the last of the water and balled up the paper cup in her hand. He'd saved her from a major injury. She'd wanted to thank him, nicely. And she would have, too, Abra thought, if he hadn't been scowling at her. "I would have gotten out of the way myself, in any case."

"Fine. Next time I'll just go about my business."

"Do that." Biting off the words, she tossed the paper cup aside. She rose and fought back a wave of giddiness. Hammers were still pounding, but more than one man was watching out of the corner of an eye. "There's no need to cause a scene."

"You've no idea the kind of scene I can cause, Wilson." He was tempted to show her, to release some of the fury that had boiled together with the fear and let her have a good long look at what he could throw. But her face was chalk white, and whether she knew it or not her hands were shaking. "If I were you, I'd have your foreman drill some safety rules into these men."

"I'll take that under advisement. Now, if you'll excuse me, I have to get back to work."

When his fingers curled around her arm, she felt the temper in them. She was grateful for it. It made her stronger. Very slowly she turned her head so that she could look at him again. Fury, she thought with a kind of edgy curiosity. The man was absolutely furious— more than a few cross words warranted. His problem, Abra told herself.

"I'm not going to keep telling you to back off, Johnson."

He waited a moment until he was sure he could speak calmly. In his mind he could still hear the sickening crack of metal hitting concrete. "That's something we can agree on, Red. You won't keep telling me to back off."

He let her go. After the briefest hesitation, she strode away.

She wouldn't keep telling him, Cody thought as he watched her disappear outside. And even if she did, it wasn't going to do her any good.

Chapter 3

He had other things to think about. Cody let the hot spray of the shower beat over his head and reminded himself that Abra Wilson wasn't his problem. A problem she undoubtedly was, but not his.

Women that skittish were best avoided, particularly when they had those pretty feminine looks that contrasted with a mean temper. The Barlow project was giving him enough headaches. He didn't need to add her to the list.

But then, she was mighty easy to look at. Cody smiled to himself as he turned off the shower. Easy to look at didn't mean easy to handle. Usually he appreciated challenges, but just now he had enough on his plate. Now that his partner was married and expecting his first baby, Cody was doing what he could to shoulder the excess. With business booming, the excess meant

twelve-hour days. In addition to overseeing the construction of the resort, there were innumerable phone
calls to make and take, telegrams to send and receive,
decisions, approvals and rejections.

He didn't mind the responsibility or the long hours.
He was grateful for them. It didn't take much prodding
for him to remember the boy who had grown up on a
muddy farm on the Georgia-Florida border. The boy
had wanted more, and the man had worked to get it.

Come a long way, Cody thought as he knotted the
towel at his waist. His body was lean, the torso tanned.
He still worked outdoors, though that was from choice
now, rather than necessity. It wasn't only drawing
boards and dreams with Cody. There was a house on a
lake in Florida that was half-built. He was determined
to finish it himself. A matter of pride now, rather than
lack of funds.

The money was there, and he'd never deny he enjoyed its benefits. Still, he'd grown up working with his
hands, and he couldn't seem to break the habit. He corrected himself. He didn't want to break the habit. There
were times when he enjoyed nothing more than the feel
of a hammer or a piece of wood in his hand.

He dragged his fingers through his wet hair. They
were callused, as they'd been since childhood. He could
run a tractor even now, but he preferred a slide rule or
a power saw.

He strode into the bedroom of his hotel suite. The
suite was nearly as big as the home he'd grown up in.
He'd gotten used to the space, to the small luxuries, but
he didn't take them for granted. Because he'd grown up

skirting poverty he'd learned to appreciate good material, good food, good wine. Perhaps he appreciated them with a more discerning eye than someone who had been born to the good life. But he didn't think about that.

Work, talent and ambition were the keys, with a bit of luck thrown in. Cody remembered that luck could change, so he never avoided work.

He had come a long way from digging in the mud to make a living. Now he could dream, imagine and create—as long as he didn't forget that making dreams reality meant getting your hands dirty. He could lay a score of brick if it was required, mix mortar, pound in a stud or drive a rivet. He'd worked his way through college as a laborer. Those years had given him not only a practical bent toward building but a respect for the men who sweated to create them.

Which brought him back to Abra. She understood construction workers. He knew firsthand that many of the people who worked at drawing boards forgot the men who hammered the nails and hauled the bricks. But not Abra. Thoughtfully he slipped into a white terry-cloth robe with the vague notion of calling room service and eating in. Abra Wilson, he mused. She would have gone to the wall to get an extra thirty minutes' break for the men. She was a fiend about checking the water supply and the salt tablets.

She was also a woman who would step in between two angry construction workers to break up a fight. Or pour beer over the head of an insubordinate employee. The memory made him grin. No drinking on the job. And she'd meant what she'd said.

He appreciated that. He was a man who preferred frankness to subtleties in both his business and his personal life. She wasn't a woman who would play flirting games or give teasing hints. She would say yes or she would say no.

As she had on the side of the road, he remembered. She'd said no, Cody mused, and she'd wanted to say yes. Discovering the reasons for the contradiction would be interesting work. It was a pity he could only fit Abra into the business slot. They might have had some fun together, he thought, dragging a hand through his still-damp hair. The trouble was, she was too uptight to settle back and have a good time. Perhaps it would be fair to say that she was too honest to take intimacy on a casual level. He couldn't fault her for that, which made one more reason to keep things on a business plane.

And there was too much friction. Friction usually led to a spark, and a spark to a blaze. He didn't have the time to fight fires just now.

With a glance at the clock on the bedside table he calculated the time back east. It was far too late to make any calls to the East Coast. That meant he'd have to get up at five, pull himself together and make all the necessary calls and connections between 6:00 and 7:00 a.m.

With a shrug, he decided that what was called for was a quick room-service meal and an early night. Just as he picked up the phone, the buzzer sounded at his door.

If there was one person he hadn't been expecting, it was Abra.

She stood there, balancing a brown grocery bag on one hip. Her hair was loose—it was the first time he'd seen it unbraided or unpinned—and curled wildly to her shoulders. She still wore jeans and a T-shirt, but she'd changed from work boots to sneakers. The next surprise was that she was almost smiling.

"Hi," she managed. It was ridiculous, but she'd never been so nervous in her life.

"Hi." He leaned against the doorframe and took a long, lazy scan. "Passing by?"

"Not exactly." Her fingers dug into the stiff brown paper bag. The telltale rattle made her relax them again. "Can I come in?"

"Sure." He stepped back, and she stepped through. From behind her, she heard the door click closed. Her heart jerked with it. "This is nice."

The living room of the suite was done in desert colors, mauves and umbers and creams. There were sketches on the walls and narrow louvered blinds at the windows. The room smelled of soap. He smelled of soap. Abra braced herself to turn.

"I wanted to apologize."

His brow lifted in an unconscious gesture as he studied her. She was doing her best, Cody realized, and hating every minute of it. Amused, he decided to draw the scene out.

"For what?"

She nearly ground her teeth. On the trip over she had prepared herself for the likelihood that he wouldn't make it easy. "For being rude and ungrateful this afternoon."

Cody slipped his hands into the pockets of his robe. "Just this afternoon?"

Venom nearly poured out, and it was hard to swallow. An apology was due, and she was damn well going to get it over with. "Yes. We're dealing with a specific instance. You helped me this afternoon, and I was ungrateful and unkind. I was wrong, and when I am I like to think I can admit it." Without asking, she moved over to the counter that separated the living space from the kitchenette. "I brought you some beer."

"To drink or to wear?" he asked when she pulled out a six pack.

"Up to you." She broke down enough to smile, really smile. The flecks in her eyes brightened. Her lips softened as if by magic. Cody felt his heart stop for two full beats. "I didn't know whether you'd eaten, so I tossed in a meatball sub and some fries."

"You brought me dinner?"

Uncomfortable, she shrugged. "It's no big deal, just a sandwich." She pulled out a twelve-inch tube wrapped in white paper.

"Some sandwich."

"Yeah." She took out the foam dish that held the french fries. If it killed her, she told herself, she was going to get the words out. And it might kill her, she thought, if he kept looking at her as though he'd rather nibble on her than the sub. "I wanted to thank you for acting so quickly this afternoon. I don't know whether I'd have gotten out of the way in time or not, but that's not the issue. The fact is, you made certain I wasn't hurt, and I never really thanked you at the time. I guess I was more shaken up than I realized."

As he had been, Cody thought. He crossed over to

stand beside her. She was holding the empty bag, folding and unfolding it. The gesture showed him more than words could have how much it had cost her to come. He took the bag from her and tossed it on the counter.

"You could have written that down in a nice little note and slipped it under the door. But I don't suppose that's your style." He resisted the urge to touch her hair, knowing it would be a mistake for both of them. He would only want to touch her more, and she already looked as though she'd jump out of her shoes at the first advance. Instead, he pulled a bottle out of the pack and turned it to read the label. "Want a beer?"

She hesitated only briefly. It looked as if he was going to make it easy for her after all. "Sure."

"Half a meatball sub?"

She relaxed and smiled again. "I could probably choke it down."

A truce, undeclared but understood, had been negotiated. They shared cold beer and spicy meatballs on Cody's terrace. A small in-ground spa swirled silently at their feet. Orange and red blossoms, their scent heavy, trailed up and along the high walls that closed them in. The sun was low, and the air was cooling.

"All the comforts of home," Abra mused as she sipped her beer.

Cody thought about his house, where everything was familiar, where so many walls were still unfinished and so many yards of trim were still unpainted. "Not quite home. But it's the next best thing."

Abra stretched the toes of her sneakers toward the water. Lord, she'd like to sink into that, close her eyes and let every muscle hum. With a soft sigh of regret, she dismissed the idea. "You do much traveling?"

"Enough. You?"

"Not really. Well, around the state. Up into Utah a couple of times. I like hotels."

"Really?"

She was relaxed enough to ignore his smirk. She bit into the sub and savored the blending of meat, sauce and cheese. "I like being able to take a shower and go out and come back to find fresh towels. Ordering room service and eating in bed. Stuff like that. You must like them, too." She watched him tilt back his beer. "You don't strike me as someone who'd keep doing something he didn't care for."

"I don't mind moving around." The fries were greasy and loaded with salt. Perfect. He took two. "I like knowing I've got some place to go back to, that's all."

She understood that very well, though it surprised her that he felt the sentiment—and the need. "Have you always lived in Florida?"

"Yeah. Can't say I care much for the snow-shoveling, finger-numbing weather in the north. I like the sun."

"Me too." She dug out fries. "It only rains here a handful of times a year. Rain's an event." With a grin, she finished off her half of the sub. The best meal, she had to admit, she'd had in weeks. It was hard to believe, but his company wasn't such a trial after all. She settled back to nurse her beer and wait for nightfall. "I'd like to see the ocean, though."

"Which one?"

"Any one."

Her eyes were gray in this light, he noted. Gray and a little sleepy. "It's a short flight to the West Coast."

"I know." She moved her shoulders and continued to watch the sky darken. "I always figured I needed a bigger reason to make the trip."

"Vacation?"

"I've been pushing pretty hard the last few years. This may be the age of women's liberation, but there are still walls to break down when you're an engineer who happens to be a woman."

"Why are you an engineer?"

He reached lazily for more fries, and so did she. Their fingers brushed companionably. "I always liked to figure out how things worked—or what to do to make them work better. I was good with numbers. I like the logic of them. If you put them together and figure out the formula, you're always going to come up with the right answer."

"The right answer's not always the best answer."

Crossing her legs at the ankles, she turned her head enough to study his face in the lowering light. "That's artistic thinking, which is why an architect needs a good engineer to keep him on track."

He took a lazy swallow of beer and smiled at her. "Is that what you're doing, Red? Keeping me on track?"

"It isn't easy. Take the design of the health club."

"I figured you'd get around to it."

Mellowed by the casual meal, she ignored his sarcasm. "The waterfall on the east wall. We'll overlook the fact that it's an impractical piece of fancy."

"You've got something against waterfalls?"

"This is the desert, Johnson."

"Ever hear of an oasis?"

She sighed, determined to be patient. It was a nice night. The food had been good, and the company more pleasant than she'd expected. "I'll give you your little whimsy."

"Bless you for that."

"But if you'd put it on the west wall, as I requested—"

"It doesn't work on the west wall," he said. "You need the windows on the west wall for the evening light, the sunsets. And the view's best in the west."

"I'm talking about logistics. Think plumbing."

"I leave that up to you. You think plumbing, I'll think aesthetics, and we'll get along fine."

Typical, typical, typical, she thought with a shake of her head. "Cody, my point is that this project could have been half as difficult as it is with a few minor adjustments."

The challenging light had come back into her eyes. He nearly smiled. The evening wouldn't have been complete without at least one argument. "If you're afraid of hard work, you should have found another profession."

That had her head snapping up, and her eyes, already filled with anger, narrowing. "I'm not afraid to work, and I'm damn good at what I do. It's people like you, who come along with your six-story egos, refusing to make any adjustments, who make things impossible."

He had a temper of his own, but he managed— barely—to check it. "It's not my ego that keeps me from making adjustments. If I made them, I wouldn't be doing the job I'd been hired to do."

"You call it professional integrity, I call it ego."

"And you're wrong," he said with deceptive calm. "Again."

She could have drawn in then and tried tact and subtlety—if she had thought of it. "Are you telling me it would have compromised your integrity to move that silly waterfall from east to west?"

"Yes."

"That's the most ridiculous thing I've ever heard. But typical," she said, rising to pace the tiny walled-in terrace. "God knows it's typical. Sometimes I think architects worry more about the color of paint than stress points."

He watched her as she paced. Her stride was long and loose, the kind that ate up ground from point to point easily. A woman going places, he mused. But he wasn't about to be walked over so that she could get there.

"You've got a bad habit of generalizing, Red."

"Don't call me Red," she muttered, then tugged an orange blossom off the vine. "I'll be glad when this project's finished and I'm out on my own. Then I can pick what architect I want to work with."

"Good luck. It might just be difficult for you to find one who's willing to put up with temper tantrums and nit-picking."

She whirled back. She knew she had a temper. She wouldn't deny it or apologize for it. But as to the rest... "I don't nitpick. It's not nit-picking to make a suggestion that would save laying an extra hundred feet of pipe. And only an egocentric, hardheaded architect would see it that way."

"You've got a problem, *Ms.* Wilson." He saw and enjoyed the way she stiffened at that. "You've got a low opinion of people in my profession, but as long as you pursue yours, you're stuck with us."

She mangled the flower she was holding. "Not everyone in your field's an idiot. There are some excellent architects in Arizona."

"So it's just architects from back east you don't like."

She wasn't going to let him put words in her mouth and make her sound like a fool. "I have no idea why Tim felt he had to hire a firm from out of state to begin with. But since he did, I'm doing my best to work with you."

"Your best could use some polishing up." Setting his beer aside, he rose. His face was in shadows, but she could tell by his stance that he was as angry as she was, and primed for a fight. "If you've got any other complaints, why don't you get them out now while there's just the two of us?"

She tossed the bruised flower, like a gauntlet, between them. "All right, I will. It infuriates me that you didn't bother to come out for any of the preliminary meetings. I was against hiring an East Coast firm, but Tim wouldn't listen. The fact that you were unavailable made things more complicated. Meanwhile, I've got to deal with Gray, who bites his fingernails and is always looking up codes or shuffling papers. Then you come out and swagger around like the cock of the walk, refusing to modify even one line of your precious design."

He took a step toward her, out of the shadows. He was angry, all right, she noted. It was just her luck that his temper made him more attractive. "In the first place,

I had a very good reason for missing the preliminary meetings. Good personal reasons that I don't feel obligated to discuss with you." He took another step. "The fact that your employer hired my firm over your objections is your problem, not mine."

"I prefer to think of it as his mistake, not mine."

"Fine." When he took the next step toward her, she had to fight back the urge to retreat. His eyes could be very dark, she discovered, very intense. He didn't remind her of a casual beachcomber now, or an easygoing cowboy. More like a gunslinger, she realized, but she held her ground. "As to Gray, he might be young and annoying, but he also works hard."

She felt a flush of shame and jammed her hands into her pockets. "I didn't mean…"

"Forget it." He took a final step that brought him so close that their bodies nearly brushed. Abra kept her jaw set and her eyes on his. "And I don't swagger."

She had a ridiculous urge to laugh, but something in his eyes warned her that that was the most dangerous thing she could do. Instead, she swallowed and lifted both brows. "You mean you don't do it on purpose?"

She was baiting him, plain and simple. He hadn't missed the light of amusement in her eyes. She wanted to laugh at him, and he'd be damned if she'd get away with it. "I don't do it at all. You, on the other hand, put on that hard hat and those steel-toed boots and stomp around the site trying to prove how tough you can be."

She opened her mouth in utter astonishment, then snapped it closed. "I don't stomp, and I don't have to prove anything to anyone. I'm doing the job I was trained to do."

"Then you do yours and I'll do mine."

"Fine. See you at sunup."

She started to spin toward the door, and he caught her by the arm. He didn't know what demon had prompted him to do it, to stop her when her angry exit would have been best for both of them. Now it was too late. The move was already made. Their faces were close, his hand was tight on her arm, and their bodies were turned toward each other. A half moon was rising. Outside the walls a woman's laugh ebbed and flowed as a couple strolled by beneath its light.

The friction had given birth to a spark—no, dozens of sparks, Cody thought as he felt them singe his skin. The heat from them was quick and dangerous, but still controllable. If he fanned them, they would flame. And then…

The hell with it, he thought as he closed his mouth over hers.

She was braced. She was ready. The desire and the intent had been plain to see as they'd stood there for that long, silent moment. Abra was honest enough to admit that the desire had been there all along. It had cut through her time and time again. So she was braced. She was ready.

It didn't do any good.

She should have been able to hold back her response, something she'd always been able to give or subdue as she chose. As *she* chose. It was frightening to learn in one split second that the choice wasn't always there.

Response ripped out of her before a decision could be made and shattered her opinion of her own free will.

She was holding on to him without any recollection of having reached out. Her body was pressed hard against his without any memory of having moved at all. When her lips parted, it was as much in demand as in invitation. His rough answer was exactly what she wanted.

He dragged her against him, amazed that need could rise from a simmer to a boil so quickly. Another surprise. What flared between them came as much from her as from him. She hadn't protested or struggled angrily away, but had met him force for force, passion for passion. With temper adding an edge to desire, he caught her hair in his hands and took as ruthlessly as his need demanded.

He nipped at her lip. Her low, throaty moan was as arousing as the play of her tongue over his. Now he gave himself freedom, letting his hands run over her, testing, tormenting, taking. Her body shuddered against his, then pressed closer. She didn't hold back, didn't seem to believe in it.

She should think, oh, she knew she should think. But it wasn't possible when her pulse was pounding in her head and her muscles were like water. How could she think when his taste was spreading through her, filling her?

He was as breathless as she when they drew apart. She was as willing as he when they came together for one last long, lingering kiss. When they parted again they stayed close, his hands on her shoulders, hers on his arms. Anger defused, passion ignited, leaving them both weak.

"What are we going to do about this?" Cody asked her.

She could only shake her head. It was too soon to think and too late not to.

"Why don't you sit down?"

She shook her head again before he could lead her to a chair. "No. No, I don't want to sit." It was harder than she'd thought it would be to step away from him. "I've got to go."

"Not quite yet." He needed a cigarette. He fumbled in the pockets of his robe and swore when he found his hands weren't steady. It amazed and infuriated him. "We have to resolve this, Abra."

She watched the match spark and flame, then drew a steadying breath. Flames could be lit, she reminded herself, and they could be put out just as easily. "It shouldn't have happened."

"That's beside the point."

It hurt, more than a little, that he hadn't disagreed with her. But of course he couldn't, she told herself. She was right. "No, I think that is the point." In frustration she dragged both hands through her hair, and he remembered all too clearly what it had felt like tangled around his own hands. "It shouldn't have happened, but it did, and now it's over. I think we're both too sensible and too professional to let it get in the way of our working relationship."

"Do you?" He should have known she'd handle this the same way she would a fouled-up order for concrete.

"Maybe you're right. Maybe. But you're an idiot if you think it won't happen again."

She had to be careful, very careful. It wasn't easy to speak calmly when her lips were still warm and swollen from his. "If it does, we'll simply have to deal with it—separately from business."

"We agree on something." Cody blew out a long stream of smoke. "What happened just now had nothing to do with business." Through the screen of smoke his eyes met hers and held them. "But that's not going to stop me from wanting you during working hours."

She felt a warning chill race up her spine. It made her straighten her shoulders. "Look, Cody, this is—was—a momentary thing. Maybe we were attracted, but—"

"Maybe?"

"All right, all right." She tried to find the right words. "I have to think of my future. We both know there's nothing more difficult, or awkward, than becoming involved with an associate."

"Life's rough," he murmured, and pitched his cigarette high over the wall. He watched the glow fly up and arc before he turned back to her. "Let's get something straight, Red. I kissed you and you kissed me right back. And it felt damn good. I'm going to want to kiss you again, and a lot more than that. What I'm not going to do is wait until it's convenient for you."

"You make all the decisions?" she snapped. "You make all the moves?"

He considered a moment. "Okay."

Fury didn't make her speechless. Taking a step forward, she poked a finger at his chest. "It's not okay, you arrogant pinhead. I kissed you back because I wanted to, because I liked it. If I kiss you again it'll be for the same reasons, not because you set the time and place. If I go to bed with you, the same rules hold. Got that straight?"

She was wonderful. Infuriating, but wonderful. He managed not to grab her. Instead, he grinned. When a woman called a spade a spade, you couldn't argue. "Straight as an arrow," he agreed. He tucked an errant strand of hair behind her ear. "Glad you liked it."

The sound that hissed out between her teeth was anything but pleased. His grin just widened. Rather than punch him in the face, she knocked his hand aside and turned for the door.

"Abra."

She yanked the door open and stood gripping the knob. "What?"

"Thanks for dinner."

The door slammed at her back, and then he did laugh. He waited ten seconds and heard the front door of the suite slam in turn. On impulse, he stripped off his robe and, turning on the timer for the spa, eased into the hot, bubbling water. He hoped it would soothe out the aches she'd left him with and clear his mind enough to let him think.

Chapter 4

Business. From now until the last tile was caulked Abra was determined to keep it strictly business between herself and Cody. Engineer to architect. They would discuss templates and curved headers, wiring and plastic pipe, concrete and thermal mass. Abra scowled at the bare bones of the health club. With luck, she thought, they would discuss nothing at all.

What had happened on that moonlit terrace was like temporary insanity. Inherited insanity, she decided as she dug her fists into her pockets. Obviously she was more like her mother than she had ever wanted to admit. An attractive man, a little stardust and *wham!* She was ready and willing to make a fool of herself.

She took the clipboard the foreman handed her, scanned the papers, then initialed them. She'd come this far without letting any congenital weaknesses muck up her life. She intended to go a lot farther. Maybe she had inherited the flaw from her mother, but unlike the sweet, eternally optimistic Jessie she had no intention of going into a romantic spin and ending up flat on her face. That moment of weakness had passed, and now it was back to business as usual.

She spent the morning running back and forth between the health club and the main building, with an occasional foray to check on the excavation work for the cabanas. The work on each section of the project was overlapping according to plan, keeping her constantly in demand to oversee, answer questions, smooth out problems.

She had a long, technical phone conversation with the mechanical engineer Thornway had assigned. He was moving more slowly than she might have liked, but his work was first-class. She made a note to go by the offices and take a good look at the dies for both the elevator and the mechanized roof over the pool.

Those were aspects of her profession she enjoyed every bit as much as the planning and figuring, and they were aspects she took every bit as seriously. She wasn't an engineer who figured her job was over once the specs were approved and the calculations checked. She'd wanted a part in the Barlow project that didn't begin and end at the drawing board. It had been given to her, and if she still winced inwardly when a shovelful of dirt was removed from the site, she had the satisfaction of being a part of its reshaping.

No one she came in contact with would have seen beneath the competent exterior to her distracted thoughts.

If she was constantly on the lookout for Cody, she told herself, it was only that she didn't care to be taken unaware. By noon she had decided he wasn't going to show. Disappointment masqueraded as relief.

She took her lunch break in the trailer with a bottle of chilled orange juice, a bag of chips and blueprints. Since her conversation with the mechanical engineer she had decided there were still a few problems to work out in the dynamics of the sliding glass roof Cody wanted over the pool. She crunched into a chip while she punched a new equation into her calculator. If it weren't for the waterfall the man insisted on having run down the wall and into the corner of the pool... Abra shook her head and tried a new angle. The man was a maniac about waterfalls, she thought. She took a long swig of juice. Basically he was just a maniac. It helped to think of him that way, as a crazy architect with delusions of grandeur, rather than as a man who could kiss the common sense right out of you.

She was going to give him his damn sliding glass arch of a roof, and his waterfalls, and his spirals and domes. Then she was going to use this foolish fancy of a design to launch her own career while he went back to his humidity and his orange groves.

Nearly satisfied, Abra sketched out a few details, then ran a new set of figures. It wasn't her job to approve, she reminded herself, it was her job to make it work. She was very good at making things work.

When the door opened, she didn't bother to glance up.

"Close that quick, will you? You'll let the heat in."

"Yes, ma'am."

The lazy drawl had her head jerking up. She straightened her shoulders automatically as Cody stooped to walk through the doorway. "I didn't think we'd see you here today."

He merely smiled and stood aside to make room for Tim Thornway and the bullet-shaped form of William Walton Barlow, Sr. Awkwardly, due to the row of cabinets over her head, Abra stood.

"Abra." Though he would have preferred to have found her knee-deep in concrete or up on the scaffolding, Tim was skilled enough to use almost any situation to his advantage. "As you can see, WW," he said, "our crew lives, sleeps and eats B and B's resort hotel. You remember Ms. Wilson, our chief structural engineer."

The little man with the thatch of white hair and the shrewd eyes held out a meaty hand. "Indeed, indeed. A Barlow never forgets a pretty face."

To her credit, Abra didn't wince, not even when Cody smirked over Barlow's head. "It's nice to see you again, Mr. Barlow."

"WW thought it was time he had a look at things," Tim explained. "Of course, we don't want to interrupt the flow or slacken the pace—"

"Don't know much about putting these places up," Barlow cut in. "Know about running them. Like what I see, though." He nodded three times. "Like the curves and arches. Classy. Barlow and Barlow stands for classy operations."

Abra ignored Cody's grin and scooted out from behind the table. "You picked a hot day to visit, Mr. Barlow. Can I get you something cold? Juice, tea?"

"Take a beer. Nothing washes away the dust like a cold beer."

Cody opened the scaled-down refrigerator himself and rooted some out. "We were about to show WW the progress on the health club."

"Oh?" Abra shook her head at the offer of a beer and was amused when Tim accepted a bottle gingerly. "Good timing. I've just been working out the final details on the pool roof. I think Lafferty and I smoothed out some of the bugs over the phone this morning."

Barlow glanced down at the blueprints and at the stacks of paper covered with figures and calculations. "I'll leave that to you. Only numbers I'm handy with are in an account book. Looks like you know your way around, though." He gestured with his bottle before taking three healthy gulps. "Thornway always said you had a head on your shoulders. Pretty shoulders, too." He winked at her.

Rather than getting her dander up, the wink made her grin. He was nearly old enough to be her grandfather and, multimillionaire or not, he had a certain rough charm. "Thank you. He always spoke highly of you."

"I miss him," Barlow said. Then he turned to the matter at hand. "Let's get on with this tour, Tim. No use wasting time."

"Of course." Tim set aside his untouched beer. "I'm giving a little dinner party for Mr. Barlow tonight. Seven. You'll escort Mr. Johnson, Abra."

Since it wasn't a question, Abra opened her mouth

with the idea of making some excuse. Cody stepped smoothly in. "I'll pick up Ms. Wilson. Why don't you start over to the health club? We'll be right with you."

"Why don't you loosen that damn tie, Tim?" Barlow asked as they stepped out of the trailer. "Man could strangle in this heat."

Cody shut the door, then leaned against it. "They *are* nice shoulders. From what I've seen of them."

From an engineering standpoint, Abra couldn't have said why the trailer seemed more crowded now than it had a moment before. Turning back to the table, she began to tidy her papers. "It isn't necessary for you to pick me up this evening."

"No." He studied her, not certain whether he was amused or annoyed by her withdrawal. He hadn't slept well, and he knew the blame lay squarely on those pretty shoulders, which were now braced for an attack. "But I will."

This was business, Abra told herself, and should be handled as such. Making up her mind, she turned to face him. "All right. You'll need an address."

He smiled again, slowly this time. "Oh, I think I can find you, Red. Same way you found me."

Since he'd brought it up, Abra told herself, it would be best to deal with it. "It's good that we have a minute here. We can clear things up."

"What things?" Cody pushed away from the door. Abra backed into the table hard. "We had a mule back home on the farm," he mused as he stepped closer. "She tended to be skittish, too."

"I'm not skittish. It's simply that I think you have the wrong impression."

"I have the right impression," he told her, reaching around to toy with the end of her braid. "Of just how your body feels when it's fitted against mine. A very right and very pleasant impression."

"That was a mistake." She would have turned away to move around him, but he tightened his grip on her hair and tugged her back.

"What was?"

"Last night." She was going to handle this calmly, Abra told herself. She was basically a calm and reasonable person. "It should never have happened."

"It?" His eyes had darkened. Abra noted that, and noted, also, that there was no anger to be seen in them. She let out a little breath of relief. Obviously he was prepared to be as reasonable as she.

"I suppose we just got caught up in the moment. The best thing to do is forget it and go on."

"Okay." She saw his smile but didn't notice how cool it was. He wasn't much of a hand at chess, but he was a killer at poker. "We'll forget last night."

Pleased at the ease with which the problem had been erased, she smiled back at him. "Well, then, why don't we—"

Her words were cut off as he dragged her against him and covered her mouth with his. Her body went rigid— from shock, she told herself. From fury. That was what she wanted to believe. Today there was none of the gentle, sensual exploration in the moonlight. This kiss was as bold and as bright as the sun that beat through the windows. And as angry, she thought as he twisted her against him and took whatever he wanted. She tried to yank free and was held fast. Those subtle muscles covered steel. Abra found herself caught up in an embrace that threatened every bit as much as it promised.

He didn't give a damn. She could stand there and talk all she wanted in that reasonable voice about mistakes. He'd made mistakes before and lived through them. She might be the biggest, she would certainly be the costliest, but he wasn't about to back off now. He remembered the way she had felt in his arms the night before, that shivering, wire-taut passion, that abrupt avalanche of emotion. Even then he'd known it was nothing he'd felt before, nothing he would feel again. Not with anyone else. He'd see them both damned before it was forgotten.

"Stop," she managed before he crushed her mouth again. She was drowning, and she knew she couldn't save herself. Drowning, she thought as she moaned against his lips. Drowning in sensations, in longings, in desires. Why was she clinging to him when she knew it was crazy? Why was she answering that hard, hungry kiss when she knew it could lead to nothing but disaster?

But her arms were around him, her lips were parted, her heart was pounding in rhythm with his. This was more than temptation, more than surrender. What she felt now wasn't a need to give but a need to take.

When they broke apart she dragged air into her lungs and braced a hand on the table for balance. She could see now that she'd been wrong. There was anger in his eyes, anger and determination and a rough-edged desire that rooted her to the spot. Still, when he spoke, his voice was mild.

"Looks as if we have another point of reference, Red." He swung to the door. "See you at seven."

There were at least a half a dozen times that evening that Abra thought of a plausible excuse and began to dial Cody at his hotel. What stopped her each time was the knowledge that if she made the call she would be acknowledging not only that there was something between them but that she was a coward. Even if she forced herself to accept the fact that she was afraid, she couldn't allow him to see it.

She was obliged to go, she reminded herself as she rummaged through her closet once again. It was really no more than a business meeting, though they would be wearing evening dress and picking at canapés on Tim's elegant patio. It was politic and necessary to show Barlow that his architect and engineer could handle a social evening together.

She had to be able to handle it. Sexual attraction aside, Cody Johnson was her associate on this project. If she couldn't handle him—and what he seemed bound and determined to make her feel—she couldn't handle the job. No slow-talking East Coast architect was going to make her admit she couldn't handle anything that came her way.

In any case, she thought with some satisfaction as she tried to decide between two dresses, once they were there there would be so many people that they would get lost in the shuffle. It was doubtful she and Cody would have to exchange more than a few words.

When the knock came, she looked at her watch and swore. She'd been talking to herself for so long that it was time to leave and she wasn't even dressed. Tightening the belt on her robe, she went out of the cramped bedroom into the tiny living area and answered the door.

Cody took one lazy look at her short cotton robe and grinned. "Nice dress."

"I'm running behind," she muttered. "You can go on without me."

"I'll wait." Without waiting for an invitation, he walked in and surveyed her apartment.

She might be a woman who dealt in precise facts and figures, but she lived in chaos. Bright pillows were tossed on a faded couch, and piles of magazines were stacked on a mismatched chair. For someone who made her living turning facts and figures into structure and form, she didn't know the first thing about decorating space—or didn't care to, Cody mused. He'd seen her work, and had admired it. If she put her mind to it, he figured, she could turn a closet into an organized and functional living area.

The room was smaller than the bedroom of his hotel suite, but no one would have called it impersonal. Dozens of pictures jockeyed for position on a long table in front of the single window. There was a comfortable layer of dust over everything except a collection of crystals that hung at the window and caught the last of the evening light.

That, more than anything else in the room, told him that she spent little time there but cared for what mattered to her.

"I won't be long," Abra told him. "If you want a drink or something, the kitchen's through there."

She escaped, clicking the door firmly behind her. God, he looked wonderful. It wasn't fair for him to look so sexy, so confident, so utterly perfect. She dragged her hands through the hair she had yet to attempt to style. It was bad enough that he looked so good in work clothes, but he looked even better in a cream-colored jacket that set off his sun-bleached hair and his tanned skin, and that didn't seem fair. Even dressed more formally for the evening he didn't lose the casual flair of the beachcomber or the masculine appeal of the cowboy. How was she supposed to fight off an attraction when every time he showed up he was that much more attractive?

The hell with it, she thought as she faced her closet again. She was going to handle him and the attraction she felt. That meant she wasn't going to wear that plain and proper blue suit after all. If she was going to play with fire, she decided, she was going to have to dress for it.

Cody found her kitchen in the same unapologetic disarray as the living room. One wouldn't have called it dirty. Something normally had to be put to use to get that way, and it was obvious that she wasn't a woman who spent a lot of time over a stove. The fact that she had a tin of cookies and a canister full of tea bags set on two of the burners made that clear.

He found a bottle of wine in the refrigerator, along

with a jar of peanut butter and one lonely egg. After a search through the cupboards he located two mismatched wineglasses and a paperback copy of a horror novel by a well-known writer.

He took a sip of the wine and shook his head. He hoped he'd have a chance to teach her a little about vintages. Carrying both glasses into the living room, he listened to the sounds of movement from the bedroom. Apparently she was looking for something and pulling out every drawer she owned in the search. Sipping gingerly, he studied her photographs.

There were some of her, one a formal shot showing that she'd been very uncomfortable in pink organdy. There was another with her standing beside an attractive blonde. Since the blonde had Abra's hazel eyes, Cody wondered if she might be an older sister. There were more of the blonde, one in what might have been a wedding dress, and another of Abra in a hard hat. There were pictures of men scattered throughout, the only one he recognized being of Thornway senior. He sipped again, wondering if any were of her father, then turned. The noises in the bedroom had stopped.

"I poured some wine," he called out. "Want yours?"

"No… Yes, damn it."

"I'll go with the yes." Walking over, Cody pushed open the bedroom door.

There was something about a long, slender woman in a black dress, Cody decided. Something that made a man's mouth water. The dress dipped low in the front, and the plunge was banded with silver in a design that was repeated again at the hem, where the skirt skimmed above her knees. The glitter was designed to draw the eye before it moved down the length of slim legs clad in sheer, smoky stockings. But it was the back that was troubling Abra. She was struggling to fasten the hooks, which stopped at her waist.

"Something's stuck."

His heartbeat, Cody thought, and he waited for it to pick up speed again. If she'd attracted him in a hard hat and a sweaty T-shirt, that was nothing compared to what she was doing to him now.

"Here." He stepped over sturdy work boots and a pair of glossy black heels that were no more than a few leather straps.

"They design these things so that you have to fight your way in and out of them."

"Yeah." He handed her both glasses and tried not to think about how much more interesting it would be to help her fight her way out of this particular scrap of black silk. "You've got the hooks twisted."

She let out an impatient breath. "I know that. Can you fix it?"

He glanced up, and their eyes met in the mirror above her dresser. For the first time since he'd seen her, she had put on lipstick. Her mouth looked slick and ripe and inviting. "Probably. What are you wearing?"

She sipped because her throat was suddenly dry. "That should be obvious. A black dress with faulty hooks."

"I mean the scent." He dipped a little closer to her neck.

"I don't know." She would have moved away, but his

fingers were busy at the waist of her dress. "Something my mother bought me."

"I'm going to have to meet your mother."

She sipped again. "Are you finished back there?"

"Not nearly." He skimmed his fingers up her back and had the pleasure of watching her reaction reflected in the mirror. "You're very responsive, Abra."

"We're very late," she countered, turning.

"Then a couple of minutes more shouldn't matter." He slid his hands lightly around her waist. In defense, she pressed both glasses against his chest. He took them patiently and set them on the dresser behind her. "You have lousy taste in wine."

"I know the difference between white and red." She lifted her hands to his shoulders as he circled her waist again. His grip was loose, just the slight pressure of his fingertips against her. But she didn't shift aside.

"That's like saying I'm a man and you're a woman. There's a lot more to it than that." He bent his head to nibble at her lips. He'd been right. They were inviting. Very inviting. "A whole lot more."

"With me things are one way or another. Cody." She arched away as she felt the floor tilt under her feet. "I'm not ready for this."

A yes or no he would have dealt with swiftly. But there was a desperation in her words that made him pull back. "For what?"

"For what's happening." There were times for flat-out honesty. "For you and what I'm feeling."

His eyes skimmed over her face and came back to hers. She'd given him the leverage. They both knew it.

Rather than applying weight, he gave her space. "How long do you need?"

"That's not a question I can answer." Her fingers tightened on his shoulders as his hands moved up and down her back. "You keep backing me into corners."

"So I do," he murmured. He moved aside and waited while she stepped into her shoes. "Abra." When she looked at him again, he took her hand. "This isn't the end of it. I have a feeling the end's a long way off."

She was absolutely certain he was right. That was what worried her. "I have a policy," she said carefully. "I like to know what the end looks like before I begin. I can't see a nice clean finish with you, Cody, so I'm not altogether sure I want to take you on—so to speak."

"Red." He brought her hand to his lips, leaving her flustered. "You already have."

By the time they arrived at the Thornway estate, the party was in full swing. The buffet was loaded with spicy Mexican cuisine, and wine and margaritas flowed. Beyond the spreading white-and-pink ranch house that Tim had had built for his bride was a sweep of carefully manicured lawn dotted with a few rustling palms. A pool glittered at the tip of a slight slope. Near it was a pretty gazebo shielded by trailing vines just beginning to bloom.

The scent from the side garden was as sweet as the moonlight.

There was a crowd mingling on the glassed-in terrace and the lawn. The cream of Phoenix society had turned out. Abra had already decided to find herself a nice quiet corner. She was always pleased to build for the upper crust, but she didn't have a clue how to socialize with them.

"A Chablis," Cody explained as he handed Abra a glass. "California. Nice clean color, sharp aroma, and very full-bodied."

Abra lifted a shoulder as she sipped. "It's white."

"And your dress is black, but it doesn't make you look like a nun."

"Wine's wine," she said, though her palate told her differently.

"Honey—" he trailed a finger down the side of her throat "—you have a lot to learn."

"There you are." Marci Thornway, Tim's wife of two years, glided up. She wore a heavily embroidered white silk caftan, and around her neck was a jeweled collar that glittered in the moonlight. She gave Abra a pat on the hand, then lifted her sapphire-blue eyes to Cody. Her voice dripped like Spanish moss. "I suppose I can understand why you were late."

"Marci Thornway, Cody Johnson."

"The architect." Marci slipped a proprietary hand through Cody's arm. "Tim's told me all about you— except he didn't mention you were so attractive." She laughed. It was a musical sound that suited her silvery blond looks and her petite frame. "But then, husbands have to be forgiven for not telling their wives about handsome men."

"Or men about their beautiful wives."

Abra made a face behind Marci's back and began to spoon up a cheese enchilada.

"You're from Florida, aren't you?" With a little sigh, Marci began leading Cody away. "I grew up in Georgia, a little town outside of Atlanta. Sometimes I swear I could pine away from missing it."

"Little magnolia blossom," Abra muttered, and turned directly into Barlow. "Oh, excuse me, Mr. Barlow."

"That's WW to you. Ought to put more on your plate, girl. Here, try these tortillas. Don't forget the guacamole."

Abra stared down at the food he had heaped on her dish. "Thanks."

"Why don't you have a seat with me and keep an old man company in the moonlight?"

Abra wasn't sure what she'd expected of this evening, but it hadn't been to enjoy a sweet and funny hour with one of the richest men in the country. He didn't, as she had half feared, make a pass, but flirted like an old family friend across the comfortable distance of thirty-five years.

They sat on a bench by the rippling waters of the pool and talked about their mutual love of movies. It was the one vice Abra allowed herself, the only pure recreation she didn't consider a waste of time.

If her attention wandered from time to time, it wasn't because she found Barlow boring, it was because she spotted Cody off and on—more often than not in Marci Thornway's company.

"Selfish," Barlow decided as he finished off his drink. "Ought to let you mingle with the young people."

Feeling guilty about her lapse, she gave him a warm

smile. "Oh, no, I like talking to you. To tell you the truth, WW, I'm not much on parties."

"Pretty thing like you needs a young man to fuss over her."

"I don't like to be fussed over at all." She saw Cody light Marci's cigarette.

Barlow was nothing if not shrewd. He followed the direction of Abra's gaze. "Now there's a pretty little thing," he observed. "Like spun glass—expensive and easy to look at. Young Tim must have his hands full."

"He's very devoted to her."

"Been keeping your architect close company this evening."

"*Your* architect," Abra said. Because she didn't like the way that sounded, she smiled. "They're both from the East—Southeast. I'm sure they have a lot in common."

"Mmm." Plainly amused, Barlow rose. "Like to stretch my legs. How about walking around the garden?"

"All right." She made a point of keeping her back to Cody as she took Barlow's arm and strolled off.

What the hell kind of game was she playing? Cody wondered as he watched Abra disappear with Barlow. The man was old enough—more than old enough—to be her father. She'd spent the entire evening cozying up to the man while he'd been trying to untangle himself from the wisteria vine called Marci Thornway.

Cody recognized a woman on the prowl, and the porcelain-cheeked Marci was definitely sending out signals—ones Cody wasn't the least bit interested in receiving. Even if he hadn't already set his sights on Abra, he wouldn't have felt the slightest tug from a woman like Marci. Married or not, she was trouble. Tim was welcome to her.

He wouldn't have judged Abra to be the kind of woman to flatter an old man, to smile and flirt with one with an eye to what it could gain her. There was no mistaking the fact that Barlow was smitten with her, or that she had just wandered off into the roses with one of the *Fortune* 500's best.

Cody lit a cigarette, then narrowed his eyes against the smoke. There was no mistaking the fact that she had wanted him. He might have initiated the kiss—might even have backed her into a corner, as she'd said—but her response had been full-blown. No one kissed like that unless she meant it.

Yet she'd pulled back. Each time. He'd thought it was because she was cautious, maybe even a little afraid of how strong the connection between them had become. And maybe he was a fool, and she held him off because she wanted to snag a bigger fish.

Almost as soon as the thought took root, he ripped it out. It was unfair, he told himself. He was allowing himself to think that way because he was frustrated—because he wanted Abra more than he had ever wanted anyone. And, most of all, because he didn't know what the hell to do about it.

"Excuse me." He cut Marci off in midsentence, sent her a quick smile and strode off toward the garden.

He heard Abra's laughter, a low whispering sound that made him think of the mist on the lake near his home. Then he saw her, standing in the beam of one of the colored lanterns the Thornways' staff had hung all over the garden. She was smiling, twirling a red blossom in her fingertips. The same kind of flower, Cody noted, that she had mangled on his terrace only the night before.

"There's not much meat," Barlow was saying as he grinned at her, "but what's there is choice."

She laughed again, then slipped the stem of the flower into his lapel.

"I beg your pardon."

Both Barlow and Abra turned—guiltily, Cody thought—at the sound of his voice.

"Well, Johnson, been enjoying yourself?" Barlow gave him a quick slap on the shoulder. "Enjoy yourself more if you took a stroll in the moonlight with someone as pretty as our Abra here. Young people don't take enough time for romance these days. Going to see if I can dig up a beer."

For a broad man, he moved quickly enough and Abra found herself alone in the festively lit garden with Cody. "I should probably go mingle—" she began, but she stopped short when Cody blocked her path.

"You haven't felt the need to mingle all evening."

Her main thought was to get out of the garden and away from him, so she just gave him a vague smile. "I've been enjoying WW. He's great company."

"I noticed. It's an unusual woman who can jump from man to man so smoothly. My compliments."

The smile turned into a look of blank confusion.

Cody found a match and cupped his hand over the

flame as he lit a cigarette. "He might be in his sixties, but two or three hundred million melt the years away, I imagine."

Abra stared at him for nearly a full minute. "Maybe you should go out and come in again. Then I might understand what you're talking about."

He tossed aside the match. In heels she was eye to eye with him. "I think I'm clear enough. Barlow's a very rich man, widowed for about ten years, and one who obviously appreciates a young, attractive woman."

She nearly laughed, but then she saw the disdain in his eyes. He was serious, she realized. It was incredibly insulting. "You could say he's certainly a man who knows how to treat a woman. Now, if you'll excuse me."

He grabbed her arm before she could storm past him. "I don't find any excuse for you, Red, but that doesn't stop me from wanting you." He pulled her around until they were once again face-to-face. "Can't say that I care for it, but there it is. I want you, and whatever goes on in that calculating head of yours I intend to have you."

"You can go straight to hell, Johnson." She jerked her arm away, but she wasn't through. "I don't care what you want, or what you think of me, but because I like Mr. Barlow too much to let you go on thinking he's some kind of senile fool, I'll let you in on something. We had a conversation tonight, the way some people do in social situations. We happened to hit it off. I wasn't coming on to him, nor he to me."

"What about that crack I heard when I walked up?"

"What?" She hesitated a minute, and then she did laugh. But her eyes were cold. "That was a line from a movie, you simpleton. An old Tracy-Hepburn movie. Mr. Barlow and I both happen to be fans. And I'll tell you something else." Temper lost, she shoved him, taking him back two steps. "If he *had* been coming on to me, it would've been none of your business. If I want to flirt with him, that's my business. If I want to have an affair with him—or anyone else—you don't have jack to say about it." She shoved him again, just for the satisfaction. "Maybe I prefer his kind of attention to the grab-and-go treatment I get from you."

"Now hold on."

"You hold on." Her eyes glowed green in the light from the lanterns. "I have no intention of tolerating this kind of insult from you, or anyone. So keep clear, Johnson, if you want that face of yours to stay in one piece."

She stormed off, leaving Cody singed. He let out a breath between his teeth as he dropped the cigarette onto the path and crushed it out.

"You had that one coming, Johnson," he muttered, rubbing the back of his neck. He knew what it was to dig a hole, and he knew he'd dug this one deep. He also knew that there was only one way out.

Chapter 5

He thought about flowers. Somehow Cody didn't think Abra was the type of woman to melt at the sight of a few roses. He considered a straight-out apology, the kind of no-frills shoot-from-the-hip *I'm sorry* one friend might offer another. But he didn't think Abra saw him as a friend, exactly. In any case, the ice she was dishing out would freeze the words before they got from his mouth to her ear. So he gave her the only thing he thought she would accept for the time being. Space.

They worked together over the next two weeks, often shoulder to shoulder. The distance between them was as great as that between the sun and the moon. Consultations were often necessary, but Abra always arranged it so that they weren't alone. With a skill he was forced to admire, she used Charlie Gray as a buffer. It couldn't have been easy, but she avoided Cody altogether whenever possible. Understanding the need for a cooling-off period, he did nothing to change the situation. Twice he made brief trips, once to the home office in Fort Lauderdale and once to work out a few bugs in a medical complex in San Diego.

Each time he returned he stuck a toe in the waters of Abra's temperament and found them still frigid.

With his hard hat in place and his eyes shielded by tinted glasses, Cody watched the glass of the dome being lowered into place.

"A nice touch. A class touch." Barlow looked up, grinning at the light that came through the glass in red-and-gold spears.

"WW." Cody relaxed a bit when the glass settled on the opening like a cap on a bottle. "Didn't know you were back in town."

"Doing some spot-checking." Barlow mopped his face with a handkerchief. "Hope they get that cooling system going."

"It's on today's schedule."

"Good. Good." Barlow turned around, wanting to take in the entire sweep of building. It pleased him. It had the look of a castle, noble and impregnable, yet at the same time was unabashedly modern. He strolled over to study the glass arch of roof that brought the mountain into the lobby. He approved of the dramatic touch here, where guests would check in and out. First and last impressions, he thought. Young Johnson was making certain they would be lasting ones. Landscapers would plant a few desert shrubs and cacti, then let nature take over. All along the west wall were wide arching windows that let in the vast arena of desert and butte. To the west, men were connecting pipe and laying the stone pool for the waterfall.

"I'll say this, boy—you deliver." It was the kind of blunt compliment Barlow gave only when it was deserved. "I'll admit I had some bad moments over the blueprints and the mock-ups, but my son saw something in all this. I went with his judgment, and I can say now he was right. You've made yourself something here, Cody. Not every man can look back on his life and say the same."

"I appreciate that."

"I'm going to want you to show me the rest." He slapped Cody on the back. "Meantime, is there a place a man can get a beer around here?"

"I think we can arrange it." Cody led the way outside to an ice chest and dug out two cans.

Barlow drank deeply and sighed. His thinning hair was covered by a straw hat with a paisley band. A porch hat, Cody's mother would have called it. It had the effect of making the millionaire look like a retired tobacco farmer.

"I'll be sixty-five my next birthday, and there's still nothing quite like a cold beer on a hot afternoon." Barlow glanced toward the health club and caught a glimpse of Abra. "Well, maybe one thing." With a quick bray of laughter he sat down on the ice chest and loosened his collar. "I like to think of myself as a student of human nature. Figure I made most of my money that way."

"Mmm-hmm," Cody responded absently. He, too, had spotted Abra. She was wearing baggy bib overalls that should have made her appear sexless. They didn't. Cody kept remembering how she'd looked in the little black dress.

"Seems to me you're a man with more on his mind than steel and glass." Barlow swigged his beer with simple appreciation. "Wouldn't have something to do with a long-legged engineer, would it?"

"Might." Cody sent him a mild look as he took out his cigarettes. He offered Barlow one, but the older man shook his head.

"Had to give them up. Damn doctors yammering at me. Took a liking to her," he continued, switching back easily to the subject of Abra. "'Course, most men take a liking to good looks, but she's got brains and grit. Might have scared me off in my younger days." He grinned and took off his hat to fan his face. "Seemed to me you two had a tiff at that do we had at Tim Thornway's."

"You could call it that." Cody sipped and considered. "I was jealous of you."

"Jealous?" Barlow had lifted the can to his lips. Now he had to set it on the ground for fear he'd drop it as he roared with laughter. Cutting loose, he rocked back and forth on the chest, mopping his streaming face with his handkerchief. "You just knocked twenty years off me, boy. I gotta thank you." He sucked in air, then let it out again in a wheeze. "Imagine a good-looking sonofabitch like you jealous of an old man." He caught his breath and leaned back, still grinning. "A rich old man. Well, well, I don't suppose the little lady took kindly to that."

"The little lady," Cody drawled, "came very close to knocking out my teeth."

"Told you she had grit." Barlow stuffed his handkerchief back in his pocket, then picked up his beer. Life still had some surprises, he thought. Thank God. "Fact is, I had her in mind for my son." At Cody's look, he chuckled and dropped the hat back on his head. "Don't get your dander up now, boy. A man can only take so much excitement in one day. 'Sides, decided against it when I saw the way she looked at you."

"That simplifies things."

"Between you and me, anyway," Barlow pointed out. "Otherwise, I'd say you were about waist-deep in quicksand."

"Pretty accurate estimate." Cody tossed his empty can in a trash barrel. "Any suggestions?"

"Better find yourself a rope, son, and haul your tail out."

"My father always used flowers," Cody mused.

"Couldn't hurt." Wincing at a few creaks in his joints, Barlow rose. "Neither would groveling." He noted Cody's expression and laughed again. "Too young for groveling yet," he said. "But you'll learn." He gave Cody a thump on the back. "Yes, indeed, you'll learn."

He wasn't about to grovel. Absolutely not. But he thought it might be time to give the flowers a shot. If a woman hadn't cooled off some in two weeks, she wasn't going to cool off at all—at least not without a little help.

In any case, Cody told himself, he owed her an apology. He laughed a little to himself as he shifted the tiger lilies to his other hand. It seemed as if they'd been bouncing apologies back and forth since the first minute they'd met. Why break the pattern? he mused as he stood in front of her door. If she didn't accept it now, he'd just stick around and drive her crazy until she did.

Each of them seemed to excel at driving the other crazy.

Besides, he'd missed her. It was as simple as that. He'd missed arguing with her about the project. He'd missed hearing her laugh the way she could when her guard was down. He'd missed the strong, uninhibited way her arms would come around him.

He glanced at the flowers in his hand. Tiger lilies were a pretty fragile rope, but they were better than none at all. Even if she tossed them in his face, it would be a change from the stiff politeness she'd dished out since the evening at Tim's. He knocked and wondered what he was going to say to get his foot in the door.

It wasn't Abra who answered, but the blonde from the photographs. She was a small, rosy-cheeked woman Cody guessed was about forty. She was dressed very simply, in a copper-colored jumpsuit that complemented her hair and her eyes, which were so much like Abra's. Cody smiled at her, as much for that as for the fact that, in her porcelain way, she was a knockout.

"Well, hello." She smiled back at him and offered a hand. "I'm Jessie Peters."

"Cody Johnson. I'm a—an associate of Abra's."

"I see." She gave him a slow, sweeping study that was laced with feminine approval. "Come in. I always love meeting Abra's…associates. Would you like a drink? Abra's in the shower."

"Sure." He remembered Abra's wine. "Something cold, if you have it."

"I've just made some lemonade. Fresh. Make yourself at home." She disappeared into the adjoining kitchen. "Was Abra expecting you?"

"No." He glanced around, noting that the apartment had had a swift but thorough tidying.

"A surprise, then. I love surprises." She walked back in with two tall glasses crackling with ice. "Are you an engineer?"

"I'm an architect."

Jessie paused for a moment. Then a smile wisped around her mouth. "*The* architect," she murmured, gesturing for Cody to sit. "I believe Abra's mentioned you."

"I'll bet." He set the flowers on the newly dusted table.

"She didn't mention you were so attractive." Jessie crossed her legs and settled back. "But it's like her to keep a thing like that to herself." She ran a fingertip down her glass as she summed him up. Her hand was pretty and fragile-looking, like the novelty magnet in Abra's car. There was a diamond on her finger, a small one in a rather ornate setting, but no wedding band. "You're from the East?"

"That's right. Florida."

"I never think of Florida as the East," she commented. "I always think of Disney World."

"Did I hear the door? I— Oh." Abra came out of the adjoining bedroom. She was wearing baggy white pants and an oversize sweatshirt with a pair of battered-looking sandals. Her hair was still damp and curled from the shower.

"You have company." Jessie rose and gathered up the flowers. "Bearing gifts."

"Yes, I see." Abra dug her hands into the deep pockets of her pants.

With her bright smile still in place, Jessie buried her face in the blooms. She recognized tension and romance. As far as she was concerned, one was wasted without the other. "Why don't I put these in water for you, sweetheart? You don't happen to have a vase, do you?"

"Somewhere."

"Of course."

Abra waited until Jessie went into the kitchen to search for it. Cautious, she kept her voice low. "What do you want?"

"To see you."

Abra's hands tightened into fists in her pockets when he rose. "You've done that. Now, if you'll excuse me, I'm busy this evening."

"And to apologize," Cody continued.

She hesitated, then let out a long breath. She had gone to him once with an apology, and he had accepted. If there was one thing she understood, it was how difficult it was to try to mend fences temper had broken.

"It's all right," she said, and managed what she hoped was a casual smile. "Let's forget it."

"Wouldn't you like an explanation?" He took a step forward. She took one backward.

"I don't think so. It might be best if—"

"I found one." Jessie came back in holding a milk bottle. "So to speak. Actually, I think they look charming in this, don't you?" She set the flowers in the center of the coffee table, then stepped back to admire them. "Don't forget to change the water, Abra. And it wouldn't hurt to lift the vase up when you dust."

"Mom…"

"Mom? You've got to be kidding." The genuine astonishment in Cody's voice had Jessie beaming.

"That's the nicest compliment I've had all day," she said. "If I didn't love her so much, I'd deny it." Raising up on her toes, she kissed Abra's cheek, then brushed lightly at the faint smear of lipstick she left behind. "You two have a nice evening. Don't forget to call me."

"But you just got here."

"I've a million things to do." Jessie gave her daughter's hand a squeeze, then offered her own to Cody. "It was lovely meeting you."

"I hope I see you again, Mrs. Peters."

"Jessie." She smiled again. "I insist that all handsome men call me Jessie." The sweep of her lashes was the gesture of a practiced flirt. "Good night, sweetheart. Oh, you're almost out of dish detergent."

Abra let out a huff of breath when the door closed.

"Are you sure that's your mother?"

"Most of the time." Abra tunneled her fingers through her hair. Jessie always left her feeling bewildered. "Look, Cody, I appreciate you coming by to clear the air."

"Now clear out?"

"I don't want to be rude. I think both of us have used up our share of rudeness for this year, but it would simplify things if we kept our contact limited to working hours."

"I never said I wanted things simple." He took a step closer. Her eyes stayed warily on his as he toyed with the damp ends of her hair. "But if you do, fine. I look at you and I want. It doesn't get much simpler than that."

"For you." If it was difficult not to step away, it was much more difficult not to step forward. "I don't want to get into all of the reasons, but when I told you that I wasn't ready I was being perfectly honest. Added to that is the fact that we just don't get along very well. We don't know each other. We don't understand each other."

"All right. So we'll get to know each other."

"You're simplifying."

"Isn't that what you just said you wanted?"

Feeling trapped, she turned away and sat down. "Cody, I told you, I have reasons for not wanting to get involved with you, with anyone."

"Let's just stick with me." He sat across from her. For the life of him he couldn't understand why he was so keyed up. He had very little time or energy to put into a relationship at this point in his life. He certainly wasn't looking for one. He corrected himself. Hadn't been. This one, one he couldn't seem to resist, had crashed onto his head. "Okay, Wilson, why don't we look at this logically? Engineers are logical people, right?"

"We are." She wished the flowers weren't sitting so bright and lovely between them.

"We have to work together for a few months yet. If there's tension between people, they don't work well. If we keep walking on eggshells around each other the way we have been the last couple weeks, the project's going to suffer."

"Okay, you have a point." She smiled. "But I'm not going to go to bed with you to ease the tension."

"And I thought you were dedicated." He sat back and braced his ankle on his knee. "If that's out..." He raised a questioning brow.

"Definitely."

"How about pizza and a movie?"

She started to speak, then stopped. She was logical. She was trained to take facts to the correct conclusion. "Nothing else?"

"That would depend."

"No." Shaking her head, Abra lifted her mother's untouched lemonade. "I prefer to deal in absolutes. If we agree to get to know each other, to try to develop a professional and a personal relationship, I have to know that the personal relationship will remain on a certain level. So we set ground rules."

He lifted a brow. "Should I get out my notepad?"

"If you like," she said mildly. "But I think we can keep it simple. We can see each other, as friends, as associates. No romantic situations."

Amused, Cody watched her. "Define 'romantic situation.'"

"I think you get the picture, Johnson. You're right in the sense that we are working closely together. If either one of us is in a snit, the work suffers. A personal understanding and respect can only lead to better professional communication."

"You ought to write that down for the next staff

meeting." He held up a hand before she could snap at him. "Okay, we'll give it a shot your way. Pals." He leaned over and offered his hand. When she took it, he grinned. "Guess I'll have to take back the flowers."

"Oh, no. You gave them to me before we set the rules." She rose, pleased with herself. "I'll buy the pizza. You spring for the movie."

It was going to work. Over the next few days Abra congratulated herself on taking a potentially volatile situation and making it into a pleasant arrangement. There were times, inevitably, that they rubbed each other the wrong way on the job. When they saw each other after working hours, they met as casual friends to enjoy a meal or a show. If she caught herself longing for more after she dropped Cody at his hotel or he left her at her apartment, she smothered the need.

Little by little she learned more about him, about the farm he had grown up on, about his struggle to finish his education. He didn't speak of the financial hardships or the backbreaking hours he'd had to put in, but she was able, as their time together went on, to hear what he didn't say through what he did.

It changed her view of him. She'd seen him as a pampered, privileged partner in a top architectural firm. She hadn't considered the fact that he had worked his way up to where he was in much the same way she had. Abra admired ambition when it was married with drive and old-fashioned hard labor.

She was more careful than he about giving away pieces of her private life. She spoke easily about her years with Thornway and about her admiration for the man who had given her her chance. But she never mentioned her family or her childhood. Though he noted the shield, Cody made no attempt to pierce it. What was growing between them was still fragile. He had no intention of pushing harder until a firm foundation had been laid.

If Abra was pleased with herself and the arrangement, Cody was growing more and more frustrated. He wanted to touch her—a fingertip to her cheek, a hand to her hair. He knew that if he made even so gentle a move the tenuous thread that was spinning between them would snap. Time and again he told himself to back off completely, to call a halt to their platonic evenings. But he couldn't. Seeing her, spending time with her, had become a habit too strong to break.

Still, he was beginning to think that whoever had said half a loaf was better than none hadn't known anything about real hunger.

Hands on hips, Abra stood and watched the crew of engineers and mechanics work on the mechanism for the sliding roof. The envelope for the glass was completed, and the glass itself would be installed at the end of the week. The sun beat mercilessly down on the smoothed concrete while she worried over her design like a mother hen.

"Darling!"

"Mom?" Her concentration broken, Abra managed to smooth her frown into a smile. "What are you doing here?"

"You talk about this place so much, I thought it was

time I came to see for myself." She tilted her hard hat at a jaunty angle. "I talked Mr. Blakerman into giving me just a smidgen longer for my lunch hour." She linked arms with her daughter as they stood in the stream of sunlight. "Abra, this place is fabulous. Absolutely fabulous. Of course, I don't know anything about these things, and all those little places over there look like a bunch of stick houses in heaps of dirt."

"Those are the cabanas."

"Whatever. But that big building I saw when I drove in. Incredible. It looks like a castle out of the twenty-fourth century."

"That about sums it up."

"I've never seen anything like it before. It's so alluring, so majestic. Just the way I've always thought of the desert."

Abra glanced back at her mother. "Really?"

"Oh, yes. I can tell you, when I first saw it I could hardly believe my own little girl had a part in something so, well…grand." She beamed as she inspected the empty pool, which was even now being faced with mosaic tiles. She didn't miss the tanned, muscular arms of the laborers, either. "Why, it's shaped like a half-moon. How clever. Everything's curved and arched, isn't it? It makes for a relaxed tone, don't you think? Just the right effect for a resort."

"I suppose," Abra murmured, hating to admit that she was beginning to see the appeal of it herself.

"What goes up there?"

Frowning again, Abra looked up through the roof at the hard blue sky. "Glass, movable glass. It'll be tinted to filter the sunlight. When it's opened, the two panels will separate and slide into the curve of the walls."

"Wonderful. I'd love to see it when it's finished. Do you have time to show me around, or should I just wander?"

"I can't leave just now. If you can—"

"Oh, look, there's your architect." Jessie automatically smoothed her skirt. She had already zeroed in on the shorter, broader man who was walking beside Cody. "And who's that distinguished-looking man with your beau?"

"He's not my beau." Abra took a swift look around to be certain no one had heard Jessie's remark. "I don't have or want a beau."

"That's why I worry about you, sweetheart."

Patience, Abra told herself. She would be patient. "Cody Johnson is my associate."

"Whatever you say, darling. But who's that with him?"

"That's Mr. Barlow. It's his resort."

"Really?" Jessie was already aiming a smile at Cody and holding out both hands. "Hello again. I was just telling Abra how much I like your design. I'm sure this is going to be the most beautiful resort in the state."

"Thank you. William Barlow, this is Abra's mother, Jessie Peters."

"Mother?" Barlow's bushy brows rose. He'd already tried, and failed, to suck in his stomach. "I didn't know Abra was only sixteen."

Jessie gave a delighted laugh. "I hope you don't mind my popping in like this, Mr. Barlow. I've been dying to see what Abra's been working on so long and hard. Now that I have, I'm convinced it's been worth it."

"We're very pleased with Abra's work. You can be proud of her."

"I've always been proud of Abra." Her lashes swept down, then up. "But tell me, Mr. Barlow, how did you ever imagine putting a resort here, and such a beautiful one?"

"That's a long story."

"Oh." Jessie sent a rueful look at Abra. "Well, I know I'm keeping everyone from their work. I'd hoped Abra could give me a little tour, but that will have to wait."

"Perhaps you'll allow me to show you around."

"I'd love it." Jessie put a hand on Barlow's beefy arm. "But I don't want to be in the way."

"Nonsense." Barlow gave her hand a quick pat. "We'll just leave everything in capable hands and have a nice stroll."

They started off, with Jessie sending a fleeting smile over her shoulder.

"There she goes again," Abra muttered.

"Hmm?"

"Nothing." With her hands jammed into her pockets, Abra turned away to watch her men. It disturbed her, and always had, to watch her mother in action. "We should have the wiring and supports finished by the end of the day."

"Good. Now do you want to tell me what's bugging you?"

Bad-temperedly she shrugged off the hand he put on

her shoulder. "I said nothing. We had some problems with the angle."

"You've worked it out."

"At considerable time and expense."

They were going to fight. Knowing it, Cody rubbed the bridge of his nose between his thumb and forefinger. "Don't you get tired of singing the same song?"

"With a slight change in degrees—"

"It would have changed the look, and the feel."

"A fly stuck on the glass wouldn't have noticed the changes I wanted."

"I would have noticed."

"You were being obstinate."

"No," Cody said slowly, struggling to pace his words well behind his temper. "I was being right."

"Stubborn. The same way you were being stubborn when you insisted we had to use solid sheets of glass rather than panes."

Without a word, Cody took her arm and dragged her away.

"What the hell are you doing?"

"Just shut up." With Abra dragging her heels, he pulled her down the steps into the empty pool. Laborers glanced over, tiles in hand, and grinned. Taking her face in his hands, he pushed her head back. "What do you see?"

"Sky, damn it. And if you don't let go you're going to see stars."

"That's right. Sky. That's what I want you to see. Whether the roof's open or whether it's closed. Not panes of glass, not a window, not a roof, but sky. It's my job to imagine, Wilson, and yours to make it work."

She shrugged out of his hold. The sides of the pool rose around them. If the water had been added, it would have been well over her head. For now the pool was like an arena.

"Let me tell you something, hotshot. Not everything that can be imagined can be engineered. Maybe that's not what people like you want to hear, but that's the way it is."

"You know the trouble with you, Red? You're too hung up to dream, too buttoned into your columns and calculations. Two and two always make four in your head, no matter how much better life might be if once in a while it came up five."

"Do you know how crazy that sounds?"

"Yeah. And I also know it sounds intriguing. Why don't you take a little time out to wonder why not instead of always assuming the negative?"

"I don't assume anything. I just believe in reality."

"This is reality," he said, grabbing her. "The wood, the glass, the steel, the sweat. That's reality. And damn it, so is this."

He clamped his mouth onto hers before either of them had a chance to think. Work around them stopped for ten humming seconds. Neither of them noticed. Neither of them cared. Abra discovered that, though the pool was indeed empty, she was still in over her head.

She'd wanted this. There was no denying it now, not when his lips were hot and demanding on hers. She curled her fingers into his work shirt, but not in protest.

In possession. She held him close as the need spiraled high inside her, very fast and, yes, very real.

He hadn't meant to touch her this way, to take what he had tried to convince himself she would give him in her own time. Patience had always been an integral part of his nature—the knowing when, the knowing how. But with her none of the old rules seemed to apply.

Perhaps if her response hadn't been so complete, if he hadn't tasted desire warm and waiting on her lips, he could have pulled back. But, like Abra, he was in over his head and sinking fast. For the first time in his life he wanted to sweep a woman up and away like some knight on a white charger. He wanted just as badly to drag her to the ground and have her like a primitive warrior reaping the spoils of victory. He wanted, like a poet, to light the candles and set the music. Most of all, he wanted Abra.

When he drew her away, she was dazed and speechless. He had kissed her before and sent the passion swimming. But there was something different, something deeper, something desperate, about this. For a moment she could only stand and stare at him, giddy with the knowledge that a woman could fall in love anywhere, anytime, even when she had barricaded her heart against it.

"That real enough for you?" Cody murmured.

She only shook her head as the buzzing in her brain cleared and separated into sounds. The whirl of drills, the slap of trowels, the murmur of men. The color rose into her cheeks quickly, and with it a combination of fury, embarrassment and self-reproach.

"How dare you do something like that here?"

He hooked his thumbs in his pockets when he realized he was still angry enough to do something rash and regrettable. "You got someplace else in mind?"

"Keep away from me, Johnson," she said under her breath. "Or you'll find yourself hauled up on sexual harassment charges."

His eyes remained very calm and very level. "We both know that what happened here has nothing to do with harassment, sexual or otherwise. It's personal, Red, and keeping my distance isn't going to make it go away."

"Fine," she said, going toe-to-toe with him. The argument interested the men around them almost as much as the kiss had. "If it's personal, let's keep it that way. Off the job, Johnson. I'm on Thornway time, and I don't intend to waste it arguing with you."

"Good."

"Good," she echoed, scrambling up the steps and out of the pool.

Cody rocked back on his heels as she stormed out of the building. They would both be off the clock soon enough.

Chapter 6

It was nearly five when Abra stopped by the trailer to splash cold water on her face. After her scene with Cody it seemed as if everything that could go wrong had. A part for the elevators had proved defective, and then there had been another tiff between Rodriguez and Swaggart. One of the carpenters had gotten a splinter in his eye, and Tim had dropped by the site to moan about the budget.

It had all started with her mother's visit, Abra thought as she wiped her dripping face with a towel. It wasn't fair to blame Jessie, but no matter when, no matter where, she was a woman who trailed complications behind her, then waited for other people to clear them up.

Maybe it wasn't right to resent the fact that her mother had hit it off so well with Barlow or to worry about the fallout. But history had a habit of repeating itself. The last thing Abra wanted added to her plate was the possibility of a romance between the owner of the project and her very susceptible mother.

Better to worry about her, Abra decided as she gathered up a load of files to take home. Jessie's varied and colorful love life was much safer to fret over than her own.

She didn't have a love life, Abra reminded herself. She didn't want a love life. Her plans, personal and professional, were all mapped out. She wasn't about to let some high-handed Florida cowboy botch them up.

What the hell had he been thinking of?

The moment the thought ran through her head, she grimaced and kicked the door open. She knew very well what he'd been thinking of, because she'd been thinking of exactly the same thing.

Rockets exploding, volcanoes erupting, tornadoes swirling. It was difficult to think of anything but power and chaos when she was in Cody's arms.

Was it that way for him, too? she wondered as she locked the trailer door. Did he lose part of himself when they came together? Did everything and everyone fade away until they seemed—no, until they *were* totally unimportant?

Of course not, she decided, and gave in enough to rest her forehead against the side of the trailer. He was just another good-looking man with a glib tongue and clever hands. The world was full of them. God knew her mother had made a science out of the search and discovery.

Not fair, Abra thought again as she straightened. Jessie's life was Jessie's life. It wasn't fair to Cody, either, she admitted, shifting the files and starting toward her car. He had initiated the kiss, but she had done nothing to stop it. That made her behavior every bit as outrageous and unprofessional as his.

She should have stopped it. A dozen times through the rest of the day she'd asked herself why she hadn't. It hadn't been shock, it hadn't even been overpowering lust. Though she would have preferred to lay the blame on either one. It had been… Just for a moment it had been as though something strange and wonderful and completely unexpected had happened. There had been more than need, more than passion, more than desire.

There had been a bang. Those rockets again, she thought ruefully, looking at the buttes, which were shadowed in the lowering sun. But with this bang something had shaken loose. She'd almost believed she had fallen in love.

Which was nonsense, of course. She dug in her pocket for her keys. She was far too levelheaded to take that route ever again. Nonsense or not, the idea was giving her some bad moments.

So, she wouldn't think about it. There were plenty of other problems to occupy her mind, and most of them were in the files she carried. With a little effort and a lot of concentration she could dig out the calculations, work the equations and find the solutions. Finding a solution to Cody was out of her sphere, so she would leave it alone and spare herself the headache.

She turned her head at the sound of a car and had another bad moment when she recognized the sporty little toy Cody had rented. He pulled up beside her, his car spewing dust, just as she yanked her own car door open.

He'd done his own share of thinking that afternoon and he'd come to his own decisions. Before she could slide behind the wheel, he was out and taking her arm.

"Let's go."

"I was just about to."

"We'll take my car."

"You take your car." She turned back to her own.

He took her keys and the files, pocketing the first and tossing the second into the back of his convertible. "Get in."

"What do you think you're doing?" Shoving him aside, she reached in to retrieve her files. "If you think I'm going anywhere with you, you need brain surgery."

"We always do it the hard way, don't we?" he said, and scooped her up.

"You are crazy." She nearly got an elbow into his ribs before she was dumped into the passenger seat. Fuming, she grabbed for the handle. His hand closed like a vise over her hers as he waited for her to toss the hair out of her eyes and glare up at him. He leaned down close, and his voice was very soft.

"You get out of this car, Wilson, and I'll make you sorry."

"Give me my keys."

"Not a chance."

She considered the possibility of wrestling the keys from him. She was mad enough, but she knew when she was outweighed. Eyes narrowed, she met him look for look. "Fine. Then I'll walk up to the road and hitch a ride."

"You already have a ride." He stepped back to walk about the hood. Abra pushed the door open. She'd no more than gotten to her feet when he shoved her back again.

"You don't scare me, Johnson."

"I should. We're off the clock, Abra, and we've got business of our own. Personal business." Reaching down, he fastened her safety belt. "I'd keep that on. It could be a rough ride."

By the time she'd fumbled the catch open, he'd slid behind the wheel. Wordlessly he jammed her belt back in its slot before he sent the car spinning up the road.

"What are you trying to prove?"

He turned off the construction road onto the highway. "I'm not sure yet. But we're going someplace quiet until I figure it out." Dust rose in plumes behind the car. It would take some time for it to settle. "The way I look at it, our first plan didn't pan out, so we go back to the drawing board."

Someplace quiet turned out to be his hotel. Abra's reaction was to slam out of the car and head across the parking lot. Cody simply picked her up and tossed her over his shoulder. Her stream of abuse trailed behind them to his door.

Cody unlocked it and pushed it open, then took the precaution of bolting it before dropping Abra into a chair.

"Want a drink?" he asked. Abra glared at him. "Well, I do." He went to the bar and opened a bottle of wine.

"A chardonnay this time. Gold highlights, a bright flavor, a bit tart. You'll like it."

She could probably have made it to the door in a dash, but she was through running. Instead, she rose very slowly, very deliberately, out of the chair. "Do you know what I would like?" she asked in a surprisingly silky voice. The tone of it alerted him even as he drew out the cork. "Do you know what I would *really* like? To see you hanging by your thumbs over a large, open fire." She advanced toward him while he poured two glasses. "A big fire, Johnson, with just enough breeze to draw the smoke away so it wouldn't dull your senses." She slapped her palms on the bar and leaned her face close to his.

"Why don't you try the wine instead?"

She snatched for the glass, but he was quicker. His fingers wrapped firmly around hers. "Red," he said in a reasonable tone, "if you pour this on me, I'm going to have to beat you up."

She jerked the glass away and downed the contents in one swallow. "Thanks for the drink." She made it to the door, dignity intact, but he was there beside her before she could unlock it.

"You'll never learn to appreciate good wine that way." Pulling her back, he shoved her into a chair. "Now sit," he told her. "We can talk this through or I can go with my more primitive instincts. Up to you."

"We have nothing to talk about."

"Fine." As quickly as he'd pushed her into the chair, he hauled her out of it. She managed one sputter of protest before she was swirled into his arms.

He kissed her as though he meant to go on kissing her forever. His mouth was hard, but skilled rather than punishing as it demanded and received response. One hand was caught in her hair, while the other roamed freely. Up and over her it stroked in one long, firm line of possession, discovering her slenderness, her softness, her weaknesses and her strengths. He'd never touched her like this before, and the result stunned both of them.

She was so alive. He could all but feel her pulse through his fingertips. An energy fueled by passion raced through her, leaving him dazed and desperate. There was no one else who had ever set off this combination of needs and sensations inside him.

No one had ever made her feel this way. No one. It terrified her. It delighted her. It was easy, almost too easy, to forget the rules she had set up for their relationship, the reason for them, and the anger he had set boiling in her only moments before. There was only now and the way her body experienced dozens of tiny explosions wherever he touched—wherever she wanted him to go on touching. With a murmur of confused pleasure, she shifted against him and offered more.

Behind them, the phone began to ring. They ignored it and listened to the pounding of their own hearts.

Cody broke away to bury his face in her hair and catch his breath. Another first, he thought. He couldn't think of another woman who had left him breathless.

He held her at arm's length to study her face. Her eyes were big and clouded and very green. He decided she looked every bit as stunned as he felt. If they moved on impulse now, their already shaky foundation would crumble.

"We'd better talk."

She nodded and sank into a chair, wondering if the strength would ever seep back into her legs. "Okay."

Turning to the bar, he poured more wine into her glass. His hand wasn't steady. Cody wondered if he'd find the energy to laugh about that later. He gave her a glass, then took his own to the chair facing hers.

She looked at him then, as she had refused to before. His hair was ruffled by the fast ride in the open car. Hours in the sun had streaked it and deepened his tan. Still, he didn't make her think of a laid-back beachcomber now. There was a sense of movement about him even when he was sitting—arrested, held in check, but ready. The energy was there, and a power she'd already experienced firsthand. If they crossed swords again while this mood was on him, she would lose.

After a long breath, she sipped. "You wanted to talk."

He had to laugh. It helped somehow to diffuse the worst of his tension. "Yeah. That was the idea."

"I don't appreciate being hauled in here this way."

He settled back but discovered that relaxing wasn't as easy as it had once been. "Would you have come if I'd asked nice?"

Her lips curved briefly. "No. But that doesn't give you the right to turn into a Cro-Magnon and haul me off by the hair."

The image of dragging Abra into a cave had a certain appeal at the moment, but she had a point. "It's not my usual style. Want an apology?"

"I think we've already passed around enough of those. You wanted to talk." She thought she was on firmer ground now. "Since I'm here, we'll talk."

"You look great in overalls, Red."

With a shake of her head, she started to rise. "If that's all—" But he held up a hand.

"I think it's fair to say that the plans we laid out about keeping our personal relationship impersonal are pretty well washed up."

Abra stared into the wine in her glass. When facts were facts, she wasn't one to evade them. "I guess that's fair."

She didn't look too thrilled by the admission, he thought, fumbling for a match. He nearly swore at his own clumsiness. Even when he dragged smoke into his lungs, all he could taste was her. "So, where do we go from here?"

She looked up then. Her eyes were calm again, calm and direct. Whatever fears were swirling inside her were carefully controlled. "You seem to have all the answers."

"Abra—" He stopped himself, knowing it would do no good to lose his temper again or to demand more than she was ready to give. "You'd like to keep things simple." He took a sip of his wine. "Do I have that right?"

Simple? she thought wildly. Things would never be simple again. Her fingers tightened on the stem of her glass, and she deliberately relaxed them. He looked so in control. "Yes. I can't imagine that either of us have time for complications at this point in our lives."

Complications. He nearly sprang out of the chair and grabbed her to show her just how complicated things already were. She looked so composed. "Then we'll deal with the facts. Fact one, I want you." He saw something—passion, fear, hope—flicker in her eyes. "Fact two, you want me." He took a moment to crush out his cigarette. "Now, if we work with those two factors and add the information that neither of us are kids, that we're both responsible adults who are smart enough to approach a relationship intellectually, as well as emotionally, we should come up with, as you said, a simple answer."

She didn't want to be intellectual. She didn't want to be smart. It had taken his practical recitation of the facts to make her realize that she just wanted to open up her arms and her heart and take him in. The hell with facts and plans and simple answers.

That was Jessie talking, Abra reminded herself as she cooled her dry throat with the wine. What worked for Jessie was never going to work for her.

She looked at Cody over the rim of her glass. He seemed so relaxed, so at ease. She couldn't see the tension that had his muscles stretched and humming like wire. She only saw the faint amusement in his eyes and the easy way he sprawled in the chair.

"Want me to run through it again for you, Red?"

"No." She set the glass aside and folded her hands. "A simple answer. We have an affair."

He didn't like the cool way she said it, as though it meant no more than the letters it took to make up the word. Yet when you cut through to the core of it, wasn't that what he wanted? To be with her. Still, it hurt, and that amazed him.

"When do you want to get started?"

His curt response had her curling her fingers hard into her palms. She had opened the door, Abra reminded herself. Now it was time to face it. "I think it's best we understand each other first. We don't let our personal life interfere with the job."

"God forbid."

Taking a deep breath, she pressed on. "It's important that we go into this knowing there are no strings, no regrets, no long-term demands. In a few weeks you'll go back to Florida and I'll stay here. It won't do either of us any good to pretend otherwise, or to act as though what we're beginning isn't going to end."

"That's clear enough," he said, toying with the idea of strangling her for being so cool, so aloof, when all he wanted to do was make love with her until they both stopped breathing. "Obviously you've been through this before."

She didn't answer. She didn't have to. Before she lowered her eyes he saw them go bleak.

"What's this?" Rising, he moved over to crouch beside her. "Someone break your heart, Red?"

"I'm glad you're amused," she began, but he cut her off by touching a hand to her cheek.

"I'm not." He curled his fingers around hers before bringing them to his lips. "I don't expect to be the first man in your life, but I'm sorry someone hurt you. Was it bad?"

The last thing she'd expected from him was sensitivity. It brought tears to her eyes that had much less to do with the past than with the present. "I don't want to talk about it."

Some wounds scar over, he thought, and others fester. He intended to find out just how deep this one had cut, but he could wait. "All right. Let's try this. Have dinner with me."

She blinked back her tears and managed a smile. "I'm not dressed to go out to dinner."

"Who said anything about going out?" Leaning over, he teased her lips with his. "Didn't you say something about liking hotels because you could order room service and eat dinner in bed?"

"Yeah." She laid a hand on his face and let herself drift with the kiss.

"I'll let you use my shower and drop the towels on the floor."

Her lips curved against his. It was going to be all right. She could almost believe it. "Sounds like a pretty good deal."

"You won't get a better one." Still holding her hand, he brought her to her feet. "You didn't mention anything about promises in your blueprints."

"I guess I missed that one."

"Then I get to make you one."

"Cody—"

He touched his lips to hers. It was his gentleness that stopped her words. It was her softness that made him speak. "Just one. I won't hurt you, Abra."

He meant it. She could see that clearly when she looked into his eyes. Too late, she thought, leaning her cheek against his. The heart she had tried so hard to hold on to was lost to him irrevocably. He was bound to hurt her now, though he would try not to. She could never let him know.

When the phone rang this time, they both heard it. Still holding Abra against him, Cody reached down for the receiver.

"Johnson." He listened a moment while he skimmed his lips over Abra's temple. "Lefkowitz, anyone ever tell you you're a pain in the neck?" Reluctantly he let Abra go and gave his attention to the phone. "You were put in charge there because we thought you could handle complications like that. You got the specs? Well, read them." Swearing, he shifted the phone to his other hand. "I hear what you're saying. Give me the number and I'll deal with it from here. Modify those blueprints and I'll break your fingers. Clear? Good. I'll take the first plane out."

When he hung up, Abra offered him his wine. "You're real smooth, Johnson."

"I leave tact and diplomacy to my partner, Nathan."

"Good thing." She toyed with her own glass and tried to be casual. "Taking a trip?"

"San Diego. Why we thought a pinhead like Lefkowitz could handle a job like that is beyond me. The man redefines the word *inept*." He moved to the closet and pulled out a small bag. "Some hotshot engineer's telling him he has to make changes in the design, and now a supplier's balking and he hasn't got the sense to bash their heads together and get on with it."

"Your design?" she asked, grinning.

"Mostly." He grabbed her braid and tugged hard enough to make her squeal. "Why don't you come with me, Wilson? You can point out all the reasons the engineer's right and I'm wrong, and then I can show you the ocean."

It was tempting—so tempting that she nearly said yes before she remembered she had a job to do. "I can't. There's no way both of us can leave the project." She turned away and tried not to show how much it mattered. "So, how long will you be gone?"

"A day or two—unless I murder Lefkowitz and stand trial. Abra." He put his hands on her shoulders and drew her gently back against him. "Is it against the rules for you to miss me?"

She turned around, covering one of his hands with hers. "I'll try to work it in."

He pulled her against him and kissed her until they were both clinging. He had an image of sinking onto the bed with her and letting the night take care of itself but, like Abra, he understood responsibility too well.

"I have to toss a few things into a bag and get to the airport. I'll drop you back by your car."

"Sure."

When she stepped back, he kept his hands on her shoulders. It was funny, he thought. Never before in his life had he thought twice about hopping a plane or moving from place to place. Somehow, in the last few minutes, he'd grown roots. "I owe you a shower—and room service."

He wasn't going off to war, Abra reminded herself. It was a business trip. There would come a time when he

would board a plane and fly out of her life. This wasn't
it. "We'll settle accounts when you get back."

It took three days, and that infuriated him. The only
thing that saved Lefkowitz was the fact that the resolu-
tions took more time and trouble than Cody had antici-
pated. Now he was cooling his heels in another hotel
room and waiting until it was time to catch his plane.
His bag was packed, but there was one item he carried
in his pocket—a choker he'd bought for Abra. Cody
took it out now and studied it.

It had been a whim, a glance in a jeweler's window
as he'd walked to an appointment. They weren't icy
white diamonds, but delicate blue-green "fancy" stones
the color of the sea. The moment he'd seen them, he'd
thought of her.

Closing the lid, he dropped the box back into his
pocket. He didn't suppose it was the kind of token two
people involved in a casual affair exchanged. The problem for him—maybe for both of them—was that his
feelings for Abra were anything but casual.

He hadn't been in love before, but he recognized
the symptoms.

She wasn't ready to hear it, he mused. For that matter, he wasn't ready to say it. Words like *love* changed
the scope of lives, the same way a single window could
change the scope of a wall.

And it might pass. He knew people who fell in and
out of love as if they were bobbing for apples. That
wasn't for him. If it was true, and if it was real, he intended to make it last. He didn't design without making

certain the building would stand the test of time. How could he do less with his own life?

With a glance at his watch, he noted that he had more than two hours before his flight. Dropping onto the bed, he plucked up the phone and called Abra. When he heard the connection click, he opened his mouth to speak. Her smooth recorded voice sounded in his ears.

"You've reached Abra Wilson. I'm sorry I can't take your call right now, but if you'll leave a message and the date and time you called, I'll get back to you as soon as possible. Thanks."

He was scowling at his watch and wondering why the hell she wasn't home when the recorder beeped. "Hi. You sound good, Red, but I'd rather talk to you in person. Listen, if you get in before seven, give me a call here at the hotel. I, ah… I hate these damn things. Don't get crazy or anything, but I missed you. A lot. Get home, will you?"

He hung up and, unsatisfied, dialed another number. The voice that answered was feminine—and real. "Hi, Jack. Cody."

"Cody. Did you get me the stuff I wanted on Monument Valley?"

"Nice to talk to you, too, Jack."

"Sorry." She laughed and changed her tone. "Cody, how the heck are you? It's great to hear from you."

"Thanks. By the way, I mailed off about ten pounds of pamphlets, pictures, souvenir books and assorted historical information on Arizona."

"My life for you. I'm halfway through the revisions

on *Lawless* and I needed some more information. I do appreciate it."

"Anytime. I like being tight with a famous novelist."

"I'm not famous yet. Give me a few more months. The historical isn't coming out until May. How's Arizona?"

"It's fine, but right now I'm in San Diego."

"San Diego?" He heard the sound of pots clattering and envisioned her in the kitchen creating some exotic meal. "Oh, that's right, I forgot. Cody…I wonder if you could pick me up some—"

"Give me a break, Jackie. Are you fat yet?"

He could almost see her running a hand over her growing belly. "Getting there. Nathan went with me last week for my exam and heard the baby's heartbeat." She chuckled again, warmly. "He hasn't been the same since."

"Is he there?"

"You just missed him. I wanted some fresh dill for dinner. He had the idea that my going out and buying it would tire the baby, so he went himself."

"Nathan wouldn't know dill from dandelions."

"I know." There was a wealth of love in those two words. "Isn't it wonderful? When are you coming back?"

"I don't know. I'm, ah…considering staying out here until the project's finished."

"Really?" She paused a moment. "Cody, do I detect a purpose other than creative control?"

He hesitated. Stupid, he thought. He hadn't called to discuss the medical complex or the resort or any other project. He'd called to talk to a friend. "There's a woman."

"No! Just one?"

He had to smile. "Just one."

"Sounds serious."

"Could be."

Because she knew him, Jackie saw through his casual air. "When am I going to meet her? You know, give her the third degree, look her over, pick her apart? Is she another architect? Wait, I know. She's a graduate student moonlighting as a cocktail waitress."

"She's an engineer."

It was several seconds before Jackie could speak. "Are you kidding? You hate them more than Nathan does. Good grief, it must be love."

"Either that or sunstroke. Listen, Jack, I wanted to let Nathan know I'd cleaned things up here and I'm heading back to Phoenix."

"I'll let him know. Cody, are you happy?"

He paused a moment, discovering there wasn't a yes-or-no answer to that. "That's going to depend on the engineer. I'll give it to you straight. I'm crazy about her, but she's dragging her heels."

"If she messes with you, I'm going to fly out and break her slide rule."

"Thanks. That ought to keep her in line. I'll keep in touch."

"You do that. And, Cody, good luck."

It was nearly nine before Abra got in. She'd had a nice, long, talky meal with her mother. That sort of thing always left her of two minds. The first was amusement, pure and simple. Jessie was great company, funny, absurd and easy to be with. No one made a better friend.

The other was worry. Those same qualities made Jessie what she was, a free spirit, a take-it-as-it-comes woman who danced from man to man without collecting any bruises. Her newest partner was W. W. Barlow—or, as her mother had taken to calling him, Willie.

Jessie had been full of him during dinner. How sweet he was, how cute, how attentive. Abra knew the signs. Jessie Wilson Milton Peters was in for another run.

Rubbing the back of her neck, Abra tossed her purse aside and stepped out of her shoes as she crossed the living room. How was she supposed to keep a professional outlook on the job if her mother was having an affair with the owner? With a laugh, she scanned the mail she'd brought in with her, then tossed that aside, as well. How was she supposed to keep that same outlook if she herself was having an affair with the architect of record?

Life had gotten very complicated in a very short time.

She would back out if she could. One of the things she was best at was untangling herself from uncomfortable situations. The trouble was, she was almost sure she was in love with him. That made it more than a situation—it made it a crisis. She'd thought she was in love once before, but...

There were no buts, Abra told herself. Just because this was more intense than anything she'd ever known, just because she couldn't seem to go more than five minutes without thinking of him, that didn't make this any different from what had happened to her years before.

Except that this time she was older and smarter and better prepared.

No one was ever going to do to her what Jamie Frye had done. She was never going to feel that small or that useless again. If love was a crisis, she could deal with it the same way she dealt with any crisis on the job. Calmly, thoroughly, efficiently. It would be different with Cody, because they were meeting on equal terms, with the rules set out clearly for both of them to read. And he was different. That much she was sure of. He wasn't shallow and insensitive, as Jamie had proved himself to be. Hardheaded, maybe. Infuriating, certainly. But there was no cruelty in him. And, she believed, no dishonesty.

When he hurt her, which she had already accepted he would do, it would happen suddenly and without intent. Hurts healed; she knew that well. She would have no reason to look back on whatever time they had together with regret or self-recrimination.

Abra shook herself. She had to stop thinking about him, or she would work herself into the blues because he wasn't there. What she needed was a nice strong cup of coffee and an hour at the drawing board.

She changed into a basketball jersey for comfort, then settled down with the hot coffee, her mind open to ideas. It was then that she noticed the message light blinking on her answering machine.

Pressing the button, Abra bit into one of the stale

cookies she'd dug out of a cupboard. The first call was from a college friend she hadn't seen for weeks. Abra made a note to return the call in the morning. The second was from Tim's secretary, setting a meeting for Monday morning. Grumbling a bit, Abra scrawled a reminder on her calender. Then she heard Cody's voice and forgot everything else.

"…if you get in before seven…"

Abra looked at her watch and sighed. It was well past that. He probably had late meetings. Even if she called the hotel she wouldn't reach him. Cupping her chin, she listened to his voice.

"…I missed you. A lot."

Ridiculously pleased, she rewound the tape and listened to the entire message again. Even though she called herself a fool, she rewound it a second time, then a third.

She worked a little and dreamed a lot during the next hour. Her coffee grew cold. Abra ran figures, then planned out how she would welcome Cody home. She'd have to go out and buy something wonderful. Tomorrow was Saturday. Surely he'd be home by the next evening, or by Sunday morning at the latest. That meant hours, and perhaps even an entire day, without the pressure of work to interfere.

She would stop by one of those fancy little boutiques the first thing in the morning and buy some glorious concoction of silk and lace. Something sexy and soft and irresistible. She'd go have a facial. Wasn't Jessie always touting the wonders of her beauty salon? Not just a facial, Abra decided. She'd go for the works. Hair, nails—what there were of them—skin, everything. When Cody got back, she'd look fantastic. Definitely black silk, she decided. A skimpy teddy or a sheer, elegant chemise.

She'd need some wine. What the devil was that brand he'd told her about? She'd have to throw herself on the mercy of the clerk in the wine shop around the corner. And flowers. Rising, Abra looked at her bedroom for the first time in days. Good God, she was going to have to clean up. Candles. She probably had candles somewhere. Caught up in her own fantasy, she began to gather up clothes and shoes. When a knock interrupted, she tossed an armful in the closet and slammed it closed.

"All right, I'm coming." Where in the hell was her robe? She found it crumpled under the bed and struggled one arm into it as she ran to the door. "Who is it?"

"Three guesses."

"Cody?"

"Right the first time," he told her as she pulled at the security chain. She yanked open the door and stared at him. Grinning, he took a long, lazy look.

Her hair was tied back with a broken shoestring. The makeup she'd applied for dinner with her mother had long since been scrubbed off. Her robe dangled open, revealing the oversize basketball jersey, which skimmed her thighs.

"Hiya, Red. Wanna shoot some hoops?"

Chapter 7

Abra blinked, wondering if he was a mirage. "What are you doing here?"

"Standing in the hallway. Are you going to let me in?"

"Yes, but—" She stepped back, and he came in and dropped his flight bag on the floor. Mirages didn't look this good. Or smell this good. Confused, she glanced back toward the bedroom and the phone machine. "I just got your message. You didn't say you were back."

"I wasn't." Since she didn't seem to be in any hurry to do so, he shut the door himself. "Now I am."

She thought of the plans she had been making. Taking a quick look around her jumbled apartment, Abra ran a helpless hand through her hair. "You should have told me you were coming back tonight. I wasn't— I'm not ready."

"What's the matter, Wilson?" To please himself, he put his hands on her shoulders, then ran them slowly up and down her arms, gradually pushing her robe aside. She was definitely giving him a whole new perspective on athletic wear. "Got another man under the bed? In the closet?"

"Don't be stupid." Frustrated, she pulled back. She knew her face was scrubbed as clean as a baby's. And her hair—she didn't need a mirror to know that was hopeless. Then there was the green-and-white jersey. Hardly the sophisticated, seductive lingerie she'd envisioned. "Damn it, Cody, you should have let me know you were coming."

He checked an impulse to gather her up and shut her up. Maybe he'd let himself get carried away thinking she'd be as glad to see him as he was to see her. And maybe he shouldn't have assumed she'd be waiting patiently and alone for him to come back.

"I might have," he said slowly, "if I'd gotten you instead of a recording. Where were you?"

"When? Oh." Her mind still racing, she shook her head. "I was out to dinner."

"I see." He stuck his hand in his pocket, and it knocked against the jeweler's box. He didn't have any claims on her. *The hell he didn't.* "Anyone I know?"

"My mother," she said absently. "What are you grinning at?"

"Nothing."

Her chin came up as she snatched at the sleeve of her robe. "I know how I look, Johnson. If you'd given me any warning at all I could have done something about it. The place is a wreck."

"It's always a wreck," he pointed out. It was all beginning to seep in. She'd wanted to set the stage, and he'd come in ahead of his cue.

"I could have cleaned up a little." Scowling, she kicked a shoe aside. "I only have lousy wine."

"Well, in that case, I'd better go." He turned away, then turned back as if he'd had a sudden thought. "Before I do, I have something to say about the way you look."

Abra folded her arms, and the glint was back in her eyes. "Watch your step."

"I guess there's only one way to handle this honestly." He stepped toward her and put a friendly hand on her shoulder. "You do want us to be honest with each other, don't you, Abra?"

"Maybe," she muttered. "Well, to a point."

"I've got to tell you something, and you should be tough enough to take it."

"I can take it." She started to shrug his hand away. "I wish you'd—"

Whatever she wished would have to wait. He jerked her forward and crushed her mouth with his. She tasted heat, waves of it that only increased when her lips parted on a half moan. In one quick movement he stripped the robe from her, then took his hands up and under the thin jersey to explore naked skin and subtle curves. Gasping, she strained against his rough hands. Then she was clinging, her knees buckling, as he sent her arrowing to the edge.

"Cody…"

"Shut up," he murmured before he pressed his lips to her throat.

"'Kay." She could manage no more than a moan as his fingers dug into her hips. Her head was spinning, but underneath the dazed pleasure was an urgency every bit as great as his. She tugged at his jacket as they began to work their way across the room. "I want you," she whispered, yanking his shirt up and over his head. In one quick, possessive stroke, she ran her hands up his chest. "Now."

Her desperate murmur triggered explosions inside him. He'd thought he'd be ready for them, but anticipation and reality were worlds apart. Desire became raw, impatient, primitive. For both, the bedroom was too far away. When they tumbled onto the couch he was still half dressed, with each of them fighting to free him. Her hands were wild, digging into him, dragging over him, while she reared up to keep her mouth fused with his. He could feel the heat radiating from her, driving him farther and farther from sanity.

With a sudden oath, he pulled the jersey down, yanking it to her waist so that he could bury his mouth at her breast. With an abandonment she'd never known before, she arched against him, pressing him closer, welcoming the dangerous scrape of teeth and tongue.

The lights burned around them. In the apartment overhead someone turned a stereo up loud, and the bass vibrated in a low, passionate rhythm. The delicate fragrance she'd splashed on an hour before mingled with the musky scent of desire.

She was going to drive him crazy. That was all Cody could think as he followed the trail of her jersey down, farther down the smooth, taut skin of her torso. Everywhere he touched, everywhere he tasted, she responded with a ripe, huge pleasure that astonished him. She pulled at his hair, and the shuddering breaths she drew in were nearly sobs.

They'd waited too long—a lifetime. Now they were together—no more evasions, no more excuses. Only impatience.

When clothing was finally stripped away, her long, graceful limbs twined around him. She could no longer think, nor did she wish to. She wanted only to feel. She wanted to murmur to him, something, anything that would tell him what was happening inside her. But the words wouldn't form. She had never wanted like this, never needed like this. Her body felt like a furnace that only he could stoke higher. There was a tremendous ache building. Instinctively she reached out, half in delight, half in defense. As if he understood, he drove her to a shuddering climax.

She gasped out his name and she felt herself falling, endlessly, weightlessly. Even as she spiraled down he caught her and sent her soaring again.

He could see her in the lamplight, her skin sheened with moisture, her eyes dazed and open. Her hair was spread out on the rug where they'd rolled. He tried to say her name, but the air in his lungs burned like fire, and the word flamed out like a curse when he crushed her lips one last time.

He watched her peak again, felt her fingers dig ruthlessly into his back. Driven to the limit, he plunged into her. She rose up to meet him with a speed that tore at his already-tattered control.

Fast, hard, hot, they raced together to a place neither of them had ever been.

Weakened, stunned, Cody collapsed onto her. He had neither the energy nor the clearheadedness to separate what had happened to him into individual actions, re-actions, sensations. It was as though one huge bubble of emotion had enclosed him and then burst, leaving him drained.

She was as soft as water beneath him, her breathing slow and shallow. He felt her hand slide off his back and fall limply to the rug. Beneath his lips her heart beat quickly, and he closed his eyes and let himself drift with the sound and the rhythm.

They didn't speak. Even if words had been possible, he wouldn't have known which ones to use to tell her what she had done to him. Done for him. He only knew that she belonged to him now and that he would do whatever was necessary to keep her.

Was this what love did? she wondered. Did it fill you with wild energy, then leave you so fragile that you thought you would dissolve from your own breath-ing? Anything she had ever felt before paled to insig-nificance compared to what she had experienced with Cody.

Everything had been new and almost unbearably in-tense. She hadn't had to think or plan or decipher. She'd only had to act on her own needs—needs she had suc-cessfully ignored until the first time he'd touched her.

It seemed he understood and accepted that. Just as it seemed he understood and accepted her. No one else ever had—not like this.

Was it love, she asked herself, or just the most over-powering of desires? Did it matter? She felt his fingers tangle in her hair and closed her eyes. It mattered—too much. Just a touch and she was tempted to toss away everything she believed, everything she'd planned, if only he would touch her again.

There was no point in denying what she felt for him, and she didn't have the courage to think about what he might feel for her.

He pressed a kiss to her throat. "You okay?"

"I don't know." It was an honest answer, she thought as she dragged in a deep, greedy breath. "I think so." Clearing her throat, she opened her eyes again. They were on the floor, she realized, wondering how they'd managed it. "How about you?"

"Fine. As long as I don't have to move for the next week or two." He turned his head so that he could nuzzle lazily at her neck. "Still mad?"

"I wasn't mad." The trace of his tongue along her already-sensitized skin had her shifting beneath him. "I just wanted things to be set up."

"Set up?" He shifted lazily to her ear.

"Yes. I was planning…" She let her words trail off as he skimmed his fingertip over her nipple. She started to say his name, but the word ended on a sigh as his lips teased hers.

"Amazing," he murmured as her slow, sinuous

movements had him hardening inside her. "Absolutely amazing."

She was as astonished as he when passion leaped out again and took control.

Sometime during the night they fell into the bed, but they didn't sleep. It was as though in the few weeks they had known each other a mountain of needs had built and tonight it had come tumbling down in an avalanche. There was no music, no flicker of candles, no seduction of silk and lace. They came together without frills, without illusions.

Energy fed on energy, desire on desire. In the darkest hour of the night they fell into an exhausted sleep, only to wake with the first light of dawn hungry for more. Passions, though satisfied again and again, remained raw until, in a tangle of limbs, they slept.

She awoke with the sun full on her face and the bed empty beside her. Groggy, she stroked a hand over the sheet, murmuring.

"Cody?" Sighing, she opened her eyes and saw that she was alone.

Abra sat straight up, looking quickly around the room. She couldn't have dreamed it, she thought. No one could have dreamed that. Rubbing her hands over her face, she tried to think.

Could he have left her? Sometime during the morning could he just have strolled out as easily as he'd strolled in? And what if he had? she asked herself as she leaned back against the headboard. They had said no strings, no commitments. Cody was free to come and go as he chose, just as she was.

If it hurt, if it left her feeling empty and miserable, it was no one's fault but her own. The trouble, Abra thought, was that she always wanted more than she had. Closing her eyes, she reminded herself that she had just been given a night no woman would ever forget. If it wasn't enough, the lack was in her.

"I was hoping you'd wake up with a smile on your face," Cody said from the doorway.

Abra's eyes flew open. In a nervous gesture she gathered the rumpled sheet to her breasts. "I thought you'd gone."

He walked over and, easing down on the mattress, offered her a cup of coffee. "Gone where?"

"I…" Feeling foolish, she sipped at the coffee and scalded her tongue. "Just gone."

His eyes darkened briefly, but then he shrugged. "You still have a very poor opinion of me."

"It's not that. I just thought you probably had things to do."

"Yeah." He shifted, sliding a leg onto the bed. He was damned if he could remember a night with a woman ever making him feel so light-headed. And awkward. Taking his time, he sipped. "Your coffee's stale, you know."

"I never seem to have time to make it in the morning." She drank again. Small talk. That seemed the best way out, and the safest. "I'd, ah, offer you breakfast, but—"

"I know. There's nothing in the kitchen but a banana and a bag of corn chips."

"There's cookies," she muttered.

"I thought they were rocks." Deliberately he put a hand under her chin. "You want to look at me?"

She did, while her free hand moved restlessly on the sheets. "I'd have gotten a few things if I'd known you were coming back."

"I don't think bacon and eggs is the issue here. Why don't you tell me what the problem is, Red?"

"There's no problem." She struggled for a casual tone. She was an adult, she reminded herself. As such she should be able to handle the morning after. But what did you say to a man in the full light of day when he'd taken you to the darkest depths of your own passions? She could hardly tell him that there had been no one who had given her so much—or taken so much.

"Would you rather I'd gone?"

"No." She said it too quickly, and she swore silently. So much for small talk, she thought, and any pretense of sophistication. "Listen, I don't know what I'm supposed to do next, what I'm supposed to say or how I'm supposed to act. I haven't had a lot of practice at this kind of thing."

"No?" Thoughtful now, he took the coffee from her and set it aside. "How much have you had?" It wasn't a question he'd known he would ask. He'd told himself that her past life was just that—her life. But he wanted to know if there was anyone, anyone at all, who had shared what he had experienced during the night.

"I don't think this is a joke."

He grabbed her shoulders before she could roll out of bed. "Am I laughing? I get the feeling you're judging what's happening here by something that happened before. I don't like it."

"Sorry," she said stiffly.

"Not good enough." He kept his hold firm so that she couldn't yank away. "This guy, the one who bounced your heart around…tell me about him."

Angry color rose to her cheeks as she tried to push him away. "I don't see that that's any of your business."

"You see wrong. Nothing new."

She struggled with the temper she was very close to losing. "I haven't asked you about any of the women you've been involved with."

"No, but you could if you thought it was important. I think this is."

"Well, you're wrong. It's not important."

But it was important. He saw it in her eyes, heard it in her voice. Both tempted him to be gentle with her. If comfort had been the answer, he would have offered it. Sometimes life and love were tough.

"If that's true, why are you upset?"

"I'm not upset."

"I thought we said something about being honest."

"Maybe we did. We should also have said something about not poking around in past relationships."

"Fair enough." He gave her a long, level look. "Unless they seep over into this one. If I'm going to be compared to someone else, I want to know why."

"You want to hear about him? Fine." She pulled away, taking the sheet with her to wrap around her body. "He was an architect." She sent Cody a humorless smile.

"Is that your basis for comparison?"

"You're the one who says I'm comparing," she countered. "You could say I have a habit of tumbling into bed with architects. I was just out of college and working full-time at Thornway. I'd been given a shot as assistant to the engineer on a small project. James was the architect. He'd just moved from Philadelphia. He was very smooth, very smart." She moved her shoulders. "I wasn't."

It was hurting her, and he found he couldn't take it. Rising, he dipped his hands into the trousers he'd pulled on earlier. "All right. I get the picture."

"No." She pulled the sheet more securely around her as they faced each other over the bed. "You wanted to hear about it, and I'm going to tell you. We started seeing each other, and I got stars in my eyes. Looking back, I can't say he promised anything, but he let me believe what I wanted. I'd always wanted to be first with someone. You know, the person someone thinks about before they think about anyone or anything else."

"Yes, I know." He would have gone to her then if he'd thought she'd accept it.

Because he sounded as though he did, she calmed down a bit. "I was very young, and I still believed things like that happened, so when he told me how much he wanted me I was ready to take him on any terms. When I went to bed with him, I was smelling orange blossoms."

"And he wasn't."

"Oh, it was more than that." She laughed, pushing the hair back from her face. "I'd like to think if it was only a matter of me wanting more than I could have I'd have swallowed hard and gone on. I'm not a whiner, Cody."

"No." Anything but, he thought. "What happened?"

"I was packing to go on a weekend trip with him. It was going to be very romantic, very intimate. A ski weekend up north—snow, roaring fires, long nights. I was certain he was going to propose. I was already picturing white picket fences. Then I had a visitor. It's funny." Her voice quieted as she looked beyond him to something only she could see. "I was nearly out the door. I don't like to think what would have happened if I'd been a little quicker. The visitor turned out to be his wife, a wife he hadn't bothered to tell me existed."

Taking a deep breath, Abra sat down behind her drawing board. "The worst part was that she loved the bastard and was coming to see me to beg me to let him go. She was ready and willing to forgive him, if only I'd take pity on her and step aside."

Abra pressed her fingers to her eyes as the memory of that scene played back all too clearly in her head, and with it the shame, the hard, bitter shame. "I'm not the other-woman type, Cody. At first I thought she was lying. I was sure of it. But she wasn't lying. That became horribly clear."

She dropped her hands, folding them loosely together. "I just stood there and listened to her tell me about herself and the three-year-old boy they had and how she wanted to save her marriage more than anything. How they had moved out west to make a new start because there had been other incidents. Other women. I felt more horrid than I ever want to feel again. Not just used, not just betrayed, but vile, really ugly and vile. She cried and begged and I couldn't say anything at all. I'd been sleeping with her husband."

Cody eased down on the bed across from her. He had to choose his words carefully. "Would you…have become involved with him if you'd known?"

"No. I asked myself that a lot after it was all over. No, I wouldn't have…couldn't have."

"Then why are you blaming yourself for something you couldn't control? He deceived you every bit as much as he deceived his wife."

"It's not just blame. I got over that, or most of it, and I got over him." It wasn't easy, but she made herself look at him. "I've never been able to forget the fact that I opened myself up to what happened to me. I never asked him any questions. I never asked myself any questions. When you make that big a mistake once, you better be careful not to repeat it. So I concentrated on my career and left the romance to Jessie."

She hadn't been with anyone else, he realized with a kind of dull amazement. There had been no one else in her life, and when he'd come into it he'd rolled in like a bulldozer. He thought of the night. It had been wonderful, exciting, overwhelming, but he hadn't been gentle, he hadn't been tender. He hadn't shown her any of the romance she was claiming she had decided to live without.

"Abra, are you afraid you're making the same mistake with me?"

"You're not married."

"No, and there's no one else." He paused when she

turned her head to look at him. "You're not a diversion or a convenience to me."

She could never explain how those words made her feel. How could she have known such a tiny flicker of hope could burn so brightly? "I'm not comparing you to James—or maybe I was, a little. It's me. I feel stupid because I don't know how to handle this kind of thing. My mother…"

"What about your mother?"

Abra rested her elbows on the drawing board and dipped her head into her hands. After a moment she straightened again. "All my life I've watched her swing from one man to another. It was always so easy for her, so light, so natural. It doesn't work for me."

He went to her to take her arm and lift her gently to her feet. "I don't want you to act any way that doesn't suit you, or be anything you're not." He brushed his lips over her brow, knowing that if he kissed her now he'd want her in the bed. She needed more than that now, whether she understood it or not. "Let's just take it from here, Red. A day at a time. I care about you. You can believe that."

"I do." She drew back. "I think I do."

He pulled her back to hug her in a way that made her eyes widen in surprise. There was something so sweet, so uncomplicated, about the gesture. "We've got the weekend ahead of us. Get dressed. I'll buy you some breakfast."

Abra was a little amazed at how easily Cody could change from the reckless lover to the casual friend. She was always surprised at how easy he made it for her to make the same transition. Breathing space, she decided as they shared a meal in a dusty diner Cody had unearthed along the highway.

She already knew his appetite—for food and other pleasures—so she barely lifted a brow when he packed away enough for two lumberjacks. It was the trip to the market, at his insistence, that left her reeling. When they returned to her apartment they were carrying what would have been for Abra a year's supply of groceries.

"What are we supposed to do with this stuff?" She dumped two bags on the counter in the kitchen, then stood back as Cody did the same.

"We eat it. At various times of the day." He began to pull out produce. "These are what's known as the basics."

"For a dormitory, maybe." She cast a dubious eye at the pile growing on the counter. "Do you cook?"

"No." He tossed her a bag of apples. "That's why you buy stuff that doesn't need it. Or…" He pulled out a can of chow mein and a frozen pizza. "Stuff that you heat and eat. As long as you have a can opener and an oven timer, you can live like a king."

She shoved a quart of milk, the apples and whatever else came to hand in the refrigerator. Cody watched her, decided she had other, more important qualities and offered her a box of corn flakes. She put those in, as well.

"Takeout's easier," she told him.

"You have to go out for takeout." He swung her around and rained kisses all over her face. A man had to love a woman who put corn flakes in the refrigerator. "You're not going anywhere until Monday morning."

Laughing, she pushed away and dug out a loaf of bread. "I was going to go buy a black silk teddy."

"Oh, yeah?" He grinned, then gripped the baggy waist of her sweats. "For me?"

"It's too late." After slapping his hand away, she tossed the bread in a drawer.

"Let's talk about this." He wrapped his arms around her waist and pulled her back against him. "I like the way you look in black silk. That's probably why I acted like a jealous maniac at Thornway's."

"Jealous?" She let out a peal of laughter. She was sure he was joking—until she turned and saw his face. "Jealous?" she repeated. "Of Mr. Barlow?"

"Don't rub it in."

"I thought you were just being insufferable and insulting."

He winced a little, then lowered his head to bite her neck. "Forget I said it."

"I don't think so," she murmured, even as she shifted to give him more access. "From where I was standing that night you seemed to be vastly entertained by Marci Thornway."

"Give me some credit." He slipped his hands under her sweatshirt to skim them up her sides. "I know a shark when I see one. No matter how pretty the teeth are, they still rip you up. Besides…" His fingers turned in to tease her breasts. "I'm not interested in cotton candy."

He had her backed against the refrigerator and was making her tremble. "As opposed to?"

"Just you, Red." He turned his head to give her a long, soul-stealing kiss. "Just you. Tell me—" he moved his hands down to mold her hips "—have you ever done anything constructive on this counter? Chopped vegetables, canned fruit, made love?"

"On the counter?" Her eyes went wide, then fluttered closed again when he ran his tongue behind her ear. "No. I haven't done any of those things."

He was moving too fast again. In a moment he wouldn't be able to pull back and give her the time and attention he wanted to. With an effort, he stepped back and brought only her hand to his lips. "We'll have to keep that in mind. I bought you something else."

"Something else?" Her breathing was almost level when she glanced around the kitchen. "What, a twenty-pound turkey?"

"No. Actually, I picked it up in San Diego."

She smiled as she took out a carton of eggs she hoped he didn't expect her to deal with. "You bought me something in San Diego? A souvenir?"

"Not exactly. Are we finished here?"

"I certainly hope so."

"Come on, then. I'll show you."

He took her by the hand to pull her out of the kitchen and into the bedroom, where his bag sat open on a chair. Reaching in, he took out a box and handed it to her.

"A present?" She felt foolishly shy as she ran a finger over the top of the box. "That was sweet of you."

"It could be an ashtray that says San Diego Padres."

"It would still be a present." She leaned over to touch her lips to his. "Thanks."

"That's the first time you've done that," he murmured.

"What?"

"Kissed me."

She laughed and would have drawn her hand away, but he reached up to hold it against his cheek. "You have a short memory."

"No." He uncurled her fingers to press his lips to her open palm. "That's the first time you've kissed me first, before I backed you into one of those corners. And you don't even know what I bought you."

"It doesn't matter. I like knowing you were thinking of me."

"Oh, I thought of you." He dipped his head to kiss her lightly, sweetly, and her lips parted in surprise. "I thought of you a lot." He checked himself again because he wanted nothing more than to gather her into his arms and show her. She needed space and time and more care than he'd bothered to show her. So instead he grinned and sat on the arm of the chair. "I would have given it to you last night, but you couldn't keep your hands off me."

She gave him an amused look before sitting on the arm beside him. "Better late than never." Then she opened the lid and sat staring and speechless.

She had expected some little token, some funny souvenir a friend might bring another after a quick trip. The gems glittered up at her, pale as water, smooth as satin. She didn't, as many women would have, recognize the glint of diamonds. What she saw were lovely stones that caught the late-afternoon light.

"It's beautiful." The amazement was still on her face

when she looked across at him. "Really beautiful. You bought this for me?"

"No, I bought it for Charlie." With a shake of his head, Cody lifted out the necklace and reached over to fasten it around her neck. "Think it'll look good on him?"

"I don't know what to say." She lifted a hand and ran it over the stones. "No one's ever given me anything so lovely."

"I guess I'll have to buy Charlie something else."

With a laugh, she sprang up to go to the mirror and look. "Oh, they are beautiful. They sparkle." Turning, she launched herself into his arms. "Thank you." She kissed him. "Thank you." And again. "Thank you."

"If I'd known it would only take a handful of glitters, I could have arranged this weeks ago."

"Laugh all you want." She pressed her cheek against his. "I really love it."

And I love you, he thought. Before too much longer, she was going to know it. "I want to see them on you," he murmured, and rose with her. With his eyes on hers, he slipped the shirt over her head. He saw the change in her face, and the invitation. He would take what she offered, but this time he would take it carefully.

"You're beautiful, Abra."

Now he saw the new change, the blank astonishment his words had brought to her. He cursed himself for a fool. Had he never bothered to tell her, or to make her believe it?

"I love the way you look in the sunlight. The first time I saw you I watched you in the sunlight."

With an easy tug he loosened the drawstring at her waist so that her pants slithered down over her hips. Now she wore only the necklace, shimmering like water around her throat. But he didn't touch her, not in any of the hot, hungry ways she'd come to expect. He framed her face as though it were made of glass and kissed her as softly as a dream.

Confused, moved to aching, she reached for him. "Come to bed."

"There's time." He kissed her again and again, lingering over it until she swayed. "This time." He peeled off his shirt so that she could feel the solid strength of his chest against her. But passion weakened now, where before it had streamed through her like fire. Her muscles trembled, then went lax. Her mind, so clear only moments before, blurred.

He only kissed her, and kissed her and kissed her.

"I don't…" Her head fell back as he deepened the kiss. "I can't…"

"You don't have to do anything. Let me show you." He swept her up, muffling her dazed protest with his lips until he lowered her to the bed.

His gentleness filled her until her limbs were too weighted to move. She would have clasped him to her and given him everything, but he linked his hands with hers and caressed her with his lips alone. Soft, moist, patient. Her mind began to float, then to soar with a pleasure far beyond the physical.

No one had ever treated her as though she were fragile, or delicate, or beautiful. He made love to her now in a way she hadn't known existed. In a way she would never forget. If the night had been flash and fire and the darkest of passions, this was quiet and cool and wonderfully light. She trembled over the first edge, then drifted like a feather in the softest of breezes.

She was exquisite. He'd seen the passion and the strength—felt them—but he hadn't seen, hadn't touched on, her fragility or her openness to love. Whatever he had felt before, in the heat of desire, was nothing compared to the intimacy of giving. Her body flowed like a river under his hands, warmed like a flower beneath his lips. When she murmured his name, the sound rippled over him, touching some deep hidden core. It was the only voice he ever wanted to hear.

He murmured to her. She heard him, responded, but she couldn't understand the words. Sensation layered over sensation, wrapping her in a cocoon of pleasure. There was the feel of his hands, the strength of them as they stroked over her skin. There was the taste of his mouth whenever he searched for hers, the warm, drugging taste of it. Over lids too heavy to lift, the sunlight beat so that vision, like her mind, was a red mist. Time spun out, inconsequential. For Abra, years might have passed without her noticing.

She felt the brush of his hair as he roamed over her, caught the scent of his skin as he skimmed over hers. If there were other things in the world, they had stopped being important. If night fell or the sun rose, it hardly mattered. Not as long as he was with her and showing her what there could be to love.

When he slipped inside her, she let out a long sigh of welcome. Still, he moved slowly, slowly, taking her gen-

tly up the wave, riding the crest. Trapped in the world
he had opened up to her, she rose to meet him, matching rhythms, merging bodies.

Promises were made, though she didn't know it. A
bond, solid and firm, was formed.

His own breath grew shallow as he dug for control.
He'd thought she'd driven him wild in the night. And
she had. Now, in surrender, she had taken him beyond
even that. His muscles trembled, then steadied with a
sweet, dark ache, and his pulse beat in hammer blows at
the back of his neck. He was driven to taste her again.
Her breath whispered into his mouth as their lips met.
Hers softened, opened, offered.

Then she opened her eyes, her lashes lifting in one
long, languid movement. Though she couldn't know it,
she had never been more beautiful than at that moment.
Though she couldn't know it, from that moment on he
was completely and irrevocably hers.

She spoke his name, and they slipped over the top
together.

Chapter 8

It wasn't so hard, this being in love. Abra thought it through as she swung her car into the parking lot at Thornway. She didn't have to act differently, live differently, be different. She wasn't required to change her life so much as open it up. Perhaps she hadn't thought it was possible for her to do even that, but Cody had proved her wrong. For that, if only for that, she would always be grateful.

If she could love him without changing who she was, didn't that mean that when the time came for him to leave she could pick up and go on as she had before? She wanted to believe it. She had to believe it.

With her keys jingling in her hand and her step very light, she crossed the lot to the building. The sun wasn't really shining brighter this morning. She knew that. But in her heart it glowed more golden, more beautiful, than ever before.

It was all a matter of perspective, she told herself as she passed through the lobby, heading toward the elevators. She knew all about perspective and planning and coming up with a workable structure.

A love affair could be engineered just like anything else. They cared about each other, enjoyed each other, respected each other. That was a solid foundation. They shared a common love of building. Even if they came at it from different angles, it was a base of sorts. From there it was a matter of adding the steel and the struts. After the weekend they had shared, Abra felt confident that progress had been made. Without the tension of work interfering, they had discovered pleasures in and out of bed.

She liked him. That seemed almost too elementary, but to her it was a revelation. It wasn't only a matter of need, attraction, falling in love. She liked who he was, how he thought, how he listened. Companionship wasn't something she'd looked for from him, any more than she'd looked for passion. In one weekend she'd discovered she could have both.

Abra pushed the button for the elevator and smiled as she remembered the way they had sprawled on her couch and watched a Cary Grant festival on television. Or the way they'd put together a meal of pizza and gingersnaps. Or the way they'd tumbled into her rumpled bed on Sunday afternoon with the radio playing jazz and the breakfast dishes neglected.

He'd made her happy. That in itself was more than she'd ever expected from a man. They were building a relationship, solid and strong. When it was time to walk away from it, she would be able to look back and remember something wonderful that had come into her life.

When the elevator doors opened, she stepped through, then felt hands encircle her waist.

"Going up?"

As the doors shut, Cody spun her around and captured her mouth with his. She held on the way he'd hoped she would. She answered the kiss the way he'd needed her to. It was hardly more than an hour since he'd left her to go back to his hotel and change for the meeting, but it seemed like days.

She'd gotten to him, he thought as he pressed her back against the side of the car. In all ways, in every way, she'd gotten to him. He was only just beginning to plan how to deal with the results.

"You taste good, Red." He lingered over her lips a moment, nibbling before he pulled back far enough to look at her. "And I like your face."

"Thanks." She lifted her hands to keep some sensible distance between them. "You were quick getting here."

"I only had to change. I could have done that at your place if you'd let me bring some things over."

She wasn't ready for that. If he lived there, really lived there over the next few weeks, the apartment would be much too empty when he left. She smiled and glanced up to check the progress of the car. They were still at lobby level. With a shake of her head she pushed the button both of them had forgotten.

"I'd hate for you to give up room service, and that neat little spa."

"Yeah." He knew she was evading him. No matter how intimate they became, she still refused to take the next step and close the final gap. He gave himself a moment to control his frustration, then pushed the button to stop the car between floors.

"What are you doing?"

"I want to ask you something before we go back to work. It's personal." He trailed a finger from the base of her neck to her waist. "As I remember, one of the rules is no mixing business with pleasure."

"That's right."

"Have dinner with me."

With a long sigh, Abra reached out to start the elevator again. Cody circled her wrist before she could press the button. "Cody, you didn't have to trap me in an elevator to ask me to have dinner."

"So you will?"

"Unless I'm stuck between the fourth and fifth floors."

"At my hotel," he added, bringing her wrist to his lips. As always, it delighted him when her response came out in a rush. "And stay with me tonight."

The fact that he had asked rather than assumed made her smile. "I'd like that. What time?"

"The sooner the better."

She laughed as she pushed the button for Tim's floor. But her pulse would be hammering for some time to come. "Then we'd better get to work."

Tim was waiting for them with a tray of coffee and Danish, which Abra ignored. It took only moments for her to recognize the signs of stress, though Tim was as jovial and expansive as ever. She was forced to stem her own impatience as details of the plans were brought out and gone over yet again. If she wasn't on the site by ten, she would miss another inspection.

When Tim set up a flow chart that diagrammed the construction sequence and the estimated dates of completion, she settled back and gave up. She'd be lucky to be on the job by noon.

"As you can see," Tim continued, "the blasting and the foundation were completed on schedule. Where we began to fall behind was on the roofing."

"There's no real problem there." Cody lit a cigarette as he studied the chart. "We were well within the usual grace period of twenty percent. In fact, it looks like we're no more off than five."

"We have another lag with the plumbing of the health club."

"No more than a day or two," Abra put in. "We'll be able to make it up with the cabanas. At this pace the resort will be built and operational within our time frame."

Tim was staring at the figures and projections. "It hasn't even been three months into construction and we're nearly ten percent behind." Tim held up a hand before Abra could speak. "Added to that is the budget. Unless we're able to take some cost-cutting methods, we're going to go over."

"The budget's not my province." Cody topped off his coffee, then filled Tim's cup. He'd seen the builder down three in the last half hour. Ulcers were made from less, he thought mildly. "And it's not Abra's. But I can tell you that from my own figures, and taking a look at the do list, you're going to come in as close to budget as it's possible."

"Cody's right. We've had no major hitches on this job. It's run more smoothly than any I've been involved with. The supplies have been delivered on time and in good order. If we've run over on a few things, such as the pool roof and the parallel windows in the main building, it's been minimal. I think that you—" She broke off when the phone rang.

"Excuse me." Tim picked up the receiver. "Julie, I want you to hold my calls until— Oh. Yes, of course." Tim pulled at the knot of his tie, then reached for his coffee. "Yes, Marci. Not yet. I'm in a meeting." He drew a long breath as he listened. "No, there hasn't been time. I know that." He gulped more coffee. "I will. By this afternoon. Yes, yes, I promise. You…" He let his words trail off, rubbing the back of his neck. "Fine, that's fine. I'll look at them when I get home. By six. No, I won't forget. Bye."

He set down the phone. Abra thought his smile was a bit forced when he turned back to them.

"Sorry about the interruption. We're planning a little trip for next month and Marci's excited about it." He gave the chart an absent glance. "You were saying?"

"I was going to point out that I think you can be very pleased with the way this job's been going." Abra paused a moment, no longer sure Tim was listening.

"I'm sure you're right." After a long breath, Tim beamed at both of them. "I want to make sure I'm on top of things. I appreciate the input." He came around the desk. "I know I'm keeping you both from your work, so we won't drag this out any longer."

"Got any idea what that was all about?" Cody asked Abra as Tim closed the door behind them.

"I'm not sure." Thoughtfully she walked toward the elevators. "I guess he's entitled to be nervous. This is the first big job he's taken on solo. Everything else he's done was already in the works when his father died."

"Thornway has a good reputation," Cody commented as they stepped inside and started down. "What's your opinion of Thornway junior?"

"I don't like to say." Uneasy about the meeting, Abra stared at the wall of the elevator. "I was very close to his father. I really loved him. He knew the building trade inside out, every angle, every corner, and he was… It was personal with him, if you know what I mean."

"I do."

"Tim's not the man his father was, but they're big shoes to fill."

They crossed the lobby and started out to the parking lot together. "How tight do you figure he bid this job?"

"Close. Maybe too close." She narrowed her eyes against the sun as she thought the problem through. "But I can't believe he'd be reckless enough to risk taking a loss on something of this size. The penalty clause is a whopper, that I do know." She fished out her keys, frowning. "Enough to put the fear of God into anyone. It's offset by a bonus if the job comes through ahead of schedule."

"So maybe he's counting too heavily on the bonus."

With a shrug, Cody leaned against Abra's car. "Seems to me his wife is an expensive tax deduction."

She gave a quick, unladylike snort. "That's a nice way to talk about a man's wife."

"Just an observation. That little dog collar she had on the other night would have set old Tim back five or six thousand."

"Thousand?" Her interest piqued, Abra stopped in the act of sliding into her car. "Was it real?"

Pulled back from his speculations, he grinned. "You're awfully cute, Red."

She almost snapped at him, but curiosity got the best of her. "Well, was it?"

"Women like that don't wear glass and paste."

"No, I suppose not," she murmured. But five thousand—she just couldn't conceive of it. That much money would go a long way toward buying a new car, or a piece of equipment, or—she could think of a dozen uses for five thousand dollars more reasonable than wasting it on something a woman wore around her neck.

"What are you thinking?"

"That he must be crazy." Then she moved her shoulders, dismissing it. "But the man's entitled to spend his money however he chooses."

"Maybe he considers it an investment." At Abra's puzzled look, Cody thought back to the night of the party and Marci's frank and unmistakable come-on. "You could say some women need a lot of incentive to stay with one man."

Because that thought made her think uncomfortably—and perhaps unfairly—of Jessie, Abra brushed it aside. "Well, it's certainly his problem. In any case, we don't have time to stand here gossiping about Tim and his wife."

"Just speculating." But he, too, brushed the subject aside. "Listen, I've got to make a stop on the way to the job. Can you follow me?"

She glanced at her watch. "Yeah, but why—?"

"There's something I have to pick up. I could use your help." He kissed her, then slid behind the wheel of his own car.

Ten minutes later, Abra drove in behind him at Jerry's Tire Warehouse. "What are you getting here?"

"A new suit. What do you think?" He pulled her out of the car and through the door. The place was a sea of tires—blackwalls, whitewalls, steel-belted radials. It smelled of rubber and grease. Behind a scarred counter piled with thick catalogs was a bald man wearing half glasses.

"Morning, folks," he shouted over the hissing and blowing of pumps and lifts. "What can I do for you?"

"See that?" Cody turned and pointed at Abra's car through the plate-glass window. "Tires, all around, and a spare."

"But I—" Before Abra could finish, the clerk was thumbing through the catalogs. He'd summed up Abra's car with one glance.

"We have some very nice budget products."

"I want the best," Cody told him, making the clerk's eyes gleam behind his dusty lenses.

"Cody, this is—"

"Well, well." Obviously seeing his commission soar,

the clerk began to write out an invoice. "I have something in stock that should do very nicely."

Cody glanced down at the invoice, noted the brand and nodded. "Can you have it ready by five?"

The clerk looked at his watch and his daily list. "Just."

"Good." Plucking the keys out of Abra's hand, Cody tossed them. "We'll be back."

Before she could complete a sentence, Abra found herself being pulled back outside. "Just what do you think you're doing?"

"Buying you a birthday present."

"My birthday's in October."

"Then I'm covered."

She managed—barely—to dig in her heels. "Listen, Cody, you have absolutely no right making decisions like this for me. You can't just—just drag somebody into a tire warehouse, for God's sake, and order tires."

"Better here than the supermarket." He put his hands on either side of her head, resting them on the roof of his car. "And I didn't drag somebody in there. I dragged somebody important to me, somebody that I won't see driving around on four tires that gave up the last of their rubber six months ago. You want to fight about that?"

Because he'd taken the wind out of her sails, she only frowned. "No. But I would have taken care of it. I've been planning to take care of it."

"When?"

She shifted her feet. "Sometime."

"Now it's done. Happy birthday."

Giving up, she leaned forward and kissed him. "Thanks."

* * *

Abra came home that evening in a dead rush. She'd missed the inspector again, but the foundations for the first set of cabanas had passed without a hitch. She'd been able to see the sliding roof in operation, and at long last the elevators were riding smoothly.

The meeting with Tim had given her some problems, enough that she had made a point of checking the foremen's daily lists. Her description of Tim to Cody had made her feel guilty. To combat that, she had decided to take a personal interest in every facet of the job. The extra time had pushed the end of her workday to six, and then she'd eaten up nearly an hour more picking up her car.

"Never ready when they say they'll be ready," she mumbled as she sprinted up the stairs of her building. When she reached her landing, she saw one more delay at her door.

"Mom. I didn't know you were coming by."

"Oh, Abra." With a little laugh, Jessie dropped a piece of paper back in her purse. "I was just going to leave you a note. Running a bit late?"

"I feel like I've been running all day." She unlocked the door and pushed it open.

"Have I come at a bad time?"

"No— Yes. That is, I'm heading back out again in a few minutes."

"I won't be long, then." Jessie gave an automatic sigh at the sight of Abra's living room. "Were you held up at work?"

"First." Abra shot straight into the bedroom. She

wasn't going to have dinner with Cody in work boots and dusty jeans. "Then I had to pick up my car."

Straightening up as she went, Jessie trailed behind her. "Did it break down again?"

"No, I was getting tires. Actually Co—a friend of mine bought me tires."

"Someone bought you tires—for a present?"

"Uh-huh." She pulled out a nile-green jumpsuit. "What do you think of this?"

"For a date? Lovely. You've always had a good sense of color. Do you have any gaudy earrings?"

"Maybe." Abra pulled open a drawer and began to search.

"Why did someone buy you tires?"

"Because mine were shot," Abra said absently as she pawed through cotton underwear and sweat socks. "And he was worried that I'd have an accident."

"He?" Jessie's ears perked up. She stopped tidying Abra's clothes and smiled. "Why, that's the most romantic thing I've ever heard of."

With a snort, Abra lifted out one silver earring with copper beading. "Tires are romantic?"

"He was worried about you and didn't want you to be hurt. What's more romantic than that?"

Abra dropped the earring back in her drawer as her lips pursed. "I didn't think about it that way."

"That's because you don't look on the romantic side of things often enough." Anticipating the reply, Jessie held up a hand. "I know, I know. I look on that side too often. That's the way I am, sweetheart. You're much more like your father was—practical, sensible, straightforward. Maybe if he hadn't died so young…" With a shrug of her slender shoulders, Jessie plumped the pillows on the bed. "That's water over the dam now, and I can't help being the kind of woman who enjoys and appreciates having a man in her life."

"Did you love him?" The moment she asked, Abra shook her head and began to search for an overnight bag. "I'm sorry. I didn't mean to ask you that."

"Why shouldn't you?" With a dreamy sigh, Jessie folded a discarded blouse. "I adored him. We were young and broke and totally in love. Sometimes I think I've never been happier, and I know it's a part of my life I'll never forget and will always be grateful for." Then the dreamy look was gone, and she set the blouse aside. "Your father spoiled me, Abra. He took care of me, cherished me in a way every woman needs to be cherished. I suppose I've looked for parts of him in every man I've ever been involved with. You were just a baby when he died, but I see him when I look at you."

Slowly Abra turned. "I never realized you felt that way about him."

"Because it's been so easy for me to form other relationships?" With competent movements, Jessie began to make the bed. "I don't like being alone. Being part of a couple is as necessary to me as your independence is to you. Flirting is like breathing to me. I'm still pretty." Smiling, she fluffed her hair as she bent to take a quick look in the mirror. "I like being pretty. I like knowing that men think I'm pretty. If your father had lived, things might have been different. The fact that I can be happy with someone else doesn't mean I didn't love him."

"It must have sounded as though I were criticizing. I'm sorry."

"No." Jessie smoothed the bedspread. "I know you don't understand me. The truth is, I don't always understand you. That doesn't mean I don't love you."

"I love you, too. I'd like you to be happy."

"Oh, I'm working on it." With a chuckle, Jessie moved around the bed to set Abra's sneakers in the closet. "I'm always working on it. That's one of the reasons I came by. I wanted you to know I was going out of town for a couple of days."

"Oh? Where?"

"Vegas. Willie's going to show me how to play blackjack."

"You're going away with Mr. Barlow?"

"Don't get that look," Jessie said mildly. "Willie is one of the sweetest men I've ever met. In fact, he's fun, considerate and a complete gentleman. He's arranged for separate suites."

"Well." Abra tried hard to accept the news. "Have a nice time."

"I will. You know, honey, if you put away all these things on your dresser you'd be able to find them when you— Oh, my." Her eye fell unerringly on the necklace. "Where did you get this?"

"It was a present." Abra smiled as Jessie scooted in front of the mirror with the necklace held around her throat. "It's pretty, isn't it?"

"It's a great deal more than that."

"I really love it."

"I don't think you should leave it lying around."

"I've got the box around here somewhere." She rummaged. "I think I'll wear it tonight."

"If it were mine, I'd never take it off. You said a present." Jessie turned from the mirror. "From whom?"

"A friend."

"Come on, Abra."

Evading only made it into something that it wasn't, Abra reminded herself. She said lightly, "Cody picked it up for me when he went to San Diego."

"Well, well…" Jessie let the choker drip from one palm to the other like a stream of stars. "You know, sweetheart, this is the kind of gift a man gives his wife. Or his lover."

As her color rose, Abra made a production of brushing her hair. "It was a thoughtful token from a friend and associate."

"Associates don't give associates diamond chokers."

"Don't be silly. They're not real."

Jessie was silent for three heartbeats. "My only daughter, and she has such a huge gap in her education."

Amused, Abra glanced around. "Diamonds are white, these aren't. Anyway, it's ridiculous to think he'd bring me diamonds. It's a lovely necklace with beautiful colored stones."

"Abra, you're a very good engineer, but sometimes I worry about you." Picking up her bag, Jessie searched out her compact. "Glass," she said, holding up the mirror. "Diamonds." She scraped the stones across the mirror, then held it up.

"It's scratched," Abra said slowly.

"Of course it's scratched. Diamonds do that. And what you have here is about five carats. Not all diamonds are white, you know."

"Oh, my God."

"You're not supposed to look terrified." Abra stood stock-still, and Jessie hooked the choker around her neck. "You're supposed to look delighted. I know I am. Oh, my, they're stunning on you."

"They're real," she murmured. "I thought they were just pretty."

"Then I think you'd better finish getting ready so that you can go thank him properly." Jessie kissed her cheek. "Believe me, sweetheart, it's just as easy to accept the real thing as it is a fake. I should know."

He was getting edgy waiting for her. He wasn't a man who kept his eye on time, but he'd looked at his watch over and over during the last ten minutes. It was after eight. The way he figured it, she should have been able to get home, toss a few things in a bag and be on his doorstep by 7:45.

So where was she?

You're getting crazy, he told himself, dropping into a chair to light a cigarette. Maybe this was normal behavior for a man in love. He'd like to think so. It was better than wondering whether he was the first and only one to go off the deep end.

He was doing this exactly the way she'd asked. While they'd been on the job he'd been completely professional. The fact that they'd nearly fallen into a shouting match twice should have reassured him. At least he hadn't lost his artistic perspective. He still thought of her as a damn annoying engineer once her hard hat was in place.

But they were off the clock now, and he was only thinking of Abra.

She looked beautiful while she slept. Soft, vulnerable, serene. He'd watched her Sunday morning until he'd been driven to touch her. He was even charmed—God help him—by the chaos of her apartment. He liked the way she walked, the way she sat, the way she got nose-to-nose with him when she started to shout.

All in all, Cody decided, he was sunk. So when she knocked he was up and at the door in three seconds flat.

"It was worth it." He relaxed the minute he saw her.

"What was?"

"The wait." Taking her arm, he drew her inside. Before he could lower his head for a kiss he saw the look in her eyes. "Something wrong?"

"I'm not sure." Feeling her way carefully, Abra stepped past him. There was a table set near the terrace doors, with candles waiting to be lit and wine chilled and ready to be opened. "This is nice."

"We can order whenever you like." He took her bag and set it aside. "What's the problem, Red?"

"I don't know that there is— Well, yes, there is, but it's probably just for me. If I'd had any idea…but I don't know a lot about these things and didn't realize what it was at the time. Now that I do, I'm not sure how to deal with it."

"Uh-huh." He sat on the sofa and gestured for her to

join him. "Why don't you run that through for me one more time, adding the details?"

She dropped down beside him, clasping her hands firmly in her lap. As beginnings went, that had been pitiful. "All right. It's this." She unlinked her hands long enough to touch the choker at her throat.

"The necklace?" With a frown, he reached out to trace it himself. "I thought you liked it."

"I did. I do." She was going to ramble again. To hold it off, she took a deep breath. "It's beautiful, but I thought it was glass or…I don't know, some of those man-made stones. My mother was by a little while ago. She's going to Las Vegas with Mr. Barlow."

Cody rubbed his temple, trying to keep up. "And that's the problem?"

"No, at least not this one. My mother said these were diamonds even though they aren't white."

"That jibes with what the jeweler said. So?"

"So?" She turned her head to stare at him. "Cody, you can't give me diamonds."

"Okay, give me a minute." He sat back, thinking it through. He remembered her reaction to the gift, her pleasure, her excitement. It made him smile, all the more now that he understood she had thought it only a glass trinket. "You're an interesting woman, Wilson. You were happy as a lark when you thought it was a dime-store special."

"I didn't think that, exactly. I just didn't think it was…" She let her words trail off, blowing out a long, frustrated breath. "I've never had diamonds," she told him, as if that explained it all.

"I like the idea that I gave you your first. Are you hungry?"

"Cody, you're not listening to me."

"I've done nothing but listen to you since you walked in. I'd rather nibble on your neck, but I've been restraining myself."

"I'm trying to tell you I don't know if it's right for me to keep this."

"Okay. I'll take it back." She sat there, frowning, while he reached around to the clasp.

"But I want it," she muttered.

"What?" It was hard to keep the smile from his voice, but he managed it. "Did you say something?"

"I said I want it." Disgusted, she sprang up and began to pace. "I'm supposed to give it back. I was going to. But I want to keep it." She paused long enough to frown at him. "It was a lousy thing for you to do, to put me in a position like this."

"You're right, Red." He rose, shaking his head. "Only a creep would go out and buy something like that and expect a woman to enjoy it."

"That's not what I meant and you know it." She paused again, this time to glare. "You're making me sound stupid."

"That's all right. It's no trouble."

She was nearly successful in stifling a giggle. "Don't be so smug. I've still got the necklace."

"Right you are. You win again."

Recognizing defeat, she turned and linked her hands around his neck. "It's beautiful."

"Sorry." He rested his hands on her hips. "Next time I'll try for cheap and tacky."

She tilted her head to study his face. He was amused, all right, she decided. It was hard not to admit he deserved to be. "I guess I should thank you for the tires, too."

He enjoyed the way her lips rubbed warm over his. "You probably should."

"My mother said they were a very romantic gift."

"I like your mother." He skimmed his hands up the length of her and down again as she traced the shape of his mouth with her tongue.

"Cody…"

"Hmm?" He lifted his hands to her face to frame it as he began to drift toward desire.

"Don't buy me any more presents, okay? They make me nervous."

"No problem. I'll let you buy dinner."

Her fingers were combing through his hair as she watched him through lowered lashes. "Are you really hungry?"

This time when she kissed him the punch of power all but brought him to his knees. "Depends," he managed.

"Let's eat later." She pressed closer.

Chapter 9

"Cody, will you get that?"

Abra sat on the side of the bed, pulling on her work boots. The knock at her door had her scowling at her watch. It wasn't often she had visitors at seven o'clock in the morning, and she was already cutting it close if she wanted to be on the site before eight.

Cody came out of the kitchen with a cup of coffee in one hand. His hair was still damp from the shower and his shirt only half buttoned when he opened the door to Abra's mother.

"Oh, hello." There was an awkward pause before Jessie smiled at him.

"Morning." Cody stepped back to let her in. "You're up early."

"Yes, I wanted to catch Abra before she left. Then I have a dozen things to do." Jessie cleared her throat as she pleated the strap of her purse. "Is she around?"

"In the other room." Cody wasn't quite sure how a man handled his lover's mother at 7:00 a.m. "Would you like some coffee?"

"Actually, I'd— Oh, there you are." She turned her nervous smile on Abra.

"Mom." The three of them stood there for a moment, forming an awkward triangle. Abra found that she didn't know what to do with her hands, so she stuck them in her pockets. "What are you doing out at this hour?"

"I wanted to see you before you left for the day." She hesitated again, then looked at Cody. "I would love a cup of coffee."

"Sure." Setting down his own, he stepped through to the kitchen.

"Abra, could we sit down a moment?"

Without a word, Abra took the chair across from the sofa. Certainly her mother wasn't going to lecture her about having a man in her apartment. "Is something wrong?"

"No, no, nothing's wrong." She took a deep breath, then accepted the cup Cody brought out to her.

"Why don't I leave you two alone?"

"No." Jessie spoke quickly, then managed a smile. Now that the initial discomfort had passed, she was glad, very glad, that her daughter had someone in her life. Someone, she thought as she studied his face, who obviously cared for her very much.

"Please, sit down, Cody. I'm sorry I've interrupted your morning, and I'm sure you both want to get to work. This won't take long." She drew a second, longer breath. "I've just gotten back from that trip with Willie."

Because she'd already resigned herself to that, Abra smiled. "Did you lose the family fortune at the crap table?"

"No." Perhaps it was going to be easier than she'd thought, Jessie decided. She plunged ahead. "I got married."

"You what?" The shock brought Abra straight up in her chair. "In Vegas? To whom?"

"Why, to Willie, of course."

Abra said nothing for ten humming seconds. When she spoke, she spoke slowly, spacing each word. "You married Mr. Barlow in Las Vegas?"

"Two days ago." She held out her hand to show off a twin set of diamonds. "When we decided it was what we wanted, there didn't seem any reason to wait. After all, neither of us are children."

Abra stared at the glittering rings, then back at her mother. "You—you hardly know him."

"I've gotten to know him very well over the last couple of weeks." No, it was going to be hard, Jessie realized as she watched Abra's face. Very hard. "He's a wonderful man, sweetheart, very strong and steady. I'll admit I didn't expect him to ask me, but when he did I said yes. We were right there, and there was this funny little chapel, so…we got married."

"You should be getting good at it by now."

Jessie's eyes flashed, but her voice remained mild. "I'd like you to be happy for me. I'm happy. But if you can't, at least I'd like you to accept it."

"I should be getting good at that, too."

The pleasure went out of Jessie's face. "Willie wanted

to come with me this morning, but I thought it best that I told you myself. He's very fond of you, speaks very highly of you as a woman and as a professional. I hope you won't make this difficult for him."

"I like Mr. Barlow," Abra said stiffly. "And I suppose I shouldn't be surprised. I'll wish you luck."

An ache passed through Jessie's heart. "Well, that's something." She rose, worrying the rings on her finger. "I have to go in early and type up my resignation."

"You're quitting your job?"

"Yes, I'll be moving to Dallas. Willie's home is there."

"I see." Abra rose, as well. "How soon?"

"We're flying out this afternoon so I can meet his son. We'll be back in a few days to tie up details." She would have stepped toward her daughter, but she thought it best to give her time. "I'll call you when we get back."

"Fine." There was no affection in the word, only a brusque dismissal. "Have a nice trip."

Cody moved to the door to open it, then touched Jessie's arm before she could pass through. "Best wishes, Jessie."

"Thank you." Jessie was grateful the office would be empty when she arrived. She could have a good, healthy cry. "Take care of her, will you?" she murmured, and walked away.

Cody shut the door, then turned to see Abra standing in exactly the same spot. "A little rough on her, weren't you?"

"Stay out of it." She would have stormed into the bedroom, but he was quick enough to grab her arm.

"I don't think so." She was as rigid as ice, and just as cold. Except for her eyes. They boiled with emotion. "What's the problem here, Abra? Don't you figure your mother's free to marry whomever she chooses?"

"Absolutely. She's always been free. I want to finish getting ready for work."

"No." He kept his grip firm. "You're not going to work or anywhere until you get this out of your system."

"All right. You want me to get it out of my system? I'll get it out. She never changes." He heard the despair under the fury and gentled his hold. "It's the same pattern with her, over and over and over. First there was Jack, my father. He died before his twenty-fifth birthday." She pulled her arm free, then snatched a picture from the table. "He was the love of her life, to hear her tell it."

Feeling his way, he spoke carefully. "He's been gone a long time. She's entitled to go on living."

"Oh, she's gone right along. *Speeding* right along. It's been hard to keep up. Husband number two. Bob." She plucked up another picture. "I was, oh, about six when she decided she was free to marry him. That one lasted two, maybe three years. Hard to keep track." She dropped those pictures to grab another. "Then we have Jim. Let's not forget Jim, husband number three. Now before him, there were three or four others, but she never got around to marrying them. Jim managed a convenience store. They met over a carton of soft drinks and were married six months later. And that's about how long they were together afterward. Jessie doesn't really count Jim. She didn't bother to keep his name.

"Then there was Bud. Good old Bud Peters. I don't seem to have a picture of him, but this is Jessie on the day they were married."

Abra swooped it up, knocking several other photographs on their faces. "Bud sold shoes and liked to putter around the house. He wasn't a man to set the world on fire, but I liked him. I guess Jessie liked him, too, before they were together almost seven years. That's a record." She set the photo back. "Good old Bud Peters holds the record."

Cody took her shoulders, massaging them gently. "It's her life, Red."

"It was my life, too," she said passionately. "Damn it, it was my life, too. Do you have any idea what it's like never knowing what last name your mother's going to use, or wondering which 'uncle' is going to be your next stepfather? What house or apartment you're going to live in? What school?"

"No." He thought of the steady and stable marriage of his parents, of the close-knit unit that was his family. "No, I don't. But you're a grown woman now. Your mother's marriage doesn't have to affect you."

"It's the same pattern, over and over. Don't you see? I've watched her fall in and out of love faster than a high-school cheerleader. And every time she gets married or divorced she says the same thing. This is going to be best for all of us. But it was never best, not for me. Now she comes here to tell me about this after it's already done. I always heard about these things after the die was cast."

He held her tighter. "If she's had poor judgment, Abra, it doesn't mean she doesn't love you."

"Oh, she loves me." Now that the venom was out, she felt hollow. Her voice sagged, and her resistance with it. "In her way. It was just never the way I needed. It's okay." She pulled back. The tears that had threatened were under control now, and so was she. "You're right. I'm overreacting. I'll talk to her, to them both, when they get back." She pushed her hands over her face and back into her hair. "I'm sorry, Cody. I took it out on you."

"No, you didn't. You just let it out."

"I guess I'm being stupid. And selfish."

"No, you're not. Just human." He stroked a hand over her cheek, wondering just how badly those early years had hurt her and how many hurts were left. "Come here." As he spoke, he pulled her into his arms and held her, just held her, until she relaxed against him. "I'm crazy about you."

He couldn't see the rush of emotions that came into her eyes. "Really?"

"Absolutely. I've been thinking that when things settle here you ought to come east—for a while," he added, not wanting to scare her off. "You can take a look at the house I'm building, give me a hard time about the design. Look at the ocean."

If she went east with him, would she ever be able to leave again? She didn't want to think about that, about endings and goodbyes. "I think I'd like that." With a sigh, she rested her head on his shoulder. "I'd like you to show me the ocean. I haven't had a chance to show you the desert yet."

"We could go AWOL today."

Her lips curved against his throat before she stepped back. He'd helped. By being there to lean on he'd helped her stand up again. "I don't think so. It wouldn't be right for me to neglect my mother's new husband's resort."

She was in a much better frame of mind by the time they reached the site. Without Cody—without his just being there—Abra knew she might have stayed depressed and angry for days. He was good for her. She wished she knew how to tell him *how* good without putting pressure on their relationship.

So far he seemed perfectly content to follow the blueprints she'd set up. There had been no promises, no talk of the future, no pretense about happy-ever-after. The invitation to visit back east had been casual enough that she felt safe in accepting.

Now, as so often happened on the site, he went his way and she hers. Later they would share the night.

She was coming to count on that, to depend on it, Abra thought as she made her way to the cabanas. It wasn't wise, it wasn't safe, but then there had to be some risks involved.

"Tunney." Abra nodded to the electrical foreman, then stood, hands on hips, studying the framework of the cabanas. "How's it going?"

"Pretty good, Ms. Wilson." He rubbed the back of his hand over his mouth. He was a big man who was running to fat, and he was sweating freely. As he watched Abra he took out a bandanna and wiped his face. "I thought you were still busy at the health club."

"I wanted to check things here." She stepped closer. Tunney kept at her shoulder. "You think the wiring's going to be done on schedule? Thornway's a little nervous."

"Yeah, sure. You might want to take a look at those units over there." He gestured to a section across what would be a courtyard. "The carpenters are really moving on it."

"Umm-hmm." Because she'd yet to find time to go through a unit, she walked forward. "I haven't checked with— Damn." She snagged her boot on a curled scrap of wire. "These places need to be squared away. Safety inspector would slap our wrists for that."

She would have reached down for the wire herself, but Tunney was ahead of her. "You gotta watch your step." He tossed the scrap into a trash drum.

"Yeah. This delivery just come in?" Abra gestured to three huge spools of wire. "As long as the suppliers keep ahead of us, we'll be fine." Absently she leaned against one of the spools.

She liked the look of the site, liked the ring of buttes and mesas constructed by time and nature that cupped the spreading growth conceived by man's imagination and sweat. This was building to her. This was what had drawn her. When a person could stand under the wide arch of sky and see progress—the right kind of progress—it brought hope, as well as satisfaction.

Though she hadn't told him yet, she'd begun to see

and understand Cody's vision. A little magic, a little fantasy, here in one of the harshest and most beautiful spots in the country. There were still coyotes in the hills, snakes in the rocks, but man belonged here. When the resort was finished, it wouldn't simply merge with the desert, it would celebrate it.

That was what he had seen. That was what she was coming to understand.

"It's going to be quite a place, isn't it?"

"Guess it is." He was shifting his weight from one foot to the other as he watched her.

"Ever take a weekend in one of these places, Tunney?"

"Nope." He wiped his face again.

"Me either." She smiled at him. "We just build them, right?"

"Guess so."

He wasn't the most expansive of men, and she sensed his impatience. "I'm keeping you from your work," she said. She tried to straighten, but the end of the wire caught at her jeans. "God, I'm a klutz today." She bent to free it before Tunney could reach her. Frowning, she pulled the length of wire out and ran it between her fingers. "Did you say this just came?"

"Right off the truck. Hour ago."

"Damn. Have you checked it?"

He looked down as she crouched to examine the wire. "No. Like I say, it was just off-loaded."

"Check it now." She waited while he bent beside her to take the cable in his hand.

"This ain't fourteen-gauge."

"No, it's not. I'd say twelve."

"Yes, ma'am." His face puckered as he straightened. "That'd be right."

Swearing, she walked over to the other reels. "These are all twelve, Tunney."

Breathing between his teeth, he pulled out his clipboard. "Fourteen-gauge on the order sheet, Ms. Wilson. Looks like somebody screwed up the delivery."

"I should have known it was too good to last." She straightened, wiping her palms on her thighs. "We can't use this, it's substandard. Call the supplier and see if they can deliver the fourteen-gauge right away. We don't want to fall behind."

"No, we sure don't. Easy mistake, though. Unit numbers almost match." He showed her the numbers on his invoice, then pointed to those stamped on the spool. "Can't tell twelve from fourteen by just looking."

"It's a good thing you can tell by feel, or else we might have had a mess on our hands." She shaded her eyes with her hands as she looked toward the cabanas. "Any chance some might have slipped by you?"

He balled the bandanna back in his pocket. "I've been in the business eighteen years."

"Right. Still, you might—" She broke off when she heard a crash of glass and a scream. "Oh, my God." She raced across the distance to the health club, following the sound of men shouting.

She was breathing hard by the time she reached it. Pushing her way through, she spotted Cody leaning over the bleeding body of one of the workers.

Her heart rose up to block her throat. "How bad?"

She thought she recognized him vaguely. He was young, maybe twenty, with a long sweep of dark hair and a tough, tanned body.

"Can't tell." Cody's voice was curt. The only thing he was sure of was that the kid was breathing. For now. "An ambulance is on the way."

"What happened?" Her boots crunched over vicious shards of broken glass as she moved to kneel beside him.

"Seems like he was on the scaffold inside, finishing some wiring. Lost his balance, took a bad step, I don't know. He went right through the window." Cody looked up, and his mouth was grim as fury and frustration ripped through him. "He fell a good twenty feet."

She wanted to do something, anything. "Can't we get him off this glass?"

"His back could be broken, or his neck. We can't move him."

Minutes later, when they heard the siren, Abra sprang into action. "Cody, get in touch with Tim. Let him know what happened. You men get back, give them room to do whatever they have to do." She wiped at the clammy skin of her brow. "What's his name?"

"It's Dave," somebody called out. "Dave Mendez."

When the ambulance pulled up, Abra waved the men back. "How about family?"

"He's got a wife." One of the men who'd seen the fall drew jerkily on a cigarette. What had happened to Mendez could have happened to any of them. "Her name's Carmen."

"I'll take care of it," Cody told her as they watched the paramedics strap Mendez to a backboard.

"Thanks. I'm going to follow the ambulance in. Somebody should be there." Because her stomach was rolling, Abra pressed a steadying hand to it. "As soon as I know anything, I'll be in touch." After a quick word to one of the ambulance attendants, she raced for her car.

Thirty minutes later she was in a waiting room, pacing uselessly.

There were other people scattered through the room. One woman waited patiently, almost placidly, with her nose in a paperback. Abra continued to pace and wondered how anyone could sit in a hospital without going slowly crazy.

She didn't even know Mendez, and yet she knew him very well. She worked with men like him every day of her professional life. It was men like him who made reality out of what she and Cody put on paper.

He wasn't family, and yet he was. As she paced the room she prayed for him.

"Abra."

"Cody." She turned, hurrying forward. "I didn't think I'd see you."

"I brought the kid's wife in. She's signing some papers."

"I feel so useless. They won't tell me much of anything." She dragged her hands through her already-tousled hair. "How's his wife?"

"Terrified. Confused. She's trying to hold on. God, I don't think she's more than eighteen."

With a nod, Abra went back to pacing. "I'll hang

around with her. She shouldn't wait alone. Did you call Tim?"

"Yes. He's upset. He said to keep him posted."

Abra opened her mouth, then shut it again. In Thornway's day, if an employee was badly hurt, he came himself. "Maybe I could talk to the doctor now." She started out of the room just as a young, pregnant woman stepped in.

"Señor Johnson?"

Cody slipped an arm around her shoulders. She was trembling as he led her to a chair. "Abra, this is Carmen Mendez."

"Mrs. Mendez." Abra reached out to take both of her hands. They were very small, like a child's—and very cold. "I'm Abra Wilson, the engineer on the project. I'm going to stay with you, if you like. Is there anyone else you want me to call?"

"Mi madre." Tears flowed down her face as she spoke. "She lives in Sedona."

"Can you give me the number?" Abra asked gently.

"Sí." But she only sat there, weeping silently.

Moving to the couch, Abra put an arm around her and began to speak in low, fluent Spanish. Nodding and twisting a tattered tissue, Carmen answered. After a moment, Abra patted her shoulder, then gestured to Cody.

"They've been married less than a year," Abra said in an undertone as they moved to the corridor. "She's six months pregnant. She was too upset to really understand what the doctor told her, but they've taken Mendez to surgery."

"Want me to see what else I can find out?"

She leaned forward to kiss his cheek. "Thanks. Oh, her mother's number." Pulling a notebook from her pocket, she scribbled in it.

Abra went back to Carmen, sitting with her, offering what comfort she could. When Cody returned he brought little new information. They spent the next four hours waiting with a television murmuring in a wall bracket nearby.

Cody poured coffee from the pot kept on a warming plate in the waiting room, and Abra urged cups of tea on Carmen. "You should eat," she murmured, closing her hand over Carmen's before she could protest. "For the baby. Why don't I get you something?"

"After they come. Why don't they come?"

"It's hard to wait, I know." The words were hardly out of her mouth when she saw the doctor, still in his surgical scrubs. Carmen saw him, too, and her fingers tightened like a vise on Abra's.

"Mrs. Mendez?" He walked over to sit on the table in front of her. "Your husband's out of surgery."

In her fear she lost her English and sent out a stream of desperate Spanish.

"She wants to know how he is," Abra said. "If he's going to be all right."

"We've stabilized him. We had to remove his spleen, and there was some other internal damage, but he's very young and very strong. He's still critical, and he lost a considerable amount of blood from the internal injuries and the lacerations. His back was broken."

Carmen closed her eyes. She didn't understand about

spleens and lacerations. She only understood that her David was hurt. "*Por favor,* is he going to die?"

"We're going to do everything we can for him. But his injuries are very serious. He's going to be with us for a while. We'll monitor him closely."

"I can see him?" Carmen asked. "I can see him now?"

"Soon. We'll come for you as soon as he's out of Recovery."

"Thank you." Carmen wiped her eyes. "Thank you. I will wait."

Abra caught the doctor before he stepped back into the corridor. "What are his chances?"

"To be candid, I would have said they were very poor when you brought him in. I had my doubts that he'd survive the surgery. But he did and, as I said, he's strong."

She would have to be content with that. "Will he walk?"

"It's early to say, but I have every hope." He flexed his fingers, which were obviously still cramped from surgery. "He'll need extensive therapy."

"We'll want him to have whatever he needs. I don't think Mrs. Mendez understands about the insurance. Thornway has excellent coverage of medical expenses."

"Then I'll tell you frankly there'll be plenty of them. But with time and care he'll recover."

"That's what we want. Thank you, Doctor."

Abra leaned against the doorway and let her body go limp.

"You okay?"

She reached for Cody's hand. "Pretty good now. I was scared. He's so young."

"You were wonderful with her."

Abra glanced back to where Carmen sat on the couch composing herself. "She just needed someone to hold her hand. If I were in her position, I'd hate to wait alone. They're just kids." Weary, she rested her head on Cody's shoulder. "She was telling me how happy they were about the baby, how they were saving for furniture, how good it was that he had steady work."

"Don't." Cody brushed a tear from her lashes. "They're going to be fine."

"I felt so helpless. I hate feeling helpless."

"Let me take you home."

She shook her head, surprised by the sudden draining fatigue. "I don't want to leave her yet."

"We'll wait until her mother gets here."

"Thanks. Cody?"

"Yeah?"

"I'm glad you hung around."

He put his arms around her. "Red, sooner or later you're going to figure out that you can't get rid of me."

Later, when the sun was going down, Cody sat in a chair in her apartment and watched her as she curled up on the couch and slept. She'd exhausted herself. He hadn't known she could. He hadn't, he added as he lit a cigarette and let his own body relax, realized a good many things about her.

The explosion he'd witnessed after her mother's announcement that morning had told him a great deal.

It hadn't been just the one incident, the one betrayal, that had made her so wary of relationships. It was her whole life.

How difficult would it be to trust yourself, to trust a man, after living in broken home after broken home? Damn near impossible, the way Cody figured. But she was with him. Maybe she still set up boundaries, but she was with him. That counted for something.

It was going to take time—more than he'd planned on—but he was going to see that she stayed with him.

Rising, he walked over to her and gathered her up in his arms.

"What?" Roused, she blinked her eyes open.

"You're worn out, Red. Let me tuck you in."

"I'm okay." She nuzzled her head in the curve of his shoulder. "I just needed a nap."

"You can finish it in bed." When he laid her down, she curled into almost the same position she'd been in on the couch. Sitting at the foot of the bed, Cody unlaced her shoes.

"I was dreaming," she murmured.

"About what?" He sat her shoes on the floor, then unbuttoned her jeans.

"I don't know exactly. But it was nice." She sighed, hoping she could find her way back to the dream. "Are you seducing me?"

He looked at the long line of her legs and at her narrow hips, which were bare but for a brief triangle of practical cotton. "Not at the moment."

She rubbed her cheek against the pillow, comfortably drowsy. "How come?"

"Mostly because I like seducing you when you're awake." He drew the sheet over her and bent to kiss the top of her head. He would have stepped back, but she reached for his hand.

"I'm awake." Her eyes were still closed, but her lips curved. "Almost."

He sat on the bed again, contenting himself with stroking her hair. "Is that a request?"

"Umm-hmm. I don't want you to go."

Cody pulled off his boots, then slipped into bed to hold her. "I'm not going anywhere."

Her arms curled around him as she settled her body against his. Then she lifted her lips to his. "Will you love me?"

"I do," he murmured, but she was already drifting with the kiss.

The light lowered, softened, glowed gold. She moved to him with the ease and familiarity of a longtime wife. Her fingers grazed him, exciting as the touch of a new lover. They didn't speak again, didn't need to.

Her lips were warm, softened by sleep, as they moved over his. Her taste was more than familiar now, it was a part of him, something he could draw in like his own breath. He lingered there, nibbling, then demanding, teasing, then taking, while she worked her way down the buttons of his shirt.

She wanted to touch him, to feel his strength beneath her hand. It was strange that she felt safe here, in his arms, when she'd never realized she needed safety. Protected, wanted, cared for, desired. He gave her all that, and she'd never had to ask. His heart beat fast and steady. The pulse of it against her was like an echo of her own.

This was what she had dreamed of—not just the pleasure, not only the excitement, but the simple security of being with the man she loved.

Cradling his face in her hands, she tried to show him what she was afraid to tell him.

She was overwhelming. Even though the loving was slow, almost lazy, she took his breath away. There seemed to be no bounds to her generosity. It flowed from her like honey, warm and thick and sweet.

No hurry. No rush. The shadows washed the room until the gold faded to a soft, soft gray. There was no sound but his lover's sigh and the quiet shifting of her body over the sheets. He looked at her as evening fell and the light faded. Her eyes, aroused now, no longer sleepy, were like the shadows—darkening, deepening.

Very slowly, as though some part of him knew he would need to remember this moment on some cold, lonely day, he combed his fingers through her hair until her face was unframed. Then he just looked and looked, while the breath trembled through her parted lips. Slowly, almost painfully, he lowered his head, his eyes on hers, watching, watching, until their lips parted, separated and were drawn back together.

With a small, helpless sound she pulled him closer, almost afraid of what his tenderness was doing to her. But the demand didn't come, only the gift. There were tears in her eyes now, and an ache in her throat, as the beauty weakened her. She spoke again, but only his name, as the emotions that were flooding her poured out.

Then they were clinging together, as survivors of a storm might cling to one another. It was as if they couldn't touch enough, couldn't take enough. Wrapped tight, mouths seeking, they rolled over the bed. Sheets tangled and were ripped aside. Their tenderness was replaced by a greed that was every bit as devastating.

With their fingers locked, their needs fused, she rose over him, sliding down to take him into her. When he filled her she arched back, crying out. Not helplessly, but triumphantly.

Caught in the last light of day, they swept each other toward dusk and the welcoming night.

Chapter 10

"I appreciate you going with me."

Cody spared Abra a brief look as he stopped the car in front of the hotel where W. W. Barlow and his new wife were staying. "Don't be stupid."

"No, I mean it." She fiddled nervously with her choker as the valet hurried to open her door. "This is my problem. A family problem." After stepping out on the curb, she took a deep breath and waited for Cody to join her. "But I'd have hated to face this dinner alone."

It continued to surprise him to find these traces of insecurity in her. This same woman who was afraid to share a quiet dinner with her mother had once stepped carelessly between two angry construction workers with fists like cinder blocks. With a shake of his head he pocketed his parking stub, then took her arm to lead her into the lobby.

"You're not alone. Still, there's no reason to go into this believing it's going to be some sort of trial by fire."

"Then how come I can already feel the heat?" she mumbled as they crossed the lobby.

"You're not being interviewed by the State Department, Wilson. You're having dinner with your mother and her new husband."

She couldn't prevent a short laugh. "And I've had tons of experience." She paused again at the entrance to the dining room. "Sorry. No snide remarks, no sarcasm and no pouting."

He cupped her face, amused by the way she had straightened her shoulders and brought up her chin. "All right. But I had planned to pout at least through the appetizers."

She laughed again, and this time she meant it. "You're good for me."

His fingers tightened as he dipped his head to give her a hard, unexpected kiss. "Red, I'm the best for you."

"Good evening." The maître d' was all smiles. He evidently had a weakness for romance. "A table for two?"

"No." Cody let his hand slip down to take Abra's. "We're joining the Barlows."

"Of course, of course." That seemed to perk him up even more. "They've just been seated. If you'll follow me?"

It was early for dinner, so the restaurant was all but empty. Salmon-colored tablecloths and turquoise napkins were pressed and waiting for the patrons who would trickle in over the next two hours. A miniature fountain shaded by palms rose up in the center. The candles on the tables had yet to be lit, as the sun still filtered through the windows. As the maître d' had said, the newlyweds were already seated. They were holding hands. Barlow spotted them first and sprang out of his chair. Abra couldn't be sure, but she thought his smile seemed a bit sheepish.

"Right on time." He grabbed Cody's hand for a quick, hearty shake. "Glad you could make it." He hesitated a moment before turning to Abra. He was wearing an obviously pricey Fioravanti suit, but he still looked like anyone's favorite uncle. "Am I allowed to kiss my new stepdaughter?"

"Of course you are." Trying not to wince at the term, she offered a cheek, but found herself gripped in a huge, hard bear hug. Instinctively at first, then with more feeling than she'd expected, she returned it.

"Always wanted a daughter," he mumbled, making a production of pulling out her chair. "Never expected to get one at my age."

Not certain what she should do next, Abra leaned over to kiss her mother's cheek. "You look wonderful. Did you enjoy your trip?"

"Yes." Jessie twisted the napkin in her lap. "I'm going to love Dallas as much as Willie does. I hope— we hope—you'll find time to visit us there."

"Always a room for you there." Barlow tugged at his tie, mangling the tidy Windsor knot. "Make it your home whenever you want."

Abra clasped and unclasped her purse. "That's kind of you."

"Not kind." Giving up his tie, Barlow smoothed what was left of his hair. "Family."

"You would like a drink before you order?" The maître d' hovered, clearly pleased to have one of the wealthiest men in the country at one of his tables.

"Champagne. Dom Perignon '71." Barlow laid a hand on Jessie's. "We're celebrating."

"Very good, sir."

Silence descended immediately, awkwardly. Cody had a quick flash of his own family meals, with everyone talking over everyone else. When Abra's hand found his under the table, he decided to give them all a little help. "I hope you'll be able to come by and check on the project before you go back to Dallas."

"Why, yes, yes. Planned to." Barlow gripped the lifeline gratefully.

Sitting back, Cody began to steer the conversation over easy ground.

Why, they're nervous, too, Abra realized as all three of them struggled to hit the right tone, find the right words. Everyone could have walked on eggshells without causing a crack. Only Cody was relaxed, hooking an arm over the back of his chair and taking the reins the others gladly relinquished. Jessie continued to twist her napkin, though she managed the occasional forced smile. Barlow ran his finger under his collar constantly, clearing his throat and reaching out to touch Jessie's hand or arm or shoulder.

Reassuring each other, Abra thought. Because of her. It made her feel small and selfish and mean-spirited. Whatever happened between Barlow and her mother, they cared for each other now. Holding back her approval or acceptance helped nothing and hurt everyone. Including her.

There seemed almost a communal sigh of relief when the wine was served. The fussy little show began with the display of the label. The cork was removed with only a whisper of sound, and a swallow was offered to Barlow for tasting. Once it was approved, wine was poured in all the glasses.

"Well, now." Barlow sent his nervous smile around the table as bubbles raced to the surface.

"I'd like to propose a toast," Cody began.

"No, please." Abra stopped him with a hand on his arm. During the strained silence, Jessie linked fingers with Barlow. "I'd like to." She couldn't think of any clever words. She'd always been better with figures. "To your happiness," she said, wishing she could do better. She touched her glass to her mother's, then to Barlow's. "I hope you'll love my mother as much as I do. I'm glad you found each other."

"Thank you." Jessie sipped, struggled to compose herself, then gave up. "I must go powder my nose. Excuse me a minute."

She hurried off, leaving Barlow grinning and blinking his eyes. "That was nice. Real nice." He took Abra's hand, squeezing tightly. "I'm going to take good care of her, you know. Man doesn't often get a chance to start over at my age. Going to do it right."

Abra rose to move over and rest her cheek against his. "See that you do. I'll be back in a minute."

Barlow watched her take the same route as Jessie.

"Guess if I were any prouder I'd bust my seams." He lifted his glass and took a long gulp. "Quite a pair, aren't they?"

"You could say that." He was feeling enormously proud himself.

"Ah, now that we've got a minute... Jessie tells me you and Abra are...close."

Cody lifted a brow. "Going to play papa, WW?"

Embarrassed, Barlow shifted in his chair. "Like I said, I never had a daughter before. Makes a man feel protective. I know Jessie would like to see that girl settled and happy. She thinks Abra's feelings might be serious. If yours aren't—"

"I love her." There. He'd said it out loud, and it felt wonderful. Cody savored it for a moment, finding it as rich and exciting as the wine. He hadn't expected it to feel good, hadn't expected the words to come so easily. As if experimenting, he said it again. "I love her. I want to marry her." The second part came as a surprise to him. It wasn't that he hadn't thought of the future, with her as a part of it. It wasn't that he hadn't thought of them spending their lives together. But marriage, the solidity of it, the absoluteness of it, came as a surprise. He found it a pleasant one.

"Well, well..." Doubly pleased, Barlow lifted his glass again. "Have you asked her?"

"No, I... When the time's right."

With a bray of laughter, Barlow slapped him on the back. "Nothing more foolish than a young man in love. Unless it's an old one. Let me tell you something, boy. You try to plan these things out—right time, right place, right mood—they never get done. Maybe you're not old enough to think about how precious time is, but take it from me, there's nothing worse than looking back and seeing how much you wasted. That girl...my daughter—" he puffed out his chest "—she's a prize. You'd better grab on before she slips away from you. Have another drink." He topped off Cody's glass. "Marriage proposals come easier if you're loose. Had to get damn near drunk to manage both of mine."

With an absent nod, Cody lifted his glass, and wondered.

Abra found Jessie in the ladies' lounge, sitting on an overstuffed white chair and sniffling into a hankie. Abra cast a helpless look around, then sat beside her.

"Did I say something wrong?"

Jessie shook her head and dabbed at her eyes. "No. You said everything right and made me so happy." She sobbed as she turned to throw her arms around Abra's neck. "I was so nervous about tonight, so afraid you'd sit there hating me."

"I've never hated you. I couldn't." Abra felt her own eyes filling. "I'm sorry. I'm sorry I made things so hard on you before."

"No, you didn't. You never have. You've always been the one thing in my life I could count on. I've always asked too much of you. I have," she insisted when Abra shook her head. "I know I've let you down, over and over again, and I regret it. But I can't go back and change it." She drew back, and her smooth cheeks were streaked with tears. "To be honest, I don't know if I would if I had the chance. I've made mistakes, sweetheart, and you've had to pay for them." She dried Abra's cheeks with her damp handkerchief. "I never thought of you first, and you have the right to resent me for that."

Sometimes she had, and sometimes the resentment had edged toward despair. Tonight wasn't the night to think of it. Instead, she smiled. "Do you remember the time, I was about ten or eleven and that boy up the street—Bob Hardy—pushed me off my bike? I came home with my knees all bloody and my shirt torn."

"That little bully." Jessie's pretty mouth thinned. "I wanted to give him a good smack."

The idea of Jessie smacking anyone, even a grubby delinquent, made Abra's smile widen. "You cleaned me all up, kissed all the scrapes and promised me a new shirt. Then you marched right off to Mrs. Hardy."

"I certainly did. When I— How do you know? You were supposed to be in your room."

"I followed you." Delighted with the memory, Abra grinned. "I hid in the bushes outside the door and listened."

Jessie's color was a bit heightened when she meticulously replaced the hankie in her purse. "You heard what I said to her? Everything?"

"And I was amazed." With a laugh, Abra took her mother's hand. "I didn't know you had even heard those kind of words, much less that you could use them so... effectively."

"She was a fat old witch." Jessie sniffed. "I wasn't going to let her get away with raising a mean, nasty boy who pushed my little girl around."

"By the time you'd finished with her she was eating out of your hand. That night she brought that mean, nasty boy to the door by his ear and made him apologize. I felt very special."

"I love you just as much now. More, really." Gently she brushed Abra's hair from her temples. "I never knew quite how to deal with a child. It's so much easier for me to talk to a woman."

Because she was beginning to understand, Abra kissed her cheek. "Your mascara's running."

"Oh, no." Jessie took one look in the mirror and shuddered. "What a mess. Willie will take one look and run for cover."

"I doubt that, but you'd better fix it before we miss out on that champagne." Abra settled back comfortably to wait.

"That wasn't so bad." Cody stripped off his tie the moment they stepped into Abra's apartment.

"No, it wasn't." She kicked off her shoes. She felt good, really good. Perhaps her mother's marriage would go the way of her others. Perhaps it wouldn't. But they had crossed a bridge tonight. "In fact, it was nice. Champagne, caviar, more champagne. I could get used to it." When he wandered to the window to look out, she frowned at his back. "You seem a little distracted. Cody?"

"What?" He turned back to stare at her. She was wearing a white sundress sashed at the waist with a vivid green scarf. She never failed to knock him out when she was wearing something slim and feminine.

Who was he kidding? She knocked him out when she was wearing dirty overalls.

A little confused by the way he was staring, Abra tried a smile. "I know I was pretty wrapped up in my-self this evening, but I did notice how quiet you got. What's wrong?"

"Wrong? Nothing. I've…got some things on my mind, that's all."

"The project? Is there a problem?"

"It's not the project." Hands in his pockets, he crossed over to her. "And I don't know if it's a problem."

She felt her hands go cold. His eyes were very dark, very intense, very serious. He was going to end it, she thought, her heart trembling. He was going to end it now and go back east. Moistening her lips, she prepared herself. She'd promised herself that she would be strong when this moment came, that she wouldn't ruin what they'd had by clinging when it was over. Quite simply, she wanted to die.

"Do you want to talk about it?"

He glanced around the apartment. It was, as always, in chaos. There was no candlelight or mood music. He didn't have a rose or a diamond ring to give her. Then again, he was hardly the down-on-one-knee, hand-on-heart type. "Yeah. I think we should—"

The phone interrupted him, making him swear and Abra jolt. As if in a dream, she moved to answer. "Hello. I… Oh, yes. Yes, he's here." Her face blank, she offered Cody the receiver. "It's your mother."

A little skip of fear raced through him as he took

the phone. "Mom? No, it's no problem. Is everything all right?"

Abra turned away. She heard snatches of his conversation, but they floated in and out of her head. If he was going to break it off, she had to be strong and accept it. As Cody had only minutes before, she walked to the window and stared out.

No, it was wrong. The whole idea was wrong and had always been wrong. She loved him. Why the hell did she have to accept that it was going to end? And why was she automatically assuming that he was going to leave? It was hateful, she thought, closing her eyes. Hateful to be so insecure over the only thing, the only person, who really mattered.

"Abra?"

"Yes?" She turned quickly, torn. "Is everything all right?"

"Everything's fine. I gave my family this number, as well as the one at the hotel."

"That's all right." Her smile was strained around the edges.

"My father had some trouble—heart trouble—a couple of months ago. It was touch and go for a while."

Compassion came instantly and wiped out her nerves. "Oh, I'm sorry. Is he okay now?"

"Looks like." He took out a cigarette, unsure how to balance his relief about his father with his nerves over Abra. "He went in for more tests today and got a clean bill of health. My mother just wanted to let me know."

"I'm so glad. It must be terrifying…" She let her words trail off as another thought sunk in. "A couple of months ago? About the time we were having our preliminary meetings?"

"That's right."

On a long breath, she shut her eyes. She could see herself perfectly, standing in the trailer on that first day and berating him for being too spoiled and lazy to leave his orange grove.

"You should have poured that beer over *my* head."

The grin helped. He walked over to tug on her hair. "I thought about it."

"You should have told me," she muttered.

"It wasn't any of your business—at the time." Taking her hand, he brought it to his lips. "Times change. Abra—"

This time the phone had him snarling.

"Yank that damn thing out of the wall, will you?"

Chuckling, she moved away to answer. "Hello. Yes, this is Abra Wilson. Mrs. Mendez? Yes, how is your husband? That's good. No, it wasn't any trouble at all. Mr. Johnson and I were glad to do it." She shifted the phone to her other ear as Cody moved behind her to nibble on her neck. "Tonight? Actually, I… No. No, of course not, not if it's important. We can be there in about twenty minutes. All right. Goodbye."

Puzzled, Abra replaced the receiver. "That was Carmen Mendez."

"So I gathered. Where can we be in about twenty minutes?"

"The hospital." Abra glanced around for the purse she'd tossed aside when they'd come in. "She sounded very strange, very nervous, yet she said that Mendez was out of Intensive Care and doing well enough. She said he needed to talk to us right away."

Since she was already putting on her shoes, Cody decided she'd made up her mind to go. "One condition."

"Which is?"

"When we get back we don't answer the phone."

They found Mendez flat on his back in a semiprivate room with his wife sitting beside him, clinging to his hand.

"It was good of you to come."

Cody noticed that Mendez's knuckles were white. The curtains between the beds were drawn. The other patient had the television on, and the squealing sounds of a car chase poured out.

"I'm glad you're doing better." Abra laid a hand on Carmen's shoulder, squeezing lightly as she studied the man in the bed. He was young, too young, for the lines of pain and trouble around his eyes. "Is there anything you need? Anything we can do for you?" She broke off, surprised and embarrassed to see his eyes fill with tears.

"No, *gracias*. Carmen told me how good you were, staying with her, taking care of all the papers and the questions."

Carmen leaned over him, murmuring in Spanish, but the words were too soft for Abra to hear.

"Sí." He moistened his lips, and though his back brace prevented him from moving, Abra thought he was set as if for a blow. "I thought I would die, and I could not die with sins on my soul. I told Carmen everything. We have talked." His eyes shifted so that he could see his wife and her nod of encouragement. "We have de-

cided to tell you." He swallowed, closing his eyes for a moment. "It didn't seem so bad, and with the baby coming we needed the money. When Mr. Tunney asked me, I knew in my heart it was wrong, but I wanted good things for Carmen and the baby. And myself."

Uneasy, Abra moved closer to the bed. Across the prone body of Mendez, she and Cody exchanged one brief look.

Cody kept his voice calm. "What did Tunney ask you?"

"Only to look the other way, to pretend not to notice. Much of the wire we use on the project is not up to code."

Abra felt her stomach sink and her blood go cold. "Tunney offered to pay you to install substandard wire?"

"*Sí.* Not all, not everywhere. Not all of the men could be trusted—not to be trusted," he said lamely. "When a delivery would come, he would assign a few of us to work with the twelve-gauge. We would be paid in cash every week. I know I can go to jail— We know. But we have decided to do what is right."

"David, this is a very serious accusation." But Abra was remembering the reels of wire she had examined herself. "That wiring was inspected."

"*Sí.* It was arranged to have the same inspector. He is paid, also. When he comes, you and Mr. Johnson are to be busy somewhere else in case you would notice something."

"How could Tunney arrange—" Abra closed her eyes. "David, was Tunney following orders?"

Mendez squeezed his wife's hand again. This was what he feared most. "*Sí*, he has orders. From Mr. Thornway." Murmuring, Carmen lifted a cup to his lips so that he could wet his dry lips.

"There is more than the wiring. I hear things. Some of the concrete, some of the steel, some of the rivets. Some," he explained. "Not all, you see? I think when I am asked that Mr. Thornway is a big builder. He is powerful, important, so this must be the way. When I tell Carmen, she is ashamed of me and says it is not our way."

"We will give back the money." Carmen spoke for the first time. Her eyes were as they had been on the day of the accident, very young and very afraid, but her voice was strong.

"I don't want you to worry about that now." Abra rubbed a hand over her temple. "Or anything else. You did the right thing. Mr. Johnson and I will take care of it. We may need to talk to you again, and you'll have to go to the police."

Carmen put an unsteady hand on her rounded stomach. "We will do what you say. *Por favor,* Señorita Wilson, my David is not a bad man."

"I know. Don't worry."

Abra stepped out of the room, feeling as though she had taken a long, nasty fall. "What are we going to do?"

"We're going to go see Tim." He put his hands on her shoulders. "I'm going to call Nathan. He needs to know about this."

She nodded, walking away as he headed to a bank of phones.

They didn't speak on the drive to Thornway's house. Abra could only think of the business Thornway had built, brick by brick, the reputation he had earned, the pride he had felt and had given her the chance to feel. In one flash the son he had handed it to had tossed it aside.

"I should have guessed," she murmured at length.

"How?" He was dealing with his own demons, and with the crumbling of his own dreams.

"The day Mendez was hurt. I was with Tunney. There had just been a delivery, and I happened to check it. It was twelve-gauge." She turned her head to look at him. "He spun me a tale about someone screwing up the invoice numbers. We were talking when the accident happened, and I never took it any further. Damn it, Cody, I never even thought of it again."

"You wouldn't have had any reason to suspect him. Or Thornway." He pulled up in front of Tim's house. "Why don't I handle this? You can wait here."

"No." She pushed open the car door. "I have to be there."

Moments later they were waiting in Tim's spacious foyer.

Elegant in a dinner jacket, Tim came down the steps. "Abra, Cody. This is a surprise. I'm afraid you just caught us. Marci and I are on our way out. She's still dressing."

"You'll have to be late," Cody said curtly. "This can't wait."

"Sounds serious." Tim checked his watch before gesturing them into his library. "I can always squeeze out a few minutes. Marci's never on time anyway." He went to a small ebony bar. "What can I get you?"

"An explanation." Abra took a step toward him, needing to see his eyes. "As to why you've been using substandard equipment on the Barlow project."

His hand shook once, and the whiskey spilled before he steadied it and poured. That was all she needed to be sure of the truth. "What in the world are you talking about?"

"I'm talking about materials that don't come up to code. I'm talking about payoffs and kickbacks and bribes." She grabbed his arm when he started to lift his drink, and her fingers dug in. "I'm talking about ruining a reputation your father spent his life building."

Whiskey in hand, Tim turned. Though the room was cool, there was already a light film of sweat beading above his mouth. "I have no idea what this is all about, but I don't appreciate being accused of any illegalities." He tossed back the whiskey, then poured another. "I realize my father had an affection for you, Abra, and that you feel a certain personal interest in my company. But that doesn't excuse this."

"Be careful." Cody's voice was too soft and too mild. "Be very careful what you say to her, or I may just decide to go with my instincts and break your arms."

The sweat was dripping now, hot and sticky down his back. "I don't have to stand here in my own house and be threatened."

Cody simply shifted in front of the door before Tim could storm out. "You're going to stand here and be a lot more than threatened. The game's up. We know about the materials, about the inspectors you bribed, about the laborers who were paid off to install and keep their mouths shut. Funny thing, Tim, it turns out that some of them have consciences."

"This is ridiculous. If someone's been skimming on the material, I intend to find out about it. You can be sure I'll initiate an investigation."

"Fine." Abra put a hand on his arm and looked him in the eye. "Call the building commissioner."

"I'll do just that."

"Do it now." Abra tightened her grip when he tried to pull away. "I imagine you have his home number. We can have a little meeting right here tonight."

Tim reached for his glass again. "I have no intention of disturbing the commissioner at home on a Saturday evening."

"I think he'd be very interested." Abra recognized the fear in his eyes and gave him one last push. "While you're at it, why don't you call Tunney, too? The commissioner's going to want to talk to him. Somehow I don't think Tunney's a man who'd be willing to take the fall alone."

Saying nothing, Tim sank into a chair. He drank again, this time in small sips, until the glass was empty. "We can work something out." He leaned forward, his hands braced on his knees. "It's business, you understand. I took a few shortcuts. Nothing that has to matter."

"Why?" She'd needed to hear him say it. Now that he had, her anger drained away. "Why would you risk everything for a few extra dollars?"

"A few?" With a laugh, he snatched the bottle from beside him and poured more whiskey. He'd already had too much and too quickly, but he badly needed more. "Thousands. It came to thousands. You skim here, cut through there, and before you know it there are thousands. I needed it." The liquor steadied his hand as he drank. "You don't know what it's like being the son, being expected to do things as well as they were always done. Then there's Marci." He glanced up as though he could see her in the room above his head. "She's beautiful, restless, and she wants. The more I give, the more she wants. I can't afford to lose her." He dropped his face into his hands. "I bid too low, way too low, on this project. I thought I could pull it off somehow. I had to. There are debts, debts to the wrong kind of people. Ever since I took over, things have been going wrong. I lost fifty thousand on the Lieterman project."

He glanced up when Abra said nothing. "It wasn't the first time. For the past nine months the business has been dropping into the red. I had to make it up. This was the best way. Cut a few corners, sweeten a few pots. If I brought this in under budget and on time I'd be in the black again."

"And when there was an electrical fire?" Cody put in. "Or the supports gave way? What then?"

"It didn't have to be that way. I had to take the chance. I had to. Marci expects to live a certain way. Am I supposed to tell her we can't go to Europe because the business is in trouble?"

Abra looked at him and felt only pity. "Yes. You're going to have to tell her a lot more than that now."

"Work isn't going to start again on Monday, Tim." Cody waited until he brought his head back up. "It's not going to start at all until after a full investigation. You bit this off, now you're going to have to swallow it. You can call the building commissioner, or we can."

Tim was getting drunk. It helped somehow. "You haven't told anyone?"

"Not yet," Abra said. "You're right that I felt close to your father and that I feel a responsibility to the business. I wanted you to have a chance to make this right yourself."

Make it right? Tim thought desperately. How in God's name could he make it right? One official inspection and everything would be over. "I'd like to speak with Marci first. Prepare her. Give me twenty-four hours."

Cody started to object, but Abra touched his arm. The wheels were already in motion, she thought. Another day wasn't going to stop what had begun. She could give him a day, because she'd cared for his father. "You'll set up a meeting at your office? For all of us?"

"What choice do I have?" His words were slurred now by drink and self-pity. "I'm going to lose everything, aren't I?"

"Maybe you'll get back your self-respect." Cody took Abra's hand. "I want to hear from you by nine tomorrow night, or we'll make that call."

Outside, Abra pressed her fingers to her eyes. "Oh, God, it's awful."

"It's not going to get better."

"No." She straightened and glanced back at the

house. The light was still burning in the library. "This was going to be my last job for them. I never expected it to end like this."

"Let's go."

Tim heard their car start up and sat listening as the sound of the engine died away in the night. His wife, his beautiful, selfish wife, was primping upstairs. In a fit of rage, he hurled his glass across the room. He hated her. He adored her. Everything he'd done had been to make her happy. To keep her. And if she left him…

No, he couldn't bear to think of it. He couldn't bear to think of the scandal and the accusations. They would crucify him, and he would lose his business, his home, his status. His wife.

Maybe there was still a chance. There was always a chance. Stumbling to the phone, he dialed a number.

Chapter 11

Perhaps it was the strain of the evening, or the discomfort of witnessing another's despair and humiliation, but they needed each other. They fell into bed in a kind of fury, saying nothing, looking for what they could bring to each other to block out the lingering anger and disillusionment.

Together they had built something strong—or thought they had. Now they had learned that it had been built on lies and deceits. If they tangled together quickly, reaching, taking, it was to assure themselves that what they had built privately was no lie.

This was real, solid, honest. She could feel it as his mouth closed hungrily over hers, as their tongues met, as their bodies fitted together. If he needed to forget what existed outside this room, this bed, for just one night, she understood. She needed it, too, and so she gave herself utterly.

He wanted to comfort her. She had looked so stricken when Tim had collapsed into confession. It was personal with Abra, and he knew, though she had said nothing, that she was taking part of the failure as her own. He wouldn't have it. But the time for straight talk was in the morning, when her feelings weren't so raw. For now, for a few hours, he would give her release in passion.

Her scent. He remembered watching her dab it on before dinner, absently, as an afterthought. It had faded as the night had worn on, and now it was no more than a whisper along her skin, and all the more intimate for that. He drew it in as he let his mouth glide over her throat and down to where her skin became impossibly soft, impossibly delicate.

Her hair. She had taken a brush through it quickly, impatiently. She was never fully satisfied with the way it looked. He thought it glorious. Now, as he combed a hand through it, he could luxuriate in the wildness of it. When she rolled over, stretching her body over his as if she couldn't get enough of him, her hair streamed over her shoulders and dipped to his.

Her lips. She had added color to them, worried it off, then replaced it. They were naked now, smooth as silk, soft as rain. He had only to touch his to them for them to part in welcome. If he asked more, she gave more.

Now, with him trapped beneath the tangle of her hair and her agile body, she took her mouth over him, giving him pleasure, seeking her own. There was an excitement in having the freedom to explore the man she loved. To touch him and feel him tremble. To taste him and hear him sigh.

The light in the hallway was still burning, so she could see him, the lean lines, the firm muscles. And his eyes. She could see his eyes as she brought her lips back to his. They were so dark, so completely focused on her.

She could sense something different but was unable to understand it. One moment he was impatient, almost brutal, in his loving. The next he held her, kissed her, as if she were precious and fragile. However his hands took, however his lips demanded, she belonged to him. Passions layered so tightly with emotions that she couldn't separate desire from love. There was no need to.

When he filled her, she found both.

It was later, much later, when she woke, disturbed by some sound or some dream. Murmuring, she shifted, reaching out—and found him gone.

"Cody?"

"I'm right here."

She saw him then, standing by the window. The end of his cigarette glowed red in the dark. "What's wrong?"

"Nothing. Can't sleep."

Sitting up, she pushed her hair away from her face. The sheet slid down to pool at her waist. "You can come back to bed. We don't have to sleep."

He laughed and tapped out his cigarette. "I never thought I'd meet a woman who could wear me out."

She threw a pillow at him. "Is that supposed to be a compliment?"

"Just an observation." He came over to sit on the side of the bed. "You're the best, Red." He wasn't talking about sex. Because she understood that, she smiled and fumbled for something to say.

"I'm glad you think so." As her eyes adjusted to the dark, she frowned. "You're dressed."

"I was going to go for a drive. I didn't know whether or not to wake you."

"Of course you should have. Where were you going?"

He took her hand, carefully, as though weighing it. "I have to see it, Abra. I might be able to get it out of my head for a few hours once I do."

Her fingers curled into his. "I'll go with you."

"You don't have to. It's late—early, I guess."

"I want to. Will you wait for me?"

"Sure." He brought her hand to his lips. "Thanks."

The air was cool and breathlessly clear. Overhead, the sky was a dark, calm sea pierced by stars. There was no traffic to dodge, only a long ribbon of road, banked first by houses and shops, then by nothing but acres of empty desert. With the windows down and the engine no more than a purr, Abra heard the lonesome call of a coyote.

"I've never driven through here at this time of night." Abra turned to look out the window at the distant buttes, which were no more than dark shadows rising and spreading. "It's so quiet. It makes you wonder."

"Wonder what?"

"That it's been this quiet, just this quiet, for centuries. I guess if we do it right it'll be just this quiet for centuries more."

"People in our business are supposed to see undeveloped land and think immediately of how it can be put to use."

She frowned a little and searched in her purse for a band or a string to tie back her hair. "Do you?"

He was silent for a moment, enjoying the drive, the quiet, the company. "There are places along the Intracoastal where the brush is so dense you can't see beyond the first foot. It's not quiet, because it's as thick with life as it is with leaves. The waterway cuts through— that's man's contribution—but some things are meant to stay as they are."

She was smiling again as she pulled her hair into a ponytail. "I like you, Johnson."

"Thanks, Wilson. I like you, too." He rested his arm on the back of the seat so that he could toy with the ends of her hair. "You said something before about the Barlow project being your last one with Thornway."

"Yeah. I've been thinking about it for a long time. After Tim took over I decided it was time to do more than think. I wish..." But it was no use wishing she had already cut her ties with the firm.

Because he understood, he massaged the tension at the back of her neck. "You got another offer?"

"No. I haven't exactly announced my resignation, but I'm not looking for another offer." She was afraid he would think her foolish, so she began to fiddle with the dial of the radio. Music poured out, as clear as the air. "I'm going to freelance, maybe start up my own business. A small one." She shut off the radio and shot him a look. "I've been putting money aside for a while now, to see me through the rough spots."

"Do you want out on your own or do you just want a change of scene?"

She considered for a moment, then shook her head. "Both, I guess. I owe a lot to Thornway. Thornway senior," she explained. "He gave me a chance, let me prove myself. Over the past year or so, things have changed. I didn't know...never had any idea Tim was into something like this, but I was never comfortable with the way he did business." Her eyes were drawn to the east, where the sky was just beginning to lighten. "He always looked at the ledger sheets instead of the overall project, the payroll instead of the men who were earning the wage. Nobody goes into business without the idea of making money, but when it's the only thing..."

"When it's the only thing you end up in a situation like the one we're in now."

"I still can't believe it," she murmured. "I thought I knew him, but this— Cody, how can a man risk everything, everything he's been given, to please a woman?"

"I'd say he loves her, obviously more than he should."

"Maybe she loves him. Maybe all the jewelry, the cars and the cruises didn't matter."

He ran a finger down the back of her neck. "They mattered, Red. With a woman like that, they always matter. It's a safe bet that when all this hits Marci Thornway takes the high road."

"That's cruel. She's still his wife."

"Remember the night of the party? She was his wife

then, too, but she invited me to…let's say she invited me to spend an afternoon with her."

"Oh." Whatever sympathy she had felt for Marci Thornway vanished. "You turned her down?"

"It wasn't a hardship. Besides, I had other things on my mind. In any case, I don't think we can dump the whole mess in Marci's lap. Tim wanted too much too soon. Maybe he'd been given too much all along. Apparently he's been going after success in all the wrong ways."

"He mentioned owing money to the wrong kind of people," Abra said.

"He wouldn't be the first businessman to make a connection with organized crime. He won't be the first to lose because of it. What's this?" As they approached the turnoff for the site, he spotted another car. It hesitated at the crossroads, then swept to the right and sped away.

"I don't know." Abra frowned at the receding taillights. "Probably kids. A lot of times construction sites end up as lovers' lanes."

"Maybe, but it's late for teenagers to be out necking." He slowed to negotiate the turn.

"Well, we're here to look around, anyway. If they were vandals we'll find out soon enough."

He parked the car by the trailer. In silence they stepped out of opposite sides and stood. The main building, with its dome and spirals, was shadowed in the predawn light. Like a sculpture, it rose up out of rock, a product of imagination. The interior was rough, and the landscaping had yet to be started, but Abra saw it now as Cody had.

In this very fragile light it looked more fanciful, yet somehow more solid, than ever before. It didn't meld with the rock and sand, nor did it harmonize. Rather, it stood with and against and for—a celebration of man's ingenuity.

Standing apart, not yet connected by the flower-bordered paths, was the health center. Castlelike, it grew out of the thin, greedy soil, its arches and curves adding a richness, even a defiance, to the stark strength of the landscape. The early light struggled over the eastern rise and sprinkled on the walls.

They stood, hands lightly linked, and scanned what they had had a part in creating.

"It's going to have to come down," Cody murmured. "All or most of it."

"That doesn't mean it can't be built again. We can build it again."

"Maybe." He slipped an arm around her shoulders. The sun had yet to rise, and the air held the clean-edged chill of the desert night. "It's not going to be easy, and it's not going to be quick."

"It doesn't have to be." She understood now, as she never had, just how much of himself he had put into this. These weren't just walls, weren't just beams and supports. This was his imagination, his contribution and, though only one who built could feel it, his heart. She turned to put her arms around him. "I guess it's time I told you the truth."

He kissed her hair, and the scent was warm, sun-drenched, though the air was cool with dawn. "About what?"

"About this place." She tilted her head up but didn't smile. He saw that her eyes were gray, like the light in the east. "I was wrong and you were right."

He kissed her, taking his time about it. "That's nothing new, Red."

"Keep it up and I won't tell you what I really think."

"Fat chance. You always tell me what you think whether I want to hear it or not."

"This time you will. You may even be entitled to gloat."

"I can't wait."

She drew away to dip her hands into her pockets and turn a slow circle. "It's wonderful."

"What?" With a hint of a smile, he gripped her shoulder. "Must be the lack of sleep, Wilson. You're lightheaded."

"I'm not joking." She pulled away to face him again. "And I'm not saying this to make you feel better—or worse, for that matter. I'm saying it because it's time I did. For the past few weeks I've been able to see what you envisioned here, what you wanted to say, how you wanted to say it. It's beautiful, Cody, and maybe it sounds overdone, but it's majestic. When it's finished— and it will be finished one day—it's going to be a work of art, the way only the best buildings can be."

He stared at her as the sun peeked over the ridges of rock and brought the first hints of daylight. "I know I'm supposed to gloat, but I can't seem to manage it."

"You can be proud of this." She rested her hands on his shoulders. "I'm proud of this, and of you."

"Abra…" He skimmed his knuckles over her cheek. "You leave me speechless."

"I'd like you to know that when it comes time to rebuild I want to be a part of it." Tilting her head, she smiled. "Not that there shouldn't be a few adjustments."

He laughed and yanked her close. He'd needed this. "There had to be that."

"Minor ones," she continued, holding on to him. "Reasonable ones."

"Naturally."

"We'll discuss them." She bit his ear. "Professionally."

"Sure we will. But I'm not changing anything."

"Cody…"

"I haven't told you that you're one of the best." Now it was her turn to look astonished. "As engineers go."

"Thanks a lot." She pulled back. "I feel better. How about you?"

"Yeah, I feel better." He ran a finger down her cheek. "Thanks."

"Let's take a look around, then. It's what we came for."

Arm in arm, they walked toward the main building. "The investigation's going to be rough," Cody began. It was easier to talk about it now. "It could mess up your plans to start your own business. At least for a while."

"I know. I guess I've been trying not to think about that. Not yet."

"You'll have Barlow behind you. And Powell and Johnson."

She smiled as he pulled open the door. "I appreciate that. I never asked you what Nathan said."

"He said he'd be on the first available plane." He paused just inside the door and looked.

The walls were up, the drywall smeared with compound and sanded smooth. Empty buckets were turned over, some of them bridged with boards to make casual seats. The elevators that had given Abra such grief were resting at ground level. The forms for the curving stairs were in place, the windows secured. Instead of the buzz and whine of tools, there was a silence, an echoing one that reached from the scarred subflooring to the brilliantly colored dome.

As they stood there she knew how he felt, even how he thought, because her own frustration at the futility of it all rose.

"It hurts, doesn't it?"

"Yeah." But he'd had to come and work his way through it. Minute by minute, it was becoming easier. "It'll pass, but I've got to say I don't want to watch when they start tearing it out."

"No, neither do I." She walked in a little farther and set her purse on a sawhorse. It did hurt. Maybe it would help for them to look beyond the immediate future to a more distant one. "You know, I've always wanted to come into a place like this as a patron." She turned with a smile because she felt they both needed it. "I'll make you a deal, Johnson. When it's done and your damn waterfalls are running, I'll treat you to a weekend."

"There's a resort I designed in Tampa that's already open."

She lifted a brow. "Does it have waterfalls?"

"A lagoon, in the center of the lobby."

"Figures. It's too dark to see much in here."

"I've got a flashlight in the car." He rocked back on his heels. "I'd like to take a closer look, make sure whoever was down here wasn't poking around where they shouldn't have been."

"Okay." She yawned once, hugely. "I can sleep tomorrow."

"I'll be right back."

She turned back into the room when he had gone. It was a waste, a terrible one, she thought, but it all hadn't been for nothing. Without this project, these buildings, she might never have met him. They said you didn't miss what you'd never had, but when she thought of Cody Abra was certain that was wrong. There would have been a hole in her life, always. She might not have known why, but she would have felt it.

Building had brought them together, and it would bring them together again. Maybe it was time she stopped sitting at the drawing board and planning out her personal life. With Cody, it might be possible to simply take, to simply act. With Cody, it might be possible to admit her feelings.

Scary, she thought, and with a nervous laugh she began to wander. She'd have to give the idea a lot of thought.

He cared for her. He might care enough to be glad if she told him she would relocate in Florida. They could go on there the way they had here. Until… She couldn't get beyond the *until*.

It didn't matter. She would deal with *until* when she

got there. The one thing she was certain of was that she wasn't going to let him walk away.

With a shrug, she glanced up at the dome. The light was trickling through, thin but beautifully tinted by the glass. Pleased, she circled around. It was lovely the way it fell on the flooring, seeped into the corners. She could almost imagine the tinkling of the waterfall, the thick, cozy chairs circled around the clear pool.

They'd come back here one day, when the lobby was filled with people and light. When they did, they would remember how it had all started. His vision, and hers.

Daydreaming, she wandered toward the pipes that ran down the walls. Fanciful, yes, but certainly not foolish. In fact, she could— Her thoughts broke off as she stared down.

At first she wondered how the drywall finishers could have been so careless as to waste a trowelful of compound. And then not to clean it up, she thought as she crouched down to inspect it. A finger of light fell over it, making her look again, then look more closely and reach out to touch.

The moment she did, her heart froze. Scrambling up, she raced for the door, screaming for Cody.

He found the flashlight in the glove compartment, then tested it as a matter of course. It was probably useless to look around. It was probably just as useless to want to rip off a few panels of drywall and see for himself.

What did it matter if the place had been vandalized at this point? Correcting the wiring would have been dif-

ficult and time-consuming enough, but if the concrete
and the steel were substandard, it all had to come down.

The anger bubbled up again, enough that he nearly
tossed the flashlight back into the car. He'd come this
far, he reminded himself. And Abra with him. They
would look, and then they would leave. After the next
day, what had once been his would be completely out
of his hands.

His thoughts were running along the same lines as
Abra's when he started back. Without the building—
whatever Tim had done to sabotage it—he would never
have met her. Whatever happened here, the moment
the mess was turned over to the proper authorities he
was going to tell her exactly what he wanted. Needed.

The hell with that, he decided, quickening his pace.
He was going to tell her now, right now, on the spot
where it had all started. Maybe it was fitting, somehow,
to ask her to marry him inside the half-finished building that had brought them together. The idea made him
grin. What could be more fitting?

When he heard her scream the first time, his head
whipped up. His heart stopped, but he was already running when she screamed again. He was close enough,
when the explosion ripped, that the wall of hot air
punched him like a fist and sent him flying in a rain of
glass and rock and sheared metal.

The fall left him dazed—five seconds, ten. Then
he was up and racing forward. He didn't feel the gash
on his temple where something sharp and jagged had
spun by close enough to tear his flesh. He didn't real-

ize that the fall and those few seconds of numbness had saved his life.

All he saw were the flames licking greedily out of the windows the explosion had blown apart. Even as he reached what had been the doorway there were other explosions, one after another until the dawn echoed like a battlefield.

He was screaming for her, so strangled by fear that he couldn't hear his own voice, couldn't feel his own heart pumping out the panic. Something else blew, and a chunk of two-by-four shot out like a bullet, missing him by inches. The wall of heat drove him back once, searing his skin. Coughing, choking, he dropped to his knees and crawled inside.

There was more than fire here. Through the thick screen of smoke he could see where walls had crumbled, where huge chunks of ceiling had fallen in. As he fought his way in he could hear the sickening sound of steel breaking free and crashing down.

Blindly he heaved rubble aside, slicing his hand diagonally from one side of the palm to the other. Blood trickled into his eyes, which were already wet from the sting of smoke and fear.

Then he saw her hand, just her hand, almost covered by a pile of rubble. With a strength born of desperation, he began to heave and toss while the fire raged around him, roaring and belching and consuming. Over and over he called out her name, no longer aware of where he was, only that he had to get to her.

She was bleeding. In the turmoil of his mind he couldn't even form the prayer that she be alive. When he gathered her up, her body was weightless. For a moment, only a moment, he lost control enough to simply sit, rocking her. Slowly, with the terror clawing inside him, he began to drag her out.

Behind them was an inferno of unbearable heat and unspeakable greed. It was a matter of minutes, perhaps seconds, before what was still standing collapsed and buried them both. So he prayed, desperately, incoherently, while his shirt began to smoke.

He was ten feet beyond the building before he realized they were out. The ground around them was littered with steel and glass and still-smoldering wood. Every breath he took burned, but he fought his way to his feet, Abra in his arms, and managed another five yards before he collapsed with her.

Dimly, as if through a long, narrow tunnel, he heard the first sirens.

There was so much blood. Her hair was matted with it, and one arm of her shirt was soaked red. He kept calling to her as he wiped the worst of the grime and soot and blood from her face.

His hand was shaking as he reached out to touch the pulse in her throat. He never heard the last thundering crash behind him. But he felt the faint thready beat of her heart.

Chapter 12

"You need some attention, Mr. Johnson."

"That can wait." The panic was down to a grinding, deadly fear in the center of his gut. "Tell me about Abra. Where have you taken her?"

"Ms. Wilson is in the best of hands." The doctor was young, with wire-framed glasses and a shaggy head of dark hair. He'd been on the graveyard shift in the ER for a week, and he was looking forward to eight hours' sleep. "If you lose much more blood, you're going to pass out and save us all a lot of trouble."

Cody lifted him off his feet by the lapels of his coat and slammed him against the wall. "Tell me where she is."

"Mr. Johnson?"

Cody heard the voice behind him and ignored it as he stared into the eyes of the first-year resident. "Tell me where she is or you'll be bleeding."

The resident thought about calling for security, then decided against it. "She's being prepped for surgery. I don't know a great deal about her condition, but Dr. Bost is heading the surgical team, and he's the best."

Slowly Cody let him down, but he maintained the grip on his coat. "I want to see her."

"You can throw me up against the wall again," the young doctor said, though he sincerely hoped it wouldn't come to that, "but you're not going to be able to see her. She needs surgery. You're both lucky to be alive, Mr. Johnson. We're only trying to keep you that way."

"She's alive." Fear was burning his throat more than the smoke inhalation.

"She's alive." Cautiously the doctor reached up to remove Cody's hands. "Let me take care of you. As soon as she's out of surgery I'll come for you."

Cody looked down at his hands. Blood was already seeping through the bandage the ambulance attendant had fashioned. "Sorry."

"Don't mention it. From what the paramedics said, you've had a rough time. You've got a hole in your head, Mr. Johnson." He smiled, hoping charm would work. "I'll stitch it up for you."

"Excuse me." The man who had spoken earlier stepped forward and flashed a badge. "Lieutenant Asaro. I'd like to speak with you, Mr. Johnson."

"You want to speak with him while he's bleeding to death?" Feeling a bit more in control, the doctor pulled open a curtain and gestured toward an examining room. "Or would you like to wait until he's patched up?"

Asaro noticed a chair near the examining table. "Mind?"

"No." Cody sat on the table and peeled off what was left of his shirt. Both his torso and his back were lashed with burns and lacerations that made Asaro wince.

"Close call, I'd say."

Cody didn't respond as the doctor began to clean the gash at his temple.

"Mind telling me what you and Miss Wilson were doing out there at dawn?"

"Looking around." Cody sucked in his breath at the sting of the antiseptic. From a few rooms down came a high, keening scream. "She's the engineer on the job. I'm the architect."

"I got that much." Asaro opened his notebook. "Don't you figure you see enough of the place during the week?"

"We had our reasons for going tonight."

"I'm going to give you a shot," the doctor said, humming a little through his teeth as he worked. "Numb this up."

Cody merely nodded to the doctor. He didn't know if he could get any more numb. "Earlier this evening we were informed that there had been discrepancies on the job. Substandard materials used."

"I see. You were informed?"

"That's right." Cody divorced his mind from his body as the doctor competently stitched the wound. "I'm not going to name the source until I discuss it, but I'll tell you what I know."

Asaro set pencil to paper. "I'd appreciate it."

Cody went through it all—the discovery, the confrontation with Tim Thornway, the confession. His anger at the deception had faded. The only thing on his mind now was Abra. He continued, speaking of the car they had seen leaving the site, their assumption that it had been teenagers taking advantage of a lonely spot.

"You still think that?" Asaro asked.

"No." He felt the slight pull and tug on his hand as his flesh was sewed together. "I think somebody planted explosives in every building on that site and blew it all to hell. It's a lot tougher to identify substandard material when there's nothing much left of it."

"Are you making an accusation, Mr. Johnson?"

"I'm stating a fact, Lieutenant. Thornway panicked and had his project destroyed. He knew Abra and I were going to the building commissioner tomorrow if he didn't. Now we can bypass that."

"How so?"

"Because as soon as Abra's out of surgery I'm going to find him and I'm going to kill him." He flexed the fingers of his bandaged hand and was vaguely relieved when they moved. He spared the doctor a brief glance. "Finished?"

"Almost." The resident continued without breaking rhythm. "You've got some glass in your back and a few nice third-degree burns."

"That's an interesting story, Mr. Johnson." Asaro rose and pocketed his book. "I'm going to have it checked out. A little advice?" He didn't wait for Cody to answer. "You should be careful about making threats in front of a cop."

"Not a threat," Cody told him. He felt the sting as the resident removed another shard of glass. He welcomed it. "There's a woman upstairs who means more to me than anything in the world. You didn't see how she looked when we got her here." His stomach tightened, muscle by muscle. "You know her only crime, Lieutenant? Feeling sorry enough for that bastard to give him a few hours to explain all of this to his wife. Instead, he might have killed her."

"One more question. Did Thornway know you were going to visit the site?"

"What difference does it make?"

"Humor me."

"No. It wasn't planned. I was restless." He broke off to press his fingers to his burning eyes. "I wanted to look at it, try to resign myself. Abra came with me."

"You ought to get yourself some rest, Mr. Johnson." Asaro nodded to the doctor. "I'll be in touch."

"We're going to check you in for a day or so, Mr. Johnson." The doctor wrapped the last burn before picking up a penlight to shine it in Cody's eyes. "I'll have the nurse give you something for the pain."

"No. I don't need a bed. I need to know what floor Abra's on."

"Take the bed, and I'll check on Miss Wilson." The look in Cody's eye had the resident holding up a hand. "Have it your way. You might not have noticed, but there are people around here who like my time and attention. Fifth-floor waiting room. Do yourself a favor," he said when Cody slid gingerly off the table. "Stop by the pharmacy." He scrawled a prescription on a pad, then ripped the sheet off. "Have this filled. Your being in pain's not going to help her."

"Thanks." Cody pocketed the prescription. "I mean it."

"I'd say anytime, but I'd be lying."

He didn't fill the prescription, not because the pain wasn't grim but because he was afraid that whatever he took might knock him out.

The waiting room was familiar. He'd spent hours there with Abra only days before, while David Mendez had been in surgery. Now it was Abra. He remembered how concerned she'd been, how kind. There was no one there now but himself.

Cody filled a large plastic cup with black coffee, scalded his already-raw throat with it and began to pace. If he could have risked leaving her alone for a time, he would have gone then to find Thornway, to pull him out of that nice white house and beat his face to a pulp on that well-groomed lawn.

For money, Cody thought as he downed the rest of the burning coffee. Abra was lying on an operating table fighting for her life, and the reason was money. Crushing the cup in his hand, he hurled it across the room. The pain that tore through his shoulder had him swearing in frustration.

She'd screamed for him. Cody dragged a hand over his face as the memory of the sound ripped through him every bit as savagely as the glass. She'd screamed for him, but he hadn't been fast enough.

Why had she been alone in there? Why hadn't he

sent her back to the car? Why hadn't he simply taken her home?

Why? There were a dozen whys, but none of the answers changed the fact that Abra was hurt and he was—

"Cody." Her hair mussed and her face drawn, Jessie ran into the room. "Good God, Cody, what happened? What happened to Abra?" She took his hands, not noticing the bandage as she squeezed. "They said there was an accident at the site. But it's Sunday morning. Why would she be out there on Sunday morning?"

"Jessie." Barlow hurried in behind her to take her hand and lead her to a chair. "Give him a chance. You can see the boy's been hurt."

Jessie's lip was trembling, and she had to bite it to steady it. She saw the bandages and the burns, and she saw the look on his face, which spoke more clearly than words of shock and fear. "Dear Lord, Cody, what happened? They said she's in surgery."

"You sit, too." Taking charge, Barlow eased Cody into a chair. "I'm going to get us all some coffee here, and you take your time."

"I don't know how she is. They wouldn't let me see her." He was going to break down, he realized, if he didn't find something to hold on to. Reaction had taken its time seeping through, but now it struck like an iron fist. "She's alive," he said. It was almost a prayer. "When I pulled her out, she was alive."

"Pulled her out?" Jessie held the cup Barlow urged on her with both hands. Still, the coffee swayed and trembled. "Pulled her out of what?"

"I was outside, on my way back. Abra was in the building when it exploded."

"Exploded?" The coffee slipped out of her hands and onto the floor.

"The fire went up so fast." He could see it, he could feel it. As he sat in the chair, in his mind he was still back in the building, blinded by smoke and searching for her. "I got through, but I couldn't find her. The place was coming down. There must have been more than one charge. She was trapped under the rubble, but when I got her out she was alive."

Barlow put a hand on Jessie's arm to calm her, and to quiet her. "I want you to take it slow, Cody. Start at the beginning."

It was like a dream now. The pain did that, and the fear. He started with the call from Carmen Mendez and continued until they had wheeled Abra, unconscious, away from him.

"I should have pushed him," Cody murmured. "I should have picked up the phone and called the authorities myself. But he was drunk and pitiful and we wanted to give him a chance to salvage something. If I hadn't wanted to go out there, to look at it, to—I don't know, soothe my pride?—she wouldn't be hurt."

"You went in after her." Jessie rubbed the heels of her hands hard over her face. "You risked your life to save hers."

"I have no life without her."

The time for tears would have to wait. She rose to take his hand. "You know, most of us never find anyone who loves us that much. She's always needed it, and I always fell short. You're not going to lose her."

"I don't suppose you'd listen to an old man and stretch out on the couch over there?" When Cody shook his head, Barlow stood. "Thought not. Got to make a few phone calls. Won't be long."

So they waited. Cody watched the clock as the minutes ticked by. When Nathan and Jackie came in ahead of Barlow an hour later, he was too numb to be surprised.

"Oh, honey..." Jackie went to him immediately, her small, sharp-featured face alive with concern. "We heard almost as soon as the plane touched down. What can we do?"

He shook his head but held on. It helped somehow just to hold on to someone who knew him. "She's in surgery."

"I know. Mr. Barlow explained everything out in the hall. We won't talk about it now. We'll just wait."

Nathan dropped a hand on his shoulder. "I wish we could have gotten here sooner. If it helps any, Thornway's already been picked up."

Cody's eyes focused, then hardened. "How do you know?"

"Barlow did some checking. The police went by to question him. The minute he was told that you and Abra had been in the explosion he fell apart."

"It doesn't matter." Cody stood up and went to the window. It didn't matter whether Thornway was in jail or in hell. Abra was in surgery, and every second was an eternity.

Nathan started forward, but Jackie laid a hand on his arm. "Let me," she murmured. She stepped up quietly beside him, waiting for him to gather his control. "She's the engineer, isn't she?"

"Yeah. She's the engineer."

"And I don't have to ask if you love her."

"I haven't even told her." He laid his forehead on the glass because he was tempted to punch his fist through it. "It was never the right time or the right place. Jack, when I pulled her out—" He needed another minute to force himself to say it out loud. "When I pulled her out, I thought she was dead."

"She wasn't. She isn't." She laid a hand gently on his wrist. "I know I have this rotten optimism that can be annoying, but I don't believe you're going to lose her. When she's better, are you getting married?"

"Yeah. She doesn't know that, either. I have to talk her into it."

"You're a good talker, Cody." She touched his cheek, then turned his head so that she could study his face. He was deadly pale, with bruises under eyes that were still swollen and red-rimmed from smoke. "You look terrible. How many stitches?"

"Didn't count."

She turned over his hands, barely managing to suppress a shudder. "Did they give you something for the pain?"

"Some prescription." Absently he touched his pocket.

"Which you didn't fill." At least this was something she could do, Jackie decided, plucking it out of his pocket. "I'm going down to have it filled now, and when I bring it up you're going to take it."

"I don't want—"

"You don't want to mess with me," Jackie told him. She kissed his cheek before she strode out of the waiting room.

He took the pills to placate her, then drank the coffeepot dry to offset the drowsiness. Another hour passed, and then another. His pain dulled to a throb, and his fear sharpened.

He recognized the doctor as the same one who had operated on Mendez. Bost came in, swept a glance over the group huddled in chairs and couches and approached Jessie.

"You're Mrs. Barlow, Miss Wilson's mother?"

"Yes." She wanted to rise but found her legs wouldn't straighten. Instead she put one hand in her husband's and the other in Cody's. "Please, tell me."

"She's out of surgery. Your daughter hasn't regained consciousness yet, and she's lost a great deal of blood. We were able to stop the hemorrhaging. She has some broken ribs, but fortunately her lungs weren't damaged. Her arm was broken in two places, and she has a hairline fracture below the right knee."

Foolishly Jessie remembered kissing scraped elbows and knees to make them better. "But they'll heal?"

"Yes. Mrs. Barlow, we're going to do a series of X rays and a CAT scan."

"Brain damage?" Cody felt his blood dry up. "Are you saying she has brain damage?"

"She suffered a severe blow to the head. These tests

are standard. I know they sound ominous, but they're our best defense against whatever other injuries she may have."

"When will you have the results?" Jessie asked.

"We'll run the tests this afternoon. They'll take a couple of hours."

"I want to see her." Cody stood, sending Jessie a brief, apologetic glance. "I have to see her."

"I know."

"She won't be awake," the doctor explained. "And you'll have to keep it brief."

"Just let me see her."

He wasn't sure what was worse—all those hours of speculation or the actuality of seeing her lying so still, so pale, with bruises standing out so harshly on her cheeks and the tubes hooking her to a line of impersonal machines.

He took her hand, and it was cool. But he could feel the pulse beating in her wrist, echoed by the monitors next to her.

There was no privacy here. She would hate that, he thought. Only a wall of glass separated her from the quiet movement of nurses and technicians in ICU. They'd given her a bed gown, something white with faded blue flowers. He resented the idea that dozens of others had worn it before.

She was so pale.

His mind kept leaping back to that, though he tried to fix it on other, inconsequential things. The faded gown, the beep of the monitors, the hush of crepe soles on the tiles beyond the glass.

Where was she? he wondered as he sat and kept her hand in his through the bars on the side of the bed. He didn't want her to get too far away. He didn't know what to say to bring her closer.

"They won't let me stay, Red, but I'll be hanging around in the waiting room until you wake up. Make it soon." He rubbed a hand absently over his chest as it tightened. "You came through okay. They want to take some more tests, but they don't amount to much. You've got a nasty bump on the head, that's all."

Please, God, let that be all.

He fell silent again, counting the monotonous beeps of the monitors.

"I was thinking we could take that trip back east once you're out of here. You can work on your tan and nag me about stress points." His fingers tightened uncontrollably on hers. "For God's sake, Abra, don't leave me."

He thought—or perhaps it was only a wish—that her fingers pressed just for an instant against his hand.

"You've got to get some rest, Cody."

He'd been staring at the same paragraph of the newspaper for twenty minutes. Now he looked up and saw Nathan. "What are you doing back here?"

"Putting my foot down with you." Nathan sat on the couch beside him. "I left Jack at the hotel. If I can't go back and tell her I convinced you to take a break, she's going to insist on coming out herself."

"I'm doing better than I look."

"You'd have to be to still be conscious."

"Be a pal, Nathan." He gave himself the luxury of sitting back and closing his eyes. "Don't push."

Nathan hesitated. He wasn't the kind of man who interfered in other people's lives. There had been a time when he'd chosen not to become involved at all. That had been before Jackie. "I remember saying almost the same thing to you once when I was confused and upset. You didn't listen, either."

"You were being too stubborn to admit your own feelings," Cody said. "I know what my feelings are."

"Let me buy you something to eat."

"I don't want to miss Bost."

"How about an update on Thornway?"

Cody opened his eyes. "Yeah."

"He made a full confession." Nathan waited while Cody lit a cigarette. The ashtray was already littered with them. "He admitted to substituting materials, the payoffs, the bribes. He claims he was drunk and in a state of panic after you and Abra confronted him. He made the call to arrange the arson with some kind of crazed idea that no one would be able to prove anything against him if the project was destroyed."

"Didn't he think there would be an investigation?" Cody expelled a quick stream of smoke. "Did he think we'd all just keep quiet about it?"

"Obviously he didn't think."

"No." Too drained even for anger, Cody stared across the room, where Jessie dozed on Barlow's shoulder. "And because he didn't think, Abra was almost killed.

Even now she could be—" He couldn't say it. He couldn't even think it.

"He's going to spend a lot of years paying for it."

"No matter how many," Cody murmured, "no matter how much, it won't be enough."

"Still up and around, Mr. Johnson?" The young resident walked in, looking as though he'd slept in a packing crate. "I'm Dr. Mitchell," he explained to Nathan. "I patched your friend up, oh—" he glanced at his watch "—about eight hours ago." He looked back at Cody. "Hasn't anybody chained you to a bed yet?"

"No."

Mitchell sat and stretched out his legs. "I pulled a double shift, but I still don't feel as bad as you look."

"Thanks."

"That was a free medical opinion. I ran into Dr. Bost up in the lab." He looked longingly at Cody's cigarette, reminded himself he was a doctor and subdued the urge to ask for one. "He was just finishing up with the results of Miss Wilson's tests."

Cody said nothing, could say nothing. Very slowly he leaned forward and crushed out the cigarette.

"It looks good, Mr. Johnson."

His mouth was dry, too dry. He couldn't find the saliva to swallow. "Are you telling me she's all right?"

"We're moving her from critical to guarded condition. The scan and the X rays don't indicate brain damage. She's got one whopper of a concussion, to couch things in unprofessional terms. Bost should be down in a few minutes to give you the details, but I thought you could use a little good news. She came to briefly," he continued when Cody remained silent. "She recited her name and address, remembered who was president and asked for you."

"Where is she?"

"It's going to be a little while before you can see her. She's sedated."

"That's her mother." Cody rubbed a hand over his face. "Her mother's sitting over there. Will you tell her? I've got to take a walk."

"I've got a bed with your name on it," Mitchell said, rising with Cody. "The best way to stay close to your lady is to check into our little hotel. I can recommend the chicken surprise."

"I'll keep that in mind." Cody found his way out and walked.

Abra wanted to open her eyes. She could hear things, but the sounds ran through her mind like water. There was no pain. She felt as though she were floating, mind and body, inches off the ground.

She remembered. If she forced her mind to focus, she remembered. There was the sun shooting in red-and-gold fingers through the dome, and a sense of contentment, of purpose. Then came the fear.

Had she screamed for him? She thought she had, but that had been before that horrible noise had thundered around her. There was another memory, but it was unclear and dreamlike. She had gone flying— Something like a hot, invisible hand had scooped her up and hurled her through the air. Then there had been nothing.

Where was he?

She thought, was almost certain, that he'd been with her. Had she spoken to him, or was that a dream, too? It seemed to her that she'd opened her eyes and seen him sitting beside her. There had been a bandage on his face, and his face had been drawn and pale. They'd spoken. Hadn't they spoken? With the drugs clouding her mind, she struggled to remember and was frustrated.

Jessie. Her mother had been there, too. She'd been crying.

Then there were strangers' faces. They'd peered down at her, shone lights in her eyes, asked her foolish questions. Did she know her name? Of course she knew her name. She was Abra Wilson and she wanted to know what was happening to her.

Maybe she was dead.

She'd lost track of time, but so had Cody. He'd spent every minute he'd been permitted to, and as many more as he could fight for, beside her. Two days had crawled by. She'd been conscious off and on, but the medication had kept her drowsy and often incoherent.

By the third day he could see that she was struggling to focus.

"I can't stay awake." For the first time he heard petulance in her voice, and he was cheered by it. Until now she had accepted everything without complaint. "What are they giving me?"

"Something to help you rest."

"I don't want any more." She turned her head so that she could look at him. "Tell them not to give me any more."

"You need to rest."

"I need to think." Annoyed, she tried to shift. She saw the cast on her arm and fought to remember. It was broken. They'd told her it was broken. There was a cast on her leg, too. She'd been confused at first, wondering if she'd been in a car accident. But it was becoming easier to remember now.

"The buildings. They're gone."

"They don't matter." He pressed his lips to her fingers. "You gave me a scare, Red."

"I know." She was beginning to feel now. Whenever she was awake for this long she began to feel. The pain reassured her. "You're hurt."

"Couple of scrapes. You're having pain." He was up immediately. "I'll get the nurse."

"I don't want any more medicine."

Patiently he leaned over and kissed her just below the bruise on her cheekbone. "Baby, I can't stand to watch you hurt."

"Kiss me again." She lifted a hand to his cheek. "It feels better when you do."

"Excuse me." The nurse bustled in, all business. "It's time for the doctor to examine you now, Miss Wilson." She shot Cody a look. He'd given her more than his share of aggravation over the past few days. "You'll have to wait outside."

"Yes, ma'am."

"I'm not taking any more medication," he heard Abra say. "If you've got any needles on you, you'd better lose them."

For the first time in days, he laughed. She was coming back.

* * *

In another week she was frantic to get out. The night nurse caught her trying to hobble into the corridor. Cody ignored her pleas to smuggle her into the elevators. The doctor scotched her compromise suggestion of outpatient care.

Abra found herself trapped, her arm covered with plaster, her leg in a cast to the knee. She'd gone through phases of anger and self-pity. Now she was just bored. Miserably bored.

When she awoke from a nap she'd taken in self-defense, she saw a woman in her room. She was small and obviously pregnant and had a wild mop of red hair. As Abra looked, she shifted around the arrangements of flowers and plants.

"Hello."

"Hi." Jackie turned and beamed a smile. "So you're awake. Now Cody's going to yell at me because I chased him downstairs to the cafeteria. He's gone from lean to skinny in a week. He'll be gaunt in another couple of days." She walked over to the bed and made herself comfortable beside it. "So how are you feeling?"

"Pretty good." It was easy to smile. "Who are you?"

"Oh, sorry. I'm Jack. Nathan's wife?" She glanced around. "Even with the flowers, hospitals are depressing, aren't they? Bored?"

"Stiff. It's nice of you to come, though."

"Cody's family. That makes you family, too."

Abra glanced toward the doorway. "How is he?"

"He gets better as you get better. We were worried about both of you for a while."

Abra glanced back and studied Jackie's face. She'd had a lot of time to study faces in the last week. This one was friendly and—thank God—cheerful. She'd spoken of Cody as family, and Abra was certain she'd meant it.

"Will you tell me something?" Abra began. "Straight?"

"I'll try."

"Will you tell me what happened? Every time I try to talk to Cody about it he changes the subject, evades or gets angry. I can remember most of it, but it's patchy."

Jackie started to evade, as well, but then she looked into Abra's eyes. Eyes that strong, she decided, deserved the truth. "Why don't you tell me how much you remember?"

Satisfied, Abra relaxed. "We'd gone out to the site, then into the main building. It was still dark, so Cody went out to the car for a light. I was looking around. You know about the switch in materials?"

"Yes."

"When I was alone and looking around, I saw what I took at first for a bunch of drywall compound. It was plastic explosive. I ran for the door." She half lifted her casted arm. "I didn't get there."

Jackie realized she'd been right about the strength. It wasn't fear she saw but determination, laced with what she imagined was a healthy dose of frustration.

"Cody was still outside when the building went up. He managed to get through and find you. I don't know the details about that—he doesn't talk about it—but it must have been terrifying. He managed to drag you out. He told me he thought you were dead."

"It must have been horrible," Abra murmured. "Horrible for him."

"Abra, he's blaming himself for what happened to you."

"What?" She shifted, fought off a twinge of pain and struggled to sit up straighter. "Why should he?"

"He has the idea that if he had dropped the ax on Thornway straight off…if he hadn't wanted to go out there that night…if he hadn't left you alone in the building. If."

"That's stupid." She found the control button and brought the head of the bed up.

"What's stupid?"

Jackie glanced over as Cody walked in. She rose and moved over to pat his cheek. "You are, honey. I'll leave you two alone. Where's Nathan?"

"Took a side trip to the nursery."

She laughed and patted her belly. "I'll join him."

"I like her," Abra said when they were alone.

"Jack's hard not to like." He handed her a rose, careful, as he had been careful for days, not to touch her. "You've got a roomful of flowers, but I thought you might like to have one to hold."

"Thanks."

His eyes narrowed. "Something wrong?"

"Yes."

"I'll get the nurse."

"Sit down." She gestured impatiently toward the chair. "I wish you'd stop treating me like an invalid."

"Okay. Want to take a quick jog around the block?"

"You're a riot."

"Yeah." But he didn't sit. Restless, he roamed the room, stopping off by the table, which was loaded with flowers. "You got some new ones."

"Swaggart and Rodriguez. They called a truce long enough to bring me carnations. They were fighting when they left."

"Some things never change."

"And some things do. You used to be able to talk to me, and to look at me when you did."

He turned. "I'm talking to you now. I'm looking at you now."

"Are you angry with me?"

"Don't be ridiculous."

"I'm not being ridiculous." She pushed herself up, wincing. Cody's jaw tightened. "You come in here every day, every night."

"I must be furious to do that." He walked to her with some idea of helping her settle comfortably.

"Stop it." She took an ill-tempered swipe at his hand. "I can do it myself. A broken arm's not terminal."

He nearly snapped back at her before he bit down on temper. "Sorry."

"That's it. *That's it.* You won't even fight with me." She gestured with her cast, which was crisscrossed with signatures. "All you do is pat me on the head or hover over me or ask me if I need anything."

"You want to go a couple rounds, fine. We'll take it up when you're on your feet."

"We'll take it up now, damn it. Right now." She pounded a frustrated fist on the bed. She couldn't even get out of bed by herself and pace off the rage. "You've treated me like some kind of slow-witted child these last few days, and I've had enough. You won't even talk to me about what happened."

"What do you want?" The strain that had stretched his emotions to the breaking point finally snapped. "Do you want me to tell you what it was like to see that building go up and know you were inside? Do you want me to describe to you what it was like to crawl through what was left, looking for you? Then to find you half buried, bleeding and broken?" His voice rose as he strode toward her, and he gripped the rail along the side of the bed, his fingers white. "Do you want me to go over how I felt waiting in this damn place, not knowing if you were going to live or die?"

"How are we going to get beyond it if we don't?" She reached for his hand, but he snatched it away. "You were hurt, too." Her own temper and frustration broke free. "Don't you know how it makes me feel to see your hand, your face, and know it happened because you went back for me? I want to talk about it, damn you. I can't standing lying here and trying to reconstruct it."

"Then stop." He waved his hand and sent a pitcher flying. There was some small satisfaction in hearing the plastic hit the wall. "It's over and it's done. When you get out of here we're not going to look back. You're never going to put me through anything like this again. Do you understand?" He whirled back to face her. "I can't stand it. I want you out of here. I want you back with me. I love you and I'm sick of lying in bed at night and sweating through what might have happened."

"What didn't happen," she shouted. "I'm here, I'm

alive, because you saw to it. You didn't cause this, you jerk. You saved my life. I love you too much to sit here and watch this eat at you. It's going to stop, Johnson. I mean it. If you can't come in here and treat me normally, don't come at all."

"Stop this." A nurse hurried in. "We can hear you arguing all the way down—"

"Get out!" both of them shouted in unison.

She did, shutting the door behind her.

"You want me to leave, I'll leave." Cody stalked toward the bed again, this time sending the railing down with a crash. "But not before I have my say. Maybe I do blame myself for this. And that's my business. You're not going to sit there and tell me how I should feel or what I should feel. I've played along with your way of doing things too long already."

Abra set her chin. "I don't know what you're talking about."

"No strings, no commitment, no long-term plans. Isn't that the way you set things up?"

"We agreed—"

"I'm through agreeing, and I'm through waiting until the time's right, the place is right, the mood's right. Did you hear what I said a few minutes ago? I said I loved you."

"You didn't say it." Abra frowned down at her hands. "You yelled it."

"Okay, I yelled it." He sat beside her, barely controlling the urge to shout again. "Now I'm saying it, and I'm saying you're going to marry me. And that's the end of it."

"But—"

"Don't." His temper vanished so abruptly that he could only press his fingers to his eyes. "Don't push me now."

"Cody, I—"

"Just shut up, will you?" He dropped his hands, thinking—hoping—he'd regained control. "It wasn't supposed to be like this, a shouting match with you flat on your back. It seems whenever we plan things out it doesn't work. So here it is, Red—no plans, no design. I need you. I want you to marry me, to come back East and live your life with me."

She looked up and took a long breath. "Okay."

With a half laugh, he rubbed his hands over his face. "Okay? That's it?"

"Not exactly. Come here." She held out her arm and took him to her. For the first time in days he held her as if he meant it. "You probably heard what I said a little while ago, about being in love with you."

"You didn't say it." His lips curved with a combination of pleasure and relief as he pressed them to her neck. She was warm and very much alive, and she was with him. "You yelled it."

"It's still true." She eased him back so that she could look at his face. "I'm sorry."

"For what?"

"For putting you through all of this."

"It wasn't your fault," Cody told her.

"No, it wasn't." She smiled, curling the fingers at the end of her cast into the fingers at the end of his bandage. "It wasn't yours, either. It's not something I'd like to go through again, but it did push you to ask me to marry you."

"I might have done it anyway." He grinned and brushed his lips over her fingers. "Maybe."

She lifted a brow. They'd crushed the rose between them. Carefully Abra smoothed out the petals. "I have a confession. I was going to come East whether you wanted me or not."

He drew away to study her face. "Is that right?"

"I thought that if I got in your way often enough you'd get used to it. In my head I told myself I was going to let you walk away, but in my heart…I wasn't going to give you a chance."

He leaned closer to kiss her. "I wasn't going anywhere."

Epilogue

Cody scrawled the information on the registration form. Behind the desk, the slope of rock was dotted with cacti just beginning to bloom. Light streamed through the arch of glass. The clerk beamed at him.

"Enjoy your stay with us, Mr. Johnson."

"I intend to." He turned, pocketing the key.

People moved in and out of the lobby, many of them in tennis clothes. Some strolled down the wide, curving staircase, others glided up and down in the silent elevators. Overhead the dome let in the sun in a fantasy of color. He watched it spread over the tile floor. A waterfall tumbled musically into a small rock pool. Smiling, he walked over to it, and to the woman who stood watching the race of water.

"Any complaints?"

Abra turned, tilting her head to study his face. "I still

remember how many feet of pipe we needed to give you your little whim."

He took her chin in his hand. "It makes a statement."

"So you always said." She'd tell him later how lovely she thought it was. "Anyway, thanks to me, it's functional." Resting her head on his shoulder, she turned back to watch the water.

"What's wrong?"

"You'll think I'm stupid."

"Red, I think you're stupid half the time." He sucked in air when her elbow connected with his ribs. "Tell me anyway."

"I miss the kids."

With a laugh he spun her around and kissed her. "That's not stupid. But I bet I can take your mind off them for a while—once we walk over to our cabana."

"Maybe." She smiled challengingly. "If you really work at it."

"I figure a second honeymoon should be even better than the first."

She linked her hands around his neck. "Then let's get started."

"In a minute." He drew her hands away to take them in his own. "Five years ago we stood in here at dawn. The place was empty, and neither of us could be sure it would ever be finished."

"Cody, it doesn't do any good to remember all that."

"It's something I'll never forget." He brought her hands to his lips. "But there's something I never told you. I was going to ask you to marry me here, that morning."

The surprise came first, even after nearly five years of marriage and partnership. Then came the pleasure and the sweetness. "I guess it's too late now. You're already stuck with me."

"Too late for that." Ignoring the people around them, he gathered her close. They might have been alone, as they had been alone that morning years before. "It's not too late for me to tell you that you're the best part of my life. That I love you more now than I did five years ago."

"Cody." She pressed her lips to his. The feeling was as strong as ever, the taste as alluring. "I'm so happy to have you, to have the family. Coming back here now makes me realize how lucky I am." She traced the faint scar along his temple. "We could have lost everything. Instead, we have everything." For a moment she held him tight. Then, breaking away, she smiled. "And I like your waterfall."

"Praise indeed, from an engineer. Here." He took a coin out of his pocket. "Make a wish."

"I don't need wishes." She tossed it over her shoulder. "Just you." The coin sank slowly into the pool as they walked away together.

* * * * *

FROM THIS DAY

Chapter 1

Spring comes late to New England. Snow lingers in isolated patches. Trees begin their greening hesitantly, tiny closed buds of leaves against naked branches. Early blooms of color burst from the earth's womb. The air is fresh with promise.

B.J. tossed open her window with a flourish and welcomed the early breeze into her room. *Saturday,* she thought with a grin, and began to braid her long, wheat-colored hair. The Lakeside Inn was half-full, the summer season three weeks away, and if all followed her well-ordered plans, her duties as manager would be light for the duration of the weekend.

Her staff was loyal, though somewhat temperamental. Like a large family, they squabbled, sulked, teased and stuck together like mortar and brick when the need arose. And I, she mused with a rueful grin, am head counselor.

Pulling on faded jeans, B.J. did not pause to consider the incongruity of the title. A small, childlike woman reflected in her glass, curves disguised by casual attire, braids hanging impishly astride a heart shaped, elfin face with huge smoky eyes dominant. Her only large feature, they swamped the tip-tilted nose and cupid's bow mouth and were prone to smolder or sparkle with the fluctuations of her mood. After lacing dilapidated sneakers, she jogged from the room, intending to check on breakfast preparations before stealing an hour for a solitary walk.

The main staircase of the inn was wide and uncarpeted, connecting its four sprawling stories without curve or angle, as straight and sturdy as the building itself. She saw with satisfaction the lobby was both tidy and deserted. The curtains were drawn to welcome the sun, needlepoint pillows plumped, and a vase of fresh wildflowers adorned the high, well-polished registration desk. The clatter of cutlery carried from the dining room as she passed through the downstairs hall, and she heard, with a long suffering sigh, the running argument between her two waitresses.

"If you really like a man with small, pig eyes, you should be very happy."

B.J. watched Dot shrug her thin shoulders with the words as she rolled a place setting in white linen.

"Wally does not have pig eyes," Maggie insisted. "They're very intelligent. You're just jealous," she added with grim relish as she filled the sugar dispensers.

"Jealous! Ha! The day I'm jealous of a squinty-eyed little runt... Oh, hello, B.J."

"Good morning, Dot, Maggie. You rolled two spoons and a knife at that setting, Dot. I think a fork might be a nice touch."

Accompanied by her companion's snickers, Dot un-rolled the linen. "Wally's taking me to a double feature at the drive-in tonight." Maggie's smug statement fol-lowed B.J. into the kitchen, and she allowed the door to swing shut on the ensuing retort.

Unlike the casual, old fashioned atmosphere of the remainder of the inn, the kitchen sparkled with twenti-eth century efficiency. Stainless steel glimmered every-where in the oversized room, the huge stove attesting that the inn's main attraction was its menu. Cupboards and cabinets stood like veteran soldiers, walls and lino-leum gleaming with fresh cleaning. B.J. smiled, pleased with the room's perfection and the drifting scent of coffee.

"Morning, Elsie." She received an absent mutter from the round woman working at a long, well-scrubbed counter. "If everything's under control, I'm going out for a couple of hours."

"Betty Jackson won't send any blackberry jelly."

"What? Well, for goodness sake why not?" Annoyed by the complication, B.J. plucked a fresh muffin from a basket and began to devour it. "Mr. Conners always asks for her jelly, and we're down to the last jar."

"She said if you couldn't be bothered to pay a lonely old woman a visit, she couldn't be bothered to part with any jelly."

"Lonely old woman?" B.J.'s exclamation was hampered by a mouthful of muffin. "She runs more news items through that house of hers than the Associated Press. Blast it, Elsie, I really need that jelly. I was too busy last week to go listen to the latest special bulletins."

"The new owner coming Monday got you worried?"

"Who's worried? I'm not worried." Scowling, she confiscated another muffin. "It's simply that as manager of the inn, I want everything to be in order."

"Eddie said you were muttering and slamming around your office after you got the letter saying he was coming."

"I was not...muttering...." Moving to the refrigerator, B.J. poured a glass of juice and spoke to Elsie's wide back. "Taylor Reynolds has a perfect right to inspect his property. It's just, blast it, Elsie, it was all those vague comments about modernizing. Mr. Taylor Reynolds better keep his hands off the Lakeside Inn and play with his other hotels. We don't need to be modernized," she continued, rapidly working herself up into a temper. "We're perfectly fine just the way we are. There's not a thing wrong with us, we don't need anything." She finished by folding her arms across her chest and glaring at the absent Taylor Reynolds.

"Except blackberry jelly," Elsie said mildly. B.J. blinked and brought herself back to the present.

"Oh, all right," she muttered and stalked toward the door. "I'll go get it. But if she tells me one more time that Howard Beall is a fine boy and good husband material, I'll scream. Right there in her living room with the doilies and chintz, I'll scream!"

Leaving this dire threat hanging in the air, B.J. stepped out into the soothing yellow sunlight.

"Blackberry jelly," she mumbled as she hopped on a battered red bike. "New owners with fancy notions...." Lifting her face to the sky, she tossed a pigtail behind her shoulder.

Pedaling down the maple lined drive, quicksilver temper ebbed, her resilient spirits were lifted with the beauty of the day. The valley was stirring with life. Small clusters of fragile violets and red clover dotted the rolling meadows. Lines of fresh laundry waved in the early breeze. The boundary of mountains was topped by a winter's coat, not yet the soft, lush green it would be in a month's time, but patched with stark black trees and the intermittent color of pines. Clouds scudded thin and white across the sky, chased by the teasing wind which whispered of spring and fresh blossoms.

Good humor restored, B.J. arrived in town with pink cheeks and a smile, waving to familiar faces along the route to Betty Jackson's jelly. It was a small town with tidy lawns, picket fences and old, well-kept homes. The dormers and gables were typical of New England. Nestled like a contented cat in the rolling valley, and the brilliant shimmer of Lake Champlain to the west, Lakeside remained serene and untouched by big city bustle. Having been raised on its outskirts had not dulled its magic for B.J.: she felt, as always when entering its limits, a gratitude that somewhere life remained simple.

Parking her bike in front of a small, green-shuttered house, B.J. swung through the gate and prepared to negotiate for her jelly supply.

"Well, B.J., what a surprise." Betty opened the door

and patted her gray permanent. "I thought you'd gone back to New York."

"Things have been a bit hectic at the inn," she returned, striving for the proper humility.

"The new owner." Betty nodded with a fortune teller's wisdom and gestured B.J. inside. "I hear he wants to spruce things up."

Resigned that Betty Jackson's communications system was infallible, B.J. settled herself in the small living room.

"You know Tom Myers is adding another room to his house." Brushing off the seat of an overstuffed chair, Betty shifted her ample posterior and sat. "Seems Lois is in the family way again." She clucked her tongue over the Myers' profligacy. "Three babies in four years. But you like little ones, don't you, B.J.?"

"I've always been fond of children, Miss Jackson," B.J. acknowledged, wondering how to turn the conversation toward preserves.

"My nephew, Howard, just loves children."

B.J. braced herself not to scream and met the bland smile, calmly. "We've a couple at the inn now. Children do love to eat." Pleased with the maneuver, she pressed on. "They've simply devoured your jellies. I'm down to my last jar. Nobody has the touch you do with jellies, Miss Jackson; you'd put the big manufacturers out of business if you opened your own line."

"It's all in the timing," Betty preened under the praise, and B.J. tasted the hint of victory.

"I'd just have to close down if you didn't keep me supplied." Gray eyes fluttered ingenuously. "Mr. Conners would be crushed if I had to serve him store-bought goods. He simply raves about your blackberry jelly. *"Ambrosia,"* she added, relishing the word. "He says it's *ambrosia."*

"Ambrosia." Betty nodded in self-satisfied agreement.

Ten minutes later, B.J. placed a box of a dozen jars of jelly in the basket of her bike and waved a cheerful goodbye.

"I came, I saw, I conquered," she told the sky with audacious pride. "And I did not scream."

"Hey, B.J.!"

She twisted her head at the sound of her name, waving to the group playing sand lot ball as she pedaled to the edge of the field. "What's the score?" she asked the young boy who ran to her bike.

"Five to four. Junior's team's winning."

She glanced over to where Junior stood, tall and gangly on the pitcher's mound, tossing a ball in his glove and grinning.

"Little squirt," she mumbled with reluctant affection. "Let me pinch hit once." Confiscating the boy's battered cap, she secured it over her pigtails and walked onto the field.

"You gonna play, B.J.?" Suddenly surrounded by young bodies and adolescent faces, B.J. lifted a bat and tested it.

"For a minute. I have to get back."

Junior approached, hands on hips, and grinned down from his advantage of three inches. "Wanna bet I strike you out?"

She spared him a brief glance and swung the bat to her shoulder. "I don't want to take your money."

"If I strike you out," he yanked a pigtail with fifteen-year-old audacity, "you gotta kiss me."

"Get on the mound, you apprentice lecher, and come back in ten years."

His grin remained unabashed, as B.J. watched, stifling a smile as he sauntered into position. He squinted, nodded, wound up and pitched. B.J. swung a full circle.

"Strike one!"

She turned and scowled at Wilbur Hayes who stood as umpire. Stepping up to the plate again, the cheers and taunts grew in volume. She stuck out her tongue at Junior's wink.

"Strike two!" Wilbur announced as she watched the pitch sail by.

"Strike?" Turning, she placed her hands on her hips. "You're crazy, that was chin high. I'm going to tell your mother you need glasses."

"Strike two," Wilbur repeated and frowned with adolescent ferocity.

Muttering, B.J. stepped again into the batter's box.

"You might as well put the bat down," Junior shouted, cradling the ball in the mitt. "You're not even coming close to this one."

"Take a good look at the ball, Junior, 'cause it's the last time you'll see it." Shifting the hat lower on her head, B.J. clutched the bat. "It's going clear to New York."

She connected with a solid crack of bat and watched the ball begin its sail before she darted around the bases. Running full steam, head down, she heard the shouts and cheers to slide as she rounded third. Scott Temple crouched at the plate, mitt opened for reception, as she threw herself down, sliding into home in a cloud of dust and frenzied shouts.

"You're out!"

"Out!" Scrambling to her feet, she met Wilbur's bland blue stare, eye to eye and nose to nose. "Out, you little squirt, I was safe by a mile. I'm going to buy you some binoculars."

"Out," he repeated with great dignity, and folded his arms.

"What we need here is an umpire with two working eyes." She turned to her crowd of supporters and threw out her hands. "I demand a second opinion."

"You were out."

Spinning at the unfamiliar voice, B.J. frowned up at the stranger. He stood leaning on the backstop, a small lift to his well-formed mouth and amusement shining from his dark brown eyes. He pushed a lock of curling black hair from his brow and straightened a long, lean frame.

"You should have been content with a triple."

"I was safe," she retorted, rubbing more dirt on her nose. "Absolutely safe."

"Out," Wilbur repeated.

B.J. sent him a withering glance before turning back to the man who approached the heated debate between teams. She studied him with a mixture of resentment and curiosity.

His features were well defined, sculptured with planes and angles, the skin bronzed and smooth, the faintest hint of red in his dark hair where the sun caught it. She saw that though his buff-colored suit was casual, it was obviously well tailored and expensive. His teas-

ing smile widened at her critical survey, and her resentment deepened.

"I've got to get back," she announced, brushing at
her jeans. "And don't think I'm not going to mention
an eye exam to your mother," she added, giving Wilbur a final glare.

"Hey, kid." She straddled her bike and looked around
idly, then smiled as she realized the man had grouped
her with the teenagers. Restraining her smile, she looked
up with what she hoped was the insolence of youth.

"Yeah?"

"How far is it to the Lakeside Inn?"

"Look, mister, my mother told me not to talk to
strange men."

"Very commendable. I'm not offering you candy and
a ride."

"Well." She frowned as if debating pros and cons.
"O.K. It's about three miles up the road." Making her
gesture vague, she finished with the obligatory codicil.
"You can't miss it."

He gave a long stare into her wide gray eyes, then
shook his head. "That's a big help. Thanks."

"Any time." She watched him wander toward a sil-
ver-blue Mercedes and, unable to prevent herself, called
after him. "And I was safe. Absolutely safe." Tossing
the borrowed hat back to its owner, B.J. cut across the
meadow and headed toward the inn.

The four stories of red brick, with their gabled roof
and neat shutters, loomed ahead of her. Pedaling up the
wide, curving drive, she noted with satisfaction that
the short cut had brought her ahead of the Mercedes.

I wonder if he's looking for a room, she thought.

Parking her bike, she hauled out her treasure of jellies from the basket. Maybe he's a salesman. No, she contradicted her own thoughts, *that was no salesman*. Well, if he wants a room, we'll oblige him, even if he is an interfering busybody with bad eyes.

"Good morning." B.J. smiled at the newlyweds who strolled across the lawn.

"Oh, good morning, Miss Clark. We're going for a walk by the lake," the groom answered politely.

"It's a lovely day for it," B.J. acknowledged, parking her bike by the entrance. She entered the small lobby, and moving behind the front desk, set down the crate of jelly and reached for the morning mail. Seeing a personal letter from her grandmother, she opened it and began to read with pleasure.

"Get around, don't you?"

Her absorption was rudely broken. Dropping the letter, she lifted her elbows from the counter and stared into dark brown eyes. "I took a short cut." Unwilling to be outmatched by his height or faultless attire, she straightened and lifted her chin. "May I help you?"

"I doubt it, unless you can tell me where to find the manager."

His dismissive tone fueled her annoyance. She struggled to remember her job and remain pleasant. "Is there some problem? There's a room available if you require one."

"Be a good girl and run along." His tone was patronizing. "And fetch the manager for me while you're about it. I'd like to see him."

Drawing herself to her full height she crossed her arms over her chest. "You're looking at her."

His dark brows rose in speculation as his eyes swept over her incredulously. "Do you manage the inn before school and on Saturdays?" he asked sarcastically.

B.J. flushed with anger. "I have been managing the Lakeside Inn for nearly four years. If there's a problem, I shall be delighted to take it up with you here, or in my office. If you require a room," she gestured toward the open register, "we'll be more than happy to oblige you."

"B.J. Clark?" he asked with a deepening frown.

"That's correct."

With a nod, he lifted a pen and signed the register. "I'm sure you'll understand," he began, raising his eyes again in fresh study. "Your morning activity on the baseball diamond and your rather juvenile appearance are deceptive."

"I had the morning free," she said crisply, "and my appearance in no way reflects on the inn's quality. I'm sure you'll see that for yourself during your stay, Mr...." Turning the register to face her, B.J.'s stomach lurched.

"Reynolds," he supplied, smiling at her astonished expression. "Taylor Reynolds."

Struggling for composure, B.J. lifted her face and assumed a businesslike veneer. "I'm afraid we weren't expecting you until Monday, Mr. Reynolds."

"I changed my plans," he countered, dropping the pen back in its holder.

"Yes, well...Welcome to Lakeside Inn," she said belatedly and flicked a pigtail behind her back.

"Thank you. I'll require an office during my stay. Can you arrange it?"

"Our office space is limited, Mr. Reynolds." Cursing Betty Jackson's blackberry jelly, she pulled down the key to the inn's best room and rounded the desk. "However, if you don't mind sharing mine, I'm sure you'll find it adequate."

"Let's take a look. I want to see the books and records anyway."

"Of course," she agreed, gritting her teeth at the stranger's hold over her inn. "If you'll just come with me."

"B.J., B.J." She watched with an inward shudder as Eddie hurtled down the stairs and into the lobby. His glasses were slipping down his nose, his brown hair was flopping around his ears.

"B.J.," he said again, breathless, "Mrs. Pierce-Lowell's T.V. went out right in the middle of her cartoons."

"Oh, blast. Take mine in to her and call Max for the repair."

"He's away for the weekend," Eddie reminded her.

"All right, I'll survive." Giving his shoulder an encouraging pat, she guided him to the door. "Leave me a memo to call him Monday and get mine in to her before she misses Bugs Bunny." Feeling the new owner's penetrating stare in the back of her head, B.J. explained apologetically. "I'm sorry, Eddie has a tendency toward the dramatic, and Mrs. Pierce-Lowell is addicted to Saturday morning cartoons. She's one of our regulars, and we make it a policy to provide our guests with what pleases them."

"I see," he replied, but she could find nothing in his expression to indicate that he did.

Moving quickly to the back of the first floor, B.J. opened the door to her office and gestured Taylor inside.

"It's not very big," she began as he surveyed the small room with desk and file cabinets and bulletin board, "but I'm sure we can arrange it to suit your needs for the few days you will be here."

"Two weeks," he stated firmly. He strolled across the room, picking up a bronzed paperweight of a grinning turtle.

"Two weeks?" she repeated, and the alarm in her voice caused him to turn toward her.

"That's right, Miss Clark. Is that a problem?"

"No, no, of course not." Finding his direct stare unnerving, she lowered her eyes to the clutter on her desk.

"Do you play ball every Saturday, Miss Clark?" He perched on the edge of the desk. Looking up, B.J. found her face only inches from his.

"No, certainly not," she answered with dignity. "I simply happened to be passing by, and—"

"A very courageous slide," he commented, shocking her by running a finger down her cheek. "And your face proves it."

Somewhat dazed, she glanced at the dust on his finger. "I was safe," she said in defense against a ridiculously speeding pulse. "Wilbur needs an optometrist."

"I wonder if you manage the inn with the same tenacity with which you play ball." He smiled, his eyes very intent on hers. "We'll have a look at the books this afternoon."

"I'm sure you'll find everything in order," she said stiffly. The effect was somewhat spoiled as she backed into the file cabinet. "The inn runs very smoothly, and as you know, makes a nice profit." She continued struggling to maintain her dignity.

"With a few changes, it should make a great deal more."

"Changes?" she echoed, apprehension in her voice. "What sort of changes?"

"I need to look over the place before I make any concrete decisions, but the location is perfect for a resort." Absently, he brushed the dust off his fingers on the windowsill and gazed out. "Pool, tennis courts, health club, a face lift for the building itself."

"There's nothing wrong with this building. We don't cater to the resort set, Mr. Reynolds." Furious, B.J. approached the desk again. "This is an inn, with all the connotations that includes. Family-style meals, comfortable lodgings and a quiet atmosphere. That's why our guests come back."

"The clientele would increase with a few modern attractions," he countered coolly. "Particularly with the proximity to Lake Champlain."

"Keep your hot tubs and disco lounges for your other acquisitions." B.J. bypassed simmer and went straight to boil. "This is Lakeside, Vermont, not L.A. I don't want any plastic surgery on my inn."

Brows rose, and his mouth curved in a grim smile. "Your inn, Miss Clark?"

"That's right," she retorted. "You may hold the purse strings, Mr. Reynolds, but I know this place, and our guests come back year after year because of what we represent. There's no way you're going to change one brick."

"Miss Clark." Taylor stood menacingly over her. "If

I choose to tear down this inn brick by brick, that's precisely what I'll do. Whatever alterations I make or don't
make remain my decision, and my decision alone. Your
position as manager does not entitle you to a vote."

"And your position as owner doesn't entitle you to
brains!" she was unable to choke back as she stomped
from the office in a flurry of flying braids.

Chapter 2

With relish, B.J. slammed the door to her room. Arrogant, interfering, insufferable man. Why doesn't he go play Monopoly somewhere else? Doesn't he already have enough hotels to tinker with? There must be a hundred in the Reynolds chain in the states alone, plus all those elegant foreign resorts. Why doesn't he open one in Antarctica?

Abruptly, she caught sight of her reflection in the mirror and stared in disbelief. Her face was smudged. Dust clung to her sweatshirt and jeans. Her braids hung to her shoulders. All in all, she thought grimly, I look like a rather dim-witted ten-year-old. She suddenly noticed a line down her cheek, and lifting her hand, recalled Taylor's finger resting there.

"Oh, blast." Shaking her head, she began to quickly unbind her hair. "I made a mess of it," she muttered and stripped off her morning uniform. "Looking like a grimy teenager and then losing my temper on top of it. Well, he's not going to fire me," she vowed fiercely and stalked to the shower. "I'll quit first! I'm not staying around and watching my inn mutilated."

Thirty minutes later, B.J. pulled a brush through her hair and studied the new reflection with satisfaction. Soft clouds of wheat floated on her shoulders. She wore an ivory dress, nipped at the waist, belted in scarlet to match tiny blazing rubies at her ears. Heels gave her height a slight advantage. She felt confident she could no longer be mistaken for sixteen. Lifting a neatly written page from her dresser, she moved purposefully from the room, prepared to confront the bear in his den.

After a brief excuse for a knock, B.J. pushed open the office door and slowly and purposefully advanced toward the man sitting behind the desk. Shoving the paper under his nose, she waited for his brown eyes to meet hers.

"Ah, B.J. Clark, I presume. This is quite a transfiguration." Leaning back in his chair, Taylor allowed his eyes to travel over the length of her. "Amazing," he smiled into her resentful gray eyes, "what can be concealed under a sweatshirt and baggy pants.... What's this?" He waved the paper idly, his eyes still appraising her.

"My resignation." Placing her palms on the desk, she leaned forward and prepared to give vent to her emotions. "And now that I am no longer in your employ, Mr. Reynolds, it'll give me a great deal of pleasure to tell you what I think. You are," she began as his brow rose at her tone, "a dictatorial, capitalistic opportunist.

You've bought an inn which has for generations maintained its reputation for quality and personal service,
and in order to make a few more annual dollars, you
plan to turn it into a live-in amusement park. In doing
so, you will not only have to let the current staff go,
some of whom have worked here for twenty years, but
you'll succeed in destroying the integrity of the entire
district. This is not your average tourist town, it's a
quiet, settled community. People come here for fresh
air and quiet, not for a brisk tennis match or to sweat
in a sauna, and—"

"Are you finished, Miss Clark?" Taylor questioned.
Instinctively she recognized the danger in his lowered
tones.

"No." Mustering her last resources of courage, she
set her shoulders and sent him a lethal glare. "Go soak
in your Jacuzzi!"

On her heel, she spun around and made for the door
only to find her back pressed into it as she was whirled
back into the room.

"Miss Clark," Taylor began, effectively holding her
prisoner by leaning over her, arms at either side of her
head. "I permitted you to clear your system for two reasons. First, you're quite a fabulous sight when your temper's in full gear. I noticed that even when I took you
for a rude teenager. A lot of it has to do with your eyes
going from mist to smoke, it's very impressive. That,
of course," he added as she stared up at him, unable to
form a sound, "is strictly on a personal level. Now on
a professional plane, I am receptive to your opinions,
if not to your delivery."

Abruptly, the door swung open, dislodging B.J.

and tumbling her into a hard chest. "We found Julius's lunch," Eddie announced cheerfully and disappeared.

"You have a very enthusiastic staff," Taylor commented dryly as his arms propped her up against him. "Who the devil is Julius?"

"He's Mrs. Frank's Great Dane. She doesn't... she won't go anywhere without him."

"Does he have his own room?" His tone was gently mocking.

"No, he has a small run in the back."

Taylor smiled suddenly, his face close to hers. Power shot through her system like a bolt of electricity down a lightning rod. With a jerk, she pulled away and pushed at her tumbled hair.

"Mr. Reynolds," she began, attempting to retrieve her all too elusive dignity. He claimed her hand and pulled her back toward the desk, then pushed her firmly down on the chair.

"Do be quiet, Miss Clark," he told her in easy tones, settling behind the desk. "It's my turn now." She stared with a melding of astonishment and indignation.

"What I ultimately do with this inn is my decision. However, I will consider your opinion as you are intimate with this establishment and with the area and I, as yet, am not." Lifting B.J.'s resignation, Taylor tore it in half and dropped the pieces on the desk.

"You can't do that," she sputtered.

"I have just done it." The mild tone vibrated with authority.

B.J.'s eyes narrowed. "I can easily write another."

"Don't waste your paper," he advised, leaning back in his chair. "I have no intention of accepting your resignation at the moment. Later, I'll let you know. However," he added slowly, shrugging, "if you insist, I shall be forced to close down the inn for the next few months until I've found someone to replace you."

"It couldn't possibly take months to replace me," B.J. protested, but he was looking up at the ceiling as though lost in thought.

"Six months perhaps."

"Six months?" she frowned. "But you can't. We have reservations, it's nearly the summer season. All those people can't be disappointed. And the staff—the staff would be out of work."

"Yes." With an agreeable smile, he nodded and folded his hands on the desk.

Her eyes widened. "But—that's blackmail!"

"I think that term is quite correct." His amusement increased. "You catch on very quickly, Miss Clark."

"You can't be serious. You," she sputtered. "You wouldn't actually close the inn just because I quit."

"You don't know me well enough to be sure, do you?" His eyes were unfathomable and steady. "Do you want to chance it?"

Silence hung for a long moment, each measuring the other. "No," B.J. finally murmured, then repeated with more strength, "No, blast it, I can't! You know that already. But I certainly don't understand why."

"You don't have to know why," he interrupted with an imperious gesture of his hand.

Sighing, B.J. struggled not to permit temper to rule her tongue again. "Mr. Reynolds," she began in what she hoped was a reasonable tone, "I don't know why you find it so important for me to remain as manager of the inn, but—"

"How old are you, Miss Clark?" He cut her off again. She stared in perplexed annoyance.

"I hardly see…"

"Twenty, twenty-one?"

"Twenty-four," B.J. corrected, inexplicably compelled to defend herself. "But I don't see what that has to do with anything."

"Twenty-four," he repeated, obviously concluding she had finished one sentence and that was sufficient. "Chronologically, I have eight years on you, and professionally quite a bit more. I opened my first hotel when you were still leading cheers at Lakeside High."

"I never led cheers at Lakeside High," she said coldly.

"Be that as it may—" he gently inclined his head "—the arithmetic remains the same. My reason for wanting you to remain in your current position at the inn is quite simple. You know the staff, the clientele, the suppliers and so forth…during this transition period I need your particular expertise."

"All right, Mr. Reynolds." B.J. relaxed slightly, feeling the conversation had leveled off to a more professional plane. "But you should be aware, I will give you absolutely no cooperation in changing any aspect which I feel affects the inn's personality. In point of fact, I will do my best to be uncooperative."

"I'm sure you're quite skillful at that," Taylor said easily. B.J. was unsure whether the smile in his eyes was real or in her imagination. "Now that we understand each other, Miss Clark, I'd like to see the place and get an idea of how you run things. I should be fairly well briefed in two weeks."

"You can't possibly understand all I've been trying to tell you in that amount of time."

"I make up my mind quickly," he told her. Smiling, he studied her face. "When something's mine, I know what to do with it." His smile widened at her frown, and he rose. "If you want the inn to remain as is, you'd best stick around and make your sales pitch." Taking her arm, he hauled her up from the chair. "Let's take a look around."

With all the warmth of a January sky, B.J. took Taylor on a tour of the first floor, describing storage closets in minute detail. Throughout, he kept a hand firmly on her arm as if to remind her of his authority. The continued contact made her vaguely uneasy. His scent was musky and essentially male and he moved with a casualness which she felt was deceptive. His voice rolled deep and smooth, and several times, she found herself listening more to its cadence than to his words. Annoyed, she added to the layers of frost coating her tone.

It would be easier, she decided, if he were short and balding with a generous middle, or, perhaps, if he had a sturdy mole on his left cheek and a pair of chins. It's absolutely unfair for a man to look the way he does and have to fight him, she thought resentfully.

"Have I lost you, Miss Clark?"

"What?" Looking up, she collected her wits, inwardly cursing him again for possessing such dark, magnetic eyes. "No, I was thinking perhaps you'd like lunch." A very good improvisation, she congratulated herself.

"Fine." Agreeably, he allowed her to lead the way to the dining room.

It was a basic, rustic room, large and rectangular with beamed ceilings and gently faded wallpaper. Its charm was old and lasting; amber globed lamps, graceful antiques and old silver. Local stone dominated one wall in which a fireplace was set. Brass andirons guarded the empty hearth. Tables had been set to encourage sociability, with a few more secluded for intimate interludes. The air was humming with easy conversation and clattering dishes. A smell of fresh baking drifted toward them. In silence, Taylor studied the room, his eyes roaming from corner to corner until B.J. was certain he had figured the precise square footage.

"Very nice," he said simply.

A large, round man approached, lifting his head with a subtle dramatic flourish.

"'If music be the food of love, play on.'"

"'Give me excess of it, that, surfeiting, the appetite may sicken, and so die.'"

Chuckling at B.J.'s response, he rolled with a regal, if oversized, grace into the dining room.

"Shakespeare at lunch?" Taylor inquired. B.J. laughed; against her will her antagonism dissolved. "That was Mr. Leander. He's been coming to the inn twice a year for the past ten years. He used to tour with a low budget Shakespearean troupe, and he likes to toss lines at me for me to cap."

"And do you always have the correct response?"

"Luckily, I've always been fond of Shakespeare, and as insurance, I cram a bit when he makes his reservation."

"Just part of the service?" Taylor inquired, tilting his head to study her from a new angle.

"You could say that."

Prudently, B.J. scanned the room to see where the young Dobson twins were seated, then steered Taylor to a table as far distant as possible.

"B.J." Dot sidled to her side, eyes lighting on Taylor in pure feminine avarice. "Wilbur brought the eggs, and they're small again. Elsie's threatening to do permanent damage."

"All right, I'll take care of it." Ignoring Taylor's questioning stare, she turned to her waitress. "Dot, see to Mr. Reynold's lunch. Please excuse me, Mr. Reynolds, I'll have to tend to this. Just send for me if you have any questions or if something is not to your satisfaction. Enjoy your meal."

Seeing Wilbur's eggs as a lucky escape hatch, B.J. hurried to the kitchen.

"Wilbur," she said with wicked enjoyment as the door swung shut behind her. "This time, I'm umpire."

A myriad of small demands dominated B.J.'s afternoon. The art of diplomacy as well as the ability to delegate and make decisions was an intricate part of her job, and B.J. had honed her skills. She moved without breaking rhythm from a debate with the Dobson twins on the advisability of keeping a frog in their bathtub to a counseling service with one of the maids who was weeping into the fresh linen supply over the loss of a boyfriend. Through the hours of soothing and listening and laying down verdicts, she was still conscious of the presence of Taylor Reynolds. It was a simple matter to avoid him physically, but his presence seemed to fol-

low her everywhere. He had made himself known, and
she could not forget about him. Perversely, she found
herself fretting to know where he was and what he was
doing. Probably, she thought with a fresh flash of resentment, probably he's even now in my office poring
over my books with a microscope, deciding where to put
in his silly tennis courts or how to concrete the grove.

The dinner hour came and went. B.J. had decided to
forego supervising the dining room to have a few hours
of peace. When she came downstairs to the lounge the
lighting was muted, the hour late. The three-piece band
hired for the benefit of the Saturday crowd had already
packed their equipment. The music had been replaced
by the murmurs and clinking glasses of the handful of
people who remained. It was the quiet time of the evening, just before silence. B.J. allowed her thoughts to
drift back to Taylor.

I've got two weeks to make him see reason, she reminded herself, exchanging goodnights as stragglers
began to wander from the lounge. That should be plenty
of time to make even the most insensitive businessman
understand. I simply went about things in the wrong
way. Tomorrow, I'll start my campaign with a brand
new strategy. I'll keep my temper under control and
use a great many smiles. I'm good at smiling when I
put my mind to it.

Practicing her talent on the middle-aged occupant in
room 224, B.J.'s confidence grew at his rapidly blinking appreciation. Yes, she concluded, smiles are much
better than claws at this stage. A few smiles, a more
sophisticated appearance, and a brisk, businesslike approach, and I'll defeat the enemy before the war's de-

clared. Rejuvenated, she turned to the bartender who was lackadaisically wiping the counter. "Go on home, Don, I'll clear up the rest."

"Thanks, B.J." Needing no second urging, he dropped his rag and disappeared through the door.

"It's no trouble at all," she told the empty space with a magnanimous gesture of one hand. "I really insist."

Crossing the room, she began to gather half filled baskets of peanuts and empty glasses, switching on the small eye-level television for company. Around her, the inn settled for sleep, the groans and creaks so familiar, they went unnoticed. Now that the day was over, B.J. found the solitude for which she yearned.

Low, eerie music poured out of the television, drifting and floating through the darkened room. Glancing up, B.J. was soon mesmerized by a horror film. Kicking off her shoes, she slid onto a stool. The story was old and well-worn, but she was caught by a shot of clouds drifting over a full moon. She reached one hand absently for a basket of peanuts, settling them into her lap as the fog began to clear on the set to reveal the unknown terror, preceded by the rustle of leaves, and heavy breathing. With a small moan at the stalking monster's distorted face, B.J. covered her eyes and waited for doom to claim the heroine.

"You'd see more without your hand in front of your eyes."

As the voice came, disembodied in the darkness, B.J. shrieked, dislodging a shower of peanuts from her lap. "Don't ever do that again!" she commanded, glaring up at Taylor's grinning face.

"Sorry." The apology lacked conviction. Leaning on

the bar, he nodded toward the set. "Why do you have it on if you don't want to watch?"

"I can't help myself, it's an obsession. But I always watch with my eyes closed. Now look, watch this part, I've seen it before." She grabbed his sleeve with one hand and pointed with the other. "She's going to walk right outside like an idiot. I ask you, would anyone with a working brain cell walk out into the pitch darkness when they hear something scraping at the window? Of course not," she answered for him. "A smart person would be huddled under the bed waiting for it to go away. Oh." She pulled him closer, burying her face against his chest as the monster's face loomed in a close-up. "It's horrible, I can't watch. Tell me when it's over."

Slowly, it dawned on her that she was burrowing into his chest, his heartbeat steady against her ear. His fingers tangled in her hair, smoothing and soothing her as though comforting a child. She stiffened and started to pull back, but the hand in her hair kept her still.

"No, wait a minute, he's still stalking about and leering. There." He patted her shoulder and loosened his grip. "Saved by commercial television."

Set free, B.J. fumbled off the stool and began gathering scattered peanuts and composure. "I'm afraid things got rather out of hand this afternoon, Mr. Reynolds." Her voice was not quite steady, but she hoped he would attribute the waver to cowardice. "I must apologize for not completing your tour of the inn."

He watched as she scrambled over the floor on her hands and knees, a curtain of pale hair concealing her face. "That's all right. I wandered a bit on my own. I finally met Eddie when not in motion. He's a very intense young man."

She shifted away from him to search for more far reaching nuts. "He'll be good at hotel management in a couple years. He just needs a little more experience." Keeping her face averted, B.J. waited for the heat to cool from her cheeks.

"I met quite a few of the inn's guests today. Everyone seems very fond of B.J." He closed the distance between them and pushed back the hair which lay across her cheek. "Tell me, what does it stand for?"

"What?" Diverted by the fingers on her skin, she found it hard to concentrate on the conversation.

"B.J." He smiled into bemused eyes. "What does it stand for?"

"Oh." She returned the smile, stepping strategically out of reach. "I'm afraid that's a closely guarded secret. I've never even told my mother."

Behind her, the heroine gave a high-pitched, lilting scream. Scattering nuts again, B.J. threw herself into Taylor's arms.

"Oh, I'm sorry, that caught me off guard." Mortified, she lifted her face and attempted to pull away.

"No, this is the third time in one day you've been in this position." One hand lifted, and traveled down the length of her hair as he held her still. "This time, I'm going to see what you taste like."

Before she could protest, his mouth lowered to hers, at once firm and possessing. His arm around her waist brought her close to mold against him. His tongue found hers, and she was unaware whether he had parted her lips or if they had done so of their own volition. He lingered over her mouth, savoring its softness, deepening the kiss until she clung to him for balance. She told herself the sudden spiraling of her heartbeat was a reaction to the horror movie, the quick dizziness, the result of a missed dinner. Then she told herself nothing and only experienced.

"Very nice." Taylor's murmured approval trailed along her cheekbone, moving back to tease the corner of her mouth. "Why don't we try it again?"

In instinctive defense, she pressed her hand into his chest to ward him off. *Lightly* she told herself, praying for the earth to stop trembling, *treat it lightly.* "I'm afraid I don't come in thirty-two flavors, Mr. Reynolds, and..."

"Taylor," he interrupted, smiling down at the hand which represented no more of an obstacle than a blade of grass. "I decided this morning, when you stalked me in the office, that we're going to know each other very well."

"Mr. Reynolds..."

"Taylor," he repeated, his eyes close and compelling. "And my decisions are always final."

"Taylor," she agreed, not wanting to debate a minor point when the distance between them was lessening despite the pressure against his chest. "Do you engage in this sort of activity with all the managers of your hotels?" Hoping to wound him with a scathing remark, B.J. was immediately disappointed when he tossed back his head and laughed.

"B.J., this current activity has nothing whatever to do with your position at the inn. I am merely indulging my weakness for women who look good in pigtails."

"Don't you kiss me again!" she ordered, struggling with a sudden desperation which surprised him into loosening his hold.

"You'll have to choose between being demure or being provocative, B.J." His tone was mild, but she saw as she backed away, his eyes had darkened with temper. "Either way we play, I'm going to win, but it would make the game easier to follow."

"I don't play this sort of game," she retorted, "and I am neither demure nor provocative."

"You're a bit of both." His hands slipped into his pockets, and he rocked gently on his heels as he studied her furious face. "It's an intriguing combination." His brow lifted in speculation. An expression of amusement flitted over his features. "But I suppose you already know that or you wouldn't be so good at it."

Forgetting her fears, B.J. took a step toward him. "The only thing I know is that I have absolutely no desire to intrigue you in any way. All that I want you to do is to keep your resort builder's hands off this inn." Her hands balled into tight fists. "I wish you'd go back to New York and sit in your penthouse."

Before he could answer, B.J. turned and darted from the room. She hurried through the darkened lobby without even a backward glance.

Chapter 3

B.J. decided that making a fool of herself the previous evening had been entirely Taylor Reynolds's responsibility. Today, she resolved, slipping a gray blazer over a white silk shirt, I will be astringently businesslike. Nonetheless, she winced at the memory of her naive plea that he not kiss her again, the absurd way her voice had shaken with the words. *Why didn't I come up with some cool, sophisticated retort?* she asked herself. *Because I was too busy throwing peanuts around the room and making a fool of myself,* she answered the question to her frowning mirror image. *Why did a simple kiss cloak my brain with layers of cheesecloth?* The woman in the mirror stared back without answering.

He had caught her off guard, B.J. decided as she arranged her hair in a neat, businesslike roll at her neck's nape. It was so unexpected, she had overreacted. Despite herself, she relived the sensation of his mouth claiming hers, his breath warm on her cheek. The knee trembling, brain spinning feeling never before experienced, washed over her again, and briskly, she shook her head to dispel it. It was simply a matter of the unexpected creating a false intenseness, like pricking your thumb with a needle while sewing.

It was important, she knew, to refrain from thinking of Taylor Reynolds on a personal level, and to remember he held the fate of the Lakeside Inn in his hands.

Dirty pool, her mind muttered, recalling his easy threat to close the inn if she pressed her resignation. Emotional blackmail. He knew he held all the aces, and waited, with that damnably appealing smile, for her to fold or call. *Well*, she decided, and smoothed the charcoal material of her skirt, *I play a pretty mean game of poker myself, Taylor Reynolds*. After trying out several types of smiles in the mirror, polite, condescending, dispassionate, she left the room with brisk steps.

Sunday mornings were usually quiet. Most of the guests slept late, rising in dribbles to wander downstairs for breakfast. Traditionally, B.J. spent these quiet hours closeted in her office with whatever paperwork she felt merited attention. From experience, she had found this particular system worked well, being the least likely time for calamities, minor or major, to befall guests or staff.

She grabbed a quick coffee in the kitchen before plunging into the sea of invoices and account books.

"How providential." She jerked slightly as a hand captured her arm, and she found herself being led to the dining room. "Now, I won't have to have breakfast alone."

The dozens of flaming retorts which sprang to mind at Taylor's presumptuousness were dutifully banked down. B.J. answered with her seasoned polite smile. "How kind of you to ask. I hope you spent a pleasant night."

"As stated in your public relations campaign, the inn is conducive to restful nights."

Waving aside her hostess, B.J. moved through the empty tables to a corner booth. "I think you'll find all my publicity is based on fact, Mr. Reynolds." Sliding in, B.J. struggled to keep her voice light and marginally friendly. Remnants of their argument in her office and their more personal encounter in the lounge clung to her, and she attempted to erase both from her mind.

"So far I find no discrepancies."

Maggie hovered by the table, her smile dreamily absent. No doubt she was thinking of her date last night with Wally, B.J. thought. "Toast and coffee, Maggie," she said kindly, breaking the trance. The waitress scribbled on her pad, her cheeks flushed.

"You know," Taylor observed after giving his order, "you're very good at your job."

B.J. chided herself for her pleasure at the unexpected praise. "Why do you say that?"

"Not only are your books in perfect order, but you know your staff and handle them with unobtrusive deftness. You just managed to convey a five-minute lecture with one brief look."

"It makes it easier when you understand your staff and their habits." Her brows lifted in easy humor. "You see, I happen to know Maggie's mind is still focused on the double feature she and Wally didn't watch last night."

His grin flashed, boyish and quick.

"The staff is very much like a family." B.J. was careful to keep her tone casual, her hands busy pouring coffee. "The guests feel that. They enjoy the informality which is always accompanied by quality service. Our rules are flexible, and the staff is trained to adjust to the individual needs of the guests. The inn is a basic place, not for those who require formal entertainment or unlimited luxury. Fresh air, good food and a pleasant atmosphere are our enticements, and we deliver."

She paused as Maggie placed their breakfast order on the table.

"Do you have a moral objection to resorts, B.J.?"

The unexpectedness of Taylor's question put her off. Blinking in confusion at the long, lean fingers as they held a knife, spreading Betty Jackson jelly on toast, she stammered, "No…why of course not." Those fingers, she recalled irrelevantly, had tangled in her hair. "No," she repeated more firmly, meeting his eyes. "Resorts are fine if they are run correctly, as yours are. But their function is entirely different from ours. In a proper resort there's an activity for every minute of the day. Here, the atmosphere is more relaxed, a little fishing or boating, skiing, and above all the menu. The Lakeside Inn is perfect exactly as it is," she concluded more fiercely than she had intended and watched one brow rise, nearly meeting the curling thickness of his hair.

"That's yet to be determined." He lifted his cup to his lips.

His tone was mild, but B.J. recognized traces of anger in the disconcertingly direct eyes. She dropped her eyes to her own cup as if enticed by the rich, black liquid.

"'The gray-eyed morn smiles on the frowning night.'"

The quote brought her head up sharply, and looking into Mr. Leander's smiling, expectant face, B.J. searched her brain. "'Chequering the eastern clouds with streaks of light.'"

Thank goodness I've read *Romeo and Juliet* a dozen times, she thought, watching his pleased saunter as he moved to his table.

"One day, he's going to catch you, and you're going to draw a blank."

"Life's a series of risks," she returned flippantly. "Better to accept its challenges."

Reaching over, he tucked a stray lock behind her ear, and she jerked away from his touch, unexpectedly shy.

"For the most part," he drew the words out with infuriating emphasis, "I believe you do. It should make things very interesting. More coffee?" His question was pleasant and easy as if they had shared the morning meal on a regular basis. B.J. shook her head in refusal.... She felt uneasily inept at parrying words with this domineering, sophisticated man....

Sunlight poured through the many-paned windows, spilling in patchwork patterns on the floor, a lawn mower hummed along the outer edges of lawn, and somewhere close, a bird sang his enjoyment of a golden day. Closeted in the office with Taylor, B.J. tuned even these small pleasures out, keeping her mind firmly on the business at hand. Here, with the impersonal wedges of invoices and account books between them, she felt confident and assured. In discussing the inn's procedure, her feet were on solid ground. Honesty forced her to admit that Taylor Reynolds knew his profession down to the finest detail. He skimmed through her books with the sharp eye of an accountant, shifted and sorted invoices with the ease of a business manager.

At least, B.J. told herself, he doesn't treat me like an empty-headed imbecile who can't tally monthly accounts. Rather, she found him listening to her explanations with attentive respect. Soothed by his obvious appreciation of her intelligence B.J. decided if he did not yet look on the Lakeside Inn as she did, perhaps that too would come.

"I see you deal with a great many small businesses and local farms."

"That's right." She searched the bottom drawer of her desk for an ashtray as he lit a cigarette. "It's advantageous on all sides. We get more personal service and fresher produce, and it boosts local economy." Finding a small ceramic ashtray under a pile of personal correspondence, B.J. placed it on the desk. "The Lakeside Inn is essential to this district. We provide employment and a market for local products and services."

"Umm."

Finding his response less than illuminating, B.J. opened her mouth to continue when the door burst open.

"B.J." Eddie stood, bottom lip trembling. "It's the Bodwins."

"I'll be right there." Suppressing a sigh, she made a mental note to tell Eddie to knock during Taylor's stay.

"Is that a natural disaster or a plague?" Taylor asked, watching Eddie's speedy exit.

"It's nothing, really." She edged toward the door. "Excuse me, I'll just be a minute."

Shutting the door behind her, B.J. hurried to the lobby.

"Hello, Miss Patience, Miss Hope." She greeted the elderly Bodwin sisters with a wary smile.

Tall and lean as two aged willows, the Bodwins were long-standing guests.

"It's so nice to see you both again."

"It's always a pleasure to come back, Miss Clark," Miss Patience announced, and Miss Hope murmured in agreement. Habitually Miss Patience announced, and Miss Hope murmured. It was one of the few things which separated them. Over the years they had melded into mirror images from their identical wire rimmed spectacles to their identical orthopedic shoes.

"Eddie, see that the luggage is taken up, please." Miss Patience flashed a knowing smile which B.J. tried not to notice. B.J. saw her sharp-eyed glance drift over her head. Turning, she spotted Taylor.

"Miss Patience, Miss Hope, this is Taylor Reynolds, the owner of the inn." Miss Patience shot her a meaningful look.

"A pleasure, ladies." Gallantly, he took each thin-boned hand in his. A blush, dormant for twenty-five years, rose to Miss Hope's wrinkled cheek.

"You're a very fortunate young man." Miss Patience

gave Taylor a thorough survey, then nodded as if satisfied. "I'm sure you know what a treasure you have in Miss Clark. I hope you appreciate her."

B.J. resisted grinding her teeth for fear the sound would be audible. With a smile, Taylor laid a hand on her shoulder.

"I'm quite convinced Miss Clark is indispensable and my appreciation inadequate."

Satisfied, Miss Patience nodded.

B.J. shook the offending hand from her shoulder and assumed a coolly professional manner. "You have your regular table, number 2."

"Of course." Miss Patience moved her lips into a smile and patted B.J.'s cheek. "You're a good girl, Miss Clark." Smiling vaguely, the two ladies drifted away.

"Surely, B.J." Taylor turned to B.J. with an infuriating smile. "You're not going to give those two dotty old girls the second table?"

"The Lakeside Inn," she said coldly, turning to precede him to the office, "makes it a habit to please its guests. I see no reason why the Bodwins shouldn't sit wherever they want. Mr. Campbell always seated them at number 2."

"Mr. Campbell," Taylor countered with infuriating calm, "no longer owns the inn. I do."

"I'm well aware of that." Her chin tilted higher in defiance. "Do you want me to turn out the Bodwin sisters and place them at the table near the kitchen? Don't they look fancy enough for you? Why don't you think of them as people rather than little black numbers in the bloody account book?"

Her tirade was sharply cut off as he gripped her shoulders. She found she had swallowed the remaining words before she could prevent herself.

"You have," he began in an ominously low voice, "a very unfortunate temper and some very odd ideas. No one tells me how to run my business. Absolutely no one. Advice is accepted upon request, but I only make the decisions, and I alone give the orders."

He moved toward her. She could only stare, fascinated and faintly terrified.

"Do we understand each other?"

B.J. nodded, wide-eyed, then gathered courage to answer audibly. "Yes, perfectly. What would you like me to do about the Bodwins?"

"You've already done it. When you do something which displeases me, B.J., I'll let you know." The underlying threat brought storm warnings to her eyes. "Of course you know," Taylor continued, his tone softening, "you're a very ingenious lady. You've managed to share my breakfast table and work with me throughout the morning without once using my name. You've skirted around it, jumped over it and crawled under it, fascinating me with the acrobatics."

"That's ridiculous." She attempted to shrug, but his hands were firm on her shoulders. "Your imagination needs re-oiling."

"Then perhaps…" His arms moved to capture her waist. She arched away only to be brought steadily closer. "You'd say it now." His mouth hovered above hers. She felt the unfamiliar sweet flow of weakness, the trembling warmth just under her skin.

"Taylor." She failed to bring her voice above a whisper.

"Very good, you'll use it more often." His mouth curved, but she saw the smile only in his eyes. "Do I frighten you, B.J.?"

"No." Her denial was faint. "No," she repeated with more firmness.

"Liar." His laugh was both amused and pleased as his mouth teased hers. It rubbed lightly, holding back the promise until with a moan she drew him closer and took it.

Her breasts crushed against his chest, her lips instinctively found his. She felt herself tumbling in helpless cartwheels down an endless shaft where lights whirled in speeding colors. His hands moved from her waist to her hips, his strong fingers discovering the secrets of subtle curves as his mouth took everything she offered. Craving more, she strained against him until her sharpened senses began to dim, and the world spun hazily around her and vanished.

Fear rose like a phoenix from the flames of passion, and she struggled away, stunned and confused. "I…I need to check how lunch is going." She fumbled behind for the doorknob.

His hands in his pockets, Taylor rocked back on his heels and held her gaze with steady assurance. "Of course.… Now run away to your duties. But you understand, B.J., that I intend to have you sooner or later. I can be patient up to a point."

Her hand connected with the knob. She found her voice. "Of all the appalling nerve! I'm not a piece of property you can have your agent pick up for you."

"No, I'm handling this strictly on my own." He

smiled at her. "I know when something's going to be mine. Acquiring it is simply a matter of timing."

"I'm not an it." More outraged than she had thought possible, she took a step toward him. "I have no intention of being acquired and added to your trophies! And timing will get you nowhere!"

His smile was maddeningly confident. B.J. slammed the door full force behind her.

Chapter 4

Mondays always kept B.J. busy. She was convinced that if a major calamity were to fall, it would fall on a Monday simply because that would be the time she would be least able to cope with it. Taylor Reynolds's presence in her office was an additional Monday morning burden. His calm statement of the previous day was still fresh in her mind, and she was still seething with resentment. In an icy voice, she explained to him each phone call she made, each letter she wrote, each invoice she filed. He would not, she decided, accuse her of being uncooperative. Frigid perhaps, she thought with wicked pleasure, but not uncooperative.

Taylor's impeccable, businesslike attitude did nothing to endear him to her. She was well aware that her cold politeness bordered on the insulting.

Never had she met a man more in control or more annoying. Briefly, she considered pouring her coffee into his lap just to get a reaction. The thought was satisfying.

"Did I miss a joke?" Taylor asked as an involuntary smile flitted over B.J.'s face.

"What?" Realizing her lapse, B.J. struggled to compose her features. "No, I'm afraid my mind was wandering. You'll have to excuse me," she went on, "I have to make sure that all the rooms are made up by this time of day. Will you be wanting lunch in here or in the dining room?"

"I'll come to the dining room." Leaning back, Taylor studied her as he tapped his pencil against the corner of the desk. "Are you joining me?"

"Oh, I'm terribly sorry." B.J.'s tone was falsely saccharine. "I'm swamped today. I recommend the roast beef, though. I'm sure you'll find it satisfactory." Satisfied with her delivery, she closed the door quietly behind her.

With ingenuity and luck, B.J. managed to avoid Taylor throughout the afternoon. The inn was nearly empty as most of the guests were outdoors enjoying the mild spring weather. B.J. was able to slip down the quiet corridors without running into Taylor. She kept her antenna tuned for his presence, however. Though she knew it was childish, she found herself enjoying the one-way game of hide and seek. It became a self-imposed challenge that she keep out of his sight until nightfall.

In the pre-dinner lull, the inn was drowsy and silent. Humming to herself, B.J. carefully checked off linens in the third floor supply room. She was confident Taylor would not venture into that area of the inn, and relaxed her guard. Her mind traveled from her task, touching on pictures of boating on the lake, walks in the woods, and long summer evenings. Though her daydreams were pleasant, they were underlined by a nagging dissatisfaction. She tried to shrug it off but found it stubborn. There was something missing from the images, or rather someone. Whom would she be boating with on the lake? Whom would she be walking with in the woods? Who would be there to make the long summer evenings special? A distressing image began to form in B.J.'s brain, and she squeezed her eyes tight until it faded.

"I don't need him," she muttered, giving a pile of freshly laundered sheets a pat. "Absolutely not." B.J. backed from the tiny room and quietly pulled the door shut. When she backed into a solid object, she shrieked and fell forward against the closed door.

"Jumpy, aren't you?" Taylor took her shoulders and turned her to face him. His expression was amused. "Muttering to yourself, too. Maybe you need a vacation."

"I...I..."

"A long vacation," he concluded, giving her cheek a fatherly pat.

Finding her tongue, B.J. responded with reasonable calm. "You startled me, sneaking around that way."

"I thought it was a rule of the house," he countered as his grin broke out. "You've been doing it all afternoon."

Furious that her cunning had fallen short of the mark, she spoke with frosty dignity. "I have no idea what you're talking about. Now, if you'll excuse me..."

"Did you know you get a half-inch vertical line between your eyebrows when you're annoyed?"

"I'm very busy." She kept her voice cool as she did her best to keep the space between her brows smooth. *Blast the man!* she thought as his engaging smile began to have its effect on her. "Taylor, if there is something specific you want…" She stopped as she saw his grin widen until it nearly split his face. "If there's some business you want to discuss—" she amended.

"I took a message for you," he informed her, then lifted a finger to smooth away the crease between her brows. "A very intriguing message."

"Oh?" she said casually, wishing he would back up so that she did not feel so imprisoned between his body and the closed store-room door.

"Yes, I wrote it down so there'd be no mistake." He took a slip of paper from his pocket and read. "It's from a Miss Peabody. She wanted you to know that Cassandra had her babies. Four girls and two boys. Sextuplets." Taylor lowered the paper and shook his head. "Quite an amazing feat."

"Not if you're a cat." B.J. felt the color lacing her cheeks. *Why would he have to be the one to take the message? Why couldn't Cassandra have waited?* "Miss Peabody is one of our oldest guests. She stays here twice a year."

"I see," said Taylor, his mouth twitching. "Well, now that I've done my duty, it's your turn to do yours." Taking her hand, Taylor began to lead her down the corridor. "This country air gives me quite an appetite. You know the menu, what do you recommend we have?"

"I can't possibly," she began.

"Of course you can," he interrupted mildly. "Just think of me as a guest. Inn policy is to give the guests what pleases them. It pleases me to have dinner with you."

Cornered by her own words, B.J. offered no argument. Within minutes, she found herself seated across from the man she had so successfully avoided during the afternoon.

B.J. thought dinner a relatively painless affair. She felt too, as it neared an end, that she had done her duty and done it superbly. It was, however, difficult to resist the pull of Taylor's charm when he chose to put it into use. The charm itself was so natural and understated that she often found herself captivated before she realized what was happening. Whenever she felt her walls of indifference crumbling, she retreated a step and shored up the holes. *What a shame he isn't someone else,* she mused as he recounted an anecdote. *It would be so nice to enjoy a quiet dinner with him if there weren't any boundaries. But there are,* she reminded herself, quickly pulling out of the range of his charm. *Very definite, very important boundaries. This is war,* she reflected, thinking of their conversation of the previous day. *I can't afford to get caught behind enemy lines.* As Taylor raised his glass and smiled at her, B.J. wondered if Mata Hari had ever been faced with a tougher assignment.

They had reached the coffee stage when Eddie approached their table. "Mr. Reynolds?" B.J. looked on with approval as Eddie neither fidgeted nor seemed ready to burst with the tidings he bore. "There's a phone call for you from New York."

"Thank you, Eddie. I'll take it in the office. I shouldn't be long," Taylor told her as he rose.

"Please, don't rush on my account." B.J. gave him a careful smile, resigning herself to the fact she was a coward. "I still have several things to see to this evening."

"I'll see you later," Taylor returned in a tone that brooked no argument. Their eyes met in a quick clash of wills. In a swift change of mood, Taylor laughed and bent down to kiss B.J. on the forehead before he strolled away.

Mouth agape, B.J. rubbed the spot with her fingertips, wondering why she suddenly felt lightheaded. Forcing herself back to earth, she drank her coffee and hurried off to the lounge.

Monday nights at the inn were an old tradition. The lounge was the center of activity for the weekly event. As B.J. paused in the doorway, she ran a critical eye over the room. The candles had been lit inside each of the coach lanterns which sat on the huddled tables. The lights flickered against the wood. Scents of polish, old wood and smoke melded. The dance floor was gently lit with amber spotlights. Satisfied that the mood was set, B.J. crossed the room and halted next to an ancient Victrola. The faithful mechanism was housed in a rich mahogany cabinet. With affection, B.J. trailed a finger over the smooth lid before opening it.

People began to wander in as she sorted through the collection of old 78s. The hum of conversation behind her was so familiar, it barely tickled her consciousness. Glasses chinked, ice rattled, and an occasional laugh echoed along the walls. With the absentminded skill of an expert, B.J. wound the Victrola into life and set a thick, black record on the turntable. The music which drifted out was scratchy, tinny and charming. Before the record was half over, three couples were on the dance floor. Another Monday night was launched.

During the next half hour, B.J. played an unbroken stream of nineteen-thirty tunes. Over the years, she had noted that no matter what the mean age of the audience, the response to a trip through the past was positive. *Perhaps,* she mused, *it's because the simplicity of the music suits the simplicity of the inn.* With a shrug, she abandoned her analysis and grinned at a couple fox-trotting over the dance floor to the strains of "Tea For Two."

"What the devil is going on in here?"

B.J. heard the demanding question close to her ear and whirled to find herself face to face with Taylor. "Oh, I see you're finished with your call. I hope there isn't any trouble?"

"Nothing important." He waited until she had switched records before he asked again, "B.J., I asked you what's going on in here?"

"Why, just what it looks like," she answered vaguely, hearing from the tone of the record that it was time to replace the needle. "Sit down, Taylor, I'll have Don mix you a drink. You know I'd swear there hasn't been time for this needle to wear out." Delving into her spares, B.J. began the task of changing needles.

"When you're finished, perhaps you'd take a look at my carburetor."

Engrossed in the intricacies of her job, B.J. remained untouched by Taylor's mockery. "We'll see," she murmured, then carefully placed the new needle on the record. "What would you like, Taylor?" As she straightened, she glanced toward the bar.

"Initially, an explanation."

"An explanation?" she repeated, finally giving him her full attention. "An explanation about what?"

"B.J." Impatience was beginning to thread through his tone. "Are you being deliberately dense?"

Liking neither his tone nor his question, B.J. stiffened. "Perhaps if you would be a bit more specific, I would be a bit less dense."

"I was under the impression that this lounge possessed a functional P.A. system."

"Well, of course it does." As she became more confused, B.J. pushed away the thought that perhaps she actually was dense. "What does that have to do with anything?"

"Why isn't it being used?" He glanced down at the Victrola. "And why are you using this archaic piece of equipment?"

"The P.A. system isn't being used," she explained in calm, reasonable tones, "because it's Monday."

"I see." Taylor glanced toward the dance floor where one couple was instructing another on the proper moves of a two step. "That, of course, explains everything."

His sarcasm caused indignation to flood through her. Clamping her teeth on a stream of unwise remarks, B.J. began to sift rapidly through records. "On Monday nights, we use the Victrola and play old records. And it is not an archaic piece of equipment," she added, unable to prevent herself. "It's an antique, a museum quality antique."

"B.J." Taylor spoke to the top of her head as she bent to change records. "Why?"

"Why what?" she snapped, furious with his ambiguity.

"Why do you use the Victrola and play old records on Monday nights?" He spoke very clearly, spacing his words as if speaking to someone whose brain was not fully operative.

"Because," B.J. began, her eyes flowing, her fists clenching.

Taylor held up a hand to halt the ensuing explanation. "Wait." After the one word command, he crossed the room and spoke to one of the guests. Seething, B.J. watched him use his most charming smile. It faded as he moved back to join her. "You're being relieved of Victrola duty for a bit. Outside." With this, he took her arm and pulled her to the side door. The cool night air did nothing to lower B.J.'s temperature. "Now." Taylor closed the door behind him and leaned back against the side of the building. He made a small gesture with his hand. "Go right ahead."

"Oh, you make me so mad I could scream!" With this dire threat, B.J. began pacing up and down the porch. "Why do you have to be so...so..."

"Officious?" Taylor offered.

"Yes!" B.J. agreed, wishing passionately that she had thought of the word herself. "Everything's moving along just fine, and then you have to come in and look down your superior nose." For some moments, she paced in silence. The romance of the moonlight filtering through the trees seemed sadly out of place. "People are enjoying themselves in there." She swung her hand toward the open window. A Cole Porter number drifted back to her. "You don't have any right to criticize it. Just because we're not using a live band, or playing top forty numbers, doesn't mean we're not entertaining the guests. I really don't see why you have to..." She broke off abruptly as he grabbed her arm.

"O.K., time's up." As he spun her around, the hair fell over B.J.'s face, and she brushed it back impatiently. "Now, suppose we start this from the beginning."

"You know," she said between her teeth, "I really hate it when you're calm and patient."

"Stick around," he invited. It began to sink into her brain that his voice was dangerously low. "You might see the other end of the scale." Glaring at him did not seem to improve her situation, but B.J. continued to do so. "If you'll think back to the beginning of this remarkable conversation, you'll recall that I asked you a very simple question. And, I believe, a very reasonable one."

"And I told you," she tossed out, then faltered. "At least, I think I did." Frustrated, she threw both hands up in the air. "How am I supposed to remember what you said and what I said? It took you ten minutes to come to the point in the first place." She let out a deep breath as she realized she did not yet have control of her temper. "All right, what was your very simple, very reasonable question?"

"B.J., you would try the patience of a saint." She heard the amused exasperation in his voice and tried not to be charmed. "I would like to know why I stepped into nineteen-thirty-five when I came into the lounge."

"Every Monday night," she began in crisp, practical tones, "the inn offers this sort of entertainment. The

Victrola was brought here more than fifty years ago, and it's been used every Monday night since. Guests who've been here before expect it. Of course," she went on, too involved in her story to realize she was being drawn closer into Taylor's arms, "the P.A. system was installed years ago. The other six nights of the week, we switch off between it and a live band, depending on the season. The Monday night gathering is almost as old as the inn itself and an important part of our tradition."

The low, bluesy tones of "Embraceable You" were floating through the open window. B.J. was swaying to its rhythm, as yet unaware that Taylor was leading her in a slow dance. "The guests look forward to it. I've found since I've worked here, that's true no matter how old or how young the clientele is." Her voice had lost its crispness. She found her trend of thought slipping away from her as their bodies swayed to the soft music.

"That was a very reasonable answer." Taylor drew her closer, and she tilted back her head, unwilling to break eye contact. "I'm beginning to see the advantages of the idea myself." Their faces were close, so close she could feel the touch of his breath on her lips. "Cold?" he asked, feeling her tremble. Though she shook her head, he gathered her closer until the warmth of his body crept into hers. Their cheeks brushed as they merged into one gently swaying form.

"I should go back in," she murmured, making no effort to move away. She closed her eyes and let his arms and the music guide her.

"Um-hum." His mouth was against her ear.

Small night sounds added to the lull of the music from the lounge; a whisper of leaves, the quiet call of a

bird, the flutter of moth wings against window glass.
The air was soft and cool on B.J.'s shoulders. It was
touched with the light scent of hyacinth. Moonlight
sprinkled through the maples, causing the shadows to
tremble. She could feel Taylor's heartbeat, a sure, steady
rhythm against her own breast. He trailed his mouth
along her temple, brushing it through her hair as his
hands roamed along her back.

B.J. felt her will dissolving as her senses grew more
and more acute. She could hear the sound of his breathing over the music, feel the texture of his skin beneath
his shirt, taste the male essence of him on her tongue.
Her surroundings were fading like an old photograph
with only Taylor remaining sharp and clear. Untapped
desire swelled inside her. Suddenly, she felt herself
being swallowed by emotions she was not prepared
for, by needs she could not understand.

"No, please." Her bid for freedom was so swift and
unexpected that she broke from Taylor's arms without
a struggle. "I don't want this." She clung to the porch
rail and faced him.

Closing the distance between them in one easy motion, Taylor circled the back of her neck with his hand.
"Yes, you do." His mouth lowered, claiming hers. B.J.
felt the porch tilt under her feet.

Longing, painfully sweet, spread through her until
she felt she would suffocate. His hands were bringing
her closer and closer. With some unexplained instinct,
she knew if she were wrapped in his arms again, she
would never find the strength to resist him.

"No!" Lifting both hands, she pushed against his
chest and freed herself. "I don't!" she cried in passion-

ate denial. Turning, she streaked down the porch steps. "Don't tell me what I want," she flung back at him before she raced around the side of the building.

She paused before she entered the inn to catch her breath and to allow her pounding heart to slow down. Certainly not the usual Monday evening at Lakeside Inn, she thought, smiling wryly to herself. Unconsciously, she hummed a few bars of "Embraceable You," but caught herself with a self-reprimanding frown before she entered the kitchen to remind Dot about the bud vases on the breakfast tables.

Chapter 5

There are days when nothing goes right. The morning, blue and clear and breezy, looked deceptively promising. Clad in a simple green shirtdress and low heels, B.J. marched down the stairs running the word *businesslike* over and over in her mind. Today, she determined, she would be the manager of the inn conducting business with the owner of the inn. There was no moonlight, no music, and she would not forget her responsibilities again. She strolled into the dining room, prepared to greet Taylor casually, then use the need to oversee breakfast preparations as an excuse not to share the morning meal with him. Taylor, however, was already well into a fluffy mound of scrambled eggs and deep into a conversation with Mr. Leander. Taylor gave B.J. an absent wave as she entered, then returned his full attention to his breakfast companion.

Perversely, B.J. was annoyed that her well-planned excuse was unnecessary. She scowled at the back of Taylor's head before she flounced into the kitchen. Ten minutes later, she was told in no uncertain terms that she was in the way. Banished to her office, she sulked in private.

For the next thirty minutes, B.J. occupied herself with busy work, all the while keeping her ears pricked for Taylor's approach. As the minutes passed, she felt a throbbing tension build at the base of her neck. The stronger the ache became, the deeper became her resentment toward Taylor. She set the reason for her headache and her glum mood at his doorstep, though she could not have answered what he had done to cause either. *He was here,* she decided, then broke the point of her pencil. *That was enough.*

"B.J.!" Eddie swirled into the office as she stood grinding her teeth and sharpening her pencil. "There's trouble."

"You bet there is," she muttered.

"It's the dishwasher." Eddie lowered his eyes as if announcing a death in the family. "It broke down in the middle of breakfast."

B.J. let out her breath in a quick sound of annoyance. "All right, I'll call Max. With any luck it'll be going full swing before lunch."

Luck, B.J. was to find, was a mirage.

An hour later, she stood by as Max the repairman did an exploratory on the dishwasher. She found his continual mutters, tongue cluckings and sighs wearing on her nerves. Time was fleeting, and it seemed to her that Max was working at an impossibly slow pace.

Impatient, she leaned over his shoulder and stared at tubes and wires. Bracing one hand on Max's back, she leaned in further and pointed.

"Couldn't you just…"

"B.J." Max sighed and removed another screw. "Go play with the inn and let me do my job."

Straightening, B.J. stuck out her tongue at the back of his head, then flushed scarlet as she spotted Taylor standing inside the doorway.

"Have a problem?" he asked. Though his voice and mouth were sober, his eyes laughed at her. She found his silent mockery infuriating.

"I can handle it," she snapped, wishing her cheeks were cool and her position dignified. "I'm sure you must be very busy." She cursed herself for hinting at his morning involvement. This time he did smile, and she cursed him as well.

"I'm never too busy for you, B.J." Taylor crossed the room, then took her hand and raised it to his lips before she realized his intent. Max cleared his throat.

"Cut that out." She tore her hand away and whipped it behind her back. "There's no need to concern yourself with this," she continued, struggling to assume the businesslike attitude she had vowed to take. "Max is fixing the dishwasher before the lunch rush."

"No, I'm not." Max sat back on his heels and shook his head. In his hand was a small-toothed wheel.

"What do you mean, no you're not?" B.J. demanded, forgetting Taylor in her amazement. "You've got to. I need…"

"What you need is one of these," Max interrupted, holding up the wheel.

"Well, all right." B.J. plucked the part from his hand and scowled at it. "Put one in. I don't see how a silly little thing like this could cause all this trouble."

"When the silly little thing has a broken tooth, it can cause a lot of trouble," Max explained patiently, and glanced at Taylor for masculine understanding. "B.J., I don't carry things like this in stock. You'll have to get it from Burlington."

"Burlington?" Realizing the situation was desperate B.J. used her most pleading look. "Oh, but, Max."

Though well past his fiftieth birthday, Max was not immune to huge gray eyes. He shifted from one foot to the other, sighed and took the part from B.J.'s palm. "All right, all right, I'll drive into Burlington myself. I'll have the machine fixed before dinner, but lunch is out. I'm not a magician."

"Thank you, Max." Rising on her toes, B.J. pecked his cheek. "What would I do without you?" Mumbling, he packed up his tools and started out of the room. "Bring your wife in for dinner tonight, on the house." Pleased with her success, B.J. smiled as the door swung shut. When she remembered Taylor, she cleared her throat and turned to him.

"You should have those eyes registered with the police department," he advised, tilting his head and studying her. "They're a lethal weapon."

"I don't know what you're talking about." She sniffed with pretended indifference while she wished she could have negotiated with Max in private.

"Of course you do." With a laugh, Taylor cupped her chin in his hand. "That look you aimed at him was beautifully timed."

"I'm sure you're mistaken," she replied, wishing his mere touch would not start her heart pounding. "I simply arranged things in the best interest of the inn. That's my job."

"So it is," he agreed, and leaned on the injured dishwasher. "Do you have any suggestions as to what's to be done until this is fixed?"

"Yes." She glanced at the double stainless steel sink. "Roll up your sleeves."

It did not occur to B.J. to be surprised that she and Taylor washed the dozens of breakfast dishes side by side until it was *fait accompli.* The interlude had been odd, B.J. felt, because of the unusual harmony which existed between them. They had enjoyed a companionable banter, an easy partnership without the tension which habitually entered their encounters. When Elsie returned to begin lunch preparations, they scarcely noticed her.

"Not one casualty," Taylor proclaimed as B.J. set the last plate on its shelf.

"That's only because I saved two of yours from crashing on the floor."

"Slander," Taylor stated and swung an arm over her shoulder as he led her from the room. "You'd better be nice to me. What'll you do if Max doesn't fix the dishwasher before dinner? Think of all those lunch dishes."

"I'd rather not. However, I've already given that possibility some consideration." B.J. found the handiest chair in her office and dropped into it. "I know a couple of kids in town that we could recruit in a pinch. But Max won't let me down."

"You have a lot of faith." Taylor sat behind the desk, then lifted his feet to rest on top of it.

"You don't know Max," B.J. countered. "If he said he'd have it fixed before dinner, he will. Otherwise, he'd have said I'll try, or maybe I can, or something of that sort. When Max says I will, he does. That," she added, seeing the opportunity to score a point, "is an advantage of knowing everyone you deal with personally."

Taylor inclined his head in acknowledgement as the phone rang on the desk. Signaling for Taylor not to bother, B.J. rose and answered it.

"Lakeside Inn. Oh, hello, Marilyn. No, I've been tied up this morning." She eased a hip down on the edge of the desk and shuffled through her papers. "Yes, I have your message here. I'm sorry, I just got back into the office. No, you let me know when you have all your acceptances back, then we'll have a better idea of how to plan the food and so on. There's plenty of time. You've got well over a month before the wedding. Trust me; I've handled receptions before. Yes, I know you're nervous. It's all right, prospective brides are meant to be nervous. Call me when you have a definite number. You're welcome, Marilyn. Yes, yes, you're welcome. 'Bye."

B.J. hung up the phone and stretched her back before she realized Taylor was waiting for an explanation. "That was Marilyn," B.J. informed him. "She was grateful."

"Yes, I rather got that impression."

"She's getting married next month." B.J. lifted a hand to rub at the stiffness in the back of her neck. "If she makes it without a nervous breakdown, it'll be a minor miracle. People should elope and not put themselves through all this."

"I'm sure there are countless fathers-of-the-bride who would agree with you after paying the expenses of the wedding." He rose, moving around the desk until he stood in front of her. "Here, let me." Lifting his hands, he massaged her neck and shoulders. B.J.'s protest became a sigh of pleasure. The word *businesslike* floated quietly out of her mind. "Better?" Taylor asked, smiling at her closed eyes.

"Mmm. It might be in an hour or two." She stretched under his hands like a contented kitten. "Ever since Marilyn set the date, she's been on the phone three times a week to check on the reception. It's hard to believe someone could get that excited about getting married."

"Well, not everyone is as cool and collected as you," Taylor remarked as he ran his thumbs along her jawline, stroking his other fingers along the base of her neck. "And, by the way, I wouldn't spread that eloping idea of yours around if I were you. I imagine the inn makes a good profit doing wedding receptions."

"Profit?" B.J. opened her eyes and tried to concentrate on what they had been saying. It was difficult to think with his hands so warm and strong on her skin. "Profit?" she said again and swallowed as her brain cleared. "Oh well…yes." She scooted off the desk and out of his reach. "Yes, usually…that is…sometimes." She wandered the room wishing the interlude in the kitchen had not made her forget who he was. "It depends, you see, on… Oh boy." She ended on a note of disgust and blew out a long breath.

"Perhaps you'd translate all that into English?" Taylor

suggested. With a twinge of uneasiness, B.J. watched him seat himself once more behind the desk. *Owner to manager* again, she thought bitterly.

"Well, you see," she began, striving for nonchalance. "There are occasions when we do wedding receptions or certain parties without charge. That is," she rushed on as his face remained inscrutable, "we charge for the food and supplies, but not for the use of the lounge..."

"Why?" The one word interruption was followed by several seconds of complete silence.

"Why?" B.J. repeated and glanced briefly at the ceiling for assistance. "It depends, of course, and it is the exception rather than the rule." *Why?* she demanded of herself. *Why don't I learn to keep my mouth shut?* "In this case, Marilyn is Dot's cousin. You met Dot, she's one of our waitresses," she continued as Taylor remained unhelpfully silent. "She also works here during the summer season. We decided, as we do on certain occasions, to give Marilyn the reception as a wedding present."

"We?"

"The staff," B.J. explained. "Marilyn is responsible for the food, entertainment, flowers, but we contribute the lounge and our time, and," she added, dropping her voice to a mumble, "the wedding cake."

"I see." Taylor leaned back in the chair and laced his fingers together. "So, the staff donates their time and talent and the inn."

"Just the lounge." B.J. met his accusatory glance with a glare. "It's something we do only a couple of times a year. And if I must justify it from a business standpoint, it's good public relations. Maybe it's even tax deductible. Ask your C.P.A." She began to storm around the office as her temper rose, but Taylor sat calmly. "I don't see why you have to be so picky. The staff works on their own time. We've been doing it for years. It's…"

"Inn policy," Taylor finished for her. "Perhaps I should have you list all the eccentricities of inn policy for me. But I should remind you, B.J., that the inn's policy is not carved in stone."

"You're not going to drop the axe on Marilyn's reception," B.J. stated, prepared for a fight to the finish.

"I've misplaced my black hood, B.J., so I can't play executioner. However," he continued before the look of satisfaction could be fully formed on her face, "you and I will have to have a more detailed discussion on the inn's public relations."

"Yes, sir," she replied in her most wintry voice, and was saved from further argument by the ringing of the phone.

Taylor motioned for her to answer it. "I'll get us some coffee."

B.J. watched him stroll from the room as she lifted the phone to her ear.

When Taylor returned a few moments later, she was seated behind the desk just replacing the receiver. With a sound of annoyance, she supported her chin on her elbows.

"The florist doesn't have my six dozen daffodils."

"I'm sorry to hear that." Taylor placed her coffee on the desk.

"Well, you should be. It's your inn, and they are actually your daffodils."

"It's kind of you to think of me, B.J.," Taylor said

amiably. "But don't you think six dozen is a bit extreme?"

"Very funny," she muttered and picked up her coffee cup. "You won't think it's such a joke when there aren't any flowers on the tables."

"So, order something besides daffodils."

"Do I look like a simpleton?" B.J. demanded. "He won't have anything in that quantity until next week. Some trouble at the greenhouse or something. Blast it!" She swallowed her coffee and scowled at the far wall.

"For heaven's sake, B.J., there must be a dozen florists in Burlington. Have them delivered." Taylor dismissed the matter of daffodils with an airy wave.

B.J. gave him an opened mouth look of astonishment. "Delivered from Burlington? Do you have any idea how much those daffodils would cost?" Rising, she paced the room while she considered her options. "I simply can't tolerate artificial flowers," she muttered while Taylor sipped his coffee and watched her. "They're worse than no flowers at all. I hate to do it," she said with a sigh. "It's bad enough having to beg for her jelly, now I'm going to have to beg for her flowers. There's absolutely nothing else I can do. She's got the only garden in town that can handle it." Making a complete circle of the room, B.J. plopped down behind the desk again.

"Are you finished?"

"No," B.J. answered, picking up the phone. "I still have to talk her out of them." Grimly, she set her teeth. "Wish me luck."

Deciding all would be explained in due time, Taylor sat back to watch. "Luck," he said agreeably and finished off his coffee.

When B.J. had completed her conversation, he shook his head in frank admiration. "That," he said as he toasted her with his empty cup, "was the most blatant con job I've ever witnessed."

"Subtlety doesn't work with Betty Jackson." Smug, B.J. answered his toast, then rose. "I'm going to go pick up those flowers before she changes her mind."

"I'll drive you," Taylor offered, taking her arm before she reached the door.

"Oh, you needn't bother." The contact reminded her how slight was her will when he touched her.

"It's no bother," he countered, leading her through the inn's front door. "I feel I must see the woman who, how did you put it? 'Raises flowers with an angel's touch.'"

"Did I say that?" B.J. struggled to prevent a smile.

"That was one of your milder compliments."

"Desperate circumstances call for desperate measures," B.J. claimed and slid into Taylor's Mercedes. "Besides, Miss Jackson does have an extraordinary garden. Her rosebush won a prize last year. Turn left here," she instructed as he came to a fork in the road. "You know, you should be grateful to me instead of making fun. If you'd had your way, we'd be eating up a healthy percentage of the inn's profits in delivery fees."

"My dear Miss Clark," Taylor drawled, "if there's one thing I can't deny, it's that you are a top flight manager. Of course, I'm also aware that a raise is in order."

"When I want a raise, I'll ask for one," B.J. snapped. As she gave her attention to the view out the side window, she missed Taylor's glance of speculation. She had not liked his use of her surname, nor had she liked being reminded again so soon of the status of their positions. He was her employer, and there was no escaping it. Closing her eyes, she chewed on her lower lip. The day had not run smoothly, perhaps that was why she had been so acutely annoyed over such a small thing. *And so rude,* she added to herself. Decidedly, it was her responsibility to offer the olive branch. Turning, she gave Taylor a radiant smile.

"What sort of raise?"

He laughed, and reached over to ruffle her hair. "What an odd one you are, B.J."

"Oh, I know," she agreed, wishing she could understand her own feelings. "I know. There's the house." She gestured as they approached. "Third from the corner."

They alighted from opposite sides of the car, but Taylor took her arm as they swung through Betty Jackson's gate. This visit, B.J. decided, thinking of the silver blue Mercedes and Taylor's elegantly simple silk shirt, should keep Miss Jackson in news for six months. The doorbell was answered before it had stopped ringing.

"Hello, Miss Jackson," B.J. began and prepared to launch into her first thank you speech. She closed her mouth as she noticed Betty's attention was focused well over her head. "Oh, Miss Jackson, this is Taylor Reynolds, the owner of the inn. Taylor, Betty Jackson." B.J. made introductions as Betty simultaneously pulled her apron from her waist and metal clips from her hair.

"Miss Jackson." Taylor took her free hand as Betty held the apron and clips behind her back. "I've heard so much about your talents, I feel we're old friends." Blushing like a teenager, Betty was, for the first time in her sixty odd years, at a loss for words.

"We came by for the flowers," B.J. reminded her, fascinated by Betty's reaction.

"Flowers? Oh, yes, of course. Do come in." She ushered them into the house and into her living room, all the while keeping her hand behind her back.

"Charming," Taylor stated, gazing around at chintz and doilies. Turning, he gave Betty his easy smile. "I must tell you, Miss Jackson, we're very grateful to you for helping us out this way."

"It's nothing, nothing at all," Betty said, fluttering her hand with the words. "Please sit down. I'll fix us a nice pot of tea. Come along, B.J." She scurried from the room, leaving B.J. no choice but to follow. Safely enclosed in the kitchen, Betty began to move at lightning speed. "Why didn't you tell me you were bringing *him?*" she demanded, flourishing a teapot.

"Well, I didn't know until…"

"Goodness, you could have given a person a chance to comb her hair and put her face on." Betty dug out her best china cups and inspected them for chips.

B.J. bit the inside of her lip to keep a grin from forming. "I'm sorry, Betty. I had no idea Mr. Reynolds was coming until I was leaving."

"Never mind, never mind." Betty brushed aside the apology with the back of her hand. "You did bring him after all. I'm positively dying to talk to him. Why don't you run out and get your flowers now before tea?" She produced a pair of scissors. "Just pick whatever you need." She dismissed B.J. with a hasty wave. "Take your time."

After the back door had closed firmly in her face, B.J. stood for a moment, torn between amusement and exasperation before heading towards Betty's early spring blooms.

When she re-entered the kitchen about twenty minutes later, armed with a selection of daffodils and early tulips, she could hear Betty laughing. Carefully placing her bouquet on the kitchen table, she walked into the living room.

Like old friends, Taylor and Betty sat on the sofa, a rose patterned teapot nestled cozily on the low table. "Oh, Taylor," Betty said, still laughing, "you tell such stories! What's a poor woman to believe?"

B.J. looked on in stunned silence. She was certain Betty Jackson had not flirted this outrageously in thirty years. And, she noted with a shake of her head, Taylor was flirting with equal aplomb. As Betty leaned forward to pour more tea, Taylor glanced over her head and shot B.J. a grin so endearingly boyish it took all her willpower not to cross the room and throw herself into his arms. He was, she thought with a curious catch in her heart, impossible. No female under a hundred and two was safe around him. Unable to do otherwise, B.J. answered his grin.

"Miss Jackson," B.J. said, carefully readjusting her features. "Your garden is lovely as always."

"Thanks, B.J. I really do work hard on it. Did you get all that you wanted?"

"Yes, thank you. I don't know how I would have managed without you."

"Well." Betty sighed as she rose. "I'll just get a box for them."

Some fifteen minutes later, after Betty had exacted a promise from Taylor that he drop by again, B.J. was in the Mercedes beside him. In the back seat were the assortment of flowers and half a dozen jars of jelly as a gift to Taylor.

"You," B.J. began in the sternest voice she could manage, "should be ashamed."

"I?" Taylor countered, giving her an innocent look. "Whatever for?"

"You know very well what for," B.J. said severely. "You very near had Betty swooning."

"I can't help it if I'm charming and irresistible."

"Oh, yes, you can," she disagreed. "You were deliberately charming and irresistible. If you'd said the word, she'd have ripped up her prize rosebush and planted it at the inn's front door."

"Nonsense," Taylor claimed. "We were simply having an enjoyable conversation."

"Did you enjoy the camomile tea?" B.J. asked sweetly.

"Very refreshing. You didn't get a cup, did you?"

"No." B.J. sniffed and folded her arms across her chest. "I wasn't invited."

"Ah, now I see." Taylor sighed as he pulled in front of the inn. "You're jealous."

"Jealous?" B.J. gave a quick laugh and brushed the dust from her skirt. "Ridiculous."

"Yes, I see it now," he said smugly, repressing a grin. "Silly girl!" With this, he stopped the car, and turning to B.J. lowered his smiling mouth to hers. Imperceptibly, his lips lost their teasing quality, becoming warm and soft on her skin. B.J.'s playful struggles ceased, and she stiffened in his arms.

"Taylor, let me go." She found it was more difficult

now to catch her breath than it had been when she had been laughing. A small moan escaped her as his lips trailed to her jawline. "No," she managed, and putting her fingers to his lips, pushed him away. He studied her, his eyes dark and full of knowledge as she fought to control her breathing. "Taylor, I think it's time we established some rules."

"I don't believe in rules between men and women, and I don't follow any." He said this with such blatant arrogance, B.J. was shocked into silence. "I'll let you go now, because I don't think it's wise to make love with you in broad daylight in the front seat of my car. However, the time will come when the circumstances will be more agreeable."

B.J. narrowed her eyes and found her voice. "You seriously don't think I'll agree to that, do you?"

"When the time comes, B.J.," he said with maddening confidence, "you'll be happy to agree."

"Fat chance," she said as she struggled out of the car. "We're never going to agree about anything." Slamming the door gave her some satisfaction.

As she ran up the front steps and into the inn, B.J. decided she never wanted to hear the word *business-like* again.

Chapter 6

B.J. was standing on the wide lawn enjoying the warmth of the spring sun. She had decided to avoid Taylor Reynolds as much as possible and concentrate on her own myriad responsibilities. Unfortunately, that had not been as easy as she had hoped: she had been forced to deal with him on a daily business basis.

Though the inn was relatively quiet, B.J. knew that in a month's time, when the summer season began, the pace would pick up. Her gaze traveled the length and height of the inn, admiring the mellowed bricks serene against the dark pines, the windows blinking in the bright spring sun. On the back porch, two guests were engaged in an undemanding game of checkers. From where she was standing, B.J. could barely hear the murmur of their conversation without hearing the words.

All too soon, this peace would be shattered by children shouting to each other as they raced across the lawn, by the purr of motorboats as they sped past the inn. Yet, somehow, the inn never lost its informal air of tranquility. Here, she mused, the shade was for relaxing, the grass invited bare feet, the drifting snow for sleigh rides and snow men. Elegance had its place, B.J. acknowledged, but the Lakeside Inn had a charm of its own. *And Taylor Reynolds was not going to destroy it.*

You've only got ten days left. He leaves in ten days, she reminded herself. She sighed.

The sigh was as much for herself as for the inn's fate. *I wish he'd never come. I wish I'd never laid eyes on him.* Scowling, she headed back towards the inn.

"That face is liable to turn guests away." Startled, B.J. stared at Taylor as he blocked the doorway. "I think it's best for business if I get you away from here for a while." Stepping forward, he took her hand and pulled her across the lawn.

"I have to go in," she protested. "I…I have to phone the linen supplier."

"It'll keep. Your duties as guide come first."

"Guide? Would you please let me go? Where are we going?"

"Yes. No. And we're going to enjoy one of Elsie's famous picnics." Taylor held up the hamper he held in his free hand. "I want to see the lake."

"You don't need me for that. You can't miss it. It's the huge body of water you come to at the end of the path."

"B.J." He stopped, turning directly to face her. "For two days you've avoided me. Now, I'm well aware we have differences in our outlook on the inn."

"I hardly see…"

"Be quiet," he said pleasantly. "I am willing to give you my word that no major alterations will be started without your being notified. Whatever changes I decide upon will be brought to your attention before any formal plans are drawn up." His tone was brisk and businesslike even while he ignored her attempts to free her hand. "I respect your dedication and loyalty to the inn." His tone was coolly professional.

"But…"

"However," he cut her off easily, "I do own the inn, and you are in my employ. As of now you have a couple hours off. How do you feel about picnics?"

"Well, I…"

"Good. I'm fond of them myself." Smiling easily, he began to move down the well worn path through the woods.

The undergrowth was still soft from winter. Beneath the filtered sunlight wild flowers were a multicolored carpet, bright against their brown background of decaying leaves. Squirrels darted up the trunks of trees where birds had already begun to nest.

"Do you always shanghai your companions?" B.J. demanded, angry and breathless at keeping pace with Taylor's long strides.

"Only when necessary," he replied curtly.

The path widened, then spread into the grassy banks of the lake. Taylor stopped, surveying the wide expanse of lake with the same absorption that B.J. had observed in him earlier.

The lake was unruffled, reflecting a few clouds above it. The mountains on its opposite edge were gently formed. They were not like the awesome, demanding peaks of the West, but sedate and well behaved. The silence was broken once by the quick call of a chickadee, then lay again like a calming hand on the air.

"Very nice," Taylor said at length, and B.J. listened for but heard no condescension in his tone. "A very lovely view. Do you ever swim here?"

"Only since I was two," B.J. answered, groping for a friendly lightness. She wished he would not continue to hold her hand as if he had done so a thousand times before, wished hers did not fit into his as if molded for the purpose.

"Of course." He turned his head, switching his study from the lake to her face. "I'd forgotten, you were born here, weren't you?"

"I've always lived in Lakeside." Deciding that setting up the picnic things was the most expedient way to break the hand contact, B.J. took the hamper and began spreading Elsie's neatly folded cloth. "My parents moved to New York when I was nineteen, and I lived there for almost a year. I transferred colleges at mid-term and enrolled back here."

"How did you find New York?" Taylor dropped down beside her, and B.J. glimpsed at the bronzed forearms which his casually rolled up sleeves revealed.

"Noisy and confusing," she replied, frowning at a platter of crisp golden chicken. "I don't like to be confused."

"Don't you?" His swift grin appeared at her frown. With one deft motion, he pulled out the ribbon which held her hair neatly behind her back. "It makes you look like my adolescent niece." He tossed it carelessly out of reach as B.J. grabbed for it.

"You are an abominably rude man." Pushing back her newly liberated hair, she glared into his smiling face.

"Often," he agreed and lifted a bottle of wine from the hamper. He drew the cork with the ease of experience while B.J. fumed in silence. "How did you happen to become manager of the Lakeside Inn?"

The question took her off guard. For a moment she watched him pour the inn's best Chablis into Dixie cups. "I sort of gravitated to it." Accepting the offered cup, she met the directness of his gaze and realized he would not be content with the vagueness of her answer. "I worked summers at the inn when I was in high school, sort of filling in here and there at first. By the time I graduated, I was assistant manager. Anyway," she continued, "when I moved back from New York, I just slid back in. Mr. Blakely, the old manager, recommended me when he retired, and I took over." She shrugged and bit into a drumstick.

"Between your education and your dedication to your career, where did you find the time to learn how to swing a bat like Reggie Jackson?"

"I managed to find a few moments to spare. When I was fourteen," she explained, grinning at the memory, "I was madly in love with this older man. He was seventeen." She gave Taylor a sober nod. "Baseball oozed from his pores, so I enthusiastically took up the game. He'd call me shortstop, and my toes would tingle."

Taylor's burst of laughter startled a slumbering blue jay who streaked across the sky with an indignant chatter. "B.J., I don't know anyone like you. What happened to the toe tingler?"

Overcome by the pleasure his laughter had brought her, she fumbled for the thread of the conversation. "Oh…he… uh…he's got two kids and sells used cars."

"His loss," Taylor commented, cutting a thin wedge of cheese.

B.J. broke a fragrant hunk of Elsie's fresh bread and held it out to Taylor for a slice of cheese. "Do you spend much time at your other hotels?" she asked, uncomfortable at the personal tone the conversation seemed to be taking.

"Depends." His eyes roamed over her as she sat cross-legged on the grass, her soft hair tumbling over her shoulders, her lips slightly parted.

"Depends?" she inquired. He stared a moment at her and she fought not to fidget under his encompassing gaze.

"I make certain my managers are competent." He broke the silence with a smile. "If there's a specific problem, I'll deal with it. First, I like to get the feel of a new acquisition, determine if a policy change is warranted."

"But you work out of New York?" The trend of the conversation was much more to her liking. The tension eased from her shoulders.

"Primarily. I've seen fields in Kansas that looked less like wheat than your hair." He captured a generous handful. B.J. swallowed in surprise. "The fog in London isn't nearly as gray or mysterious as your eyes."

B.J. swallowed and moistened her lips. "Your chicken's getting cold."

His grin flashed at her feeble defense but his hand relinquished its possession of her hair. "It's supposed to be cold." Lifting the wine bottle, Taylor refilled his cup. "Oh, by the way, there was a call for you."

B.J. took a sip of Chablis with apparent calm. "Oh, was it important?"

"Mmm." Taylor moved his shoulders under his cream colored tailored shirt. "A Howard Beall. He said you had his number."

"Oh." B.J. frowned, recalling it was about time for her duty date with Betty Jackson's nephew. Her sigh was automatic.

"My, you simply reek of enthusiasm."

Taylor's dry comment brought on a smile and a shrug. "He's just a man I know."

Taylor contented himself with a slight raising of his brow.

The sky was now an azure arch, without even a puff of cloud to spoil its perfection. Replete and relaxed, B.J. rolled over on her back to enjoy it. The grass was soft and smelled fresh. Overhead, the maple offered a half-shade. Its black branches were touched with young, tender leaves. Through the spreading cluster of trees, dogwoods bloomed white.

"In the winter," she murmured, half to herself, "it's absolutely still here after a snowfall. Everything's white. Snow hangs and drips from the trees and carpets the earth. The lake's like a mirror. The ice is as clear as rain water. You almost forget there's any place else in the world, or that spring will come. Do you ski, Taylor?" She rolled over on her stomach, her elbows supporting her head to smile at him, all animosity forgotten.

"I've been known to." He returned her smile, studying the soft drowsy face, rosy from the sun and the un-accustomed wine.

"The skiing's marvelous here." She tossed back her hair with a quick movement of her shoulders. "Snow skiing's so much more exciting than water skiing, I think. The food at the inn brings the skiing crowd. There's nothing like Elsie's stew after a day on the slopes." Plucking a blade of grass, she twirled it idly.

Taylor moved to lie down beside her. She was too content to be alarmed at his proximity.

"Dumplings?" he inquired, and she grinned down into his face.

"Of course. Hot buttered rum or steaming chocolate."

"I'm beginning to regret I missed the season."

"Well, you're in time for strawberry shortcake," she offered in consolation. "And the fishing's good year round."

"I've always favored more active sports." His finger ran absently up her arm, and B.J. tried hard to ignore the pleasure it gave her.

"Well." Her brow creased as she considered. "There's a good stable about fifteen miles from here, or boats for rent at the marina, or..."

"Those aren't the sports I had in mind." With a swift movement, he dislodged her elbows and brought her toppling onto his chest. "Are they the best you can do?" His arms held her firmly against him, but she was already captured by the fascination of his eyes.

"There's hiking," she murmured, unaware of the strange husky texture of her own voice.

"Hiking," Taylor murmured, before altering their positions in one fluid motion.

"Yes, hiking's very popular." She felt her consciousness drifting as she gazed up at him and struggled to retain some hold on lucidity. "And…and swimming."

"Mmm." Absently, his fingers traced the delicate line of her cheek.

"And there's…uh…there's camping. A lot of people like camping. We have a lot of parks." Her voice faltered as his thumb ran over her lips.

"Parks?" he repeated, prompting her.

"Yes, a number of parks, quite a number. The facilities are excellent for camping." She gave a small moan as his mouth lowered to tease the curve of her neck.

"Hunting?" Taylor asked conversationally as his lips traveled over her jawline to brush the corner of her mouth.

"I, yes. I think…what did you say?" B.J. closed her eyes on a sigh.

"I wondered about hunting," he murmured, kissing closed lids as his fingers slid under her sweater to trace her waist.

"There's bobcat in the mountains to the north."

"Fascinating." He rubbed his mouth gently over hers as his fingers trailed lightly up her flesh to the curve of her breast. "The chamber of commerce would be proud of you." Lazily, his thumb ran over the satin swell. Pleasure became a need as warmth spread from her stomach to tremble in her veins and cloud her brain.

"Taylor." Unable to bring her voice above a whisper, her hand sought the thick mass of his hair. "Kiss me."

"In a minute," he murmured, obviously enjoying the taste of her neck, until with devastating leisure, he moved his mouth to hers.

Trembling with a new, unfamiliar hunger, B.J. pulled him closer until his mouth was no longer teasing but avid on hers. Warmth exploded into fire. His tongue was searching, demanding all of her sweetness, his body as taut as hers was fluid. He took possession of her curves with authority, molding them with firm, strong hands. His mouth no longer roamed from hers but remained to devour what she offered. The heat grew to an almost unbearable intensity, her soul melting in it to flow into his. For a moment, she was lost in the discovery of merging, feeling it with as much clarity as she felt his hands and mouth. Soaring freedom and the chains of need were interchangeable. As time ceased to flow, she plunged deeper and deeper into the all-enveloping present.

His hands took more, all gentleness abandoned. It flashed across the mists in her brain that beneath the control lay a primitive, volatile force from which she had no defense. She struggled weakly. Her protests were feeble murmurs against the demands of his mouth. Feeling her tense, Taylor lifted his head, and she felt the unsteady rhythm of his breathing on her face.

"Please, let me go." Hating the weak timbre of her own voice, she sank her teeth into the lip still tender from his.

"Why should I do that?" Temper and passion threatened his control. She knew she had neither the strength nor the will to resist him if he chose to take.

"Please."

It seemed an eternity that he studied her, searching the smoky depths of her eyes. She watched the anger fade from his eyes as he took in the fair hair spread across the grass, the vulnerable, soft mouth. Finally, he released her with a brief, muttered oath.

"It appears," he began as she scrambled to sit up, "that pigtails suit you more than I realized." He took out a cigarette and lit it deliberately. "Virginity is a rare commodity in a woman your age."

Color flooded her cheeks as B.J. began to pack up the remains of the picnic. "I hardly see what business that is of yours."

"It doesn't matter," he countered easily and she cursed him for his ability to retain his composure so effortlessly while her entire body still throbbed with need. "It will simply take a bit more time." At her uncomprehending stare, he smiled and folded the cloth. "I told you I always win, B.J. You'd best get used to it."

"You listen to me." Storming, she sprang to her feet. "I am not about to be added to your list. This was… this was…" Her hands spread out to sweep away the incident while her brain searched for the proper words.

"Just the beginning," he supplied. Rising with the hamper, he captured her arm in a firm grip. "We haven't nearly finished yet. I wouldn't argue at the moment, B.J.," he warned as she began to sputter. "I might decide to take what you so recently offered here and now, rather than giving you some time."

"You are the most arrogant—" she began. Her voice sounded hopelessly childish even to her own ears.

"That's enough for now, B.J." Taylor interrupted pleasantly. "There's no point saying anything you might regret." He leaned down and kissed her firmly before helping her to her feet. With an easy swing, he reached for the hamper. B.J. was too dazed to do anything but meekly follow him as he led the way toward the homeward wooded path.

Chapter 7

Once back at the inn, B.J. wanted nothing more than to disengage her arm from Taylor's grasp and find a dark, quiet hole in which to hide. She knew all too well that she had responded completely to Taylor's demands. Moreover, she knew she had made demands of her own. She was confused by her own reactions. Never before had she had difficulty in avoiding or controlling a romantic interlude, but she was forced to admit that from the moment Taylor had touched her, her mind had ceased to function.

Biology, she concluded, darting Taylor a sidelong glance as they approached the skirting porch. It was simply a matter of basic biology. Any woman would naturally be attracted to a man like Taylor Reynolds. He has a way of looking at you, B.J. mused, that makes your mind go fuzzy, then blank. He has a way of touching you that makes you feel as though you never had been touched before. He's nothing like any other man I've ever known. And *I asked him to kiss me.* Color rose to her cheeks. *I actually asked him to kiss me.* It must have been the wine.

Soothed by this excuse, B.J. turned to Taylor as they entered the side door. "I'll take the basket back to the kitchen. Do you need me for anything else?"

"That's an intriguing question," he drawled.

B.J. shot him a quelling glance. "I have to get back to work now," she said briskly. "Now, if you'll excuse me?"

B.J.'s dignified exit was aborted by a flurry of activity in the lobby. Curiosity outweighing pride, she allowed Taylor to lead her toward the source.

A tall, svelte brunette stood by the desk, surrounded by a clutter of shocking pink luggage. Her pencil-slim form was draped in a teal blue suit of raw silk. The scent of gardenias floated toward B.J.

"If you'll see to my luggage, darling, and tell Mr. Reynolds I'm here, I'd be very grateful." She addressed these requests in a low, husky voice to Eddie who stood gaping beside her.

"Hello, Darla. What are you doing here?"

At Taylor's voice, the dark head turned. B.J. noted the eyes were nearly the same shade as the exquisite suit.

"Taylor." Impossibly graceful on four-inch heels, Darla glided across the lobby to embrace Taylor warmly. "I'm just back from checking on the job in Chicago. I knew you'd want me to look this little place over and give you my ideas."

Disengaging himself, Taylor met Darla's glowing

smile with an ironic smile. "How considerate of you. B.J. Clark, Darla Trainor. Darla does the majority of my decorating, B.J. manages the inn."

"How interesting." Darla gave B.J.'s sweater and jeans a brief, despairing glance and patted her own perfectly styled hair. "From what I've seen so far, my work is certainly cut out for me." With a barely perceptible shudder, Darla surveyed the lobby's hand hooked rugs and Tiffany lamps.

"We've had no complaints on our decor." B.J. leaped to the inn's defense.

"Well." She was given a small, pitying smile from deeply colored lips. "It's certainly quaint, isn't it? Rather sweet for Ma and Pa Kettle. You'll have to let me know, Taylor, if you plan to enlarge this room." Transferring her attention, Darla's expression softened and warmed. "But, of course, red's always an eye-catcher. Perhaps red velvet drapes and carpeting."

B.J.'s eyes darkened to flint. "Why don't you take your red velvet drapes and..."

"I believe we'll discuss this later," Taylor said diplomatically, tightening his hold on B.J.'s arm. Struggling to prevent herself from crying with the pain, B.J. found argument impossible.

"I'm sure you'd like to get settled in," she forced out between clenched lips.

"Of course." Darla viewed B.J.'s brief outburst with a fluttering of heavy lashes. "Come up for a drink, Taylor. I assume this place has room service."

"Of course. Have a couple of martinis sent up to Miss Trainor's room," Taylor said to Eddie. "What's your room number, Darla?"

"I don't believe I have one yet." Again using her extensive lashes to advantage, Darla turned to a still dazed Eddie. "There seems to be a small communication problem."

"Give Miss Trainor 314, Eddie, and see to her bags." The sharp command in B.J.'s voice snapped Eddie's daydream, and he scurried to comply. "I hope you find it suitable." B.J. turned her best managerial smile on her new and unwelcome guest. "Please let me know if there's anything you need. I'll see to your drinks."

Taylor's hand held her still another moment. "I'll speak with you later."

"Delighted," B.J. turned, feeling the circulation slowly returning to her arm as he released it. "I'll wait to be summoned at your convenience, Mr. Reynolds. Welcome to the Lakeside Inn, Miss Trainor. Have a nice stay."

It was a simple matter to avoid a private meeting with Taylor as he spent the remainder of the day in Darla Trainor's company. They were closeted in 314 for what seemed to B.J. a lifetime. To boost her ego B.J. decided to phone Howard. They arranged a date for the following evening. *Well, at least Howard doesn't closet himself downing martinis with Miss Glamorpuss,* she thought. Somehow this knowledge was not as comforting as it should have been.

The dress B.J. had chosen for dinner was black and sleek. It molded her subtle curves with a lover's intimacy, falling in a midnight pool around her ankles, with a gentle caress for thighs and calves. Small pearl buttons ran from her throat to her waist. The high, puritanical neckline accentuated her firm, small breasts and emphasized her slender neck. She left her hair loose to float in a pale cloud around her shoulders. She touched her scent behind her ears before leaving her room to descend to the dining room.

The candle-lit, corner table where Taylor sat with Darla was intimate and secluded. Glancing in their direction, B.J. could not suppress a scowl. There was no denying that they were a handsome couple. *Made for each other,* she thought bitterly. Darla's vermilion sheath plunged to reveal the creamy swell of her breasts. Taylor's dark suit was impeccably cut. In spite of herself, B.J.'s eyes were drawn to the breadth of his shoulders. She drew in her breath sharply, recalling the feel of his corded muscles now expertly concealed by the fine tailoring, and shivered involuntarily.

Taylor glanced over, his expression indefinable as he made a slow, exacting survey, his eyes lingering on the gentle curves draped in the simplicity of unrelieved black. Though her skin grew warm, B.J. met his eyes levelly. Examination complete, Taylor lifted one brow, whether in approval or disapproval, she could not determine. With a brief gesture of his hand, he ordered B.J. to his table.

Fuming at the casual insolence of the command, she schooled her features into tranquility. She wove her way through the room, deliberately stopping to speak with diners along the route.

"Good evening." B.J. greeted Taylor and his companion with a professional smile. "I hope you're enjoying your meal."

"As always, the food is excellent." Taylor rose and pulled up a chair expectantly. His eyes narrowed in challenge. It was not the moment to cross him, B.J. decided.

"I trust your room pleases you, Miss Trainor," she said pleasantly, as she sat down.

"It's adequate, Miss Clark. Though I must say, I was rather taken aback by the decorating scheme."

"You'll join us for a drink," Taylor stated, motioning a waitress over without waiting for B.J.'s consent. She glared at him for a moment before she glanced up at Dot.

"My usual," she said, not feeling obliged to explain this was a straight ginger ale. She turned back to Darla, coating her voice with polite interest. "And what is it about the decorating which took you aback, Miss Trainor?"

"Really, Miss Clark," Darla began as though the matter was obvious. "The entire room is *provincial,* don't you agree? There are some rather nice pieces, I admit, if one admires American antiques, but Taylor and I have always preferred a modern approach."

Fighting her annoyance and an all too unwanted spasm of jealousy, B.J. said sarcastically, "I see. Perhaps you'd care to elaborate on the modern approach for this country bumpkin. I so seldom get beyond the local five and dime."

Dot set B.J.'s drink in front of her and scurried away, recognizing storm warnings.

"In the first place," Darla began, immune to her frosty gray eyes, "the lighting is all wrong. Those glass domed lamps with pull chains are archaic. You need wall to wall carpeting. The hand hooked rugs and faded Persians will have to go. And the bathroom... Well, needless to say, the bathroom is hopeless." With a sigh, Darla lifted her champagne cocktail and sipped. "Footed tubs belong in period comedies, not in hotels."

B.J. chewed on a piece of ice to keep her temper from boiling over. "Our guests have always found a certain charm in the baths."

"Perhaps," Darla acknowledged with a depreciating shrug. "But with the proper changes and improvements, you'll be catering to a different type of clientele." She drew out a slim cigarette, giving Taylor a brief flutter of lashes as he lit it.

"Do you have any objections to footed tubs and pull chains?" B.J. asked him, voice precise, eyes stormy.

"They suit the present atmosphere of the inn." His voice was equally precise, his eyes cool.

"Maybe I've got a few fresh ideas for you, Miss Trainor, if and when you pull out your little book of samples." Setting down her glass, B.J. watched from the corner of her eye as Taylor flicked his lighter at the end of his cigarette. "Mirrors should be good on the ceiling in particular. Just a light touch of decadence. Lots of chrome and glass to give the rooms that spacious, symmetrical look. And white, plenty of white as well, perhaps with fuchsia accents. The bed, of course," she continued with fresh inspiration. "A large circular bed with fuchsia coverings. Do you like fuchsia, Taylor?"

"I don't believe I asked for your advice on decorating tonight, B.J." Taylor drew casually on his cigarette. The smoke traveled in a thin column toward the exposed beam ceiling.

"I'm afraid, Miss Clark," Darla commented, spurred on by Taylor's mild reproof, "that your taste runs to the vulgar."

"Oh really?" B.J. blinked as if surprised. "I suppose that's what comes from being a country bumpkin."

"I'm sure whatever I ultimately decide will suit you, Taylor." Darla placed a hand with easy familiarity on his as B.J.'s temper rose. "But it will take a bit longer than usual as the alterations will be so drastic."

"Take all the time you need." B.J. gestured with magnanimity as she rose. "In the meantime, keep your hands off my footed tubs."

The dignity of her exit was spoiled by a near collision with Dot who had been discreetly eavesdropping.

"An order of arsenic for table three…on the house," B.J. muttered, skirting around the wide eyed waitress and sweeping from the room.

B.J.'s intention to stalk straight to her room and cool off was undone by a series of small, irritating jobs. It was after ten when the last had been dealt with and she was able to shut the door to her room and give vent to suppressed temper.

"Country bumpkin," she hissed through clenched teeth. Her eyes rested on a William and Mary table. *She'd* probably prefer plastic cubes in black and white checks. Her eyes moved from the dower chest to the schoolmaster's desk and on to the Bostonian rocker and wing chair in softly faded green. Each room of the inn was distinctive, with its own personality, its own treasures. Closing her eyes, B.J. could clearly see the room which Darla now occupied, the delicate pastel of the flowered wallpaper, the fresh gleam of the oak floor, the charm of the narrow, cushioned window seat. The pride of that particular room was an antique highboy in walnut with exquisite teardrop pulls. B.J. could not recall an occasion when a guest who had stayed in that room had done other than praise its comforts, its quiet charm, its timeless grace.

Darla Trainor, B.J. vowed, *is not getting her hands on my inn.* Walking to the mirrored bureau, she stared at her reflection, then let out a long disgusted breath. She's got a face that belongs on a cameo, and mine belongs on a milk commercial, she thought. Picking up her brush, she told herself that these reflections had nothing to do with the problem at hand.

How am I going to convince Taylor that the inn should stay as it is when she's already rattling off changes and giving him intimate smiles? I suppose, B.J. continued, giving her reflection a fierce scowl, *she's not just his decorator.* The kiss she gave him when she arrived wasn't very businesslike. I don't believe for a moment they spent all that time in her room discussing fabrics.

That's no concern of mine, she decided with a strong tug of the brush. But if they think they're going to start steaming off wallpaper without a fight, they're in for a surprise. She put down her brush and turned just as the door swung open to admit Taylor.

Before her astonished eyes, he closed and locked her door before placing the key in his pocket. As he advanced toward her, she could see that he was obviously angry.

"Being the owner doesn't give you the right to use the

master key without cause," she snapped, as she backed against the bureau.

"It appears I haven't made myself clear." Taylor's voice was deceptively gentle. "You have, for the time being, a free hand in the day to day managing of this inn. I have not, nor do I desire to infringe upon your routine. However—" He took a step closer. B.J. discovered her hands were clutching the edge of the bureau in a desperate grip. "All orders, all decisions, all changes in policy come from me, and only me."

"Of all the dictatorial…"

"This isn't a debate," he cut her off sharply. "I won't have you issuing orders over my head. Darla is employed by me. I tell her what to do, and when to do it."

"But surely you don't want her to toss out all these lovely old pieces for gooseneck floor lamps and modular shelving. The server in the dining room is Hepplewhite. There're two Chippendale pieces in your room alone, and…"

The hand which moved from the back of her neck to circle her throat halted B.J.'s furious rush of words. She became uncomfortably aware of the strength of his fingers. No pressure was applied, but the meaning was all too evident.

"Whatever I want Darla to do is my concern, and my concern only." He tightened his grip, bringing her closer. Now B.J. read the extent of his anger in his eyes. Like two dark suns, they burned into hers. "Keep your opinions to yourself until I ask for them. Don't interfere or you'll pay for it. Is that understood?"

"I understand perfectly. Your relationship with Miss Trainor has overruled any opinion of mine."

"That—" his brow lifted "—is none of your business."

"Whatever concerns the inn is my business," B.J. countered. "I offered you my resignation once, and you refused it. If you want to get rid of me now, you'll have to fire me."

"Don't tempt me." He lowered his hand and rested his fingers on the top button of her bodice. "I have my reasons for wanting you around, but don't push it. I agreed to keep you abreast of any alterations I decide on, but if you persist in being rude to others in my employ, you'll be out on your ear."

"I can't see that Darla Trainor needs protection from me," B.J. remarked resentfully.

"Don't you?" His temper appeared to drift toward amusement as he scanned her face. "A couple of centuries ago, you'd have been burned at the stake for looking as you do at this moment. Hell smoke in your eyes, your mouth soft and defiant, all that pale hair tumbling over a black dress." Deftly, his fingers undid the top button and moved down to the next as his eyes kept hers a prisoner. "That dress is just puritanical enough to be seductive. Was it accident or design that you wore it tonight?"

With casual ease, he unloosed half the range of buttons, continuing his progress as his gaze remained fixed on hers.

"I don't know what you mean." Yet her traitorous feet refused to walk away. B.J. found herself powerless to move. "I want…I want you to go."

"Liar," he accused quietly, his hands slipping inside the opened front of her dress. His fingers traced lightly over her skin. "Tell me again you want me to go." His hands rose, his thumbs moving gently under the curve of her breasts. The room began to sway like the deck of a ship.

"I want you to go." Her voice was husky, her lids felt heavy with a tantalizing languor.

"Your body contradicts you, B.J." His hands claimed her breasts briefly before sliding to the smooth skin of her back. He brought her hard against him. "You want me just as much as I want you." His mouth lowered to prove his point.

Surrendering to a force beyond her understanding, B.J. rested in his arms. His demands increased with her submission, his mouth drawing the response she had no strength to withhold. While her mind screamed no, her arms drew him closer. The warnings to run were lost as his lips moved to the vulnerable skin of her throat, teasing the softness with tongue and teeth. She could only cling and fret for more. Mouth returned to mouth. While his hands roamed, arousing fresh pleasure, hers slipped under his jacket.

With a suddenness that gave her no time for defense, no thought of resistance, he fell deep into her heart. He claimed its untouched regions with the deftness of a seasoned explorer. The emotion brought B.J. to a spinning ecstasy which vied with a crushing, hopeless despair. To love him was certain disaster, to need him, undeniable misery, to be in his arms, both the darkness and the light. Trapped in the cage of her own desire, she would never find escape.

Helpless to do other than answer the hunger of his mouth, submit to the caressing journey of his hands, she felt the sting of emptiness behind her closed lids.

Her arms pulled him closer to avert the insidious chill of reason.

"Admit it," he demanded, his lips moving again to savage her throat. "Admit you want me. Tell me you want me to stay."

"Yes, I want you." The words trembled on a sob as she buried her face in his shoulder. "Yes, I want you to stay."

She felt him stiffen and burrowed deeper until his hand forced her face to his. Her eyes were luminous, conquering the darkness with the glimmer of unshed tears. Her mouth was soft and tremulous as she fought the need to throw herself into his arms and weep out her newly discovered love. For eternity, he stared, and she watched without comprehension as his features hardened with fresh temper. When he spoke, however, his voice was calm and composed and struck like a fist on the jaw.

"It appears we've gotten away from the purpose of this meeting." Stepping away, his hands retreated to his pockets. "I believe I've made my wishes clear."

She shook her head in confusion. As her hand lifted to her tousled hair, the opening of her dress shifted in innocent suggestion over creamy skin. "Taylor, I…"

"Tomorrow—" she shivered as the coolness of his voice sapped the warmth from her skin "—I expect you to give Miss Trainor your complete cooperation, and your courtesy. Regardless of your disagreement, she is a guest of the inn and shall be treated as such."

"Of course." The hated tears began to flow as pain and rejection washed over her. "Miss Trainor shall be given every consideration." She sniffed, brushed at tears and continued with dignity. "You have my word."

"Your word!" Taylor muttered, taking a step toward her. B.J. streaked to the bath and locked the door.

"Go away!" No longer able to control the sobs, one small fist pounded impotently against the panel. "Go away and leave me alone. I gave you my promise, now I'm off duty."

"B.J., open this door."

She recognized both anger and exasperation in his tone and wept more desperately. "No, go away! Go keep Miss Perfect company and let me alone. Your orders will be carried out to the letter. Just go. I don't have to answer to you until morning."

Taylor's swearing and storming around the room were quite audible, though to B.J. his muttered oaths and comments made little sense. Finally, the bedroom door slammed with dangerous force. In an undignified huddle on the tiled floor, B.J. wept until she thought her heart would break.

Chapter 8

"Well, you did it again, didn't you?" B.J. stared at her reflection as the morning sun shone in without mercy. *You made a total fool of yourself.* With a weary sigh, she ran a hand through her hair before turning her back on the accusing face in the mirror. *How could I have known I'd fall in love with him?* she argued as she buttoned a pale green cap-sleeved blouse. *I didn't plan it. I didn't want it.*

"Blast," she muttered and pulled on a matching skirt. *How can I control the way he makes me feel? The minute he puts his hands on me, my brain dissolves. To think that I would have let him stay last night knowing all he wanted from me was a quick affair! How could I be so stupid?* And then, she added, shame warring with injured pride, *he didn't want me after all.* I suppose he remembered Darla. Why should he waste his time with me when she's available?

The next ten minutes were spent in fierce self-flagellation as B.J. secured her hair in a roll at the base of her neck. These tasks completed, she squared her shoulders and went out to meet whatever task the day brought.

A casual question to Eddie informed her Taylor was already closeted in the office, and Darla Trainor had not yet risen. B.J. was determined to avoid them both and succeeded throughout the morning.

The lunch hour found her in the lounge, conducting an inventory on the bar stock. The room was quiet, removed from the luncheon clatter. She found the monotony soothing on her nerves.

"So, this is the lounge."

The intrusion of the silky voice jolted B.J.'s calm absorption. She whirled around, knocking bottles of liquor together.

Darla glided into the room looking elegantly businesslike in an oatmeal colored three piece suit, a pad and pencil in perfectly manicured hands. She surveyed the cluster of white clothed tables, the postage stamp dance floor, the vintage upright Steinway. Flicking a finger down the muted glow of knotty pine paneling, she advanced to the ancient oak bar.

"How incredibly drab."

"Thank you," B.J. returned in her most courteous voice before she turned to replace a bottle on the mirrored shelves.

"Fix me a sweet vermouth," Darla ordered, sliding gracefully onto a stool and dropping her pad on the bar's surface.

B.J.'s mouth opened, furious retorts trembling on her tongue. Recalling her promise to Taylor, she clamped it shut and turned to comply.

"You must remember, Miss Clark," Darla's triumphant smile made B.J.'s hand itch to connect with ivory skin, "I'm merely doing my job. There's nothing personal in my observations."

Attempting to overcome her instinctive dislike, B.J. conceded. "Perhaps that's true. But, I have a very personal feeling about the Lakeside Inn. It's more home than a place of business to me." She set the glass of vermouth at Darla's fingertips before turning back to count bottles.

"Yes, Taylor told me you're quite attached to this little place. He found it amusing."

"Did he?" Feeling her hand tremble, B.J. gripped the shelves until her knuckles whitened. "What a strange sense of humor Taylor must have."

"Well, when one knows Taylor as I do, one knows what to expect." Their eyes met in the mirror. Darla smiled and lifted her glass. "He seems to think you're a valuable employee. What did he say…rather adept at making people comfortable." She smiled again and sipped. "Taylor demands value from his employees as well as obedience. At times, he uses unorthodox methods to keep them satisfied."

"I'm sure you'd know all about that." B.J. turned slowly, deciding wars should be fought face to face.

"Darling, Taylor and I are much more than business associates. And I, of course, understand his…ah…distractions with business."

"How magnanimous of you."

"It would never do to allow emotion to rule a relationship with Taylor Reynolds." Drawing a long, enameled nail over the rim of her glass, Darla gave B.J. a knowledgeable look. "He has no patience with emotional scenes or complications."

The memory of her weeping spell and Taylor's angry swearing played back in B.J.'s mind. "Perhaps we've at last reached a point of agreement."

"The first warning is always friendly, Miss Clark." Abruptly, Darla's voice hardened, throwing B.J. momentarily off balance. "Don't get too close. I don't allow anyone to infringe on my territory for long."

"Are we still talking about Taylor?" B.J. inquired. "Or did I lose part of this conversation?"

"Just take my advice." Leaning over the bar, Darla took B.J.'s arm in a surprisingly strong grip. "If you don't, the next place you manage will be a dog kennel."

"Take your hand off me." B.J.'s tone was soft and ominous, as the well-shaped nails dug into her flesh.

"As long as we understand each other." With a pleasant smile, Darla released B.J.'s arm and finished her drink.

"We understand each other very well." Taking the empty glass, B.J. placed it under the bar. "Bar's closed, Miss Trainor." She turned her back to recount already counted bottles.

"Ladies." B.J. stiffened and watched Taylor's reflection enter the room. "I hadn't expected to find you at the bar at this time of day." His voice was light, but the eyes which met B.J.'s in the glass did not smile.

"I've been wandering around making notes," Darla told him. B.J. watched her hand rub lightly over the back of his. "I'm afraid the only thing this lounge has going for it is its size. It's quite roomy, and you could easily fit in double the tables. But then, you'll have to let me know if you want to go moody, or modern. Actually, it might be an idea to add another lounge and do both, along the lines of your place in San Francisco."

His murmur was absent as he watched B.J. move to the next shelf.

"I thought I'd get a good look at the dining room if the luncheon crowd is gone." Darla's smile was coaxing. "Why don't you come with me, Taylor, and you can give me a clearer picture of what you have in mind?"

"Hmm?" His attention shifted, but the imperceptible frown remained. "No, I haven't decided on anything yet. Go ahead and take a look, I'll get back to you."

Well arched brows rose at the dismissive tone, but Darla remained cool and composed. "Of course. I'll bring my notes to your office later and we can discuss it."

Her heels echoed faintly on the wooden floor. Her heavy perfume scent lingered in the air after she faded from view.

"Do you want a drink?" B.J. questioned, keeping her back to him and her voice remote.

"No, I want to talk to you."

With great care, B.J. avoided meeting his eyes in the mirror. She lifted a bottle, carefully examining the extent of its contents. "Haven't we covered everything?"

"No, we haven't covered everything. Turn around B.J., I'm not going to talk to your back."

"Very well, you're the boss." As she faced him, she caught a flash of anger in his eyes.

"Do you provoke me purposely, B.J., or is it just an accidental talent?"

"I have no idea. Take your choice." Suddenly, she was struck by inspiration. "Taylor," she said urgently, "I *would* like to talk to you. I'd like to talk to you about buying the inn. It can't be as important to you as it is to me. You could build a resort farther south that would suit you better. I could raise the money if you gave me some time."

"Don't be ridiculous." His abrupt words cooled her enthusiasm. "Where would you come up with the kind of money required to buy a property like this?"

"I don't know." She paced back and forth behind the bar. "Somewhere. I could get a loan for part of it, and you could hold a note for the rest. I've some money saved…"

"No." Standing, he skirted the bar and closed the distance between them. "I have no intention of selling."

"But, Taylor…"

"I said no. Drop it."

"Why are you being so stubborn? You won't even consider changing your mind? I might even be able to come up with a good offer if you gave me time—" Her voice trailed off uncertainly.

"I said I wanted to *talk* to you. At the moment I don't care to discuss the inn or any part of it."

He gripped her arm to spin her around, connecting with the flesh tender from Darla's nails. B.J. gave a cry of pain and jerked away. Taylor loosened his hold immediately, and she fell into the shelves, knocking glasses in a crashing heap on the floor.

"What the devil's got into you?" he demanded as her

hand went automatically to nurse her bruised arm. "I barely touched you. Listen, B.J., I'm not tolerating you jumping like a scared rabbit every time I get close. I haven't hurt you. Stop that!" He pulled her hand away, then stared in confusion at the marks on her arm. "Good Lord. I didn't...I'd swear I barely touched you." Astonished, his eyes lifted to hers, darkened with emotions she could not understand. For a moment, she merely stared back, fascinated by seeing his habitual assurance rattled.

"No, I did it before." Dropping her eyes, B.J. busied herself by resecuring the pins in her hair. "It's just a bit sore. You startled me when you grabbed it."

"How did you do that?" He moved to take her arm for a closer examination, but B.J. stepped away quickly.

"I bumped into something. I've got to start looking where I'm going." She began to gather shards of broken glass, fresh resentment causing her head to ache.

"Don't do that," Taylor commanded. "You'll cut yourself."

Like an echo to his words, B.J. jerked as a piece of glass sliced her thumb. Moaning in pain and disgust, she dropped the offending glass back into the heap.

"Let me see." Taylor pulled her to her feet, ignoring her struggles for release. "Ah, B.J." With a sigh of exasperation, he drew a spotless white handkerchief from his pocket, dabbing at the cut. "I'm beginning to think I have to keep you on a very short leash."

"It's nothing," she mumbled, fighting the warmth of his fingers on her wrist. "Let me go, you'll have blood all over you."

"Scourges of war." He brought the wounded thumb

briefly to his lips, then wrapped the cloth around it. "You will continue to bind up your hair, won't you?" With his free hand, he dislodged pins, clattering them among broken glass. Studying the flushed face and tumbled hair, his mouth lifted in a smile which brought B.J. new pain. "What is it about you that constantly pulls at my temper? At the moment, you look as harmless as a frazzled kitten."

His fingers combed lightly through her hair, then rested on her shoulders. She felt the sweet, drawing weakness seeping through her limbs. "Do you know how close I came to kicking in that foolish bathroom door last night? You should be careful with tears, B.J., they affect men in strange ways."

"I hate to cry." She lifted her chin, terrified she would do so again. "It was your fault."

"Yes, I suppose it was. I'm sorry."

She stared, stunned by the unexpected apology. In a featherlight caress, he lowered his mouth to brush hers. "It's all right...It doesn't matter." She backed away, frightened by her own need to respond, but found herself trapped against the bar. Taylor made no move toward her, but merely said, "Have dinner with me tonight. Up in my room where we can talk privately."

Her head shook before her lips could form a refusal. He closed the space between them before she could calculate an escape.

"B.J., I'm not going to let you run away. We need to talk somewhere where we won't be interrupted. You know that I want you, and..."

"You should be satisfied with your other acquisitions," she retorted, battling the creeping warmth.

"I beg your pardon?" At her tone, his face hardened. The hand which had lifted to brush through her hair dropped back to his side.

"I'm sure you'll understand if you give it a bit of thought." She lifted her own hand to the sore flesh of her arm as if to keep the memory fresh. His eyes followed her gesture in puzzlement.

"It would be simpler if you elaborated."

"No, I don't think so. Just don't let your ego get out of hand, Taylor. I'm not running from you, I simply have a date tonight."

"A date?" He slipped his hands into his pockets as he rocked back on his heels. His voice was hard.

"That's right. I'm entitled to a personal life. I don't think it's included in my job contract that I have to spend twenty-four hours at your beck and call." Adding salt to her own wound, she continued, "I'm sure Miss Trainor will fill your requirements for the evening very well."

"Undoubtedly," he agreed with a slow nod. Stung by the ease of his answer, B.J.'s ice became fire.

"Well then, that's all decided, isn't it? Have a delightful evening, Taylor. I assure you, I intend to. If you'll excuse me, I've work to do." She brushed by him, only to be brought up short by a hand on her hair.

"Since we're both going to be otherwise engaged this evening, perhaps we can get this out of the way now."

His mouth took hers swiftly, and she could taste his smoldering fury. She made a futile attempt to clamp her lips tightly against his. Ruthlessly, his hand jerked her hair. As she gasped in pained surprise he invaded her mouth, conquering her senses one by one. Just as she had abandoned all semblance of resistance, he drew back, his hands moving with slow insistence from her waist to her shoulders.

"Are you through?" Her voice was husky. Despising the longing to feel his mouth again, she forced herself rigid, keeping her eyes level.

"Oh no, B.J." The tone was confident. "I'm a long way from through. But for now," he continued as she braced herself for another assault, "you'd best tend to that cut."

Too unnerved to answer, B.J. rushed from the lounge. She had left dignity to lay with the scattered pieces of glass.

She felt the kitchen would be the quietest sanctuary at that time of day and entered on the pretext of wanting a cup of coffee.

"What did you do to your hand?" Elsie's question was off-handed as she completed the assembly line production of apple cobblers.

"Just a scratch." Frowning down at Taylor's handkerchief, B.J. shrugged and advanced on the coffee pot.

"Better put some iodine on it."

"Iodine stings."

Tongue clucking, Elsie wiped her hands on her full apron before foraging in a small cabinet for medical supplies. "Sit down and don't be a baby."

"It's just a scratch. It's not even bleeding now." Helplessly, B.J. dropped into a chair as Elsie flourished a small bottle and a bandage. "It's nothing at all. Ouch! Blast it, Elsie! I told you that wretched stuff stings."

"There." Elsie secured the bandage with a satisfied smile. "Out of sight, out of mind."

"So you say." B.J. rested her chin on her hand and stared into the depth of her coffee cup.

"Miss Snooty tried to get into my kitchen," Elsie announced with an indignant sniff.

"Who? Oh, Miss Trainor." Throbbing thumb momentarily forgotten, B.J. gave her cook her full attention. "What happened?"

"I tossed her out, of course." Elsie flicked flour from her abundant bosom and looked pleased.

"Oh." Leaning back in her chair, B.J. laughed at the picture of Elsie ordering sophisticated Darla out of her kitchen. "Was she furious?"

"Fit to be tied," Elsie returned pleasantly. B.J.'s grin widened before she could prevent it. "Going out with Howard tonight?"

"Yes." Her answer was automatic, not even vaguely surprised that communications had delivered this information to Elsie's ears. "To the movies, I think."

"Don't know why you're wasting your time going off with him when Mr. Reynolds is around."

"Well, it keeps Betty Jackson happy, and…" B.J. stopped and frowned as the complete sentence seeped through. "What does Taylor…Mr. Reynolds have to do with it?"

"I don't see why you're going out with Howard Beall when you're in love with Taylor Reynolds." Elsie's statement was matter-of-factly delivered as she poured herself a cup of coffee.

"I am not in love with Taylor Reynolds," B.J. de-clared, gulping down coffee and scalding both tongue and throat.

"Yes, you are," Elsie corrected, adding cooling cream to her own cup.

"I am not."

"Are too."

"I am not. I am absolutely not! Just what makes you so smart?" she added nastily.

"Fifty years of living, and twenty-four of knowing you." The reply was smug.

"La de da." B.J. attempted to appear sublimely unconcerned.

"Be real nice if you got married and settled down right here." Ignoring B.J.'s fit of choking, Elsie calmly sipped her coffee. "You could keep right on managing the inn."

"Stick to chicken and dumplings, Elsie," B.J. advised when she had recovered. "As a fortune teller, you're a complete failure. Taylor Reynolds would no more marry me and settle here than he would marry a porcupine and live on the moon. I'm a bit too countrified and inexperienced for his taste."

"Hmph." Elsie sniffed again and shook her head. "Sure does a lot of looking in your direction."

"I'm sure in the vast wisdom you've amassed in your famous fifty years, you know the difference between a physical attraction and the urge to marry and settle down. Even in our sheltered little town, we learn the difference between love and lust."

"My, my, aren't we all grown up and sassy," Elsie observed with the mild tolerance of an adult watching a child's tantrum. "Finish your coffee and scoot, I've got a prime rib that needs tending. And don't worry that bandage off your thumb," she ordered as B.J. swung through the door.

Obviously, B.J. decided as she prepared for her date that evening, I don't project an imposing enough authority figure. She frowned again as she recalled Elsie dismissing her like a bad tempered child. A breeze wafted through her opened window, billowing the curtains and wafting in the smell of freshly mowed grass. B.J. shrugged off her black mood. I'll simply change my image a bit.

She rooted through her closet and pulled out her birthday present from her grandmother. The blouse was pure white silk and plunged deep to cling provocatively to every curve and plane before it tapered to the narrow waist of sleek black pants. The slacks continued a loving embrace over hips and down the length of shapely legs, molding her shape with the accuracy of a second skin.

"I'm not sure I'm ready for a new image," she muttered, turning sideways in front of her mirror. "I'm not sure Howard's ready either." The thought brought an irrepressible giggle as Howard's pleasantly homely face loomed in her mind.

He had the eyes of a faithful puppy, made all the more soulful by the attempt of a moustache which hung apologetically over his top lip. The main problem, B.J. decided, concentrating on his image, is that he lacks a chin. His face seemed to melt into his neck.

But he's a nice man, B.J. reminded herself. A nice, uncomplicated, predictable, undemanding man. Easing her feet into leather slides, she grabbed her bag and scurried from the room.

Her hopes to slip unseen outside to await Howard's arrival were shattered by a panic-stricken Eddie.

"B.J. Hey, B.J.!" He loped across the lobby and cornered her before she could reach the door.

"Eddie, if the place isn't burning down, hold it until tomorrow. I'm just leaving."

"But, B.J.," he continued, grabbing her hand and ignoring her unconscious search of the room for a tall, dark man. "Dot told Maggie that Miss Trainor is going to redecorate the inn, and that Mr. Reynolds plans to make it into a resort with saunas in every room and an illegal casino in the back." Horrified, his hand clung to hers for reassurance, his eyes pleading behind the thickness of his glasses.

"In the first place," B.J. began patiently, "Mr. Reynolds has no intention of running an illegal casino."

"He has one in Las Vegas," Eddie whispered in confidence.

"Gambling is a prerequisite in Las Vegas, it's not illegal."

"But, B.J., Maggie said the lounge is going to be done in red and gold plush with nude paintings on the walls."

"Nonsense." She patted his hand in amusement as color rose to his cheeks. "Mr. Reynolds hasn't decided anything yet. When he does, I'm sure it won't run to red and gold plush, and nudes!"

"Thank you," Taylor said at her back. B.J. jumped. "Eddie, I believe the Bodwin sisters are looking for you," he added.

"Oh, yes, sir." Face flaming, Eddie shot off, leaving B.J. in the very position she had sought to avoid.

"Well, well." Taylor surveyed her, an encompassing, thoroughly male examination, lingering on the point where her blouse joined above her breasts. "I trust your date has a high boiling point."

She started to snap that Howard had no boiling point at all, but changed her mind. "Do you really like it?" Tossing clouds of hair over her shoulder, B.J. gave Taylor the benefit of a melting, sultry smile.

"Let's say I might find it appealing under different circumstances," he said dryly.

Pleased to observe he was annoyed, B.J. recklessly gave his cheek a brief pat and glided to the door. "Good night, Taylor. Don't wait up now." Triumphant, she stepped out into the pink-clouded evening.

Howard's reaction to her appearance caused her ego to soar yet higher. He swallowed, eyes blinking rapidly, and stammered in small, incoherent sentences the entire distance to town. Finding this a pleasant change from self-assured amusement, B.J. basked in his admiration as she watched the hazy sun sink beyond the hills through the car window.

In town, the streets were already quiet with the midweek, mid evening hush which isolates small towns from the outside world. A few windows glowed like cats' eyes in the dark, but most of the houses had bedded down for the night like so many contented domestic pets.

At the far end of town where the theater was, there were more signs of activity. Howard pulled into the parking lot with his usual, plodding precision. The neon sign glowed somewhat ludicrously against the quiet sky. The *L* in PLAZA had been retired for the past six months.

"I wonder," B.J. mused as she alighted from Howard's sensible Buick, "if Mr. Jarvis will ever get that sign fixed or if each of the letters will die a quiet death." Howard's answer was muffled by the car door slam. She was faintly surprised as he took her arm with a possessive air and led her into the theater.

An hour through the feature, B.J decided Howard was not at all himself. He did not consume his popcorn with his usual voracity, nor did he shift throughout the film on the undeniably uncomfortable seats the Plaza offered. Rather, he sat in a glazed-eyed state that seemed almost catatonic.

"Howard." Keeping her voice low, B.J. placed her hand on his. To her surprise he jumped as though she had pinched him. "Howard, are you all right?"

Her astonishment changed to stunned disbelief when he grabbed her, scattering popcorn, and pressed a passionate if fumbling kiss to her mouth. At first, B.J. sat stunned. All other advances by Howard had consisted of a brotherly embrace at the door of the inn. Then, hearing a few snickers from the back of the theater, she wiggled from his arms and pushed against his stocky chest.

"Howard, behave yourself!" She gave an exasperated sigh and straightened in her seat.

Abruptly, Howard gripped her arm and pulled her to her feet, dragging her up the aisle and out of the theater.

"Howard, have you lost your mind?"

"I couldn't sit in there any more," he muttered, bundling her into his car. "It's too crowded."

"Crowded?" She blew an errant curl from her eyes. "Howard, there couldn't have been more than twenty people in there. I think you should see a doctor." She patted his shoulder then tested his brow for signs of fever. "You're a bit warm and not at all yourself. I can get a ride back, you'd better just go home."

"No!" There was no mistaking the vehemence of his tone.

B.J. gave Howard a long, searching stare before settling back uneasily into her seat. Though it was too dark to tell much, he appeared to be concentrating on his driving. He drove rapidly over the winding country road. Soon B.J. was able to distinguish the blinking lights of the hotel.

Suddenly, Howard pulled off the road and seized her. In the beginning, B.J. was more surprised than angry. "Stop it! Stop this, Howard! What in the world has gotten into you?"

"B.J." His mouth searched for hers, and this time his kiss was neither fumbling nor brotherly. "You're so beautiful." His groping hand reached for her blouse.

"Howard Beall, I'm ashamed of you!" B.J. remonstrated, pushing Howard firmly away and sliding toward the car door. "You get home right now and take a cold shower and go to bed!"

"But, B.J.—"

"I mean it." She wrenched open the car door and jumped out. Standing by the road, she tossed back her hair and adjusted her clothes. "I'm walking right back to the inn before you grow fangs again. Consider yourself lucky if I don't say something to your aunt about your temporary bout of insanity." Turning, she began the half-mile hike to the hotel.

Ten minutes later, shoes in hand and muttering disjointed imprecations toward the entire male sex, B.J. panted up the steep hill. The shadowy trees sighed softly in the moonlight. A lone owl hooted above her. But B.J. was in no mood for the beauties of the evening. "You be quiet," she commanded, glaring up at the bundle of feathers.

"I haven't said anything yet," a deep voice answered.

On the verge of screaming, B.J. found a hand over her mouth. Struggling to escape, she found a hard arm gripping her around the waist. "What the—?"

"Out for a stroll?" Taylor inquired mildly, releasing her. "It does seem an odd place to take a walk," he commented.

"Very funny." She managed two outraged steps before he caught her wrist.

"What's the matter? Your friend run out of gas?"

"Listen, I don't need this right now." Realizing she had dropped her shoes in her fright, B.J. searched the ground. "I've just walked a hundred miles after wrestling with a crazy man."

"Did he hurt you?" The grip on her wrist increased, as Taylor examined her more closely.

"Of course not." Tossing back her hair, B.J. let out a sigh of exasperation. "Howard wouldn't hurt a fly. I don't know what came over him. He's never acted like that before."

"Are you really that artless, or am I watching the second feature?" At her baffled expression, Taylor took her shoulders and administered a brief shake. "Grow up, B.J.! Look at yourself, the poor guy didn't have a chance."

"Don't be ridiculous." She shrugged out of his hold. "Howard's known me forever. He's never behaved like this before. He's just been reading too many romances or something. Good grief, I used to go skinny dipping with him when I was ten years old."

"Has anyone bothered to point out that you're no longer ten years old?"

Something in his voice made her raise her eyes to his.

"Stand still, B.J." He spoke in quiet command, and she felt her knees tremble. "I feel like a mountain lion stalking a house kitten."

For a moment, they stood apart, the stars glimmering above their heads, the moon a pale white guardian. Somewhere, a nightbird called to its mate, a plaintive sound. It echoed into silence as she melted in his arms.

She rose on her toes to offer him the gift of her mouth, her sigh of surrender merging with the wind's murmur. Her breasts crushed against his chest as his hands molded her hips closer. For this moment, she was his. Her heart sought no past or future but only the warmth and knowledge of now—the eternity of the present. She moaned with pleasure as his mouth sought the curve of her neck. Her fingers tangled with his dark hair as his mouth met hers again and she opened her lips to his kiss.

Locked together, they were oblivious to the sounds of night; the sigh of wind, the mellow call of an owl and the chirp of crickets. With a harsh suddenness, the inn door opened, pooling them in artificial light.

"Oh, Taylor, I've been waiting for you."

B.J. pulled away in humiliation as Darla leaned against the doorway, draped in a flowing black negligee. Her ivory skin gleamed against the lace. Her smooth, raven hair fell loose and full down her back.

"What for?" Taylor's question was abrupt.

Darla pouted and moved lace clad shoulders. "Taylor, darling, don't be a bear."

Devastated that he should have used her so blatantly while he had another woman waiting, B.J. stooped to retrieve her shoes.

"Where do you think you're going?" Taylor captured her wrist and aborted her quick escape.

"To my room," B.J. informed him with her last vestige of calm. "It appears you have a previous engagement."

"Just a minute."

"Please, let me go. I've done my quota of wrestling for one evening."

His fingers tightened on her flesh. "I'm tempted to wring your neck." Taylor tossed her wrist away as though the small contact was abhorrent.

Turning on bare heels, B.J. rushed up the steps and past a sweetly smiling Darla.

Chapter 9

B.J. moved her files to her room. There, she determined, she could work in peace without Taylor's disturbing presence. She immersed herself in paperwork and tried to block all else from her mind. The gray, drizzling rain which hissed at her windows set the stage for her mood. Thick, low hanging clouds allowed no breath of sun. Still, her eyes were drawn to the misty curtain, her mind floating with the clear rivulets which ran down the glass. Shaking her head to bring herself to order, B.J. concentrated on her linen supply.

Her door swung open, and she turned from the slant top desk. With sinking heart, she watched Taylor enter.

"Hiding out?"

It was apparent from the set of his mouth that his mood had not mellowed since her departure the previous evening.

"No." The lifting of her chin was instinctive. "It's simply more convenient for me to work out of my room while you need the office."

"I see." He towered menacingly over her desk, making her feel small and insignificant. "Darla tells me you two had quite a session yesterday in the lounge."

B.J.'s mouth opened in surprise. She could not believe Darla would have disclosed her own behavior so readily.

"I warned you, B.J., that as long as Darla is a guest at the inn, you're to treat her with the same courtesy you show all other guests."

B.J. was astonished. "I'm sorry, Taylor, perhaps I'm dim. Would you mind explaining that?"

"She told me you were inexcusably rude, that you made some comments on her relationship with me, refused to serve her a drink, made yourself generally unpleasant, and told the staff not to cooperate with her."

"She said that, did she?" B.J.'s eyes darkened with rage. She set her pen down carefully and rose despite Taylor's proximity. "Isn't it odd how two people can view the same scene from entirely different perspectives! Well." She stuck her hands in her pockets and planted her feet firmly. "I have news for you—"

"If you've another version," Taylor returned evenly, "I'd like to hear it."

"Oh!" Unable to prevent herself, she lifted her fist to give his chest a small, inadequate punch. His eyes dropped to it in amused indulgence. "How generous of you. The condemned man is given a fair trial." Whirling, she paced the room in a swirl of agitation, debating whether to give him a verbatim account of her meeting with Darla. Finally, her pride won over her desire to clear herself in Taylor's eyes. "No thanks, your honor. I'll just take the fifth."

"B.J." Taylor took her shoulders and spun her to face him. "Must you constantly provoke me?"

"Must you constantly pick on me?" she countered.

"I wouldn't have said I was doing that." His tone had changed from anger to consideration.

"That's your opinion. I'm the one who's constantly in the position of justifying myself. I'm tired of having to explain my every move, of trying to cope with your moods. I never know from one minute to the next if you're going to kiss me or sit me in the corner with a dunce hat. I'm tired of feeling inadequate, naive and stupid. I never felt like any of those things before, and I don't like it."

Her words tumbled out in a furious rush while Taylor merely looked on, politely attentive.

"And I'm sick of your precious Darla altogether. Sick of her criticizing every aspect of the inn, sick of her looking at me as though I were some straw-chewing hick from Dogpatch. And, I resent her running to you with fabricated stories, and, I detest your using me to boost your over-inflated ego while she's floating around half naked waiting to warm your bed. And... Oh, blast!"

Her torrent of complaints was interrupted by the shrill ringing of the phone. Ripping the receiver from its cradle, B.J. snapped into it.

"What is it? No, nothing's wrong. What is it, Eddie?" Pausing, she listened, her hand lifting to soothe the back of her neck where tension lodged. "Yes, he's here." She turned back to Taylor and held out the phone. "It's for you, a Mr. Paul Bailey."

He took the receiver in silence, his eyes still on her face. As she turned to leave the room, his hand caught her wrist. "Stay here." Waiting for her nod of agreement, he released her. B.J. moved to the far side of the room and stared out at the insistent rain.

Taylor's conversation consisted of monosyllabic replies which B.J. blocked from her mind. Frustrated by the inability to complete her outburst, she now felt the impetus fading. Just as well, she admitted with a sigh of weary resignation. I've already said enough to insure the job at that dog kennel Darla mentioned. Blast! She rested her forehead on the cool glass. Why did I have to fall in love with an impossible man?

"B.J." She started at the sound of her name, then twisted her head to watch Taylor cradle the phone. "Pack," he said simply and moved to the door.

Closing her eyes, she tried to tell herself it was better that she leave, better not to be connected with him even as an employee. Nodding mutely, she turned back to the window.

"Enough for three days," he added in afterthought as his hand closed over the knob.

"What?" Thrown into confusion, she turned, staring with a mixture of grief and bewilderment.

"We'll be gone for three days. Be ready in fifteen minutes." Halting, Taylor's features softened suddenly at her clouded expression. "B.J., I'm not firing you. Give me credit for a bit more class than that."

She shook her head, washed with relief and the

knowledge of the inevitable. He started to cross the room, then paused and merely leaned against the closed door.

"That was a call from the manager of one of my resorts. There's a bit of a problem, and I've got to see to it. You're coming with me."

"Coming with you?" Her fingers lifted to her temple as if she could smooth in understanding. "What on earth for?"

"In the first place, because I say so." He folded his arms across his chest and became the complete employer. "And secondly, because I like my managers well rounded. No pun intended," he added, smiling as her color rose. "This is a good opportunity for you to see how my other hotels are run."

"But I can't just leave at a moment's notice," she objected, as her mind struggled to cope with the new development. "Who'll take care of things here?"

"Eddie will. It's about time he had a bit more responsibility. You let him lean on you too much. You let all of them lean on you too much."

"But we have five new reservations over the weekend, and…"

"You're down to ten minutes, B.J.," he informed her with a glance at his watch. "If you don't stop arguing, you'll only have the clothes on your back to take with you."

Seeing all of her objections would be overruled, she tried not to think of what going away with Taylor would do to her nervous system. *Business,* she reminded herself. *Just business.*

Somewhat annoyed that he was already walking

through the door, having taken it for granted that she was going with him, she called after him, "I can't simply pack because you say to."

He turned back, his temper fraying. "B.J."

"You never said where," she reminded him. "I don't know if I need mukluks or bikinis."

A ghost of a smile played on his lips before he answered. "Bikinis. We're going to Palm Beach."

B.J. was to find her surprises were not yet over for the morning. First, her last minute flurry of instructions was cut off by Taylor's order as she was bundled out of the dripping rain and into his car. On the drive to the airport, she mentally reviewed every possible disaster which could occur during her absence. She opened her mouth to enlighten Taylor only to be given a quelling look which had her suffering in silence.

At the airport, she found herself confronted not with a commercial jet, but with Taylor's private one, already primed for take-off. B.J. stood motionless staring at the small trim plane as he retrieved their luggage.

"B.J., don't stand in the rain. Go on up."

"Taylor." Unmindful of the rain which pelted her, B.J. turned to him. "I think there's something you should know. I'm not very good at flying."

"That's all right." He secured cases under his arm and grabbed her hand. "The plane does most of the work."

"Taylor, I'm serious," she objected, as he dragged her inside the plane.

"Do you get air sick? You can take a pill."

"No." She swallowed and lifted her shoulders. "I get

paralyzed. Stewardesses have been known to stow me in the baggage compartment so I don't panic the other passengers."

He rubbed his hands briskly through her hair, scattering rain drops. "So, I've found your weakness. What are you afraid of?"

"Mostly of crashing."

"It's all in your head," he said easily as he helped her off with her jacket. "There's a term for it."

"Dying," she supplied, causing him to laugh again. Miffed by his amusement, she turned away to examine the plush luxury of the cabin. "This looks more like an apartment than a plane." She ran a hand over the soft maroon of a chair. "Everyone's entitled to a phobia," she muttered.

"You're absolutely right." His voice trembled on the edge of laughter. B.J. turned to snap at him but found his smile too appealing.

"You won't think it's so funny when I'm lying in a moaning heap on your shag carpet."

"Possibly not." He moved toward her and she stiffened in defense. Brooding down at her a moment, he searched her wary gray eyes. "B.J.," he began, "shall we call a moratorium on our disagreements? At least for the duration of the trip?"

"Well, I…" His voice was soft and persuasive, and she lowered her eyes to study the buttons of his shirt.

"An armed truce?" he suggested, capturing her chin between his thumb and forefinger and lifting her face. "With negotiations to follow?" He was smiling, his charming, utterly disarming smile. She knew resistance was hopeless.

"All right, Taylor." Unable to prevent her own smile from blossoming, she remained still as his finger lifted to trace it.

"Sit down and fasten your seat belt." He kissed her brow with an easy friendliness which left her weak.

B.J. found that the easy flow of his conversation from the moment of take off eased her tension. Incredibly, she felt no fear as the plane soared into the air.

"It's so flat and so warm!" B.J. exclaimed as she stepped off the plane steps and looked around her.

Taylor chuckled as he led the way to a sleek black Porsche. He exchanged a few words with a waiting attendant, accepted the keys, unlocked the door, and motioned B.J. inside.

"Where is your hotel?" she asked.

"In Palm Beach. This is West Palm Beach. We have to cross Lake Worth to get to the island."

"Oh!" Enchanted by roadside palms, she lapsed into silence.

The white, sandy soil and splashes of brilliant blossoms were so far removed from the scenery of her native New England, she felt as though she had entered another world. The waters of Lake Worth, separating Palm Beach from the mainland, sparkled blue and white under the afternoon sun. The oceanside was lined with resort hotels. B.J. recognized the elaborate initials *T.R.* atop a sleek white building which rose twelve stories over the Atlantic. Hundreds of windows winked back at her. Taylor pulled into the semi-circular macadam drive and stopped the car. B.J. narrowed her eyes against the streaming rays of the sun. The archway which formed the entrance was guarded by palms and semi-tropical plants, their tangle of color obviously well planned and scrupulously tended. The lawn spread, perfectly level and unbelievably green.

"Come," said Taylor, coming around to open the door for her. He helped her out of the car and led her inside.

To B.J. the lobby was a tropical paradise. The floor was flagstoned, the walls a half-circle of windows at the front. A center fountain played over a rocky garden, dotted with lush plants and ferns. B.J. saw that the interior was round, an open circle spiraling to the ceiling where a mural emulating the sky had been painted. The effect was one of limitless space. *How different from the cozy familiarity of the Lakeside Inn!* she thought.

"Ah, Mr. Reynolds." Her meditation was interrupted by the appearance of a slender, well dressed man with a shock of steel gray hair and a lean, bronzed face. "So good to see you."

"Paul." Taylor accepted the proffered hand and returned the smile of greeting. "B.J., this is Paul Bailey, the manager. Paul, B.J. Clark."

"A pleasure, Miss Clark." B.J.'s hand was engulfed by a smooth, warm grasp. His eyes surveyed her fresh, slender beauty with approval. She found herself smiling back.

"See to our bags and I'll take Miss Clark up. After we've settled in a bit, I'll get back to you."

"Of course. Everything's quite ready." With another flash of teeth, he led the way to the registration desk and secured a key. "Your bags will be right up, Mr. Reynolds. Is there anything else you'd like?"

"Not at the moment. B.J.?"

"What?" B.J. was still admiring the luxurious lobby.

"Would you like anything?" Taylor smiled at her and brushed a curl from her cheek.

"Oh…no, nothing. Thank you."

With a final nod for Bailey, Taylor secured her hand in his and led her to one of the three elevators. They glided up in a cage of octagon glass high above the cluster of greenery.

When they reached the top floor, Taylor moved along the thick carpeting to unlock the door. B.J. entered and crossing the silent plush of ivory carpet, stared down from the dizzying height at the white beach which jutted out into an azure span of sea. In the distance, she could see the churning whitecaps and the flowing grace of gulls as they circled and dove.

"What an incredible view. I'm tempted to dive straight off the balcony." Turning, she caught Taylor watching her from the center of the room. She could not decipher the expression in his eyes. "This is lovely," she said to break the long silence.

She ran a finger over the smooth surface of an ebony bar and wondered if Darla had decorated the room. Grudgingly, she admitted to herself if this were the case, Darla had done a good job.

"Would you like a drink?" Taylor pushed a button cunningly concealed in the mirror tiles on the wall behind the bar. A panel slid open to reveal a fully stocked bar.

"Very clever," B.J. smiled. "Some club soda would be nice," she said, leaning elbows on the bar.

"Nothing stronger?" he asked as he poured the soda

over crackling ice. "Come in," he responded to the quiet knock on the door.

"Your luggage, Mr. Reynolds." A red-and-black-uniformed bellboy carried in the cases. B.J. was conscious of his curious gaze and blushed self-consciously.

"Fine, just leave them there." He accepted the tip from Taylor and vanished, closing the door with quiet respect.

B.J. eyed the cases. Taylor's elegant gray sat neatly beside her practical brown. "Why did he bring it all in here?" Setting down her glass, she lifted her eyes. "Shouldn't he have just taken mine to my room?"

"He did." Taylor secured another bottle and poured himself a portion of Scotch.

"But, I thought this was your suite." B.J. glanced around the luxurious room again.

"It is."

"But you just said…" She faltered, as her color rose. "Surely you don't think I'm going to—to…"

"What did you have in mind?" Taylor inquired with infuriating amusement.

"You said you wanted me to see how one of your other hotels was run, you never said anything about… about…"

"You really must learn to complete a sentence, B.J."

"I'm not sleeping with you," she stated very positively, her eyes like two summer storm clouds.

"I don't believe I asked you to," he said lazily before he took an easy sip of Scotch. "There are two very adequate bedrooms in this suite. I'm sure you'll find yours comfortable."

Embarrassment flooded her cheeks. "I'm not stay-

ing in here with you. Everyone will think that I'm...
that we're..."

"I've never known you to be quite so coherent." His
mockery increased her wrath, and her eyes narrowed
to dangerous slits. "In any case," he continued unper-
turbed, "the purity of your reputation is already in question. As you're traveling with me, it will naturally be
assumed that we're lovers. As we know differently,"
he went on as her mouth dropped open, "that hardly
matters. Of course, if you'd like to make rumor fact, I
might be persuaded."

"Oh, you insufferable, egotistical, conceited..."

"Name calling can hardly be considered persuasion,"
Taylor admonished, patting her head in an infuriating
manner. "I assume, therefore, you'll want your own
bedroom?"

"As this is off season," B.J. began, gaining a tenuous grip on her temper, "I'm sure there are a surplus of
available rooms."

Smiling, he ran a finger down her arm. "Afraid you
won't be able to resist temptation, B.J.?"

"Of course not," she said though her senses tingled
at his touch.

"Then that's settled," he said, finishing off his drink.
"If you're harboring the notion that I'll be overcome
by lust, there's a perfectly sturdy lock on your bedroom door. I'm going down to see Bailey; why don't you
change and grab some time at the beach? Your room's
the second door on your left down the hall." He pointed
as he moved to the door and slipped through before she
had time to frame a response.

* * *

Before lifting her case and beginning to unpack, B.J. thought of at least a half a dozen withering remarks she should have made. However, she soon regained her sense of proportion.

After all, it wasn't every day that she had the opportunity to indulge in such luxury. She might as well enjoy it. Besides, the suite was certainly large enough for both of them.

Slipping into brief tan shorts and a lime green halter, B.J. decided to finish her unpacking later and head for the beach.

Taylor had certainly made the most of nature's gift, offering a luxury playground with an ocean and sky backdrop. B.J. had seen the huge mosaic tiled pool for those who preferred its filtered water to the sea. On her way to the beach, she glimpsed at the expanse of tennis courts with palms and flowering shrubs skirting about the entrance gate. She had seen enough of the hotel's interior to be certain that Taylor left his guests wanting for nothing.

From the beach B.J. shaded her eyes and studied again the perfection of the imposing resort. It was, she admitted with a sigh, elegantly appealing. As far out of her realm as its owner. *Egg noodles and caviar,* she thought ruefully, reflecting both on the comparison between inn and resort and Taylor and herself. They simply don't belong on the same plate.

"Hello."

Startled, B.J. turned, blinked against the brilliant sun and stared at an even white smile in a bronzed face.

"Hello." Returning the smile with a bit more caution, B.J. studied the attractive face surrounded by thick masses of light, sun bleached hair.

"Aren't you going to give the ocean a try?"

"Not today."

"That's very unusual." He fell into step beside her as she began to cross the sand. "Usually everyone spends their first day roasting and splashing."

"How did you know it was my first day?" B.J. asked.

"Because I haven't noticed you here before, and I would have." He gave her an encompassing and intensely male survey. "And because you're still peaches and cream instead of parboiled."

"Hardly the time of year," B.J. commented, admiring the deep, even tan as he shrugged on his shirt. "I'd say you've been here for some time."

"Two years," he returned, with an appealing grin. "I'm the tennis pro, Chad Hardy."

"B.J. Clark." She paused on the tiled walkway which led to the hotel's beach entrance. "How come you're on the beach instead of the courts?"

"My day off," he explained and surprised her by winding the tips of her hair around his finger. "But if you'd like a private lesson, it could be arranged."

"No, thanks," she declined lightly and turned again toward the door.

"How about dinner?" Chad captured her hand, gently but insistently bringing her back to face him.

"I don't think so."

"A drink?"

She smiled at his persistence. "No, sorry, it's a bit early."

"I'll wait."

Laughing, she shook her head and disengaged her hand. "No, but I appreciate the offer. Goodbye, Mr. Hardy."

"Chad." He moved with her through the archway into the hotel's coolness. "What about tomorrow? Breakfast, lunch, a weekend in Vegas?"

B.J. laughed; such ingenuous charm was hard to resist. "I don't think you'll have any trouble finding a companion."

"I'm having a great deal of trouble securing the one I want," he countered. "If you had any compassion, you'd take pity on me."

With a rueful smile, B.J. surrendered. "All right, I wouldn't mind an orange juice."

In short order, B.J. found herself seated at an umbrella table beside the pool.

"It's not really that early," Chad objected when she adhered to her choice of fruit juice. "Most of the crowd is straggling in to wash off the sand and change for dinner."

"This hits the spot." She sipped from the frosted glass. Then, gesturing with one slender hand, she glanced around at green fan palms and scarlet blooms. "You must find it easy to work here."

"It suits me," Chad agreed, swirling his own drink. "I like the work, the sun." He lifted his glass and smiled with the half toast. "And the benefits." His smile widened. Before she had the opportunity to draw them away, his hand captured her fingers. "How long will you be here?"

"A couple of days." She let her hand lie limp, feeling

a struggle would make her appear foolish. "This was actually a spur-of-the-moment trip rather than a vacation."

"Then I'll drink to spur-of-the-moment trip," said Chad.

The friendly, polished charm was potent, and B.J. could not resist beaming him a smile. "Is that your best serve?"

"Just a warm-up." Returning the smile, his grip on her hand tightened slightly. "Watch out for my ace."

"B.J."

Twisting her head, she stared up at Taylor, frowning above her. "Hello, Taylor. Are you finished with Mr. Bailey?"

"For the moment." His glance shifted to Chad, drifted over their joined hands and returned to her face. "I've been looking for you."

"Oh?" Feeling unaccountably guilty, B.J. nibbled her lip in a tell-tale sign of agitation. "I'm sorry, this is Chad Hardy," she began.

"Yes, I know. Hello, Hardy."

"Mr. Reynolds," Chad returned with a polite nod. "I didn't know you were in the hotel."

"For a day or two. When you've finished," he continued, giving B.J. the full benefit of a cold disapproving stare, "I suggest you come up and change for dinner. I don't think that outfit's suitable for the dining room." With a curt nod, he turned on his heel and stalked away.

"Well, well." Releasing her hand, Chad leaned back in his chair and studied B.J. with new interest. "You might have told me you were the big man's lady. I'm rather fond of my job here."

Her mouth opened and closed twice. "I am not Taylor's lady," B.J. spurted on her third try.

Chad's lips twisted in a wry grin. "You'd better tell him that. A pity." He sighed with exaggerated regret. "I was working on some interesting fantasies, but I steer clear of treading on dangerous ground."

Standing, he lifted her chin and gave her a rather wistful smile. "If you find yourself down here again without complications, look me up."

Chapter 10

The emphatic slamming of the suite's door gave B.J. small satisfaction. Advancing with purpose on Taylor's bedroom, she pounded on his door.

"Looking for me?" The voice was dry.

She whirled around. For a moment, she could only gape at the sight of Taylor leaning against the bathroom door, clad only in a dark green towel tied low over lean hips. His hair fell in tendrils over the lean planes of his face.

"Yes, I..." She faltered and swallowed. "Yes," she repeated with more firmness as she recalled Chad's comments. "That was an uncalled for exhibition out there. You deliberately left Chad with the impression that I was your..." She hesitated, eyes darkening with outraged impotence, as she searched for the right word.

"Mistress?" Taylor suggested amiably.

B.J.'s pupils dilated with fury. "He at least used the term lady." Forgetting the corded arms and dark mat of hair covering his chest, she stalked forward until she stood toe to toe. "You did it on purpose, and I won't tolerate it."

"Oh, really?" Had she not been so involved venting her own anger, B.J. might have recognized the dangerous pitch of his voice. "It appears by the speed with which Hardy lured you into his corner, you're remarkably easy prey. I feel it's my obligation to look out for you."

"Find someone else to protect," she retorted. "I'm not putting up with it."

"Just what do you intend to do about it?" The simple arrogance of the question was accompanied by a like smile which robbed B.J. of all coherency. "If giving Hardy and others of his type the impression that you're my property keeps you from making a fool of yourself, that's precisely what I'll do. Actually," he continued, "you should be grateful."

"Grateful?" B.J. repeated, her voice rising. "Your property? *A fool of myself?* Of all the arrogant, unspeakable gall!"

Her arm pulled back with the intention of connecting her fist with his midsection, but she found it twisted behind her back with astonishing speed. Her body was crushed against the hard undraped lines of his.

"I wouldn't try that again." The warning was soft. "You wouldn't like the consequences." His free hand lowered to her hip, bringing her closer as she tried to back away. "Don't do that," he ordered, holding her still and trapped against him. "You'll just hurt yourself. It seems we've broken our truce." His words were light, though she saw the signs of lingering temper in his eyes.

"You started it." Her declaration was half-defiant, half-defensive. She kept her eyes level with sheer determination.

"Did I?" he murmured before he took her mouth.

She was washed by the familiar flood of need. Offering no struggle, she went willingly into the uncharted world where only the senses ruled. His hand released her arm in order to roam over the bareness of her back, and she circled his neck, wanting only to remain in the drifting heat and velvet darkness.

Abruptly, he set her free. She stumbled back against the wall, thrown off balance by the swiftness of her liberation.

"Go change." He turned and gripped the knob of his door.

B.J. reached out to touch his arm.

"Taylor…"

"Go change!" he shouted. She stumbled back again, eyes round and wide at the swift flare of violence. He slammed the door behind him.

B.J. retreated to her room to sort out her feelings. Was it injured pride? Or was it rage? She could not for the life of her tell.

The early sky lightened slowly from black to misty blue. The stars faded, then died as the sun still lay hidden beneath the horizon. B.J. rose, grateful the restless night was behind her.

She had shared an uncomfortably polite dinner with Taylor, the elegance of the dining room only adding to

the sensation that she had stood aside and watched two
strangers go through the motions of dining. Taylor's
solicitous and unfamiliar formality had disturbed her
more than his sudden seething fury. Her own responses
had been stilted and cool. Immediately after dinner she
pleaded fatigue and crept off unescorted to pass the
evening hours alone and miserably awake in her room.

It had been late when she had heard Taylor's key in
the lock, his footsteps striding down the hall to pause
outside her room. She had held her breath as if he might
sense her wakefulness through the panel. Not until she
had heard the muffled sound of his door closing had
she let it out again.

B.J. felt no better the next morning. The events of the
day before had left her with a lingering sense of loss and
sorrow. Though she knew that there was little hope, she
had finally acknowledged to herself that she was in love
with Taylor. But there was no point thinking about it.

She slipped on her bikini, grabbed a terry robe, and
tiptoed from her room.

The view from the wide window in the living room
drew her. With a sigh of pleasure, she moved closer to
watch the birth of day. The sun had tinted the edge of
sea and sky with rose-gold streaks. Pinks and mauves
shot through the dawning sky.

"Quite a view."

With a gasp, B.J. spun around, nearly colliding with
Taylor whose footsteps had been hidden by the thickness of carpet. "Yes," she returned as their hands lifted
simultaneously to brush back the fall of her hair which
tumbled to her cheek. "There's nothing so beautiful as

a sunrise." Disturbed by his closeness, she found her own words silly.

He was clad only in short denim cut-offs, frayed at the cuffs.

"How did you sleep?" His voice was politely concerned.

She shrugged off his question, evading a direct lie. "I thought I'd take an early swim before the beach gets crowded."

Deliberately, he turned her to face him, while he searched her face with habitual thoroughness. "Your eyes are shadowed." His finger traced the mauve smudges as a frown deepened the angles of his face. "I don't believe I've ever seen you look tired before. You seem to have some inner vitality that continually feeds itself. You look pale and fragile, quite unlike the pigtailed brat I watched sliding into home plate."

His touch was radiating the weakness through her so she stepped back in defense. "I…It's just the first night in a strange bed."

"Is it?" His brow lifted. "You're a generous creature, B.J. You don't even expect an apology, do you?"

Charmed by his smile, her weariness evaporated. "Taylor, I want…I'd like it if we could be friends." She finished in an impulsive rush.

"Friends?" he repeated as the sudden boyish grin split his face. "Oh, B.J., you're sweet, if a bit slow." Taking both hands in his, he lifted them to his lips before speaking again. "All right, friend, let's go for a swim."

But for gulls, the beach was deserted, a stretch of white pure and welcoming. The air already glowed with the promise of heat and light. B.J. stopped and gazed around, pleased with the quiet and the solitude.

"It's like everyone went away."

"You're not much for crowds, are you, B.J.?"

"No, I suppose not." She turned to him with a lift of bare shoulders. "I enjoy people, but more on a one to one level. When I'm around people, I like to know who they are, what they need. I'm good with small problems. I can shore up a brick here, hammer a nail there. I don't think I'm equipped to construct an entire building the way you are."

"One can't keep a building standing without someone shoring up bricks and hammering nails."

She smiled, so obviously pleased and surprised by his observation that he laughed and tousled her hair. "I'll race you to the water."

Giving him a considering look, B.J. shook her head in reluctance. "You're a lot taller than I am. You have an advantage."

"You forget, I've seen you run. And—" His eyes dropped to the length of shapely legs. "For a small woman, you have amazingly long legs."

"Well." She drew the word out, lips pursed. "O.K." Without waiting for his assent, she streaked across the sand and plunged into the sea, striking out with long strokes.

She was brought up short by hands on her waist. Laughing, she struggled away, only to be caught and submerged in the ensuing tussle.

"Taylor, you're going to drown me," she protested as her legs tangled with his.

"That is not my intention," he informed her as he

drew her closer. "Hold still a minute or you'll take your-self under again."

Relaxing in his hold, B.J. allowed him to keep them both afloat. She permitted herself a few moments of ecstasy cradled in his arms as the water pooled around them like a cool satin blanket. The change began like a gradual drizzle as she became more aware of his shoul-der beneath her cheek, the possessive hold of the arm which banded her bare waist. Powerless to resist, she floated with him as his lips descended to the sleek cap of her hair, then wandered to tease the lobe of her ear with tongue and teeth before moving to the curve of her neck. His fingers traced the low line of the bikini snug at her hips as his mouth roamed her cheek in its journey to hers.

Her lips parted before he requested it, but his kiss remained gentle, the passion simmering just below the surface. His hand touched and fondled, slipping easily under the barrier of her brief top to trail over the curve of her breast. The water sighed gently as flesh met flesh.

What with gentle caresses, the drifting buoyancy of the sea, and the growing heat of the ascending sun B.J. fell into a trancelike state. Perhaps, she thought, mind and limbs lethargic, she was meant to float forever in his arms. She shivered with pleasure.

"You're getting cold," Taylor murmured, drawing her away to study her face. "Come on." He released her, leaving her without support in the sighing sea. The magic shattered. "We'll sit in the sun."

B.J. started for the shore with Taylor swimming eas-ily beside her.

On the beach, she fanned her hair in the sun while

Taylor stretched negligently beside her. She tried not
to look at the strong planes of his face, his bronzed,
glistening skin.

He told me how it would be, she reminded herself.
Right from the beginning. I don't seem to be able to
do anything about it and if I don't, I'll end up being
just another Darla in his life. Bringing her knees to
her chest, she rested her chin on them and stared at the
distant horizon. He's attracted to me for some reason,
perhaps because I'm different from other women in his
life. I haven't their sophistication or experience and I
suppose he finds that appealing and amusing. I don't
know how to fight both loving him and wanting him.
If it were just physical, I could avoid being hurt. If it
were only an attraction, I could resist him.

She recalled suddenly his quick violence of the previous day and realized he was a man capable of em-
ploying whatever means necessary to gain an objective.
At the moment, she knew he was playing her like a patient fisherman casting his line into calm waters. But
ultimately, they both knew she would be captured in
his net. Though it might be silk, it would still lead to
eventual disaster.

"You're very far away." Sitting up, Taylor tangled
his fingers in her damp hair and turned her to face him.

Silently, she studied every plane and angle of his
face, engraving them on both heart and mind. *There
is too much strength there,* she thought, rocked by a
surge of love. Too much virility, too much knowledge.
She scrambled to her feet, needing to postpone the inevitable.

"I'm starving," she claimed. "Are you going to spring for breakfast? After all, I did win the race."

"Did you?" He rose as she pulled the short robe over the briefness of her bikini.

"Yes," she said, "positively." Picking up Taylor's light blue pullover, she held it out. "I was the undisputed winner." She watched as he dragged the snug, crew necked shirt over his head then bent to retrieve the towels.

"Then you should buy my breakfast." Smiling, he held out his hand. After a brief hesitation, she accepted.

"How do you feel about corn flakes?"

"Unenthusiastic."

"Well." Her shoulders moved in regret. "I'm afraid my funds are rather limited as I was hauled to Florida without ceremony."

"Your credit's good." He released her hand and swung a friendly arm around her shoulders. They moved away from the sea.

By mid afternoon, B.J. felt euphoric. There was a new, charming friendliness about Taylor that made her realize she liked him every bit as much as she loved him.

She was given a thorough if belated tour of the hotel, allowed to wander through the silver and cobalt lounge, linger in the two elegantly stocked boutiques and examine the enormous expanse of the steel and white kitchen. In the game room, she was provided with an endless supply of change as Taylor watched her reckless enthusiasm with tolerance.

Leaning against a machine, he looked on as she steered her computer car to another horrendous wreck.

"You know," he commented as she held her hand for another quarter, "by the time you've finished, you'll have spent every bit as much as that dress in the boutique cost. Why is it, you'll take the money for these noisy machines, but you refuse to let me buy you that very appealing dress?"

"This is different," she said vaguely, maneuvering the car around obstructions.

"How?" He grimaced as she narrowly missed an unwary pedestrian and skidded around a corner.

"You never said if you worked out the problem," B.J. murmured as she twisted the wheel to avoid a slow moving vehicle.

"Problem?"

"Yes, the one you came down here to see to."

"Oh, yes." He smiled and brushed an insistent wisp from her cheek. "It's working out nicely."

"Oh, blast!" B.J. frowned as her car careened into a telephone pole, flipped through the air and landed with an impressive show of computer color and sound.

"Come on." Taylor grabbed her hand as she looked up hopefully. "Let's have some lunch before I go bankrupt."

On the sundeck above the pool, they enjoyed quiche Lorraine and Chablis. A handful of people splashed and romped in the pale blue water. Toying with the remains of her meal, B.J. stared down at the swimmers and sun bathers. Her gaze swept to include the curve of beach before returning to Taylor. He was watching her, a small secret smile on his lips and in his eyes. She blinked in confused embarrassment.

"Is something wrong?" Battling the urge to wipe her

cheek to see if it was smudged, she lifted her glass and sipped the cool wine.

"No, I just enjoy looking at you. Your eyes are constantly changing hues. One minute they're like peat smoke, and the next clear as a lake. You'll never be able to keep secrets; they say too much." His smile spread as her color rose. Her eyes shifted to the golden lights in her glass. "You're an incredibly beautiful creature, B.J."

She lifted her head, her eyes wide in surprise.

With a light chuckle, he captured her hand and brought it to his lips. "I don't suppose I should tell you that too often. You'll begin to see how true it is and lose that appealing air of innocence."

Rising, he maintained possession of her hand, pulling her to her feet. "I'm going to take you to the Health Club. You can get a first hand impression of how this place works."

"All right, but…"

"I'm leaving instructions that you're to have the complete routine," he interrupted. "And when I meet you at seven for dinner, I don't want to see any shadows under your eyes."

Transferred from Taylor's authority to a perfectly shaped brunette, B.J. was whirlpooled, saunaed, pummeled and massaged. For three hours, she was alternately steamed and sprayed, plied with iced fruit juice and submerged in churning water. Her first instinct was to retrieve her clothes and quietly slip out. After finding they had been conveniently cached out of sight, she submitted, and soon found tensions she had been unaware of possessing seeping out of her.

Stomach down on a high table, she sighed under the magic hands of the masseuse and allowed her mind to float in the twilight world of half sleep. Dimly, the conversation of two women enjoying the same wonder drifted across to her.

"I happened to be staying here two years ago…so incredibly handsome…what a marvelous catch…All that lovely money as well…The Reynolds empire."

At Taylor's name, B.J.'s eyes opened and her inadvertent eavesdropping became deliberate.

"It's a wonder some smart woman hasn't snagged him yet." An auburn haired woman tucked a bright strand behind her ear and folded her arms under her chin.

"Darling, you can be sure scores have tried." Her brunette companion stifled a yawn and smiled with wry humor. "I don't imagine he's averse to the chase. A man like that thrives on feminine adulation."

"He's got mine."

"Did you see his companion? I caught a glimpse last night and again today by the pool."

"Mmm, I saw them when they arrived, but I was too busy looking at him to take much notice. A blonde, wasn't she?"

"Um-hum, though I don't think that pale wheat shade was a gift of nature."

B.J.'s first surge of outrage was almost immediately replaced by amusement. So, she decided, if I'm to be Taylor's temporary, if fictional mistress, I might as well hear the opinion of the masses.

"Do you think this one will get her hooks in? Who is she, anyway?"

"That's precisely what I attempted to find out." The brunette grimaced and mirrored her companion's position of chin on arms. "It cost me twenty dollars to learn her name is B.J. Clark of all things. Beyond that, not even dear Paul Bailey knows anything. She just popped up out of the blue. She's never been here before. As for getting her hooks in." Elegantly tanned shoulders shrugged. "I wouldn't bet either way. His eyes simply devour her; it's enough to make you drool with envy."

B.J. raised a skeptical eyebrow.

"I suppose," the brunette went on, "huge gray eyes and masses of blond hair are appealing. And she is rather attractive in a wholesome, peaches and cream sort of way."

B.J. rose on her elbows and smiled across the room. "Thank you," she said simply, then lowered her head and grinned into the ensuing silence.

Chapter 11

Refreshed and pleased with herself, B.J. entered Taylor's suite, carrying a dress box under her arm. Though she had lost the minor tussle with the sales clerk in the boutique, she remained in high spirits. After her session in the spa, she had returned to the shop. Pointing to the gown of silver silk which Taylor had admired, she was prepared to surrender a large hunk of her bank account only to be told Mr. Reynolds had left instructions that any purchases she made were to be billed to him.

Annoyed by his arrogance, however generous, B.J. had argued with the implacable salesgirl. Ultimately, she had left the shop with the dress in hand vowing to see to the monetary details later.

If, she decided, pouring a substantial stream of bath salts under the rushing water of the tub, she was to por-tray the image of the mysterious lady from nowhere she was going to dress the part. She lowered herself into hot, frothy water and had just begun to relax when the door swung open.

"So, you're back," Taylor said easily, leaning against the door, "Did you enjoy yourself?"

"Taylor!" B.J. slid down in the tub, attempting to cover herself with the blanket of bubbles. "I'm having a bath!"

"Yes. I can see that, and little else. There's no need to drown yourself. Would you like a drink?" The question was pleasant and impersonal.

Recalling the overheard conversation in the spa, B.J.'s pride rallied. It's time, she decided, to give him back a bit of his own.

"That would be lovely." Fluttering her lashes, she hoped her expression was unconcerned. "Some sherry would be nice, if it's no bother."

Watching his brow lift in surprise, B.J. felt decidedly smug. "It's no trouble," he said as he retreated, leaving the door ajar. She prayed fervently the bubbles would not burst until she had a chance to leave the tub and slip into her robe.

"Here you are." Reentering, Taylor handed her a small glass shimmering with golden liquid.

B.J. gave him a smile and sipped. "Thanks. I'll be finished soon if you want the bath."

"Don't rush," he returned, delighted to see her coolness had somewhat rattled him, "I'll use the other."

"Suit yourself," she said agreeably, making sure her shrug was mild and did little to disturb her peaceful waters. Relieved that the door closed behind him, B.J. expelled a long breath and set the remains of her drink on the edge of the tub.

For a full five minutes, B.J. stared at her reflection in the full-length mirror. Silver silk draped crossways over the curve of each breast, narrowing to thin straps over her shoulders before continuing down her sides to leave her back bare to the waist. The skirt fell straight over her slender hips and legs, one side slit to mid-thigh. She had piled her hair in a loose knot on top of her head, allowing a few curling tendrils to escape and frame her face.

B.J. found the stranger in the mirror intimidating. With a flash of intuition, she knew B.J. Clark could not live up to the promises hinted at by the woman in the glass.

"Almost ready?" Taylor's knock and question jolted her out of her reverie.

"Yes, just coming." Shaking her head, she gave the reflection a reassuring smile. "It's just a dress," she reminded both B.J. Clarks and turned from the mirror.

Taylor's hand paused midway in the action of pouring pre-dinner drinks. He lifted his cigarette to his lips, inhaling slowly as he surveyed B.J.'s entrance. "Well," he said as she hesitated, "I see you bought it after all."

"Yes." With a surge of confidence, she crossed the room to join him. "As a woman of ill fame I felt my wardrobe inadequate."

"Care to elaborate?" He handed B.J. a delicate glass.

She accepted automatically. "Just a conversation I overheard in the spa." Her eyes lit with amusement, she set her glass on the bar. "Oh, Taylor, it was funny. I'm sure you have no idea how ardently your...ah...affairs are monitored." Describing her afternoon at the spa, she was unable to suppress her giggles.

"I can't tell you how it boosts the ego to be envied and touted as a woman of mystery! I certainly hope it's not discovered that I'm a hotel manager from Lakeside, Vermont. It would spoil it."

"No one would believe it anyway." He did not appear to be amused by her story as, frowning, he sipped at his drink.

Confused by his expression, B.J. asked, "Don't you like the dress after all?"

"I like it." He took her hand, the smile at last taking command of his mouth. "Obviously, we'll have to have champagne. You look much too elegant for anything else."

They began their meal with oysters Rockefeller and champagne. Their table sat high in the double level dining room, in front of a wide wall aquarium. As the London broil was served, B.J. sipped her wine and glanced around the room.

"This is a lovely place, Taylor." She gestured with a fine-boned hand to encompass the entire resort.

"It does the job." He spoke with the smooth confidence of one who knew the worth of his possessions.

"Yes, it certainly does. It runs beautifully. The staff is efficient and discreet, almost to the point of being invisible. You hardly know they're there, yet everything's perfect. I suppose it's elbow to elbow in here during the winter."

With a movement of his shoulders, he followed her gaze. "I try to avoid hitting the resorts during the heavy season."

"Our summer season will begin in a few weeks," she began, only to find her hand captured and her glass replenished with champagne.

"I've managed to keep you from bringing up the inn all day; let's see if we can finish the evening without it. When we get back tomorrow, we can talk about vacancies and cancellations. I don't discuss business when I'm having dinner with a beautiful woman."

B.J. smiled and surrendered. If only one evening remained of the interlude, she wanted to savor each moment.

"What do you discuss over dinner with a beautiful woman?" she countered, buoyed by the wine.

"More personal matters." His finger traced the back of her hand. "The way her voice flows like an easy river, the way her smile touches her eyes before it moves her mouth, the way her skin warms under my hand." With a low laugh, he lifted her hand, lips brushing the inside of her wrist.

Glancing up warily, B.J. asked, "Taylor, are you making fun of me?"

"No." His voice was gentle. "I have no intention of making fun of you, B.J."

Satisfied with his answer, she smiled and allowed him to lead the conversation into a lighter vein.

Flickering candles, the muted chink of crystal and silver, the low murmur of voices, Taylor's eyes meeting hers—it was an evening B.J. knew she would always remember.

"Let's go for a walk." Taylor rose and pulled back her chair. "Before you fall asleep in your champagne." Hand in hand they walked to the beach.

They walked in silence, enjoying each other and the night. Merging with the aroma of the sea and the night was the tenuous scent of orange blossoms. B.J. knew the fragrance would be forever melded with her memory of the man whose hand lay warm and firm over hers. Would she ever look at the moon again without thinking of him? Ever walk beneath the stars without remembering? Ever draw a breath without longing for him?

Tomorrow, she reflected, it would be business as usual, and a handful of days after, he would be gone. Only a name on a letterhead. Still, she would have the inn, she reminded herself. He'd said no more about changes. She'd have her home and her work and her memories, and that was much more than some ever had.

"Cold?" Taylor asked, and she shivered, afraid he had read her mind. "You're trembling." His arm slipped around her shoulders, bringing aching warmth. "We'd better go back."

Mutely, she nodded and forced tomorrows out of her mind. Relaxing, she felt the remnants of champagne mist pleasurably in her head.

"Oh, Taylor," she whispered as they crossed the lobby. "That's one of the women from the spa this afternoon." She inclined her head toward the brunette watching them with avid interest.

"Hmm." Taylor pushed the button for the glass enclosed elevator.

"Do you think I should wave?" B.J. asked before Taylor pulled her inside.

"No, I've a better idea."

Before she realized his intent, he had her gathered into his arms, silencing her protest with a mind-spinning kiss. Releasing her, he grinned down at the openly staring brunette.

B.J. turned to Taylor as the door of the suite shut behind him. "Really, Taylor, it's a crime I haven't a lurid past she could dig up."

"It's perfectly all right, she'll invent one for you. Want a brandy?" He moved to the bar and released the concealing panel.

"No, my nose is already numb."

"I see; is that a congenital condition?"

"It is," she stated, sliding onto a bar stool, "my gauge for the cautious consumption of liquor. When my nose gets numb, I've already had one more than my limit."

"I see." Turning, he poured amber liquid into a solitary snifter. "Obviously, my plans to ply you with liquor is doomed to fail."

"I'm afraid so."

"What's your weakness, B.J.?" The question was so unexpected she was caught unaware. *You,* she almost answered but caught herself in time. "I'm a pushover for soft lights and quiet music."

"Is that so?"

Magically, the lights lowered and music whispered through the room.

"How did you do that?"

He rounded the bar and stood in front of her. "There's a panel in back of the bar."

"The wonders of technology." Nerves prickling, she tensed like a cornered cat when his hand took her arm.

"I want to dance with you." He drew her to her feet. "Take the pins out of your hair. It smells like wildflowers; I want to feel it in my hands."

"Taylor, I..."

"Ssh." Slowly, he took out the pins until her hair tumbled free over her shoulders. Then, his fingers combed through the length of it before he gathered her close in his arms.

He moved gently to the music, keeping her molded against him. Her tension flowed away, replaced by a sleepy excitement. Her cheek rested naturally in the curve of his shoulder, as if they had danced countless times before, would dance countless times again.

"Are you going to tell me what B.J. stands for?" he murmured against her ear.

"No one knows," she responded hazily as his fingers followed the tingling delight along her bare skin. "Even the F.B.I. is baffled."

"I suppose I'll have to get it from your mother."

"She doesn't remember." She sighed and snuggled closer.

"How do you sign official papers?" His hand caressed the small of her back.

"Just B.J., I always use B.J."

"On a passport?"

She shrugged, her lips unconsciously brushing his neck, her cheek nuzzling the masculine roughness of his chin. "I haven't got one. I've never needed one."

"You need one to fly to Rome."

"Yes, I'll make sure I have one the next time I do. But

I'd sign it Bea Jay." She grinned, knowing he would not realize she had just answered his question. She lifted her face to smile at him and found her lips captured in a gentle, teasing kiss.

"B.J.," he murmured and drew her away before her lips were satisfied. "I want…"

"Kiss me again, Taylor." Sweet and heavy, love lay on her. "Really kiss me," she whispered, shutting out the voice of reason. Her eyes fluttered closed as she urged his mouth back to hers.

He said her name again, the words soft on the lips which clung to his in silent request. With a low groan, he crushed her against him.

He swept her feet off the floor as his mouth took hers with unbridled hunger. In dizzying circles, the room whirled as she felt herself lowered to the thick plush of carpet. Unrestrained, his mouth savaged the yielding softness of hers, tongue claiming the sweet moistness. His hand pushed aside the thin silk of her bodice, seeking and finding the smooth promise for more, his mouth and hands roaming over her, finding heat beneath the cool silk, fingers trailing up the slit of her skirt until they captured the firm flesh of her thigh.

Tossed on the turbulent waves of love and need, B.J. responded with a burst of fire. His possession of her mouth and flesh was desperate. She answered by instinct, moving with a woman's hidden knowledge as he took with insatiable appetite the fruits she offered. Her own hands, no longer shy, found their way under his jacket to explore the hard ripple of muscles of his back and shoulders, half-terrified, half-delighting in their strength. From the swell and valley of her breasts, his mouth traveled, burning, tantalizing, to burrow against her neck. Her own lips sought to discover his taste and texture, to assuage her new and throbbing hunger.

His loving had lost all gentleness, his mouth and hands now bringing painful excitement. Her fragile innocence began to dissolve with the ancient cravings of womanhood. B.J. began to tremble with fear and anticipation.

Taylor's mouth lifted from the curve of her neck, and he stared into the eyes cloudy with desire and uncertainty. Abruptly he rose and pulled her to her feet. "Go to bed," he commanded shortly. Turning to the bar, he poured himself another brandy.

Dazed by the abruptness of the rejection, B.J. stood frozen.

"Didn't you hear me? I said go to bed." Downing half his brandy, Taylor pulled out a cigarette.

"Taylor, I don't understand. I thought…" A hand lifted to push at her hair, her eyes liquid and pleading. "I thought you wanted me."

"I do." He drew deep on his cigarette. "Now, go to bed."

"Taylor." The fury in his eyes caused her to flinch.

"Just get out of here before I forget all the rules."

B.J. straightened her shoulders and swallowed her tears. "You're the boss." She ignored the swift flame of temper in his eyes and plunged on. "But I want you to know, what I offered you tonight was a one-time deal. I'll never willingly go into your arms again. From now on, the only thing between you and me is the Lakeside Inn."

"We'll leave it at that for now," he said in curt agreement as he turned away and poured another drink. "Just go to bed."

B.J. ran from the room and turned the lock on her door with an audible click.

Chapter 12

B.J. threw herself into the inn's routine like a bruised child returning to a mother's arms. She and Taylor had flown from Florida to Vermont in almost total silence, he working on his papers while she had buried herself in a magazine. Avoiding Taylor for the next two days was easy. He made no effort to see her. Annoyance made hurt more tolerable. B.J. worked with dedication to construct a wall of resentment to shield the emptiness she would experience when he left both the inn and her.

Furthering her resentment was the stubborn presence of Darla Trainor. Although B.J. observed Taylor was not often in her company, her mere existence rubbed the sore of wounded pride. Seeing Darla was a constant reminder of B.J.'s uncomfortable and confusing relationship with Taylor.

B.J. knew she could not have mistaken the desire he

had felt for her the last night in Florida. She concluded, watching Darla's sensuous elegance, that he had ultimately been disappointed in her lack of experience in the physical demands of love.

Wanting to avoid any unnecessary contact with Taylor, B.J. established her office in her room for the duration of his stay. Buried to her elbows in paperwork one afternoon, she jumped and scattered receipts as the quiet afternoon was shattered by screams and scrambling feet above her head. Racing to the third floor, B.J. followed the sounds into 314. For a moment she could only stand in the doorway and gape at the tableau. In the center of the braid rug, Darla Trainor was engaged in a major battle with one of the housemaids. A helpless Eddie was caught in the middle, his pleas for peace ignored.

"Ladies, ladies, please." Taking her life in her hands, B.J. plunged into the thick of battle and attempted to restore order. Hands and mixed accusations flew. "Louise, Miss Trainor is a guest! What's gotten into you?" She tugged, without success, on the housemaid's arm, then switched her attention to Darla. "Please, stop shouting, I can't understand." Frustrated because she was shouting herself, B.J. lowered her voice and tried to pull Darla away. "Please, Miss Trainor, she's half your size and twice your age. You'll hurt her."

"Take your hands off me!" Darla flung out an arm, and by accident or design, her fist connected, sending B.J. sprawling against the bedpost. The light shattered into fragments, then smothered with darkness as she slid gently to the floor.

"B.J." A voice called from down a long tunnel. B.J.

responded with a moan and allowed her eyes to open into slits. "Lie still," Taylor ordered. Gingerly, she permitted her eyes to open further and focused on his lean features. He was leaning over her, his face lined with concern while he stroked the hair away from her forehead.

"What happened?" She ignored his command and attempted to sit up. Taylor pushed her back against the pillow.

"That's precisely what I want to know." As he glanced around, B.J. followed his gaze. Eddie sat on a small settee with his arm around a sniffling Louise. Darla stood by the window, her profile etched in indignation.

"Oh." Memory clearing, B.J. let out a long breath and shut her eyes. Unconsciousness, she decided, had its advantages. "The three of them were wrestling in the middle of the room. I'm afraid I got in the path of Miss Trainor's left hook."

The hand stroking her cheek stopped as Taylor's fingers tensed against her skin. "She hit you?"

"It was an accident, Taylor." Darla interrupted B.J.'s response, her eyes shining with regret and persecution. "I was simply trying to take these tacky curtains down when this…this maid—" she gestured regally toward Louise "—this maid comes in and begins shouting and pulling on me. Then he's shouting—" She fluttered a hand toward Eddie before passing it across her eyes. "Then Miss Clark appears from nowhere, and she begins pulling and shouting. It was a dreadful experience." With a long, shuddering sigh, Darla appeared to collect herself. "I only tried to push her away. She had no business coming into my room in the first place. None of these people belong in my room."

"She had no business trying to take down those curtains," Louise chimed in, wringing Eddie's handkerchief. She waved the soggy linen until all eyes shifted to the window in question. The white chintz hung drunkenly against the frame. "She said they were out-of-date and impractical like everything else in this place. I washed those curtains myself two weeks ago." Louise placed a hand on her trembling bosom. "I was not going to have her soiling them. I asked her very nicely to stop."

"Nicely?" Darla exploded. "You attacked me."

"I only attacked her," Louise countered with dignity, "when she wouldn't come down. B.J., she was standing on the Bentwood chair. Standing on it!" Louise buried her face in Eddie's shoulder, unable to go on.

"Taylor." Tucking an errant lock behind her ear, Darla moved toward him, blinking moist eyes. "You aren't going to allow her to speak to me that way, are you? I want her fired. She might have injured me. She's unstable." Darla placed a hand on his arm as the first tear trembled on her lashes.

Infuriated by the display of helpless femininity, B.J. rose. She ignored both Taylor's restraining hand and the throbbing in her head. "Mr. Reynolds, am I still manager of this inn?"

"Yes, Miss Clark."

B.J. heard the annoyance in his voice and added it to her list of things to ignore. "Very well. Miss Trainor, it falls under my jurisdiction as manager of the inn to oversee all hirings and firings. If you wish to lodge a formal complaint, please do so in writing to my attention. In the meantime, I should warn you that you will be held responsible for any damages done to the furnishings of your room. You should know, as well, that the inn will stand behind Louise in this matter."

"Taylor." Nearly sputtering with anger, Darla turned back to him. "You're not going to allow this?"

"Mr. Reynolds," B.J. interrupted, wishing for a bottle of aspirin and oblivion. "Perhaps you'll take Miss Trainor to the lounge for a drink, and we can discuss this matter later."

After a brief study, Taylor nodded. "All right, we'll talk later. Rest in your room for the remainder of the day. I'll see you're not disturbed."

B.J. accepted the display of gratitude and sympathy by both Eddie and Louise before trudging down to her room. Stepping over scattered papers, she secured much needed aspirin then curled up on the quilt of her bed. Dimly, she heard the door open and felt a hand brush through her hair. The grip of sleep was too strong, and she could not tell if the elusive kiss on her mouth was dream or reality.

When she woke up the throbbing had decreased to a negligible ache. Sitting up, B.J. stared at the neat stack of papers on her desk. Maybe it was a dream, she mused, confused by the lack of disorder on her floor. She touched the back of her head and winced as her fingers contacted with a small lump. Maybe I picked them up and don't remember. It's always the mediator who gets clobbered, she thought in disgust, and prepared to go downstairs to confront Taylor. In the lobby, she came upon Eddie, Maggie and Louise in a heated, low-voiced debate. With a sigh, she moved toward them to restore order.

"Oh, B.J." Maggie started with comical guilt. "Mr. Reynolds said you weren't to be disturbed. How are you feeling? Louise said that Miss Trainor gave you a nasty lump."

"It's nothing." She glanced from one solemn face to the next. She moved her shoulders in resignation. "All right, what's the problem?"

The question produced a jumble of words from three different tongues. Pampering her still aching head, B.J. held up a hand for silence. "Eddie," she decided, choosing at random.

"It's about the architect," he began, and she raised her brows in puzzlement.

"What architect?"

"The one who was here when you were in Florida. Only we didn't know he was an architect. Dot thought he was an artist because he was always walking around with a pad and pencil and making drawings."

Resigning herself to a partially coherent story, B.J. prompted, "Drawings of what?"

"Of the inn," Eddie announced with a flourish. "But he wasn't an artist."

"He was an architect," Maggie interrupted, unable to maintain her silence. Eddie shot her a narrow-eyed frown.

"And how do you know he was an architect?" After asking, B.J. wondered why it mattered. Her wandering attention was soon drawn back with a jolt.

"Because Louise heard Mr. Reynolds talking to him on the phone."

B.J.'s gaze shifted to the housemaid as a hollow feeling grew in the pit of her stomach. "How did you hear, Louise?"

"I wasn't eavesdropping," she claimed with dignity, then amended as B.J. raised her brows. "Well, not really, until I heard him talking about the inn. I was going to dust the office, and since Mr. Reynolds was on the phone, I waited outside. When I heard him say something about a new building, and he said the man's name, Fletcher, I remembered Dot talking about this man named Fletcher making sketches of the inn." She gave the group a small smile in self-reward for her memory. "Anyway, they talked awhile, technical sort of things about dimensions and timber. Then Mr. Reynolds said how he appreciated the Fletcher person not letting on he was an architect until he had everything settled."

"B.J.," Eddie began urgently, grabbing her arm. "Do you think he's going to remodel the inn after all? Do you think he's going to let us all go?"

"No." Feeling her head increase its throbbing, B.J. repeated more emphatically, "No, it's just some mix up, I'll see about it. Now, you all go back to work and don't spread this around anymore."

"It's no mix up." Darla glided over to the group.

"I told you three to go back to work," B.J. ordered in a voice which they recognized as indisputable. They dispersed, waiting until a safe distance before murmuring among themselves. "If you'll pardon me, Miss Trainor, I'm busy."

"Yes, Taylor's quite anxious to see you."

Cursing herself, B.J. nibbled at the bait. "Is he?"

"Oh, yes. He's ready to tell you about his plans for

this little place. It's quite a challenge." She surveyed the lobby with the air of one planning a siege.

"What exactly do you know of his plans?" B.J. demanded.

"You didn't really think he intended to leave this place in this condition simply because you want him to?" With a light laugh, Darla brushed away a fictional speck of dust from her vivid blue blouse. "Taylor is much too practical for grand gestures. Though, he might keep you on in some minor capacity once the alterations are complete. You're hardly qualified to manage one of his resorts, but he does seem to think you have some ability. Of course, if I were you, I'd pack up and bow out now to spare myself the humiliation."

"Are you saying," B.J. began, spacing words with great care, "that Taylor has made definite plans to convert the inn into a resort?"

"Well, of course." Darla smiled indulgently. "He'd hardly need me and an architect otherwise, would he? I wouldn't worry. I'm sure he'll keep the bulk of your staff on, at least temporarily."

With a final smile, Darla turned and left B.J. staring at her retreating back.

After the first flow of despair, fury bubbled. She took the steps two at a time and slammed into her room. Minutes later, she sped out again, taking stairs in a headlong flight and stomping into the office unannounced.

"B.J." Rising from the desk, Taylor studied her furious face. "What are you doing out of bed?"

For an answer, she slammed the paper on his desk.

He lifted it, scanning her resignation. "It seems we've been through this before."

"You gave me your word." Her voice trembled at the breach of trust but she lifted her chin. "You can tear that one up too, but it won't change anything. Find yourself a new patsy, Mr. Reynolds. I quit!"

Streaking from the room, she collided bodily with Eddie, brushed him aside and rushed up the stairs. In her room, she pulled out her cases and began to toss articles in them at random. Clothing, cosmetics, knick-knacks, whatever was close at hand was dumped, until the first case overflowed.

She stopped her frantic activities to whirl around at the metallic click of the lock. The door opened to admit Taylor.

"Get out!" she commanded, wishing fleetingly she was big enough to toss him out. "This is my room until I leave."

"You're making one beautiful mess," he observed calmly. "You might as well stop that, you're not going anywhere."

"Yes, I am." She caught herself before she tossed her asparagus fern among her lingerie. "I'm leaving just as fast as I can pack. Not only is working for you intolerable, but being under the same roof is more than I can stand. You promised!" She spun to face him, cursing the mist which clouded her eyes. "I believed you. I trusted you. How could I have been so stupid! There's no way I could have prevented you once you'd made your decision, and I would have adjusted somehow. You could have been honest with me."

Tears were spilling over with more speed than she

could blink them away, and impatiently she brushed at them with the back of her hand. "Oh!" She spun away to pull pictures from the wall. "I wish I were a man!"

"If you were a man, we'd have had no problem to begin with. If you don't stop tearing up the room, I'll have to stop you. I think you've been battered enough for one day."

She heard it in his voice, the calm control, the half-amused exasperation. Despair for her abiding love merged with fury at his betrayal.

"Just leave me alone!"

"Lie down, B.J., and we'll talk later."

"No, don't you touch me," she ordered as he made to take her arm. "I mean it, Taylor, don't touch me!"

At the desperation in her voice, he dropped his hand to his side. "All right then." The first warning signals of anger touched his face. In the cool precision of his voice, she could hear the danger. "Suppose you tell me what exactly it is I've done?"

"You know very well."

"Spell it out for me," he interrupted, moving away and lighting a cigarette.

"That architect you brought here while we were in Florida."

"Fletcher?" Taylor cut her off again, but this time he gave her his full attention. "What about him?"

"What about him?" B.J. repeated incredulously. "You brought him here behind my back, making all his little drawings and plans. You probably took me to Florida just to get me out of the way while he was here."

"That was a consideration."

His easy admission left her speechless. A wave of pain washed over her, reflecting in her eyes.

"B.J." Taylor's expression became more curious than angry. "Suppose you tell me precisely what you know."

"Darla was only too happy to enlighten me." Turning away, she assuaged the hurt with more furious packing. "Go talk to her."

"She's gone by now. I told her to leave, B.J., did you think I'd let her stay after she hit you?" The soft texture of his voice caused her hands to falter a moment. Quickly, she forced them to move again. "What did she say to you?"

"She told me everything. How you'd brought in the architect to draw up plans for turning the inn into a resort. That you're going to bring in someone to manage it, how…" Her voice broke. "It's bad enough you've been lying to me, Taylor, bad enough you broke your word, but that's personal. What is more important is that you're going to change the whole structure of this community, alter dozens of lives for a few more dollars you don't even need. Your resort in Palm Beach is beautiful and perfect for where and what it is, but the inn…"

"Be quiet, B.J." He crushed out his cigarette then thrust his hands in his pockets. "I told you before, I make my own decisions. I called Fletcher in for two reasons." A swift gesture of his hand haltered her furious retort. "One, to design a house for a piece of property my agent picked up for me last week. It's about ten miles outside of town, five acres on a hill overlooking the lake. You probably know it."

"Why do you need…"

"The second purpose," he continued, ignoring her,

"was to design an addition to the inn, adhering to its present architecture. The office space is just too limited. Since I plan to move my base from New York to the inn after we're married, I require larger accommodations."

"I don't see…" Her words stumbled to a halt, as she stared into calm brown eyes. A medley of emotions played through her, eradicating the ache in her head. "I never agreed to marry you," she managed at length.

"But you will," he countered and leaned against her desk. "In the meantime, you can ease the various minds downstairs that the inn will remain as is, and you'll remain in the position of manager with some adjustments."

"Adjustments?" She could only parrot his last word and sink into a chair.

"I have no problem basing my business in Vermont, but I won't base my marriage in a hotel. Therefore, we'll live in the house when it's completed, and Eddie can take over some of your duties. You'll also have to be free to travel from time to time. We leave for Rome in three weeks."

"Rome?" she echoed him again, dimly remembering his speaking of Rome and passports.

"Yes, your mother's sending your birth certificate so you can see to getting a passport."

"My mother?" Unable to sit, B.J. rose and paced to the window, trying to clear the fog which covered her brain. "You seem to have everything worked out very neatly." She struggled for control. "I don't suppose it occurred to you to ask my feelings on the matter?"

"I know your feelings." His hands descended to her

shoulders, and she stiffened. "I told you once, you can't keep secrets with those eyes."

"I guess it's very convenient for you that I happen to be in love with you." She swallowed, focusing on the gleam of the sun as it filtered through the pines on the hillside.

"It makes things less complicated." His fingers worked at the tension in her shoulders but she held herself rigid.

"Why do you want to marry me, Taylor?"

"Why do you think?" She felt his lips in her hair and squeezed her eyes shut.

"You don't have to marry me for that, and we both know it." Taking a deep breath, she gripped the windowsill tighter. "That first night you came to my room, you'd already won."

"It wasn't enough." His arms circled her waist and brought her back against him. She struggled to keep her mind clear. "The minute you swaggered into the office with invisible six guns at your hips, I made up my mind to marry you. I knew I could make you want me, I'd felt that the first time I held you, but the night in your room, you looked up at me, and I knew making you want me wasn't enough. I wanted you to love me."

"So—" she moved her shoulders as if it was of little consequence "—you comforted yourself with Darla in the meantime."

She was spun around so quickly, her hair flew out to fall over her face, obscuring vision. "I never touched Darla or anyone from the first minute I saw you. That little charade in the nightgown was strictly for your benefit, and you were stupid enough to fall for it. Do you think I could touch another woman when I had you on my mind?"

Without giving her time to answer, his mouth closed over hers, commanding and possessive. His arms banded her waist, dragging her against him. "You've been driving me crazy for nearly two weeks." Allowing her time to draw a quick breath, his mouth crushed hers again. Slowly, the kiss altered in texture, softening, sweetening, his hand moving with a tender lightness which drugged her reason.

"B.J.," he murmured, resting his chin on her hair. "It would be less intimidating if you owned a few more pounds and inches. I've had a devil of a time fighting my natural instincts. I don't want to hurt you, and you're too small and much too innocent." Lifting her chin, he framed her face with his hands. "Have I told you yet that I love you?"

Her eyes grew wide, her mouth opening, but powerless to form sound. She shook her head briskly and swallowed the obstruction in her throat.

"I didn't think I had. Actually, I think I was hit the minute you stood up from home plate, turned those eyes on me and claimed you were absolutely safe." He bent down and brushed her lips.

She threw her arms around his neck as though he might vanish in a puff of smoke. "Taylor, why have you waited so long?"

Drawing her away, he lifted a brow in amusement, reminding her of the brevity of their relationship.

"It's been years," she claimed, burying her face in his shoulder as joy washed over her. "Decades, centuries."

"And during the millennium," he replied, stroking

fingers through her hair, "you've been more exasperating than receptive. The day I came into the lounge and found you ticking off bourbon bottles, I had hoped to start things along a smooth road, but you turned on the ice very effectively. The next day in your room, when you switched to fire, it was very illuminating. The things you said made a great deal of sense, so I decided a change of setting and attitude were in order. Providentially, Bailey called from Florida."

"You said you had to go to Palm Beach to help him with a problem."

"I lied," he said simply, then laughed with great enjoyment at her astonishment. "I had planned," he began, dropping into a chair and pulling her into his lap, "to get you away from the inn for a couple of days. More important to have you to myself. I wanted you relaxed and perhaps a bit off guard." He laughed again and nuzzled her ear. "Of course, then I had to see you sitting with Hardy and looking like a fresh peach ripe for picking."

"You were jealous." Indescribably pleased, she sighed and burrowed closer.

"That's a mild word for it."

They spent the next few minutes in mutually agreeable silence. Taylor lingered over the taste of her mouth, his hand sliding beneath the barrier of her shirt. "I was quite determined to do things properly, hence the dinner and wine and soft music. I had fully intended to tell you I loved you and ask you to marry me that last night in Florida."

"Why didn't you?"

"You distracted me." His lips trailed along her cheek, reminding her of the power of their last night together.

"I had no intention of allowing things to progress the way they did, but you have a habit of stretching my willpower. That night it snapped. Then, I felt you trembling, and your eyes were so young." He sighed and rested his cheek on her hair. "I was furious with myself for losing control of the situation."

"I thought you were furious with me."

"It was better that you did. If I had told you then how I felt about you, nothing would have stopped me from taking you. I was in no frame of mind to introduce you gently to the ways of love. I've never needed anyone so much in my life as I needed you that night."

Round and liquid with love, her eyes lifted to his. "Do you need me, Taylor?"

His hand lifted to brush back her hair. The arm cradling her shifted her closer. "You look like a child," he murmured, tracing her lips with his finger. "A child's mouth, and I can't seem to do without the taste of it. Yes, B.J., I need you."

His mouth lowered, featherlight, but her arm circled his neck and demanded more. The pressure increased, and the door opened to the world of heat and passion. She felt his hand on her breast, never aware that the buttons of her shirt had been loosened. Her fingers tightened in his hair, willing him to prolong the ecstasy.

His mouth moved to her brow, then rested on her hair, his fingers tracing lightly over her bare skin. "You can see why I've been keeping away from you the last day or so."

With a soft sound of agreement, she buried her face against his shoulder.

"I wanted to get everything set up before I got near

you again. I could have done with one more day; we still need a marriage license."

"I'll talk to Judge Walker," she murmured, "if you want one quickly. He's Eddie's uncle."

"Small towns are the backbone of America," Taylor decided. He pulled her close to cover her mouth again when a frantic knock sounded on the door.

"B.J." Eddie's voice drifted through the panel. "Mrs. Frank wants to feed Julius, and I can't find his dinner. And the Bodwin sisters are out of sunflower seeds for Horatio."

"Who's Horatio?" Taylor demanded.

"The Bodwins' parakeet."

"Tell him to feed Horatio to Julius," he suggested, giving the door a scowl.

"It's a thought." Lingering on it briefly, B.J. cast it aside. "Julius's dinner is on the third shelf right hand side of the fridge," she called out. "Send someone into town for a package of sunflower seeds. Now, go away, Eddie, I'm very busy. Mr. Reynolds and I are in conference." With a smile, she circled Taylor's neck again. "Now, Mr. Reynolds, perhaps you'd like my views on the construction of this house you're planning as well as my educated opinion on the structure of your office space."

"Be quiet, B.J."

"You're the boss," she agreed the moment before their lips met.

* * * * *

New York Times bestselling author

DIANA PALMER

The life of a paid mercenary makes sense to Special Forces officer Winslow Grange. The jungles of South America may make his former job as a ranch manager for his friend Jay Pendleton look like a cakewalk, but it's nothing that the former Green Beret can't handle.

A woman's heart, however—that's dangerous territory. Back in Texas, Grange's biggest problem was avoiding Peg Larson and all the complications being attracted to the daughter of his foreman would entail. Now Grange will need all his training to help General Emilio Machado gain control of the tiny South American nation of Barrera; when Peg arrives unannounced, she's a distraction he can't avoid. She's determined to show Grange she can be useful on and off the battlefield. Once she breaks through his armor, traversing the wilds of the Amazon will prove an easier task than defending himself against her winning charms….

Available wherever books are sold!

Be sure to connect with us at:

Harlequin.com/Newsletters

Facebook.com/HarlequinBooks

Twitter.com/HarlequinBooks

REQUEST YOUR FREE BOOKS!

2 FREE NOVELS
FROM THE ROMANCE COLLECTION
PLUS 2 FREE GIFTS!

YES! Please send me 2 FREE novels from the Romance Collection and my 2 FREE gifts (gifts are worth about $10). After receiving them, if I don't wish to receive any more books, I can return the shipping statement marked "cancel." If I don't cancel, I will receive 4 brand-new novels every month and be billed just $6.24 per book in the U.S. or $6.74 per book in Canada. That's a savings of at least 22% off the cover price. It's quite a bargain! Shipping and handling is just 50¢ per book in the U.S. and 75¢ per book in Canada.* I understand that accepting the 2 free books and gifts places me under no obligation to buy anything. I can always return a shipment and cancel at any time. Even if I never buy another book, the two free books and gifts are mine to keep forever.

194/394 MDN F4XY

Name   (PLEASE PRINT)

Address   Apt. #

City   State/Prov.   Zip/Postal Code

Signature (if under 18, a parent or guardian must sign)

Mail to the Harlequin® Reader Service:
IN U.S.A.: P.O. Box 1867, Buffalo, NY 14240-1867
IN CANADA: P.O. Box 609, Fort Erie, Ontario L2A 5X3

Want to try two free books from another line?
Call 1-800-873-8635 or visit www.ReaderService.com.

* Terms and prices subject to change without notice. Prices do not include applicable taxes. Sales tax applicable in N.Y. Canadian residents will be charged applicable taxes. Offer not valid in Quebec. This offer is limited to one order per household. Not valid for current subscribers to the Romance Collection or the Romance/Suspense Collection. All orders subject to credit approval. Credit or debit balances in a customer's account(s) may be offset by any other outstanding balance owed by or to the customer. Please allow 4 to 6 weeks for delivery. Offer available while quantities last.

Your Privacy—The Harlequin® Reader Service is committed to protecting your privacy. Our Privacy Policy is available online at www.ReaderService.com or upon request from the Harlequin Reader Service.

We make a portion of our mailing list available to reputable third parties that offer products we believe may interest you. If you prefer that we not exchange your name with third parties, or if you wish to clarify or modify your communication preferences, please visit us at www.ReaderService.com/consumerchoice or write to us at Harlequin Reader Service Preference Service, P.O. Box 9062, Buffalo, NY 14269. Include your complete name and address.

**If you build it, love will come...
to Hope's Crossing.**

USA TODAY Bestselling Author

RaeAnne Thayne

Alexandra McKnight prefers a life of long workdays and short-term relationships, and she's found it in Hope's Crossing. A sous-chef at the local ski resort, she's just been offered her dream job at an exclusive new restaurant being built in town. But when it comes to designing the kitchen, Alex finds herself getting up close and personal with construction foreman Sam Delgado....

At first glance, Sam seems perfect for Alex. He's big, tough, gorgeous—and only in town for a few weeks. But when Sam suddenly moves into a house down the road, Alex suspects that the devoted single father of a six-year-old boy wants more from her than she's willing to give. Now it's up to Sam to help Alex see that, no matter what happened in her past, together they can build something more meaningful in Hope's Crossing.

Available wherever books are sold!

Be sure to connect with us at:

Harlequin.com/Newsletters

Facebook.com/HarlequinBooks

Twitter.com/HarlequinBooks

www.Harlequin.com

PHRT747

NORA ROBERTS

28594	O'HURLEY'S RETURN	___	$7.99 U.S.	___	$9.99 CAN.
28592	O'HURLEY BORN	___	$7.99 U.S.	___	$9.99 CAN.
28590	SWEET RAINS	___	$7.99 U.S.	___	$9.99 CAN.
28588	NIGHT TALES: NIGHT SHIELD & NIGHT MOVES	___	$7.99 U.S.	___	$9.99 CAN.
28587	NIGHT TALES: NIGHTSHADE & NIGHT SMOKE	___	$7.99 U.S.	___	$9.99 CAN.
28586	NIGHT TALES: NIGHT SHIFT & NIGHT SHADOW	___	$7.99 U.S.	___	$9.99 CAN.
28583	WORTH THE RISK	___	$7.99 U.S.	___	$9.99 CAN.
28167	CHARMED AND ENCHANTED	___	$7.99 U.S.	___	$9.99 CAN.
28166	PLAYING FOR KEEPS	___	$7.99 U.S.	___	$9.99 CAN.
28165	CAPTIVATED AND ENTRANCED	___	$7.99 U.S.	___	$9.99 CAN.
28164	FIRST IMPRESSIONS	___	$7.99 U.S.	___	$9.99 CAN.
28163	GOLDEN SHORES	___	$7.99 U.S.	___	$9.99 CAN.
28162	A DAY AWAY	___	$7.99 U.S.	___	$9.99 CAN.
28161	MYSTERIOUS	___	$7.99 U.S.	___	$9.99 CAN.
28160	THE MacGREGOR GROOMS	___	$7.99 U.S.	___	$9.99 CAN.
28159	THE MacGREGOR BRIDES	___	$7.99 U.S.	___	$9.99 CAN.
28158	ROBERT & CYBIL	___	$7.99 U.S.	___	$9.99 CAN.
28156	DANIEL & IAN	___	$7.99 U.S.	___	$9.99 CAN.
28155	BENNETT & CAMILLA	___	$7.99 U.S.	___	$9.99 CAN.
28154	GABRIELLA & ALEXANDER	___	$7.99 U.S.	___	$9.99 CAN.
28152	WESTERN SKIES	___	$7.99 U.S.	___	$9.99 CAN.
28150	IRISH HEARTS	___	$7.99 U.S.	___	$9.99 CAN.
28134	THE MacGREGORS: ALAN & GRANT	___	$7.99 U.S.	___	$9.99 CAN.
28133	THE MacGREGORS: SERENA & CAINE	___	$7.99 U.S.	___	$9.99 CAN.

(limited quantities available)

TOTAL AMOUNT	$	_____
POSTAGE & HANDLING	$	_____
($1.00 FOR 1 BOOK, 50¢ for each additional)		
APPLICABLE TAXES*	$	_____
TOTAL PAYABLE	$	_____

(check or money order—please do not send cash)

To order, complete this form and send it, along with a check or money order for the total above, payable to Harlequin Books, to: **In the U.S.:** 3010 Walden Avenue, P.O. Box 9077, Buffalo, NY 14269-9077; **In Canada:** P.O. Box 636, Fort Erie, Ontario, L2A 5X3.

Name: _____

Address: _____ City: _____

State/Prov.: _____ Zip/Postal Code: _____

Account Number (if applicable): _____

075 CSAS

*New York residents remit applicable sales taxes.
*Canadian residents remit applicable GST and provincial taxes.

Silhouette®
™ *Where love comes alive*™

Visit Silhouette Books at www.Harlequin.com

PSNR0513BL